*The fiery brilliance of the Zebra Hologram Heart which you see on the cover is created by "laser holography." This is the revolutionary process in which a powerful laser beam records light waves in diamond-like facets so tiny that 9,000,000 fit in a square inch. No print or photograph can match the vibrant colors and radiant glow of a hologram.*

*So look for the Zebra Hologram Heart whenever you buy a historical romance. It is a shimmering reflection of our guarantee that you'll find consistent quality between the covers!*

## LIGHTNING HEAT

Rand launched himself forward from the saddle, knocking the gun from the youth's grip and tumbling him to the ground. The momentum of his assault sent them rolling down the slight, rocky incline, and when a boulder stopped their descent with bone-jarring suddenness, Rand rolled to pin his opponent; spread-eagled, to the ground.

But instead of the angular boniness of a young boy, he felt the softness of a woman's body beneath him. As a jagged bolt of lightning split the sky, he recognized the burnished tangle of curls and the wide, beautiful eyes. "You!" he snorted in disbelief.

The feel of her, so soft and helpless as she squirmed against his overpowering weight, created a fire of unbidden desire within Rand. He could not restrain himself from taking what she seemed, despite her struggles, to be offering. He lifted her hips, holding her tightly to him as his mouth claimed hers.

"No, you mustn't . . ." she protested. But desire was blossoming in the sweet heat of her. His touch ignited previously unexplored fires within her, and she began to respond hungrily to his every move.

Then there was no more thought . . . only feeling.

## ROMANCE FOR ALL SEASONS
### from Zebra Books

**ARIZONA TEMPTRESS** (1785, $3.95)
by Bobbi Smith

Rick Peralta found the freedom he craved only in his disguise as El Cazador. Then he saw the exquisitely alluring Jennie among his compadres and the hotblooded male swore she'd belong just to him.

**RAPTURE'S TEMPEST** (1624, $3.95)
by Bobbi Smith

Terrified of her stepfather, innocent Delight de Vries disguised herself as a lad and hired on as a riverboat cabin boy. But when her gaze locked with Captain James Westlake's, all she knew was that she would forfeit her new-found freedom to be bound in his arms for a night.

**WANTON SPLENDOR** (1461, $3.50)
by Bobbi Smith

Kathleen had every intention of keeping her distance from the dangerously handsome Christopher Fletcher. But when a hurricane devastated the Island, she crept into Chris's arms for comfort, wondering what it would be like to kiss those cynical lips.

**GOLDEN GYPSY** (2025, $3.95)
by Wanda Owen

When Domonique consented to be the hostess for the high stakes poker game, she didn't know that her lush body would be the prize—or that the winner would by the impossibly handsome Jared Barlow whose fortune was to forever crave the *Golden Gypsy*.

**GOLDEN ECSTASY** (1688, $3.95)
by Wanda Owen

Nothing could match Andrea's rage when Gil thoroughly kissed her full trembling lips. She was of his enemy's family, but they were forever enslaved by their precious *Golden Ecstasy*.

*Available wherever paperbacks are sold, or order direct from the Publisher. Send cover price plus 50¢ per copy for mailing and handling to Zebra Books, Dept. 2010, 475 Park Avenue South, New York, N.Y. 10016. Residents of New York, New Jersey and Pennsylvania must include sales tax. DO NOT SEND CASH.*

# DESERT HEART

## Bobbi Smith

**ZEBRA BOOKS**
**KENSINGTON PUBLISHING CORP.**

ZEBRA BOOKS

are published by

Kensington Publishing Corp.
475 Park Avenue South
New York, NY 10016

Copyright © 1987 by Bobbi Smith

All rights reserved. No part of this book may be reproduced
in any form or by any means without the prior written
consent of the Publisher, excepting brief quotes used in
reviews.

First printing: March 1987

Printed in the United States of America

*This book is dedicated to two cavalier gentlemen who keep me on the move, Charlie Lesseg and Kevin Berra, and to their ladies, Elsie and Debbie*

*Author's note of thanks:*

*To Ellen and John McCrea, my real life guides to Phoenix and gold mines, and to Bobbie Suncelia, who again helped immeasurably with the research. Thanks!*

# Prologue

The moonlight sifted through the gauzy veil of curtains at the window silvering the lithe bodies of the man and woman heatedly entwined on the softness of the wide bed. They were a study in sensuous contrast as they moved together in fervid joining: he, dark and powerfully lean; she, small and ethereally blond. Yet, despite her obvious delicateness, she did not hold back in their loveplay. She met her partner's every caress, every thrust; and she reveled in the feelings of abandon his demanding touch aroused. Driven by their need to possess each other, the pair sought ultimate passion, that mindless ecstasy in which all is forgotten save need. They strained desperately together as the tide of their desire crested into waves of unequalled rapture. Then, in the aftermath of those moments, they lay in each other's arms, overwhelmed by the sensations they'd shared.

"I had always known you would be this way." A knowing smile curved Lydia Douglas' perfect lips and her tone was husky with satisfaction as she gazed at her lover, the handsome Rand McAllister, a young man

7

seven years her junior. She had desired him since the first moment she'd seen him, and she was glad now that she'd risked allowing him in her bed.

"What way?" At nineteen, Rand was no untried youth, but he had never before encountered a woman as wanton and enthralling as the Widow Douglas. He was enthralled by her beauty, and her sensuality held him spellbound.

"Perfect," she purred, trailing an exploratory hand over his chest and then his abdomen. "You're everything I've ever wanted in a man." She pressed her lips to his throat just as her hand intimately touched him, and she growled contentedly as he responded readily to her expert manipulations.

Rand was amazed when her skillful caress sent the heat flooding back to his loins. Ready and eager for her once again, he lifted her above him, kissing her deeply and savoring the intoxicating wine of her desire.

Lydia was pleased by the power she had over Rand. The knowledge that she could arouse his youthful passion so easily added to her excitement. Feeling totally in control, she urged him on, guiding him without his being aware of it, to total fulfillment and back.

Lying quietly beside him in the afterglow of their explosive union, Lydia reflected on her life and knew, regretfully, that no matter how much she enjoyed being with Rand, there could never be more to their relationship than what they now shared. She wanted another husband, true; but she was determined to marry a wealthy man this time. Available females were at a premium here in town, and the lovely Lydia had every intention of using her considerable charms to the best of her calculating ability. She was resolved to ensnare the man of her choice and Rand, attractive though he might be, was only a poorly paid deputy sheriff. His family did own a good-size ranch outside of town, but Rand and his father were not on the best of terms so she could not be certain of their relationship in the future.

Lydia had always prided herself on being logical, and now she was determined to marry only when she found a man who could satisfy *all* her desires. Being innately selfish, however, she refused to give up the joys of sharing her bed with her youthful, virile lover until she found the perfect husband.

Rand could not believe his good fortune in winning Lydia's attentions. Regardless of the fact that she was older than he, she was the most beautiful woman in town and he'd been hoping to court her ever since she'd come out of mourning for her husband. The fact that he was now sharing her bed had him totally beguiled.

In his opinion, Lydia was a wonderful woman— sensuous, loving, kind—and she wanted him as much as he wanted her. For the first time in his young life, Rand knew he could lose his heart.

Rolling onto his side, he levered himself up on one elbow to stare down at the woman he so revered. She appeared to be sleeping so he took the time to study her, committing to memory the lush thickness of her long blond hair as it spilled out across the bed in sensual disarray, the pale luminescence of her flawless skin, and the sultry, natural pout that pursed her delectable lips even in repose. Thinking of the wild, exciting things she could do with her mouth sent a thrill through him, and without conscious thought, Rand bent slowly to her and captured her lips.

Lydia had sensed his intense regard and had remained quiescent until he'd kissed her. Delighted that he was so enamored of her, she sighed in pleasurable contentment as she looped her arms about his neck and arched invitingly against him.

"Ah, Lydia," he whispered hoarsely, "I've never known another woman as exciting as you."

She smiled up at him, victoriously, and laughed throatily. "Do I really excite you, Rand?" Her taunt was deliberate, her tone breathless with anticipation. "Show me how much."

And he loved her through the balance of the night, not tearing himself from her torrid embrace until dawn's first light stained the eastern horizon with night-devouring shades of red and gold.

Lydia curled on her side and watched with open interest as Rand pulled on his clothing. His body was magnificent, she decided as her gaze tracked avidly over his broad, muscle-corded shoulders and then dropped to the tapered leanness of his flanks. She had never bedded a man so physically arousing before, and she knew she would have to have him again.

"Morning came too fast." Her tone was throaty and she gave him a contented smile when he turned to find her eyes upon him.

The emotions that this woman had stirred within Rand were too new and too strong for him to deal with effectively. He only knew that he did not want to leave her and that, if he could, he would remain with her forever. Nothing else mattered except the splendor of their lovemaking.

"When can I see you again?" he asked as he moved to stand by the bed. Wanting once more to test the strength of her sensual sorcery, Lydia reached out purposefully to caress the taut hardness of his thigh. The tensing of his body testified to her power and her lips curved in a triumphant secret acknowledgment. She drew back then, not wanting, at that moment, to encourage him further.

"I don't know," she answered evasively, not wanting to suggest to him that he alone had her favor. "It's

10

dangerous . . . I don't want anyone to know about us."

For a moment, Rand was angered by her reply, for he thought she was ashamed of having slept with him, but her further explanation somewhat allayed his irritation. She was worried about her reputation and rightfully so. He knew that a good woman was not a loose woman.

"You don't have to worry about me," he assured her. "I won't tell anyone. I care about you Lydia. I wouldn't let anything or anyone harm you in any way."

His pledge of silence pleased her, and she rose to her knees before him. "Thank you, Rand."

Pushed beyond control by her seemingly humble, trusting manner, Rand swept her into his arms and crushed her to his chest, kissing her fervently. It was only with herculean effort that he was able to release her moments later.

"I have to go," he apologized, but Lydia was secretly glad of that. It was far better that he left still desiring her. She would then be on his mind for some time to come.

"I'll contact you when the time is right to be together again, but we must be cautious," she urged.

"I'll be waiting." He nodded tersely as he buckled on his gunbelt. Then, with one last glance at her as she sat gloriously nude amidst the rumpled sheets of the bed, he turned and was gone.

When the door closed behind him, Lydia plumped the pillows behind her and sat back to ponder the night just passed. Sex with Rand had been marvelous, but she had to remind herself that sex was all it was. She could not allow herself the luxury of loving him. Her plans were set and she was satisfied with them. She would use Rand at her own convenience, keeping him entirely off balance in their relationship, and when he wanted to marry her, she would end it. Settling down

11

onto the bed, she drew the sheet up over her and sought rest, the passion-filled hours in Rand's arms having left her spent.

The next weeks passed slowly for Rand. It seemed in every waking moment he was tortured by exciting memories of making love to Lydia, yet he was forced to bide his time and restrain himself from pursuing her too ardently. When they met at several social gatherings, she was polite but nothing came of their encounters so his frustration mounted.

Only the ball being given by the Mallorys gave him any hope of being with her again. He had met her purely by chance as she'd come out of the general store one afternoon, and when he'd mentioned the upcoming party, she'd flashed him an encouraging smile accompanied by a low, suggestive, "I'll be looking forward to seeing you then."

Rand's heart had soared at the promise in her tone and he'd practically counted the hours until that Saturday night. Donning his best clothes, a dark frock coat, dark pants, and a white dress shirt, he arrived on time for the party and then lingered by the refreshment table with several other young bucks. While bantering with them, he watched for Lydia's arrival, and a clutch of excitement seized him when she finally came through the doorway.

He suppressed his eager desire to go to her and made a point of asking one of the eligible Mallory girls to dance. Though he had Peggy Mallory in his arms, all his thoughts were on the Widow Douglas and he was particularly glad when the music came to an end. With deceptive casualness, Rand approached Lydia. She was engaged in conversation with several bachelors, and he felt a surge of irritation as she laughed delightedly at someone's remark.

"Good evening, Rand," she said as he joined them. "It's good to see you again."

"Hello, Lydia," he replied, taking great care to mask the emotions charging through him. The gown she was wearing was new, an off-the-shoulder creation of deep rose silk with a daringly low cut. He wanted to feast his eyes on the mesmerizing display of her breasts, wanted to scoop them free from the nest of her bodice and press hot, devouring kisses over their silken sweetness. Instead, he smiled easily and tried to think of something other than the way she felt when she was beneath him in bed, writhing and crying out in her passion. "Would you care to dance?" Rand asked when the small group of musicians struck up another tune.

"I'd love to, but I've already promised my next three to these gentlemen. Perhaps later?" She laughed lightly as one of the men took her arm and led her out onto the dance floor, and it was all Rand could do to keep from forcefully dragging her out of the room and away from her ardent suitors.

He was heading toward the refreshment table again to partake of the stronger punch when the sound of his father's voice halted his progress.

"Hello, Rand."

Conflicting feelings assaulted him as he turned slowly to face Will McAllister.

"Father." He greeted him brusquely. "What brings you to town?"

"You don't sound particularly pleased to see me," Will McAllister chided his only offspring.

Rand managed a shrug. "If you remember, the last time we spoke, we didn't part on the best of terms."

Will bristled at the reminder of their heated argument over Rand's taking the job as deputy sheriff.

He had wanted his son to stay on the ranch and help run things, but Rand had been insistent on pursuing a career as a lawman. "It's a damn fool thing for you to be doing. I thought so then and I think so now."

"That, sir"—Rand was curt—"is your opinion, and you are entitled to it. If you'll excuse me?"

Without another word, Rand moved away, leaving his father frustrated and angry. Forsaking the punch he'd originally sought, Rand joined the men gathered in the study and availed himself of the fine bourbon his host had had freighted in from St. Louis. A card game was in progress, and when the opportunity arose, Rand sat in, glad for the diversion.

Later, returning to the ball after his sojourn in the study, he paused in the doorway to survey the room. His dark-eyed gaze ignoring the virginal maidens who would swoon for a kind word from him, he searched out the one woman who had haunted his dreams during these last, long weeks. Catching sight of Lydia chatting with a group of matrons on the far side of the room, he approached her, boldly, his ardor warmed by the potent liquor.

"I believe this is our dance," he announced courteously and Lydia, realizing that she could hold him at bay no longer, accepted gracefully.

He drew her into his embrace as they moved out onto the dance floor, and it was an effort for him to keep his touch impersonal.

"I've missed you, Lydia."

"I've missed you, too, Rand," she responded, glancing up at him from beneath lowered lashes as they swirled about the room. He was devastatingly handsome in his dress clothing, and she felt a primitive urge to make him once again her own. She had passed some time during his absence from the ballroom in the company of some of the younger, single women and

14

their eager speculation as to which of them would be favored by Rand with a dance had left her inwardly gloating. It pleased her to know that he was hers for the taking, and this was one night she fully intended to take! She had been too long without a man.

At her answer, Rand smiled down at her, his eyes acknowledging his need.

"I plan to leave the ball at midnight . . ." Her words trailed off alluringly.

"I'm not due back on duty until noon tomorrow," he responded.

No further words were spoken for no words were needed, and they parted nonchalantly when the music ended. Lydia was quickly claimed for the next dance by another ardent suitor, but Rand made his excuses to the Mallorys and left. He returned to his room over the Sidewinder Saloon and waited there, impatient for the interminably long hours to pass so he could once again be with Lydia.

Moments after he'd left the McCreas Lydia approached her hostess discreetly, her manner was confidential as she drew the other woman aside. "Emmie, darling, may I speak with you for a moment?"

"Why, Lydia dear, what is it?" Emmie Mallory asked when they had moved slightly away from the others.

"Nothing's wrong," Lydia insisted smoothly. "I was just wondering if you could tell me who that tall gentleman is who's talking to your husband?"

"That's Will McAllister, Lydia. He owns the Lazy Ace," Emmie confided, and she smiled as she considered how perfect a romance between those two would be—the long-time widower and Lydia, the lovely widow. "Come with me; I'll introduce you. I'm surprised you two haven't met before."

The rest of the ball passed in a haze of excitement for Lydia. The moment her eyes had met Will's, she'd known she'd finally found the right man. Mature, still handsome, and quite well-to-do, Will McAllister was the answer to her dreams, and she had every intention of going to the altar with him. Thoughts of a passionate night of lovemaking with Rand faded before Will's gentlemanly courtship and Lydia concentrated totally on captivating the good-looking rancher. It was near two in the morning when he escorted her home, and when he left her, it was with a promise that he would come calling again, soon.

Lydia's heart was light as she entered her small house, and she didn't even bother to light a lamp as she made her way to the bedroom. When the cold sound of Rand's angry voice cut through her happy musings she realized that he'd been waiting here for her since midnight.

"Rand!" she gasped, feeling suddenly trapped in her own home.

"Who was he?" Rand demanded, barely controlling his fury.

"That," she emphasized the word as she quickly regained her composure. "Is none of your business, Rand McAllister."

"I'm making it my business!" He was seething as he stalked forward to confront her.

"Don't," she replied succinctly, turning her back on him and starting to walk toward her dressing table, but Rand's emotions were in turmoil and he grabbed her forcefully by the arms and pulled her back against him.

"Don't ever walk away from me again, Lydia," he snarled, jealousy searing his soul for he'd heard her returning with another man and he feared what little control he'd had over her was lost. Holding her tightly, her back to his chest, his hands cupped her breasts as he pressed kisses along her neck and exposed shoulders.

"Rand! Let me go!" She struggled briefly to be free

of his domination, but as his hand dipped within the low confines of her bodice, the heat of his touch sent a flood of arousal through her and her knees went weak with desire. A small moan of desire escaped her as she leaned heavily against him.

It infuriated her that he could excite her so easily, and she cringed inwardly at the thought that one day soon she might be his stepmother. Determinedly pushing that thought aside, she gave herself over to the ecstasy of his caresses and it was some hours before her thoughts returned to her own future.

Nestling disarmingly against Rand, Lydia asked softly, "Tell me about your family."

Her question surprised him, and he hoped that she was considering that they might have a future together. If this feeling of never being able to get enough of her was love, then he was definitely ready to claim her for his own. "There's not much to tell. I'm an only child. My mother died when I was young."

"And your father?" The inquiry was deceptively innocent so he continued, supplying all the information she'd needed.

"My father never remarried. He dedicated himself to making the Lazy Ace into one of the finest ranches around, and he succeeded."

"You helped him, I'm sure; the Lazy Ace is a big spread. Why did you leave it?"

"I was offered the job as deputy here in town, and when I accepted, Father was furious."

"Oh, you had words?"

"You could say that." Rand smiled sardonically in the darkness as he remembered their heated clash of wills. His father had refused to acknowledge that he was his own man and had threatened to disinherit him if he took the job. Unmoved by the threat, Rand had gone ahead and accepted the post.

"Will you ever reconcile your differences?" Lydia prodded.

"I don't know," he shrugged, and then, not wanting to think about his father anymore, he drew her to him igniting the spark between them once more.

They made love throughout the night, and only with the advent of dawn did Rand tear himself from her side. Lydia was elusive about when they would meet next, and her refusal to arrange another assignation disturbed Rand. He wanted her with a desperation that sometimes frightened him, but he knew he would wait, forever if necessary, for their next rendezvous.

On her part, much as she had delighted in their night of love, Lydia was glad when Rand finally departed. She had many things to think about, many plans to make, and she wanted to plot her strategy for becoming Mrs. Will McAllister as quickly as possible.

When Rand entered the sheriff's office that afternoon, he was surprised to find that the Deputy U.S. Marshal Lou Moran was waiting for him along with Sheriff John McCrea.

"Lou, good to see you," he shook hands with the marshal and then cast a questioning look toward McCrea. "Trouble?"

"Nothing major, but Lou is in need of some help and I've told him you're the man for the job," John explained.

"What can I do for you?" Rand asked.

"I've got two of the Benton brothers, Cody and Pat, in custody and I'm on my way to Prescott to turn them in."

"That means there's still one of them on the loose." The notoriety of the vicious Benton gang was widespread, and Rand was well aware of their reputation. They were bloodthirsty killers who had left a trail of death and destruction across the entire territory.

"Right. Matt got away. He's the youngest and the worst of the lot."

"If there is a worst," Rand agreed. "When do we leave?"

"As soon as you're ready." Able peace officer that he was, Lou was relieved to have Rand's assistance. The young deputy was known for his steady nerves and good judgment, not to mention his ability with his sidearm. "I'll wait here for you."

Rand felt conflicting emotions as he left the office to return to his room and pack for the trip. He didn't like the idea of being away from Lydia for any length of time, but he found the prospect of transporting the Benton brothers challenging. Ready to do his duty, he finished packing his saddlebags and, grabbing his bedroll and rifle, set out for the stable. He felt lucky indeed when, on his way, he came across Lydia in the company of Emmie Mallory.

"Afternoon, ladies." His greeting was courteous, and both women responded to it with a warm smile.

"Why, Rand, are you off somewhere?" Emmie asked. She thought him a fine young man and hoped that one day he would court one of her daughters.

"Yes, ma'am. Marshal Moran and I are transporting two prisoners to Prescott."

"Well, have a safe trip," she cautioned.

"Yes, Rand, do be careful." Lydia pretended concern, but in truth she was glad that he would be out of town for the next few weeks. Her plan couldn't be going better! She'd wondered how she could keep her interest in his father from him, but now that had been taken care of.

"Thank you for your concern, ladies. I'll be seeing

you." He tipped his hat and moved on. He regretted not having a private moment with Lydia, but there'd been no way to manage it. At least, she would know where he was and, he hoped, would anxiously await his return.


After manacling Cody and Pat Benton, Lou led the infamous duo from the Phoenix jail.

"We got some company going along with us, boys." Lou chuckled when he noticed his prisoners' surprised expressions upon seeing Rand mounted and waiting for them.

"He ain't gonna be no help to ya when young Matt comes to get us," Cody sneered as he spat disgustedly into the dirt at the marshal's feet.

"Well, we'll just see about that, now won't we?" Lou's eyes narrowed as he regarded the savage pair. They were little better than animals and he would be glad to be rid of them when they reached Prescott. "This here is Deputy Rand McAllister. I think you boys might have heard of him."

"Naw, I ain't. 'Sides, he don't even look dry behind the ears, does he, Pat?"

Pat Benton turned his cold-eyed gaze to Rand, and after sizing him up for a minute, he shrugged indifferently. "Don't matter who ya got to ride along, Moran, neither one of you is gonna live to see Prescott."

Though Lou felt a prickle of fear run down his spine, he revealed no weakness to the murdering jackals in his custody. "I don't think you can predict that, Benton. Now, shut up and mount up. We got some miles to make before sundown."

Rand, too, sensed the danger of their undertaking, and he steeled himself to be constantly on the alert for some sign of Matt Benton and the rest of the Benton gang during the journey north.

The first days of the trek were uneventful, but as the hours and the miles passed, Lou and Rand became more apprehensive. Matt Benton, wildman that he was, would not allow his brothers to go to trial without making some effort to free them, he would be making his move soon, while they were on the trail and away from the relative security of Prescott. It was on their third night out, that their worst fears were realized.

In the bright luminescence of the moon the Joshua trees and cacti stood in sharp relief, but their dark shadows wove mysterious and elusive patterns across the loneliness of the desert. In the strained peace of their camp, Lou and Rand took extra precautions as they prepared to bed down for the night. They built no campfire, not wanting to provide Matt Benton—if he was around—with an easy target, and they manacled and gagged their prisoners to effectively insure their silence. Lou took first watch as had been the custom, leaving Rand to settle in and try to get some rest before it was his turn to take over.

Sleep had just overtaken Rand, when the touch of Lou's hand on his shoulder brought him fully awake. He could barely make out his companion's features in the night, but he could sense the tension in the older man's grip.

"What is it?"

"I'm not sure." Lou was crouched, gun in hand, beside Rand, his senses alert and attuned to the desert around them. "A sound . . . it could have been nothing, but my instincts tell me—"

Rand had just grabbed his rifle when the gunfire erupted. The fusillade would have meant instant death had they been caught unaware, and Rand was grateful for Lou's alertness. Protective cover was minimal so they fired rapidly in the direction of the flashing guns as they raced from shadow to shadow in search of a better vantage point.

An agonized scream split the night as one of Rand's shots found it's target and gunfire from that source ceased. His joy was short-lived, however, for another round of shooting drew a tortured cry from Lou. Ammunition running low, his situation desperate, Rand tried to manuever himself closer to his prisoners, and then the bullet caught him, grazing his forehead and sending him tumbling to the ground, unconscious.

The three remaining gunmen slowly emerged from their hiding places, and they cautiously made their way toward the two bound members of their gang. When he was certain that everything was quiet, Matt strode swaggeringly ahead of the others.

"I done good, eh Cody?" he asked, his mood triumphant as he knelt before his brothers and began to loosen their gags.

"Check those bastards and make sure they're dead!" Cody snarled as soon as he could speak.

"Mick! Ty! Make sure them lawmen are dead and then find me the key for these here chains they done put on my brothers!" Matt ordered. "Ain't never gonna be any Benton arrested again. We gonna kill every lawman we find from now on!"

"This here one is still breathin'," Mick called out as he bent over Lou.

"Put a bullet in his head. I want that to be our callin' card from now on. Any sheriff or marshal messes with a Benton, he's gonna know he'll have to pay the price!" Cody vowed savagely.

His head pounding from the bullet graze, Rand regained consciousness just in time to hear the end of

22

their deadly conversation and the sound of the gunshot that snuffed out the last flicker of life in Lou Moran. Groping in the darkness, Rand sought his sidearm. He said a silent prayer of thanks when his hand touched the coldness of the metal and, grasping it firmly, he rolled onto his back, in one violent, desperate move, and fired. His first two shots took out the startled Mick and Ty. Matt, panicking, drew his gun, but Rand was too quick for him and his well-aimed bullet tore through the murderer's body, killing him instantly as his brothers looked on in helpless fury.

Rand was oblivious to the threats screamed at him by the two surviving Bentons as he bound his own bleeding head wound with a bandana and then set about burying the body of his friend. Lou's murder filled him with rage, and he swore to himself that he would see these two face their day of judgment. At first light, he set out for Prescott, his two prisoners, still manacled and once again gagged, in tow.

Marshal Bryce in Prescott, though saddened by the loss of Moran, was impressed by Rand, who had single-handedly brought in the two remaining members of the Benton gang, and he quickly offered him the now-vacant job of U.S. Deputy Marshal for the territory. The offer appealed to Rand, but he knew that before he gave Bryce a definite answer, he had to see Lydia again. He didn't want to take a job that would keep him away from her for months at a time if she was interested in deepening their relationship, and he hoped that she was.

It was over three weeks later when Rand finally returned to Phoenix. His experience with the Bentons had hardened him, but he still felt good about coming home—Lydia was there.

While in Prescott, Rand had sent Sheriff McCrea word of the ambush, and the Phoenix sheriff was delighted when Rand strode back into his office that afternoon.

"Rand! Good to see you!" he declared cheerfully, glad to have his deputy back safe and sound.

"And it's good to see you, John," Rand replied sincerely. "I just got back, and I thought I'd check in with you before I head back to the Sidewinder and get cleaned up." He knocked some of the trail dust from his clothes before dropping into the chair in front of John's desk.

"Everything taken care of in Prescott?"

"Yes," Rand replied grimly. "The trial was short and sweet. Those two won't be getting out of jail for a long, long time."

"Good."

A moment of silence fell over them as they thought of Lou.

"Anything happen while I was gone?" Rand asked casually, and McCrea's answer caught him by surprise.

"Well, I don't know if it's my place to tell you, but you'll find out soon enough anyway. Your Pa went and got himself married."

"Pa? Married?" The news shocked and baffled Rand. For years, Will McAllister had been a confirmed bachelor. He wondered what woman had caught his eye. "That was quick. Who did he marry?"

"Why, the most sought-after young widow in town."

Rand felt a sudden lurch in his vitals, but McCrea continued.

"The Widow Douglas. Must have been love at first sight for them. Got married just last week, they did. Not much of a courtship, but then I certainly wouldn't waste any of my time making up my mind about Lydia Douglas either, had I had a chance to marry her!" John chuckled to himself.

"Now, you know Ellen wouldn't want to hear that

24

kind of talk from you," Rand managed to quip as he tried to deal with his stunned disbelief. Lydia had married his father? How could this have happened? She was his! He loved her. My God, he was certain that she loved him! They'd slept together, yet she'd gone ahead and married his father.

"You're right, she might just have my hide," John laughed, then looked up and noticed Rand's troubled expression. "You all right?"

"Yeah. Sure. Just surprised, is all. I'd never expected the old man to marry again and especially not so quickly." As nonchalantly as he could, he stood up. "Well, I think I'll go wash up and then take a ride out to the ranch. It seems congratulations are in order. When will you need me again?"

"Tomorrow afternoon will be fine."

"I'll see you then." Rand left the office without a backward look.


Alone with his thoughts, the ride to the Lazy Ace seemed interminable. Lydia had married his father. Though Rand knew in his heart that it was true, consciously he wanted to deny it. How could she have done it after what they'd shared? Had she just been using him? Allowing him to warm her bed and keep her satisfied until a man with a bigger bank account showed some interest in her? His jaw tensed as he realized the truth and the possibility that he might not have been the only man she was sleeping with jarred him even more deeply. How many lovers had she had? Was that why she'd been so elusive? Because others had demanded her time . . . and body?

He felt no hatred toward his father. What man in his right mind wouldn't want Lydia? But Lydia . . . Disgust settled over him as he thought of seeing her again, but he knew he had to do it in order to rid himself of any possible romantic notion that, somehow, she hadn't entered willingly into the marriage. Though his emotions were in turmoil, he reflected outward calm as he rode down the road that led to the secluded Lazy Ace.

The McAllister ranch house was a single-story adobe structure with a red roof and a sprawling design. From the two-room home of Rand's childhood, it had grown, as time and money had dictated, to impressive proportions, and Rand now felt a tinge of melancholy as he fended off memories of the happy years he'd spent there. He wondered briefly if there would ever be a time when the breach between his father and himself would heal. That seemed impossible, now that Lydia stood between them. Tossing the reins of his mount to the waiting servant boy, Rand strode purposefully up the few steps to the shaded gallery and entered the house that was no longer his home.

"Rand! You heard the good news and you've come home!" the shrill call of Juana, the McAllister's housekeeper greeted him as he was swept into the older woman's hardy embrace. "It is so good to see you! And it is time you returned!" There was a stern touch of disapproval in her tone. She had thought the differences between father and son, who had once been so close, ridiculous, and she hoped, now, that everything would be right between them.

"I'm not here to stay," he told her, noting her disappointment. "I've only come to extend my congratulations to my father and my best wishes to his new bride."

"That is appropriate," she declared, ushering him down the wide coolness of the tiled hall and into the main sitting room. "Come. Join the gathering. Mr.

Spencer is here, visiting with his daughter. We will have a big dinner tonight and celebrate, *si?*"

Rand didn't respond as he followed her into the familiar surroundings of the parlor where his father, Lydia, and George Spencer and his eleven-year-old daughter Lorelei were gathered.

"Rand!" Will came to his feet and went to shake his hand.

"Hello, Father. George, Lorelei." He paid scant attention to his father's other guests. Then, pinning Lydia with a fathomless gaze, he spoke to her, "Lydia."

"I'm so glad you've come. You've heard the news?" Will asked, then glanced back to where his new wife sat and motioned for her to come to his side.

"Yes, John told me when I got back from Prescott. Congratulations are in order, I understand," his expression was carefully blank as he watched the woman he'd thought he loved step into his father's warm embrace. He was sorely tempted to tell his father about his affair with Lydia, but he refrained.

"Thank you, Rand. Your good wishes mean a lot to me," Will admitted. "Lydia and I . . . well, it must have been love at first sight."

"I can certainly understand that," Rand replied blandly, and as his father looked down at Lydia with open adoration, Rand let his gaze roam insultingly over her well-remembered curves. How he hated her and her conniving, scheming ways! Never again would he allow himself to care for a woman. No doubt they were all alike—shrewd, deceitful and not above using their bodies to gain whatever ends they were after. No, Rand resolved, he would never be taken in by a female again. He would use women as Lydia had used him. From now on he would be the one to walk away. He would never allow his emotions to be touched.

27

"Stay and join us. Spend the night," Will offered, glad that the rift between them seemed healed. "George and Lorelei are on their way to town and they've agreed to stay until morning. If you stay, we can have a real celebration dinner tonight. What do you say?"

Rand noticed Lydia's carefully schooled features tense at his father's request so, determined to play the role of the reconciled son to the hilt, he answered, "Fine." He found it slightly amusing that she didn't want him to spend the night, and it gave him a perverse pleasure to know his presence would make her uncomfortable.

"That's wonderful! Juana, Rand will be staying for dinner!" Will called.

They passed the next hour in polite conversation, talking with George Spencer about his luck at prospecting and discussing his plans for the future. Lorelei grew bored with the adult small talk, and after asking permission, she went out to the McAllister stables to admire the fine line of horses raised there.

When she'd left the room, Will remarked, "She'll make a lovely woman one day, George. Her red-gold hair and green eyes are truly stunning."

"Yes, I know," Spencer replied somewhat sadly. "She looks so much like Elizabeth . . . but I worry about her, Will."

"Why? She seems perfectly happy, and she's certainly a well-mannered child."

"I want a good life for her, Will. If I don't make a strike soon, she'll have no chance for a better life than the one I gave her mother." George's expression grew somber as he recalled losing his wife Elizabeth to a devastating fever.

"Don't be ridiculous, George. Happiness isn't measured in money. Elizabeth loved you."

Sighing, the prospector smiled faintly at his friend. "I know. It's just that sometimes I feel as though I've failed her by not providing Lorelei with a more traditional upbringing."

"Nonsense!" Will protested indignantly. "You've raised Lorelei to be an honest, forthright child, and she's going to grow into a mature, sensible woman. You'll see."

"You're right, I'm sure." Spencer felt relieved by his friend's reassurance.

"Of course, I'm right. Now, let's drink to your next venture," McAllister proposed, and they lifted their glasses in salute.

Dinner was a sumptuous affair when it was served a short time later; the cook having outdone herself in honor of the wedding and Rand's return. Lydia, slightly unnerved by his presence, kept the conversation flowing and no one, save Rand, noticed her nervousness. Outwardly he seemed to be enjoying himself, but his thoughts were black as he remembered the nights she'd spent in his arms and their passionate lovemaking. From time to time his gaze hardened as he glanced at Lydia and he could not conceal the disgust he felt for her.

Lorelei, in the romantic way of young girls, found Will's and Lydia's impromptu marriage exciting, and she imagined herself being carried away by some handsome prince to live happily ever after as the characters did in some of the books her mother had left for her. She observed the couple's open affection and hoped that someday she could be as happily married.

When her gaze settled on Rand, whom she considered handsome but as unattainable as the princes in her fairy tales, she was surprised to find his eyes filled with loathing as he looked at his new stepmother. His expression quickly changed, but she couldn't help but be puzzled by it.

Shortly thereafter, the meal finished, the adults retired to the parlor, and Lorelei bid them good night and went to the guest chamber the housekeeper had assigned to her.

It was almost midnight when Rand announced the decision he'd made upon hearing the news of his father's marriage, "There was another reason for my visit here besides extending my good wishes."

"Oh?" The mood in the room was mellow and Will was not prepared for what came next.

"When I was in Prescott, I was offered Deputy Moran's job and I've decided to take it. I'll be leaving Phoenix soon."

"What?" Will was shocked. "But Rand—"

"It's already decided." Rand cut him off sharply. "I'll be heading back to Prescott in the next day or so, but I wanted you to be among the first to know."

"You know how I feel about your being a lawman," Will began awkwardly, then he stopped. "Well, good luck with it."

"Yes, good luck," George added. He admired Rand and felt the young man would make a fine deputy marshal.

"Thank you. Now, if you'll excuse me, I'd better call it a night. I've got to get an early start in the morning."

They shook hands all around, and then, as casually as he could, Rand kissed Lydia on the cheek before retiring.

Lydia was terrified. How she'd managed to get through the evening, she never knew. Fear ate at her, fear that at any moment Rand would tell his father about them and ruin her marriage at the start. Desperate for a chance to be alone with Rand, she knew that in the morning she would wait for him in the stable for she was desperate to find out if he had any intention of telling Will about their affair.


The first light of dawn found her dressed and sneaking quietly from the bedroom she shared with Will. Luckily, Will had had too much to drink the night before and she did not awaken him. Shivering in anticipation of the upcoming confrontation, she crept into the stable to await Rand's coming.

Just being with his father and Lydia for that short a time had been tortuous for Rand and he couldn't wait to be away from the Lazy Ace. Striding almost eagerly into the stable, he headed for the stall where his mount was kept.

"Rand . . ." Lydia's voice, though soft, cut through him like a knife and he stopped dead in his tracks.

"What do you want?" His tone was unemotional.

"I want to talk with you."

"I don't think there's anything to be said. You've made your decision." His movements were jerky as he started to saddle his horse.

"Rand, I'd just like to ask a favor of you."

He turned to her, outwardly calm. "What?"

"I was hoping to convince you not to tell Will of our previous relationship."

"Oh?" he asked cynically, and viciousness provoked him to ask, "What's my continued silence worth to you?"

Lydia had never expected him to be so coldly indifferent, but she took a step toward him, willing to give the only thing she had to bargain with—her body—to insure his cooperation. Sinuously, she linked her arms about his neck and pressed herself fully against him before drawing his head down to hers.

Lorelei had fallen asleep early the night before so she awakened with the dawn. Slipping unnoticed from her room, she headed to the stables to see the horses again. Unaware of the intrigue within, she entered, undetected by Lydia and Rand. The sight of Lydia McAllister in Rand McAllister's arms startled her, and she stood in stunned silence near the door, watching the passionate embrace. This seemed to her the most terrible of betrayals that Lydia could be newly married to Will and yet make love to Will's son. Angry, confused and disgusted by what she saw, she rushed away.

The scent of her, the taste of her . . . Lydia was an aphrodisiac to him, but Rand succumbed only momentarily to her brazen offering of herself. Tearing her arms from him, he thrust her forcefully away as if repelled by her very nearness.

"Lydia, don't prostitute yourself," he snarled. "Your sordid past is safe with me, although I pity my father."

Lydia was infuriated by Rand's rejection and she swung at him, fully intending to slap him, but he caught her arm and twisted it behind her.

"I wouldn't advise it, Lydia," he told her dispassionately. "Now, if you'll excuse me? I have a job to do."

Pushing her slightly away from him, he led his horse from the stall and swung up into the saddle. Then, without a glance in her direction, he put his heels to his horse, his heart hardened against women and their ways for all time.

Lorelei, safely hidden from view, watched as Rand rode away and she wondered what had gone on in the privacy of the stables after she'd left. She considered telling her father what she'd witnessed, but decided the best course of action was to say nothing. Sometimes too much hurt could come from such revelations. Returning to the house and her own room, Lorelei longed for her lost innocence and was anxious to be gone from the ranch.

# Chapter One

*Phoenix, Seven Years Later*

The knock at the door of Josh Taylor's private office interrupted his work. Slightly irritated, he looked up from his massive desk. "What is it?"

Horace Wright, a young clerk who worked at the bank, opened the door and peered into the bank officer's personal haven. "George Spencer is here, Mr. Taylor."

"Fine, fine," Josh remarked with real enthusiasm as he immediately came to his feet. "Send him in, Wright."

"Yes, sir," the clerk replied smartly.

Josh mentally rubbed his hands together as he thought of George Spencer's gold mine, the Triple Cross, and the glowing assayer's report on the quality of the new vein discovered there. Spencer had come to the bank several days earlier with a request for a loan and Josh had tentatively agreed, pending the findings of an independent assayer. He had received the results yesterday and the finding had been as exciting as Spencer's original report. The newly discovered lode in the Triple Cross was definitely of good quality and

34

promised to be a rich one. Now, Josh thought wickedly, if everything works out as I plan . . . His musings were interrupted as the mine owner entered the room, and he smiled a warm welcome.

"Spencer! Good to see you!" Josh moved around his desk to shake the older man's hand. "Have a seat."

"Thanks," George settled in the chair he indicated. "I judge by the message you sent, that you have your report and you've come to some decision?"

"Yes and I appreciate your responding so promptly," Taylor told him as he sat behind his desk. Shuffling through the stack of papers there, he withdrew an official-looking document and handed it to Spencer. "These are the results of the assay I required."

George avidly scanned the report.

"As you can see, it confirms your findings," Josh went on. "On the basis of these reports, I'll be more than glad to loan you the money you've requested."

Though George Spencer was not enthusiastic about borrowing large sums of money, he knew this was the one time he had to do it. "Thanks," he told him gruffly.

"I have here the paper you need to sign." He handed George the loan document. "It's been made out as you stipulated—$20,000, with the total amount plus interest due in full by the first of September. Are you sure that you want only six months time before payback?"

"Positive," George answered as he quickly signed it. He was certain that the mine would be producing enough bullion by the fall to pay the loan off without a problem.

"The money will be deposited in your account within twenty-four hours," Taylor stated. Then both men stood and shook hands again.

"I appreciate all your help," Spencer declared as he started from the office.

"You're more than welcome. By the way, how is your

35

lovely daughter? She's in school back East, isn't she? St. Louis?" Josh asked.

"Yes. Lori is doing just fine." There was a note of loneliness in Spencer's voice.

"That's wonderful. I imagine she's quite a lady now."

"That she is. She turns eighteen at her next birthday, and she's due to graduate from that finishing school this June."

"You must be very proud."

"I am. She's even garnered a proposal from one of the finest young men in town."

"Did she accept?"

"As of her last letter, no, but a woman's perogative . . ." Both men laughed. "Well, thanks again, Taylor. I'll be speaking to you soon, I'm sure."

"I wish you the best of luck in your endeavor."

Josh watched George leave the bank, and then he turned back into his office and closed the door. His smile had a feral quality as he sat down behind and picked up the paper George had so recently signed. "Yes, sir, George Spencer, if ever a person needed luck, you will." Taylor's chuckle was malevolent.


The Sidewinder Saloon was bustling and noisy, filled with miners and ranchhands who were relaxing. The piano player was pounding out a raucous melody on his out-of-tune instrument, liquor flowed freely, and the stakes were running high in the card games at the various tables. Hard-working men were taking advantage of their time off.

Only in the back corner of the bar was the mood somber. The two men who faced each other across the secluded table were tense and equally distrustful of one another.

36

Harley Oates's eyes narrowed as he regarded Josh Taylor levelly. "What's in this for me—*if* I decide to help you out?"

Josh turned an icy gaze on the grubby-looking little man who worked at the Triple Cross Mine. "Let me put it to you this way, Oates, it's what's going to happen to you if you don't help me that you should be concerned about. You still owe me over five hundred dollars in gambling debts, remember?"

"Wait a minute, Taylor! Payin' you back, doesn't include murder!" Oates protested, regretting the day he'd allowed himself to become indebted to this cold-hearted bastard.

"Shut up and listen!" Josh snarled and when Harley fell silent, he continued coolly, "You misunderstand me. I don't want anyone hurt at the Triple Cross; I just don't want things to run on schedule up there, that's all."

Harley knew he had no choice except to go along with Taylor's scheme, but it angered and frustrated him. He liked George Spencer and wanted things to go well at the mine. "But why?"

"That is none of your business," Taylor replied cuttingly. "Just do everything I tell you to do and don't ask any questions. Do I make myself clear?"

"Very."

"Good. I'll expect to be hearing some distressing news about the mine in the next several weeks."

"Right." The little man got up to leave.

"And, Oates . . ."

"What?"

"This conversation never took place," Josh ordered calmly, smiling at the nervous man.

Oates wanted to say more, but he knew it would do him no good. Turning away, he stalked across the room to the bar and ordered a double whiskey to help numb the pangs of conscience that were assaulting him.

It was almost a week later that Lydia McAllister came to town. Will, having decided to pay a visit to his old friend George Spencer, had approved of her overnight excursion to Phoenix as long as Jack Barlow, the Lazy Ace's foreman, went along to protect her.

Lydia felt as if she'd just been freed from a gilded cage, and as she checked into the hotel, she eagerly looked forward to a day of shopping—and a night of illicit love. It had been a long time since she'd been able to arrange a rendezvous with her lover, Josh Taylor, and this night promised to be an exciting one. With dispatch, she sent a note off to the bank. Though it was strictly businesslike, she knew Josh would interpret her missive correctly and come to her late that night.

Lydia passed the afternoon in a whirlwind of activity, visiting with friends and shopping. The Harpers, long-time friends of the McAllisters, invited her to dine with them and she accepted gratefully. It was almost midnight before she managed to return to the hotel and she wondered if she had missed Josh.

Unlocking the door to her room, she thanked Abe Harper for escorting her safely back and then swept into the darkened room and quickly closed the door behind her. She was shocked and almost cried out when two strong arms embraced her from behind, but her fear dissolved as she recognized Josh's touch. Turning in his arms, she met his welcoming kiss passionately, and they came together in a heated joining. When the excitement of their longed-for reunion was spent, they lay on the still-made bed, their clothing in disarray.

"I've missed you desperately, Josh," Lydia told him huskily as she moved to kiss him once more.

"And I you, darling," he professed. "I wish there was some way we could be together more often."

"It's impossible. It is only by the rarest stroke of luck that I come to be here tonight. Will went to visit an old friend, but before he left, I got him to agree to my 'shopping' excursion in town."

"How?" Josh knew how possessive Will McAllister was where his beautiful, young wife was concerned, and he was surprised that she'd been allowed out of his sight.

"I had to agree to allow Jack Barlow to accompany me."

"The man's nothing but a damned watchdog," Josh complained bitterly. He resented the older man's claim on her and longed for the day when he could make her his own.

"No, darling, not a watchdog . . . more a protector of my virtue." She laughed. "As if my virtue needs protecting."

"Lydia, I love you so!" With impatient fingers, Josh stripped away her garments and once again made breathless love to her, taking her to the peak of pleasure and satisfying her craving for fulfillment.

Later, as they rested, limbs sensuously entwined, Josh caressed the softness of her cheek as his eyes met hers searchingly. "Do you love me, Lydia?"

"How can you ask after all we've been to each other?" Lydia hoped that she sounded appropriately outraged at his doubt.

He nodded solemnly, "I promise you, love, that within a few short months I will have more wealth than we ever dreamed of and when I do"—he paused and took a deep breath—"I want you to run away with me."

"Run away?" Lydia was shocked by the suggestion.

Josh was a good lover, but he was only a dalliance to her, a diversion to keep her life interesting.

"Yes. Leave the old man and come with me. We'll go to San Francisco and live as we should. Gossips be damned! We don't need anyone but each other and with all the money I'll have—" Josh was becoming excited as he imagined them living as man and wife.

"But where is all this money coming from?" she pressed, curious.

"I can't tell you right now, but as soon as things begin to take shape you'll be the first to know. Promise me that you'll leave McAllister and go away with me."

"You know I'd do anything for you, Josh." Lydia lied prettily, and fool that he was, he believed her.

Several days later the shocking news reached Phoenix: George Spencer and Will McAllister had been killed in a rock slide near the Triple Cross Mine. The town was stunned by the death of two such prominent citizens and even Josh was taken aback by the revelation.

Though Josh hadn't considered the possibility of George's death, it did make things much easier for him where the mine was concerned. He was certain that he would be able to convince young Lori Spencer to sell and then the mine would be his.

Josh considered Will's death a bonus; he couldn't have imagined things turning out any better. Lydia would be free now, and he felt sure that she would marry him after a reasonable amount of time for mourning.

Never before had things gone so well for him. Josh was confident that everything was going to turn out even better than he'd planned. He would contact George's daughter in St. Louis, making an offer for the mine. He was convinced that she would agree to sell, for the amount he had in mind would allow her to continue living back East in considerable comfort. So he sent off the telegram, extending his condolences on her recent loss and stating what he'd pay for the Triple Cross.

# Chapter Two

The single, deadly shot rang out with devastating clarity in the cactus-studded land. Holstering his sidearm, Rand McAllister stared down at the carcass of his horse for a moment before turning away in complete disgust. As he moved to pick up his gear, he cursed his reason for being here and the freak accident that had broken his horse's leg, leaving him now afoot in the Arizona desert.

Shading his eyes from the harsh glare of the hot midmorning sun, he studied the horizon and tried to calculate the shortest route to civilization. As best as he could judge, the road from Maricopa to Phoenix was only a half-day's walk from his present position so in the hope of finding help on that trek, he shouldered his saddle and his other belongings and started off.

As Rand trudged across the barren landscape, the occurrences of the past week assailed him. Lydia's letter informing him of his father's death had finally caught up with him in Tucson. It had been with great sorrow that he'd learned the news; he had always hoped that someday he would make peace with his father, but now he'd never have the chance. At his request, Marshal Duke had granted him a leave of absence to see to his personal business, and he was now on his way home to the Lazy Ace which he'd left years before.

Though he had no desire to see Lydia, Rand knew there was no way he could avoid the upcoming reunion. According to her missive, his father had left them a sixty/forty joint ownership of the Lazy Ace, with Rand holding the majority interest. He'd decided right off to try to buy her forty percent. Knowing what an opportunistic bitch Lydia was, he hoped she'd jump at his offer. But much as he loved the Lazy Ace, he was still committed to his job, and once he secured sole title, he wanted to leave the ranch in the hands of its capable foreman Jack Barlow and then return to his duties as Deputy U.S. Marshal.

The weight of his saddle slowed his progress, and Rand shifted the burden uncomfortably as he trudged onward, his mind on his upcoming confrontation, his gaze searching the distance for a sign of the Maricopa-Phoenix road.


Above the stark southern Arizona landscape, the glittering sun shone with unchallenged intensity in the cloudless sky. Though it was only late spring, the heat was already oppressive, and the three occupants of the Phoenix-bound Gilmer Stage were suffering accordingly.

Dressed in their long-sleeved, high-necked traveling gowns of dark nondescript colors, the two young female passengers had long ago discarded their fashion-dictated gloves and hats, and were stoically enduring the sweltering confines of the rumbling coach in a manner that would have made the instructors at their Eastern finishing school proud. The young man accompanying them was also dressed in the Eastern style, in a tailored suit, tie, and derby; but he seemed unaffected by the weather as he gazed intently out the window at the passing scenery. Ever the outdoorsman back home in St. Louis, Roger Westlake was finding the desert panorama most fascinating, and had this trip to Arizona been made under different circumstances, he was certain he would have found it most enjoyable.

Turning back to the ladies—Lorelei Spencer, the beautiful young woman he planned to wed as soon as she would have him, and Sally Westlake, his cousin and Lori's best friend—he remarked, "I'm sorry your homecoming is occasioned by such sad circumstances, Lori."

Lorelei smiled softly at Roger's thoughtfulness, "So am I, Roger. I wish my father were still alive so you could meet him. You would have liked him."

"I'm sure I would have," Roger agreed, his dark eyes meeting hers in quiet sympathy. Ah, those eyes. A man could lose his soul in them, he thought as he took in the fathomless depths of her green-eyed gaze and the burnished beauty of her copper-colored tresses, now tightly coiled in a practical bun at the base of her slender neck. How he longed to free the glory of her hair from its confines, to run his fingers through her luxurious silken tresses! Knowing that this was hardly the time to fantasize about making love to Lori, he shook himself mentally and, with an effort, dragged his thoughts back to the present.

The memory of her father had brought tears to her eyes, and Lori sighed as the events of the last two weeks overtook her. First, there had been the letter informing her of her father's death; then, the following day, a letter from a Mr. Taylor of the Phoenix Bank had arrived, offering to buy the Triple Cross at what seemed a substantial price, and finally, she had decided to leave school early, before graduation, and return to Phoenix.

At first, Lori had seriously considered not going back, for without her father, there was really nothing for her in Arizona; but the memory of what the Triple Cross had meant to George Spencer convinced her that she could not let go of his dream so lightly. She resolved to meet with Hal Johnson, her father's trusted friend and the long-time supervisor of the Triple Cross, and then to choose an appropriate course of action. Certainly, Mr. Taylor's generous offer was not to be dismissed easily. She knew she would have to weigh all her options carefully before making any decision regarding the mine.

Lori was truly grateful for company. She knew she could trust Roger and Sally. Their counsel would be valuable should any problems arise. They had been tremendously supportive throughout her entire trauma, and when they had offered to accompany her on her trip back home, she had gladly accepted. Glancing across the close confines of the stifling stage to where her two companions sat, she studied them fondly.

Roger, in his mid-twenties, was devastatingly handsome. With black hair and dark eyes, he was one of the richest, most sought-after bachelors in St. Louis. Through her friendship with Sally, Lori had made his acquaintance, and he had begun to court her after their initial introduction. Adventuresome and rakish, he had thoroughly charmed her. Still, though they'd been enjoying one another's company regularly from the first, Lori had been caught totally by surprise when Roger had declared his love and had proposed to her a month ago. Knowing his reputation as a man about town, she had not suspected that he was that serious about her. Bewildered by his unexpected ardency, she had hesitated to respond. True, Lori found him attractive and fun to be with, but she wasn't sure that she loved him. Until she could be certain, she knew it

45

was best not to commit herself.

Roger had accepted her hesitation with remarkable equilibrium, considering he'd never proposed to a woman before, and because her initial response had been so warmly yet demurringly given, he had been left with the hope that one day soon, she might, indeed, change her mind. For that reason, he had volunteered to come with her. He loved her and he wanted to show her just how much by being at her side whenever she needed him.

Sally, at eighteen, was tall and slim with the same dark good looks as Roger, and if one were not acquainted with them, the pair could easily be mistaken for brother and sister instead of just cousins. Popular in her social set, Sally was ever the perfect lady. Her serenity and warmth drew people to her.

Lori smiled as she considered how very different Roger and Sally were. She, herself, was hardly the polite sophisticate Mrs. Harding, their instructress in the fine art of deportment, wanted her to be. True, Lori knew she had acquired a certain veneer during her four years at school, but beneath it she was the same young girl her father had affectionately nicknamed Wildcat because she'd loved the unrestricted life she'd led in the Arizona wilderness.

"How much longer do we have to go?" Sally asked, her query interrupting Lori's thoughts.

"At least another seven or eight hours," Roger answered after taking out his pocket watch and checking the time. "We left Maricopa at sunup and it's only a little after two now."

"The trip takes sixteen hours," Lori stated.

Sally stifled a groan and smiled weakly. "Somehow, I never thought sixteen hours could last so long," she said as the stage suddenly slowed its pace.

Exhausted, Rand stood in the middle of the road,

waving his arms over his head as the stage slowed and finally came to a stop a short distance away from him. Glad that he was still wearing his marshal's badge, he walked slowly toward the coach, taking care to keep his hands clear of his gun.

"Thanks for stopping. It's been one helluva day for a walk," he declared as he gestured to where his gear lay.

Brady Barclay, the Wells Fargo express messenger who was riding shotgun, leveled his rifle at Rand's chest as he eyed him and his badge warily. "What's your name stranger?"

"I'm Deputy U.S. Marshal McAllister and I'm on my way to Phoenix," Rand explained. Understanding their distrust, he made no move toward them. "My horse went down early this morning and I had to shoot him. Been walkin' ever since."

"McAllister, huh? Any connection to the McAllisters of the Lazy Ace?" Pops Dawson, the driver, asked.

"Will McAllister was my father," Rand replied, and as the guard lowered his gun, he smiled. "All right if I throw my gear up top?"

"Fine, Marshal. We only got three passengers this run—two fine ladies and an Eastern dude—so there's room inside. Just let me tell the folks what's happening," Brady told him.

"Thanks. I appreciate it." Rand removed his rifle from his saddle scabbard and then began to load the rest of his belongings on the stage as Brady jumped down to speak with the passengers.

Lori, Sally, and Roger had all tried to figure out what was going on, but they could only make out snatches of the conversation between the guard, the driver, and the stranger who'd evidently flagged them down. Lori was aware of the possible danger from bandits or renegade Indians here in the territory, and when they had stopped so unexpectedly, she had

47

carefully positioned her drawstring purse upon her lap and had slipped a hand inside to grip with practiced expertise the gun her father had always insisted she carry when traveling.

"Ladies, no cause to be alarmed," Brady explained cordially as he came to stand at the door of the stage. His gaze met Sally's.

"What's going on?" Roger asked.

Brady looked away from the dark-haired beauty and replied, "We're just picking up a U.S. Marshal who's lost his horse. He's going to be riding into town with us."

"Oh, that's a relief." Sally smiled brightly at the guard.

"Yes, ma'am." He returned her smile and then took his seat beside the driver.

Rand finished stowing his belongings and then jumped down from the top. Throwing open the door, he climbed in.

After the guard's explanation, Lori had relaxed. Now she was glad that her defensive gesture had not been noticed by her companions. Reassuming a ladylike demeanor, she looked up just as the stagedoor opened, and her emerald gaze collided and then locked with the stranger's dark eyes.

"Afternoon, ma'am," Rand began as he entered, his eyes meeting those of the young woman sitting alone on the seat to his left. His first thought was that she was absolutely gorgeous. Her hair, though pulled back in a restrictive style, was a halo of fiery splendor about her pale, perfect features, and Rand was not the first man to wonder how she would look naked on a bed, her tresses spread out around her.

Lori was caught off guard by the intensity of this stranger's glance and for an instant, she was totally unaware of anything save his overwhelming presence as Rand's broad shoulders completely filled the entrance of the carriage. Deeply tanned, sporting several day's growth of beard, and covered with trail dust, there was nothing civilized about him as he levered his large frame inside the cramped stage; still, Lori felt an attraction to him more powerful than any feeling she'd ever known before . . . and it disturbed her greatly.

Though he kept his expression inscrutable, Rand noticed the slight widening of her eyes as if she'd experienced the same sensual recognition he had, and it took a concerted effort to tear his gaze from hers. He braced his rifle against the side of the seat, and was about to speak to the sedate couple sitting on the opposite side of the coach when the stage lurched forward.

Pops was anxious to keep to his schedule and as soon as he saw Rand disappear inside, he put the whip to his team. Caught unprepared by the sudden movement, Rand lost his balance and started to fall. Only by sheer luck did he manage to prevent himself from landing on top of Lori, and she, seeing what was happening, gasped and threw up her arms to break his fall. The contact of her hands on the hard wall of his chest was electric, and the position Rand found himself in was so intimate, arms braced on either side of her shoulders, his face hovering near hers, that they stared at each other for a moment in startled amazement. Fleetingly, he considered kissing her, for her lips were soft and inviting and so close to his, but the panicked cries of her companions banished the thought.

"Lori! Are you all right?" Roger asked as he saw the large man leaning over her.

"Excuse me, ma'am," Rand managed as he pushed himself away from her and settled onto the seat beside her. "I hadn't expected the driver to start moving so soon or I'd have been more prepared." His smile was slightly mocking as he looked down at her, and Lori couldn't help but suspect that he was thoroughly enjoying himself.

"Obviously, Sheriff," she remarked with dry sarcasm, trying to draw away from his overwhelming nearness. There had been something so disturbing about the contact between them a moment ago. . . .

"It's marshal, ma'am," Rand corrected easily. Then, noticing her nervous movements, he added in a courtly tone, "I hope I didn't frighten you?" he drawled as his gaze traveled knowingly over her full curves.

"Hardly," she replied crisply. "I'm just fine now that you've removed yourself from my person, thank you." Turning away from his derisive look, she directed her attention out the window, all the while wishing fervently that it was Sally beside her and not this lawman, who certainly was no gentleman. Why, just the way he was looking at her left her oddly breathless and she found the sensation quite irritating.

Considering her frigid reply, Rand thought the name "Lori" too sweet for this prickly female. Shrugging, he glanced over at the man and woman sitting opposite him, "Afternoon."

"Hello. I'm Sally," Sally spoke cautiously for she sensed the tension that had erupted between Lori and this stranger and she wondered at it. "And this is my cousin, Roger."

Rand nodded cordially at Roger and said cautiously, "Ma'am."

Roger, however, had read Rand's expression accurately, and he did not hesitate to speak up, "Perhaps, sir, you would like to switch seats with my cousin. It might be more comfortable for us men to sit together."

The possessiveness in Roger's tone could not be misinterpreted so Rand answered with a casualness that was deceptive, "Fine." Taking up his rifle, he

50

shifted his position in order to trade seats with Sally, his thigh accidentally brushing against Lori's in the process and sending a shock of awareness through both of them.

As quickly as possible, Rand sat down directly across from Lori, and then a stilted silence fell upon the group. Tipping his hat low across his eyes in a pretense of trying to rest, he quietly observed the two women, marveling at the contrast between the dark-haired woman's sedate, gentle attractiveness and the copper-tressed Lori's startling beauty. He sensed something special—something untamed—about this flame-haired female, and he knew it would take quite a man to tame her, should any man be foolish enough to even try.

Lovely and desirable though she might be, Rand knew he wanted nothing to do with her. He'd had one "good" woman in his life—Lydia—and that had been enough. For the past seven years, he'd avoided "nice" females. He'd wanted no personal involvement, not since taking his job as a marshal. It bothered him now to find that with just a glance and an innocent touch this unknown woman had stirred him as no other had in years. Annoyed by the direction of his thoughts, Rand closed his eyes, glad that in just a few hours the trip would be over and he'd be free of her disturbing presence.

Lori had been unnerved by the lawman's accidental touch. Glancing at him now as he sat opposite her, his long legs stretched out as far as possible in the confined space, she wondered at her own reaction to him. What was there about this one man that such a harmless contact between them could provoke in her such confusion? She was no silly chit! She'd been kissed by Roger several times, but his embrace had never wreaked such havoc on her senses as the single touch of this man's thigh against her own.

51

Her catlike eyes narrowed as she surreptitiously gazed at him. Lori didn't understand why she felt it was necessary to hide her interest in this stranger, but she did and she was glad that he had his eyes closed and was obviously resting. She didn't want him to catch her staring and favor her with that mocking, derisive smile.

Intrigued, Lori let her gaze sweep over him as she studied him with concealed curiosity. She knew she couldn't fairly judge his looks, but travel-weary and unkempt as he was, she could tell that he was tall, lean, and muscular. His eyes, when they'd met hers earlier, had been dark and fathomless, but a heavy growth of beard camouflaged much of his face. Lori tried to imagine him clean-shaven, but she met with little success.

He was a Deputy U.S. Marshal, she knew that. She had called him sheriff to slight him, and his refusal to take offense had surprised her. Probably, she reasoned, he considered her a light-headed female who didn't know the difference between a federal marshal and a local official. That possibility irked her, and she couldn't help but wonder why, for after this short trip to Phoenix she'd never see him again.

Frustrated and not understanding the cause of it, she turned to Sally and engaged her friend in pleasant chatter, wanting to distract herself in the hopes of putting an end to her strange mood.

As the hours passed, the heat within the coach grew ever more stifling. Lori and Sally both longed to loosen the buttons at the necks of their gowns, but with the men present, they knew modesty must prevail. Only the promise of a bath that night when they finally reached Phoenix held them in restraint as sweat beaded their brows and further stained their travel-soiled dresses.

Finally their conversation dulled as the suffocating, cloying heat sapped what little energy they had left, and they lapsed into silence, too exhausted to even chat.

Cody and Pat Benton exchanged satisfied looks as they crouched among a stand of huge boulders some distance from the trail.

"That's got to be the stage," Cody pointed toward the rolling cloud of dust a mile or so away down the Maricopa to Phoenix road.

"Nearly on time, too." Pat's smile showed his relief at realizing their plan was about to come to fruition.

"Yes, sir," Cody reflected vengefully. "Once we get ourselves some pocket money, we can start looking for ol' Marshal McAllister and I'm going to enjoy myself when we find him."

"Me, too," Pat agreed. "I've had seven long years to think about how I'm gonna kill him when I meet up with him again."

"You suppose he knows we done broke out of prison?"

"Don't know, but I hope not. I want to catch him by surprise. 'Course if we don't, it don't matter. Either way, he's a dead man."

They threw back their heads and laughed with a kind of insane glee, knowing that one day real soon, they would have the vengeance they sought.

"C'mon, let's get the others and take out this stage. There's bound to be some money in the cashbox, and once we divvy it up, we can start lookin' for McAllister."

"Right."

Moving back down to where their horses were tied, they summoned the other two members of their newly formed gang—Angelo and Juan—and tying bandanas about their faces to hide their identity, they prepared to attack the approaching coach.

The shots, when they came, brought a bellow of pain from up top, and the stage was jolted as Pops urged the horses forward at breakneck speed in an attempt to get away from the four bandits who followed in hot pursuit.

Rand, who just moments before had finally managed to doze off, came awake at the first sound of gunfire, and in a single smooth motion, his gun was drawn and he was firing rapidly out the window at the approaching riders.

"What's happening?" Sally cried, terrified, as she was thrown wildly about in the careening coach.

"Holdup," Rand bit out between shots.

"A holdup?" she squeaked in fright.

"Right and unless you've got a gun and know how to use it, get down on the floor and stay there!" he ordered as he snatched up his rifle, pushed open the stagedoor and started the precarious climb up to the driver's box.

Momentarily dumbstruck at the thought of being robbed, Sally watched his dangerous move with awe before diving to the floor as a new volley of shots struck the sides of the coach, spewing splinters in all directions.

Roger, unaccustomed to wearing a sidearm, was carrying only a two-shot derringer with him, but realizing the seriousness of their situation, he drew it and took up a position on his side of the coach. Though a capable marksman, Roger had never used a gun against another man. He knew a moment of hesitation as he considered the possibility that he might actually kill someone, but when a bullet struck the window frame near his head, his doubt was swept away.

Her early years in the untamed territory had prepared Lori for such incidents, and she methodically pulled her gun from her purse, checked the chambers, and prepared to fire out of the window.

"Lori! What are you doing?" Sally demanded as she saw the gun in her friend's hand, and even Roger turned from his vigil to look at Lori.

"I'm trying to keep us from being murdered!" she shouted above the din. "Now stay down Sally!"

"Lori?" Roger's look was questioning.

"I've been a practiced shot since I was eight years old, Roger. Don't worry!" she responded, and not giving him or propriety another thought, she turned back to her window.

Having shot the guard, the masked bandits felt confident that the stage was theirs for the plucking, and they galloped after the fleeing coach, heady from the ease of their conquest. Firing incessantly, they urged their mounts to even greater speeds in their quest to overtake their quarry.

Pat and Cody concentrated on catching up with the lead horses so they could stop the stage as their two sidekicks rode in closer in the hope of being able to climb aboard and overpower the driver.

Muscles straining, Rand levered himself onto the roof of the careening stage only to find that the guard had been shot and the driver was fighting to regain control of his panicked team.

"Stay down and don't stop!" Rand shouted to Pops as he sought a secure position.

The sight of a passenger scrambling up to help the driver gave the desperadoes pause, but it did not deter them. The two bandits reached the coach at about the same time. Launching themselves at the stage, they gained handholds and started to pull themselves up, one on Lori's side of the stage and one over the back.

Rand got off one shot, but it went astray as the stage hit a bump. Forced to physically grapple with the masked robber who came scrambling up on top over the back, Rand managed to land a few vital punches

55

and finally knocked the man clear of the coach just as his cohort, clinging to the side, took careful aim at Rand's unguarded back.

Lori had turned to her window just in time to see the bandit jump from his horse and cling to the side of the coach, gun in hand. She could hear the sounds of a struggle above, and realizing that he was about to shoot the deputy, she didn't hesitate. She fired point-blank at the man's torso.

The sound of the gunshot caused Rand to turn quickly, and he saw the bandit, gun in hand, his expression one of tortured surprise, lose his grip and fall away from the coach, a gaping bullet hole in his midsection.

Cody and Pat glanced back toward the stage just in time to see their companions done in, and not wanting to take any unnecessary risks now that the passenger on top was firing in place of the guard and there was shooting coming from within the stage, they gave up. Turning their horses quickly away from the racing vehicle, they fled the scene.

Rand had been totally stunned by the unexpected help of the passenger, and he knew he would have to thank the man for saving his life once they reached safety.

Bending over the wounded Brady, Rand shouted to Pops, "He's still breathing! Don't stop until we get to the next relay station!"

"How bad is it?" the driver asked worriedly.

"The shot took him in the chest."

"What about the passengers? Were any of them hurt?"

"I'll check." Hanging over the side so they could hear him, Rand shouted. "Anyone hurt inside?"

Lori glanced from Roger to Sally, who was fine but deathly pale after seeing Lori shoot the outlaw, and

called back quickly, "No! We're fine." She was surprised to find that the sound of his voice sent a pang of
relief through her. She was glad to know that he was
not hurt. "Is it over? Are you and the others all right?"

"They're gone, but the guard's been wounded. We're
not going to stop until we get to the relay station,"
Rand explained. Then he turned back to try to help the
guard.

"They're not hurt?" Pops asked.

"No," he answered as he ripped Brady's shirt away
and tried to staunch the flow of blood.

"Good. Let's get Brady to Riley's. If anyone can
help him, Riley can."


Pushing off the scarves that had effectively disguised
them, Pat and Cody circled back the way they'd come,
rounding up the other men's horses as they went. They
found a bruised and battered Angelo leaning over
Juan's body.

"He dead?" Cody asked as he dismounted.

"Sí," Angelo snarled. "Someone inside had a gun."

"Leave him," Pat instructed flatly. "Let's get out of
here."

Angelo stood up slowly, his anger at having been
beaten obvious. "I will get even with whoever killed
Juan, and I will take care of that lawman, too!"

"Lawman?" Cody and Pat exchanged quixotic
glances. "Are you saying there was a lawman on that
stage?"

"Sí. He was the one who crawled up on top after we
shot the guard!"

"Damn!" The Bentons were furious that their robbery attempt had failed, but they were also worried
that a posse might be coming after them.

"What are we gonna do?"

"First, we're gonna make tracks. No sense waiting around here to see if they get a posse together once they reach Phoenix. Nobody can identify us, so it should be safe enough to double around and head into town."

"What about money?"

"I've still got twenty dollars," Cody told them. "We'll sell Juan's horse and then find us a red-hot poker game. Who knows what kind of information we might pick up in a saloon."

"Right," his *compadres* agreed, and eager for a night of drinking and whoring, they started off.

# Chapter Three

As the stage raced on through the blazing afternoon heat, Lori leaned back against the seat and drew a deep, ragged breath. She had never shot anyone before, but she did not regret doing so. Looking up, she found both Roger's and Sally's eyes upon her.

"Lori?" Sally ventured. "Are you all right?"

"I'm fine, Sally, really." She smiled wanly.

"What you did was so brave," Sally declared, her admiration for her friend growing as she realized the enormity of Lori's act.

Lori shrugged as if her deed had been unimportant, but her hand shook as she put the gun back into her reticule. "I learned how to shoot when I was very young for this very reason," she explained. "My father always insisted that I carry a gun with me when I traveled."

"I'm glad he did," Roger remarked, his respect for this young woman increasing. Not only was Lori beautiful and intelligent, she was capable of acting when the situation required it. In his experience, that was a trait few women possessed. "I only had two shots in my derringer, and I missed both times." He smiled wryly. "Maybe I'd better invest in a sidearm when we get to town."

59

"I doubt that you'll need one while we're in Phoenix, but if we go up to the mine, it might not be a bad idea," Lori agreed.

"The marshal said that the guard had been wounded." Sally's concern was obvious. "Will they be able to help him at the relay station? The ones we've stopped at seemed so primitive."

"I don't know," Lori replied. "I guess it depends on how badly he was wounded."

"I hope we get there soon." Sally said softly, remembering the courteous greeting the big, blond-haired man had given her when she'd boarded the stagecoach in Maricopa and the special look they'd exchanged earlier when the marshal had boarded. "He seemed like a nice man."

"They'll do everything they can for him, I'm sure," Roger assured her, and then they fell silent as they reflected on the danger they'd just faced.

It was almost an hour later when they finally pulled up in front of the way station. At Pops' cry Riley ran from the small adobe house.

"What's happened?" he shouted.

"Bandits. We managed to get away, but they shot Brady!" Pops explained as he quickly tied the reins and turned to help Rand lift the wounded guard down.

"How is he?" Riley came to their aid, and the three men carried Brady out of the heat and into the relative coolness of the station.

"It doesn't look good," Rand said as they took him back to the station's single bedroom and placed him on the bed.

Riley hurriedly stripped off Brady's shirt. Then he examined the wound, noting that the bullet had entered his lower right side and had passed through his body, exiting out his lower back.

"He was lucky on one account," Riley told them

gruffly. "It's a clean wound—went right on through. Let me get my doctorin' supplies."

"Is he gonna live?" Pops demanded. He and Brady had been riding together ever since the young man had signed on with Wells Fargo.

"Cain't tell yet, Pops."

"Should I get him into town?"

"I wouldn't move him," Riley answered quickly. "He's lost a lot of blood and jostlin' him around in that stage won't do him a bit of good. Might even kill him. Besides, it's too late now for you to make town before dark. Spend the night here, and we'll see how he is in the morning."

"I'd better get word to town," Pops began.

"If you've got a spare horse I'll be glad to ride ahead and notify the stage line and the Wells Fargo of what's happened," Rand offered. "By the way, I'm Marshal McAllister." He shook hands with the relay station manager.

"Good to meet ya." Riley eyed Rand appreciatively. "Good thing you was on this stage."

"Sure was," Pops reported. "Why, if it hadn't been for McAllister, here, we'd probably all be dead in the middle of the desert. It was great luck that we picked him up."

"Picked you up?" Riley asked.

"My horse broke a leg early this morning and I had to shoot him. I started walking and finally managed to flag down the stage."

"Stroke of fate," Riley murmured, nodding. "Pops, why don't you take him on out to the stable and fix him up with a mount. Take whatever gear you need, Marshal, and then when you get to town, leave the horse with the stage company people."

"Be glad to. Do you want me to have them send any help out to you?"

"Have them send a doctor. I'll do my best for Brady, but I don't know if it'll be good enough." As he left the room, the two men followed. Getting his medical supplies from a cupboard, he started toward the back of the house, but the sound of voices outside stopped him. "You had passengers too?"

"Three of them," Pops replied. "Two women and a man. They're not hurt."

"Good, one patient's about all I can handle," Riley growled as he disappeared into the bedroom to see to Brady. "Tell 'em to make themselves comfortable. I don't know how long I'll be."

"Right."

Outside, Roger had gotten out of the stagecoach and was helping the women out of its sweltering interior. "I don't know that it's any cooler out here, but it's got to be better than sitting in there," he was saying as he handed Sally and then Lori down.

"Thank you," they murmured as they stretched wearily, exhausted from the heat and the emotional letdown after their encounter with the robbers.

The first thing Rand saw as he emerged from the house with Pops was Lori, hands on her hips, arching her back and stretching in what looked to be a sensual invitation. His gaze locked on the firm thrust of bosom straining against the dark material of her gown, and he longed to see her in the same position, unclad. Swearing silently, he cursed his own folly at even contemplating such an encounter. Then, scowling blackly, he strode forward, the driver at his side, to claim his gear off the stage.

Lori watched the marshal's approach with real interest. It was the first time she'd seen him outside the confines of the coach and she couldn't help but admire the fine figure of a man he was. It was only as he drew near that she noticed his thunderous look, and she wondered at the fierceness of his expression.

Roger, too, noticed Rand's somber manner and as Pops joined them, he asked, "How's the guard?"

"The stationmaster is looking after him," Pops explained.

"Will he live?" Sally queried.

"Don't know, missy. The marshal here is gonna ride into town right away to notify the stage line and have them send out a doctor."

Lori glanced at Rand, who was busy taking his gear down from the stage, and her spirits flagged as it occurred to her that, more than likely, she would never see him again.

When Rand had unloaded his saddle, he turned to Roger and extended a hand in friendship. "I want to thank you for your help during the shootout. That was a tight scrape I was in and you probably saved my life."

"I'd like to take the credit, Marshal, but I'm afraid I'm not the one you should be thanking."

"What do you mean?" Rand frowned.

"I only had my derringer, and I was shooting out the opposite side of the stage. Lori's the one who—"

"You're the one who shot the bandit?" Pops broke in, incredulous that such a pretty young Eastern woman could have been so heroic.

Lori had tolerated the condescending attitudes of the men she'd met in St. Louis society, but it irritated her to discover that these two Westerners equated femininity with helplessness. Her smile was strained as she faced them.

Though he found it hard to believe that she could have shot a man, Rand recovered quickly from his shock and said smoothly, "Then I thank you, ma'am. That was some lucky shot."

*Lucky shot!* How dare this man presume that she didn't know how to handle a gun! Thank heaven she

63

would have no more to do with him, attractive or not. At least Roger appreciated her prowess. He knew her shot had not been a lucky one.

"Yes, I suppose it was lucky—for you." She kept her tone cool.

Rand felt the bite of her words, and he glanced at her quickly as Sally went on.

"And we thank you, Marshal," Sally declared, not noticing how his last statement had infuriated her friend. "You were so brave to go up and help the driver the way you did. Why, I hate to think what would have happened to us if you hadn't been along!"

Lori was nauseated by Sally's prattle.

"I was glad to be of service, ma'am," Rand was saying as Pops interrupted him.

"You'd better be gettin' on, if you're gonna make town before sundown."

"You're right," Rand agreed, shouldering his saddle.

"You take the ladies and go on in the house," Pops told Roger. "Riley's busy takin' care of Brady in the back bedroom, but I'll be back with you in a few minutes."

"Is there anything we can do to help?" Lori and Sally offered.

"I don't think so, not right now. Riley'll let us know, later."

"Fine," Roger agreed. "Again, Marshal, thanks."

Rand tipped his hat in their direction before picking up his rifle, and then he and Pops strode off toward the stable.

"What a nice man," Sally said to Roger as they started toward the station, and Lori was forced to bite back a sarcastic retort.

"Ooeee!" Pops chuckled when they were out of earshot. "That redhead is somethin' else, ain't she? They didn't make 'em like that when I was young!

64

Gorgeous and gun-totin', both!"

"Yeah, but that tongue of hers is sharp."

"Naw," Pops denied. "She jes' needs a good man to straighten her out a bit. She'd be a tame little filly with the right handlin'."

Rand was inclined to argue the point, but he let it pass. What did it matter anyway? He'd never see her again, and as far as he was concerned, that was just fine.

"Well, I wish him luck, whoever he may be," he drawled as he threw his saddle on the back of the horse Pops had pointed out.

"You be careful now."

"I will. I'll leave the horse with the stage company."

"Fine and tell them to send that doctor as quick as they can. I'm worried about Brady."

"Will do," Rand assured him as he gathered the reins and swung up onto the horse's back.

"Thanks, McAllister."

"You're welcome, Pops. I'll probably be seeing you in town."

"Probably," the old man murmured as he watched him ride from the stable.

Anxious to relay the news about the attempted holdup, Rand headed toward Phoenix, unaware that Lori was watching him from the shade of the station's veranda. As irritated as she was by his arrogance, Lori did not know why she was driven to watch him leave, but she was. And she stood there until he was out of sight, gone from her life.

"Do either of you ladies know anythin' about nursin'?" A gruff voice broke into Lori's thoughts and she turned about to see the man she presumed was Riley, standing in the doorway to the bedroom.

"I know a little," Sally offered, rising from her seat beside the plank table.

65

"I could sure use your help, ma'am," Riley continued. "Brady isn't lookin' good, and it's gonna be several hours before any help can git here from town."

"I'll be glad to help. Just tell me what you want me to do." Already Sally was on her way to his side.

"Thank you," he said gratefully as he gestured her into the room.

Roger almost protested, but he realized that they were in the territory now and not on some fashionable St. Louis outing. Judging from the experiences they'd had today, he'd already concluded that cooperation was necessary for survival.

"Is there anything we can do?" He asked as Lori came to stand beside him.

"Not right now," Riley replied before following Sally into the bedroom.

When the stationmaster had disappeared into the sickroom with Sally, Lori glanced up at Roger and was surprised to find his intent gaze upon her. "Roger? Is something wrong?"

"No, sweetheart. Nothing's wrong. I was just thinking how very fortunate we were to get out of the robbery attempt unscathed." With a gentle caress, he touched her cheek. "I wouldn't have been able to live with myself if anything had happened to you or Sally."

Lori was touched by his words. "Nonsense. It wouldn't have been your fault."

"Of course, it would have! I'm supposed to be traveling with you to protect you, but what good was I? If it hadn't been for the deputy and your own quick thinking—"

"Roger, nothing happened to us, so there's nothing to blame yourself for!"

"It's not going to happen again, Lori. I promise you. I won't let you down again," Roger pledged earnestly, and he bent to her, kissing her quickly, softly, to seal

66

his vow.

When he drew back, she told him, "You're a very sweet man, Roger. I'm lucky to have you."

"I know." He grinned, suddenly his old self. "Why don't you marry me and make me your own?"

Put on the spot, Lori found herself wavering. Certainly Roger would make a far better husband than any other man she'd met. She respected him and liked him . . . but the memory of the lawman's innocent, yet devastating, touch left her wondering.

"Roger . . . I . . ."

"Don't," he said more sharply than he'd intended. "I'm not pressuring you. Not at all. I just want you to know how I feel, want you to know that I'll always be here for you."

"I know," Lori said gently, and they moved apart as Pops returned.


After Lydia entered Josh's office, he silently closed and locked the door.

"It's perfectly respectable that I should pay a visit to my banker, don't you think?" she asked archly as she went into his arms.

"Absolutely," he responded, kissing her ardently. "I couldn't believe it when I heard yesterday that you'd come to town."

"I couldn't bear it out there on the ranch." She pouted prettily. "It's so boring . . ."

"I can't tell you how glad I am that I'm handling your affairs here at the bank. It's the perfect ruse, and in just a few months when the commotion over Will's death has faded, we can be married." He pressed heated kisses along the sensitive cords of her neck as he busily worked at the tiny buttons at her bodice.

The illicitness of their meeting sent a thrill of

excitement through Lydia, and when Josh parted the material of her black mourning gown to caress the fullness of her bosom, she groaned in ecstatic anticipation. "Oh, Josh . . . I've been so lonely."

"I know." Desperate, his eyes glazed with passion, he glanced quickly around his office. "Here." He drew her with him and, lifting her, seated her before him on the massive desk. "Now . . ."

Heatedly, they embraced. The danger of discovery only adding to their exhilaration. Brushing her skirts aside, Josh brought her to him, wrapping her legs about his hips as he moved sensuously against her.

"I can't wait until we can be together like this—always," he told her, kissing the silken fullness of her breasts.

Lydia surrendered willingly to his need, moving with him passionately when he freed himself from his trousers and entered her welcoming heat. Their fervid joining, heightened by their fear of discovery, was explosive and they collapsed into each other's arms.

"You're marvelous, Lydia." Josh kissed her again, before moving slightly away to straighten his own clothing. "I wish this charade of your mourning was over, so we could marry."

"I know, darling." She soothed him, wishing fervently that he would stop talking about it. She had no intention of jumping into another marriage now that she was financially secure. Besides, Rand was coming back. The thought of her young lover of long ago brought a smile to her lips, and Josh mistook her look for one of invitation.

"I'm glad I please you, Lydia." He caressed her still bare breasts and then regretfully covered them. "But it's much too dangerous to press our luck any further."

"Of course, Josh," Lydia replied, amazed at how egotistical he was. Just because she'd smiled, he'd thought she was ready to make love with him again. Buttoning her bodice, she slipped from the desktop and smoothed her skirts. "I do hate black." She grimaced distastefully.

"Frankly, my dear," Josh said callously, "I am quite delighted to see you wearing it. You're a free woman, Lydia."

Her eyes were bright with that knowledge as she looked up at him. "And for the first time in my life, I don't have to worry about money. Thanks to my dear, departed Will."

"Yes. Your portion of the Lazy Ace is worth a small fortune, but do you plan on keeping the place?"

Lydia shrugged. "I haven't given it much thought yet. There's no point in rushing a decision when I've got better than five months of mourning to go. I don't particularly like living there, but I doubt that I would be happier anywhere else, given the circumstances. I've got to play out this charade and make the best of it—for now."

"Have you heard from Rand yet?"

"Not a word and it's been almost two weeks since I sent the letter." Her answer did not reveal the depth of her concern about Rand. Surely he'd received her letter by now. Where was he? Why hadn't he come back? Had he been killed in the line of duty? Over the past seven years, she had had minimal contact with him. He had never returned to the ranch, a fact that had distressed Will greatly and had left her curious as to the reason. Had he been staying away because of her? And, if so, was that why he wasn't responding even now on the occasion of his father's death?

"Don't worry, he'll show up. He'd be a fool not to. Why, he's a rich man now. He owns sixty percent of the Lazy Ace," Josh took her in his arms tenderly. "You can sell him your share and move into town, and then we can be together."

Hiding her disgust at his continued persistence, she returned his kiss and then moved away from him. "I suppose you're right." She sighed, aware that her helpless female ploy was working.

"Of course I'm right," he replied arrogantly. "You'll see."

"I'd better be going." Lydia hoped she sounded regretful, but in reality she couldn't wait to be away from Josh now that he'd satisfied her needs. "I told Jack that I'd only be gone about a half-hour. We're returning to the ranch today."

"Do you know when I'll be able to see you again?" he pressed.

"No. It'll just depend on when Rand shows up and how often I can think of a reason to come to town."

"I understand." Josh was not pleased by her answer, but he felt it was the most definite one she could give him.

As Lydia started for the door, she said in her most businesslike tone of voice, "Thank you for your kindness, Mr. Taylor, and your help."

"Any time, Mrs. McAllister. Please feel free to call on me." His eyes were dark with desire as he opened the office door for her.

"I'm sure I'll be speaking with you as soon as my stepson arrives. We must go over the details of my husband's affairs with him."

"Just let me know and we'll arrange a meeting at your convenience." Josh's manner was professional as he bid her good day, and none of his employees suspected that the Widow McAllister had just made torrid love to their boss in the privacy of his office.

\*     \*     \*

70

It was several hours later, nearly dusk, when Rand emerged from the office of the Gilmer Stage Company.

"Thanks again for the information, Marshal. We'll send a doctor out to the relay station at once."

"Good. Barclay's condition looked pretty serious," Rand told him. "You'll let the Wells Fargo people know?"

"Right away, sir."

"I'll check in with Sheriff McCrea now and see how he feels about getting a posse together."

"Well, keep us informed."

"I will." Rand strode down the dusty street in the direction of the sheriff's office.


John McCrea couldn't believe his eyes when he looked up from where he sat behind his desk, "Rand! By God, it's been a long time!" He hurried to greet his old friend, clapping him jovially on the back. "I must say even though you look like hell, you are a sight for sore eyes!"

"I don't know if that's a compliment or not," Rand chuckled, rubbing his bearded chin as he sat down in the chair in front of the desk. "But after the day I've had, I'm not up to arguing the point."

"What happened?" John returned to his seat.

"I got word from Lydia of Father's death while I was in Tucson and—"

"Terrible thing, Will and George dying like that," McCrea said in quiet sympathy.

"George?" Rand frowned.

"Lydia didn't tell you?" At Rand's negative nod, he explained. "Your father was with George Spencer, out near his mine, and they were caught in the landslide. It was a terrible shock for everyone. I'm sorry, Rand."

71

"So am I. He was a good man." Rand was silent for a moment as he thought of his father and his good friend. Then he went on. "Anyway, I was on my way home this morning when my horse broke his leg. I ended up on foot near the Maricopa stage line. To make a long story short, I managed to flag down the stage, but there was a holdup attempt on our way in, a little south of Riley's relay station."

"Was anyone hurt?"

"The Wells Fargo guard, Brady Barclay, was shot, but he's still alive. I told the men down at the stage office and they're going to send a doctor out to him at Riley's. The driver's holding the stage there overnight."

"That's good to know." John frowned. "Who were they? Did you get a good look at them?"

"No, damn it. There were four of them, but they were all wearing bandanas. I didn't recognize any of them. One of the passengers shot one, but the other three got away."

"Did you have time to check on the one who was shot?"

"No. With Barclay looking as bad as he was, it was more important to get him to help."

"There's no point in trying to put a posse together now, but I think I'll ride out at dawn and see what I can find. Come with me?"

"Sure," Rand agreed. He'd waited this long to see Lydia, another day wouldn't make any difference.

John was pleased by his acceptance. "Good. It'll be like old times."

"Well, I'm going over and get a room at the hotel. Maybe in the morning, once I'm cleaned up, you'll recognize me." He laughed as he came to his feet, then, as he thought of his father, his mood darkened. "Do you know where Lydia had my father buried?"

72

"Yes. He was buried in the cemetery here in town."

"Thanks. I'll see you in the morning."

Even in the fading evening light, Rand had no trouble locating the newly dug gravesite, and hat in hand, he stood solemnly staring down at the headstone. It occurred to him as he did so that he knew very little about his father's death. Lydia's letter had been short and lacking in detail. He knew he would have to find out exactly what had happened when he met with her. His heart heavy with memories of happier times when he and his father had been close, Rand headed back to the Gardiner's Hotel to take a room for the night.

He bathed, shaved, and then ate dinner in the hotel dining room before retiring for the night. The room was clean and boasted a wide, comfortable bed, but the softness of the mattress seemed foreign to him after so many nights on the trail. He lay awake for a long time, thinking of his father, the Lazy Ace, and Lydia. Only when he was finally drifting off to sleep did the vision of a flame-haired vixen with flashing green eyes slip disturbingly into his thoughts.

Night had fallen and in the lamplit interior of the way station conversation was muted as travelers and stationmaster alike tensely awaited the doctor's report on Brady's condition. Doc Simpson, accompanied by an armed escort, had arrived from town only a short while before, and he had gone straight into the bedroom to see to his patient.

Sally had been grateful when the physician had finally arrived for she had been tending Brady since that afternoon and had become quite concerned about his condition. Despite her best efforts and Riley's, the

73

guard had not been doing well. He had lost a considerable amount of blood and she feared that if he developed an infection and a fever took him, he might not make it through the night.

The realization that this man Brady Barclay might die upset her greatly, and she wondered at her own reaction as she sat at the plank table in the station's main room with Lori and Roger. Sally had been courted by many men in St. Louis—rich ones, handsome ones, sophisticated ones—but none of them had stirred any great emotion within her. Yet this giant of a cowboy had intrigued her from the first moment they'd spoken back in Maricopa when she had boarded the stagecoach. Though he was not handsome in the classic way—his craggy features were more plain than handsome; his massive build, she knew, would look out of place in a drawing room—she sensed something special about him and she wanted to get to know him better.

Roger, noting his cousin's grim expression, touched her arm.

"I'm fine," she answered. "I'm just worried about the guard. The doctor's been in there a long time."

As she spoke, the door opened and Doctor Simpson came out with Riley.

"How is he?" Sally asked quickly, and Roger and Lori exchanged puzzled looks for she was displaying an unusual concern for this stranger.

"He's going to come through it," Riley related happily. "'Course he ain't woke up yet, but the doc says he should by morning."

"Yes, I believe he'll recover," the physician put in.

"Is there anything else that we can do to help?" Roger asked.

"No. It's just a matter of waiting now. Then, once

he's a little stronger, we can move him into town." Turning to Riley, he asked, "Do you have a place where we can bed down for the night?"

"I don't usually get overnighters, but I figure the men can sleep in the stable and I'll fix up a curtained-off area for the ladies in here," the stationmaster explained.

"Fine. We'll have to take turns sitting with Barclay. It wouldn't do for him to regain consciousness and try to get up. I'll sit with him first."

The day having been a long, eventful one, the rest of the men retired to the stable shortly thereafter, but not before Riley fashioned a small private area in a corner of the main room for the women.

After washing up as well as they could, Lori and Sally lay down on the makeshift pallet that was serving as their bed, but tired though she was, Lori was unable to sleep. Tossing uncomfortably, she finally gave up the quest for rest and moved silently to the open window to stare out across the night-shrouded desert she loved so much.

"Lori?" Sally's voice was soft, yet questioning, in the darkness of the room.

"I'm all right."

"You're sure?"

"Yes. Go to sleep."

"Well, good night."

"'Night."

Gazing out at the moon-kissed darkness, Lori sensed for the first time that she was home and it felt good to her. She wondered sadly why she had ever let her father convince her to go away to school in the first place. She supposed she had done it to please him, and though she had not hated her time in the East, she had not realized until now how much she missed the life she'd shared with him here in the territory.

Sighing, Lori didn't even try to stifle her tears of sorrow. She would never see him again, never hear his deep laugh or feel the warmth of his fatherly embrace. For long minutes there in the shadows of the night, she let herself quietly grieve until her emotions were spent.

Lori had wanted her father to be proud of her so she knew now what she had to do. She would not settle his affairs and go back East, never to be heard from again. She was George Spencer's daughter and she knew as much, if not more, about hard-rock mining than most men. The Triple Cross had been a paying mine before his death, and she would see to it that it continued to pay. It had been his dream and she would carry on that dream.

Her decision made, a new determination took possession of her, and she felt a lightness of spirit she hadn't known for a long time. She loved the territory, and she would stay. A thought of Roger and his proposal came to mind, but she dismissed it. She liked him, but she loved the West and the life she could live here. She would not give it up again. Maybe, in time, if her feelings for him deepened and he came to love the West as much as she did, then she would think about marrying him.

Still, Lori wondered about her feelings for Roger. When he had kissed her so briefly earlier that afternoon, there had been no passion in her response, only a warm sense of being cared for. That did not compare to the electrifying touch of the deputy. She wrinkled her nose in childish distaste as she thought of the lawman and the unusual effect he had had on her senses. She didn't know why she had reacted so violently to his presence, but she had and the re-membrance of it still bothered her, even now. A shiver of some as yet unknown recognition quivered down her spine, and she hurried back to her pallet,

76

trying to push all thoughts of the arrogant man from her mind. Lying back down beside an already sleeping Sally, Lori pulled the light-weight cover up to her chin and tightly closed her eyes, but even as she curled on her side to seek sleep, the memory of the lawman's dark-eyed gaze and of her own breathless excitement taunted her.

## Chapter Four

The first light of day found Lori up, dressed, and eager to be on her way. The feeling of confidence that had possessed her during the long, dark hours of the night was even stronger in the brightness of the new day, and she was anxious to reach the Triple Cross and begin her new life. All else paled beside her new-found determination to complete her father's dream, and she watched impatiently as Pops and Riley hitched the team to the stage in preparation for the last leg of their journey to Phoenix.

"Lori?" Sally called as she appeared in the doorway of the bedroom. Since the doctor had left with his own guard at sunup, she had been sitting with Brady while Riley took care of his morning chores. "Are they ready for us to leave yet?"

"Not quite." Lori turned from the window. "How's the guard doing?"

"He still hasn't regained consciousness, but the doctor didn't seem too concerned when he was talking to Riley before he left. He seemed to think he'd recover because an infection hadn't developed."

"And he's not feverish?" Roger asked from where he was sitting at the table.

78

"Not in the least," Sally told them. "Call me when they're ready."

"I will," Lori promised. Then she watched her friend disappear into the bedroom.

Only a few moments passed before they heard Sally call, "Lori! Roger!"

They rushed to the bedroom doorway.

"Get Riley! He's starting to stir." Sally exclaimed, and as they hurried to find the stationmaster, she again turned her attention to the guard only to find him awake and watching her intently.

"I knew you were an angel when I first saw you," Brady rasped as he stared up at the dark-haired vision of loveliness hovering over him.

"Thank heaven, you're better!" She couldn't hide her pleasure. The doctor had been right. He was going to make it.

Brady tried to change his position, but the effort made him grimace. "Damn!" Realizing suddenly that she was real and no apparition, he quickly apologized for his profanity, "Oh, sorry, miss."

"Just relax and don't worry about a thing. We've been so worried about you."

"You have?" Though he was still groggy, her statement penetrated his haze of discomfort.

Sally flushed becomingly, and though she wanted to tell him of her very real concern for him, she was frightened of her response to him. "We *all* have, sir."

Her answer was evasive. Had Brady been well he would have pressed the point, but fatigue was overpowering him, dulling his senses, and making it difficult even to carry on a conversation.

Sally was relieved when Riley and Pops came charging into the room, and she quietly made her exit, leaving the three men to their heartfelt reunion. When Pops came into the outer room a short time later, his mood was considerably improved.

"Yep, he's gonna be just fine," he told them, grinning widely.

"That's wonderful, Pops," they agreed.

"I sure do appreciate all that deputy did to help us yesterday. Brady wouldn't have had a chance if it hadn't been for McAllister," he remarked. "I hope he's still in town when we get there 'cause I'm gonna buy him a beer!"

Lori started. Deputy? McAllister? She frowned and couldn't stop herself from asking, "Do you know him very well?"

"Nope, why?"

"Oh, nothing." She tried to sound casual, but Roger's eyes were suddenly upon her. "Except that I remember a man named Rand—Rand McAllister. He lived on the Lazy Ace with his father, and I think he was a sheriff, or something."

"Why yes, ma'am," Pops said, slightly surprised. "That was him."

"It was?" Her eyes rounded at the news.

"Yep. I asked him, when we stopped to pick him up, if he was related to the McAllisters of the Lazy Ace and he said that Will McAllister was his father."

"Oh." Lori blinked in confusion.

"You didn't recognize him?" Pops asked.

"I was only eleven the last time I saw him. It's been seven years," she replied distractedly, remembering with vivid clarity the last time she'd seen him—there in the stable . . . kissing his own stepmother. Lori had to suppress a shiver of disgust.

"Well, maybe you'll see him again in town. For now, we'd better get on the road, we still got some distance to cover this morning."

At Pops' instigation they began to gather up their belongings in preparation for leaving.

Within a half hour, they were in the stagecoach and rolling out of the relay station at a brisk pace, destination Phoenix. Roger had elected to ride on top with Pops for the balance of the journey, and Lori and Sally had settled themselves inside. Each young woman was now lost in thought.

Lori silently pondered the revelation that the man she'd faced yesterday in this very same coach had been Rand McAllister. Odd that she hadn't recognized him, she thought, but it had been a long time. At eleven, she had thought him a demigod and had worshipped him from afar until she'd discovered the sordid truth about his relationship with his stepmother. She grimaced mentally at the remembrance. How devastated she'd been—and how confused. It had hurt to find out that the man she'd idolized and imagined to be perfect was in truth an unprincipled rogue.

Lori thought of her own reaction to Rand when she had not known who he was, the heat of delayed embarrassment warmed her cheeks. If she had thought him handsome seven years ago, she found him even more so now, and she hoped fervently that she would not run into him again. He was an arrogant womanizer with the scruples of an alley cat and she wanted absolutely nothing to do with him.

Lori knew that she would have to pay a visit to the ranch to see Will McAllister for he'd always been like an uncle to her, but before she went, she was going to make sure that Rand would not be there. The last thing she wanted or needed was to see him with Lydia and his father. She'd been relieved, during those first years after witnessing the scene in the stable, that he had never been at the Lazy Ace when she and her father had visited, and she only hoped that her luck would continue for despite her newly acquired courtesy, it would be difficult to disguise her feelings. Hoping that

81

that problem would never arise, she stopped worrying and stared out the window at the cactus-studded countryside.

Oblivious to Lori's troubled thoughts, Sally pondered her own confusing emotions. She didn't understand how Brady Barclay could have come to be so important to her in such a short period of time, but when he'd awakened that morning and called her an angel, she'd been thrilled. Leaving the relay station had been one of the most difficult things she'd ever done and now she feared she might never see him again. Though Sally had never been one to connive to win a man's attention—she had disdained such practices in St. Louis—she now knew the desperation that could drive a woman to plot ways to catch her man, and she felt a surge of feminine power. Somehow, somewhere, she was going to meet Brady Barclay again, and when she did, she was going to win him for her own. Imagining him sweeping her into her arms and declaring his love for her, Sally enjoyed her pleasant daydreams as the rumbling, rocking stage headed for town.

They had been traveling for almost an hour when Pops caught sight of two riders approaching in the distance. "Grab the rifle," he told Roger, as he tightened his hold on the reins.

"Who are they?" Roger asked, taking a firm grip on the firearm.

"I'm not sure, but after yesterday, I'm not taking any chances," Pops grumbled, squinting into the brightness of the morning sun. Long, tense minutes passed before the riders drew close enough for him to recognize them. "It's okay," he finally told Roger.

"Good." Roger was relieved. "Who is it?"

"It's Marshal McAllister and Sheriff McCrea from town. Mornin'," Pops called as he slowed the stage to

82

a stop.

"Good morning, Pops, Roger," Rand greeted them as he reined in the mount John had loaned him.

"McAllister . . . Sheriff," they returned cordially.

"We ran into the doc on the trail a little earlier and he told us that Barclay's going to recover. That's good news."

"Yep," Pops said thankfully. "He came to a little before sunup and though he ain't feelin' too pert yet, he's gonna make it."

"Rand, here, told me about the hòldup attempt. Must have been pretty rough for you," John was saying.

Lori and Sally were both startled to feel the coach slow and come to a stop, and as they glanced nervously at each other, Lori once again reached into her reticule.

"What do you think is wrong?" Sally asked, still unnerved by the previous day's experience.

"I don't know but—" Rand's voice jolted her and she tried not to groan. "It's the marshal and another lawman."

"Thank goodness," Sally laughed. "I was afraid it was the outlaws coming back to try again."

"I know," Lori tried to sound relieved, but right then, if she'd had a choice, she might have preferred the outlaws to Rand. Hopefully, McAllister would go right on by after speaking with Pops and Roger, and there would be no contact between them.

"Don't you want to tell the marshal that you know him?" Sally never suspected that Lori wouldn't want to renew her acquaintance.

"Heavens no!" Lori blurted out the response so quickly that Sally looked puzzled.

"Why not? He seemed like such a nice man."

"I was just a child the last time I saw him. Besides it was his father who was close to my father. We were

83

never friends. He was a man then and I was only a little girl. He barely noticed me."

"All the more reason to let him know what a beautiful woman you've become," Sally said encouragingly.

"Not right now. I'll have to pay a visit to his father soon enough, and if he's there, I'll introduce myself. Otherwise, it really doesn't matter. I hardly think that we'll be moving in the same social circles here in town," Lori responded.

"If you say so."

"I do."

Outside, Pops was asking, "Why'd you two ride out this morning?"

"After I reported the holdup attempt, John thought it would be a good idea for us to take a look around," Rand explained. "No doubt the outlaws are gone by now, but we might be able to find something that will give us a clue as to who they were."

"I hope so, 'cause I sure don't like gettin' shot at and this here is my regular run. Good luck to you."

"See you, Pops, Roger," Rand started to ride away, but for some perverse reason he rode closer to the coach, reining in beside the passenger window and smiling widely at both Lori and Sally. "Afternoon, ladies." He greeted them easily, and his eyes swept over Lori. Damn! he thought with real irritation. She's as lovely as I remembered.

Lori stifled an inward groan at coming face to face with him again, yet she couldn't tear her gaze away from him. Clean-shaven and no longer looking like a saddle bum, he was definitely the Rand McAllister she remembered from her childhood, darkly handsome, tall and lean. She realized that he had changed little over the past seven years; even so, Lori sensed there was something different about him, a hardening of his personality, perhaps. It was reflected in his guarded expression.

"Hello, Marshal McAllister," Sally returned warmly.

"Marshal," Lori said with cool nonchalance, yet when he tipped his hat in her direction and wheeled his horse around to ride away, she suddenly felt very alone.

"I don't understand why you're hesitant to renew your acquaintance with him. He certainly seems personable enough," Sally remarked as she watched Rand ride off with the other rider.

"I'm sure he is. I just have other things on my mind right now." Her answer was sharp and Sally wondered at her mood.

"Whatever you say, Lori," she replied. "Now, how soon do you think we'll get to town?"


The sun-drenched town of Phoenix was an oasis of acequias and cottonwood trees, and Lori gazed excitedly about, finding it hard to believe that this sprawling, vital community was the one she'd left four years before. The advent of the railroad to Maricopa had made supplies available for potential builders in Phoenix, and now that the townspeople were no longer limited to adobe bricks, many handsome structures had sprung up. Impressed by the changes, Lori was convinced that she'd made the correct decision the night before so, when the stagecoach pulled up in front of the stage office, she descended from it eagerly, not bothering to wait for either of the men to help her.

"Roger, it's changed so much!" she exclaimed looking around.

Used to the lush attractiveness of the Mississippi River valley and the sophistication of St. Louis, Roger reserved judgment on this thriving desert community.

"It's certainly much larger than I'd expected and

85

seems more civilized, too. After Maricopa." He grinned ruefully remembering the boom town they'd passed through the day before. Then, as he helped Sally down from the coach and took their bags from Pops who unloaded them from the rear boot, he asked, "Where's the best place to stay here in town, Pops?"

"Gardiner's Hotel," Pops answered. "Just a couple of blocks over."

"Thanks. Can you have the luggage delivered there?" Roger stared down at the mound of baggage they'd brought along.

"Sure enough," the old man drawled as he started into the office to take care of his business. "See you folks."

"Thanks again, Pops, and good luck on your return run."

Pops raised an arm in friendly farewell as Roger accompanied Lori and Sally in the direction of the hotel.

"Now that we're finally here, Lori, what are your plans?" Sally wondered aloud.

"First, I need to send word to Hal out at the mine."

"Will it take long to hear from him?"

"It shouldn't. It's less than a day's ride to the Triple Cross, so we should receive a reply by the end of the week. I want to meet with Mr. Swartz, he's the lawyer who informed me of Father's death, and a Mr. Taylor at the bank, too. He made a very generous offer for the mine; I need to discuss that with him."

"I guess we'd better get settled in as quickly as possible so you can set up appointments with them."

"The sooner, the better," Lori agreed.


In the oppressive afternoon heat, Rand and John rode slowly in the direction of town. Their search for clues had turned up only the remains of the dead outlaw, and since he'd been exposed to the elements for a day, it was impossible for them to identify him.

"Where the hell was this guy when your passenger shot him?" John asked as they hastily dug a grave for the bandit. "Near to blew a hole clean through him."

"He was climbing on the side of the stage, trying to get on top."

"That Eastern tenderfoot really shot him at close range." John declared.

"Hardly," Rand said stiffly. "One of the women did it."

"A woman?"

Rand nodded curtly, remembering Lori's cutting comment.

"That was some brave woman, and she must know something about guns, too, because that wasn't any little derringer that put such a hole in him," John remarked after they'd finished burying the body.

As Rand considered his friend's words, he felt a reluctant admiration for the woman who'd haunted his sleep last night. Gorgeous and proficient with a gun . . . It was a devastating combination, just as Pops had said. He thought briefly of how she'd looked when he'd greeted her in the stage earlier, and he had to admit she was a cool one. She seemed a prim and proper miss, but her actions indicated otherwise.

"Are you going to ride back into town with me or take the cutoff out to the Lazy Ace?" John was asking so Rand forced his thoughts away from the green-eyed vixen.

"I left some things at the hotel, so I think I'll spend one more night in town before heading out to the ranch."

"Good. I'll enjoy your company on the ride back."

As they headed toward town, Rand knew that he could no longer put off his confrontation with Lydia.

Tomorrow, he would have to return to the Lazy Ace.

The night was hot, unusually so for this time of year, and though Roger and Sally had retired several hours before, Lori found herself, again, unable to sleep. Alone in her private room, she gazed out the window at the moonswept courtyard with the splashing pool in the center. Her excitement at being home had faded to a comfortable glow, and she was anticipating with confidence her scheduled meetings with the lawyer and the banker the next day.

Too keyed up to rest, Lori found the temptation of the cool, gurgling waters too difficult to resist so she left her room to seek the quiet serenity of the hotel's deserted courtyard. The chance for a few peaceful moments under the stars had great appeal, and she was pleased when she encountered no one on the way out. An impish feeling of daring came over her as she stood beside the inviting waters, and after a furtive glance around to be sure she was alone, Lori quickly slipped off her shoes and stockings. Hiking up her skirts, she sat down on the edge of the pool and dangled her feet over the side, relishing the coolness of the water. For a moment she was even tempted to go for a swim, but she decided that would be too risky. Stifling a giggle, she leaned back, and bracing herself with her arms, she closed her eyes, breathing deeply of the sweet freshness of the night air.

Rand had passed the evening with John, sharing a few drinks and some reminiscences at the Last Chance Saloon before returning to the hotel. Restless, he decided not to go directly to his room, but made his way instead to the hotel's private patio to enjoy a cheroot before turning in for the night.

He saw her as soon as he stepped silently out into the

night's concealing darkness. Forgetting about the cheroot, he stood unmoving near the building, watching her as she sat so comfortably on the side of the pool. Rand found it intriguing that she presented such a priggish façade to the world yet she could sit by a pool in the moonlight with her skirts up over her knees in a very unladylike pose and enjoy the waters with the enthusiasm of a child. But nothing else was childish about her as she sat there, head thrown back, body arched in imagined supplication to the silvered moonlight. Her glorious hair was unbound. Freed from the confines of the prim style she had been wearing, it was tied back from her face by just a single thin ribbon. Rand felt an unbidden urge to release that small restraint and run his hands through her lush curls.

Denying that desire, he tried to hold himself in restraint. He knew she was not a woman to be trifled with, and since he had no desire to become entangled with anyone wanting more from a relationship than a fleeting night of pleasure, he started to walk away. It was then that the soft sound of her song came to him—an entrancing, lilting melody that was haunting in its beauty. It wove a spell around him, holding him a willing captive. His iron-willed self-control weakened by his drinking and the silver splendor of the night, Rand found himself walking toward her, instead of away.

"You could be a siren," he murmured appreciatively as he stopped several steps behind her.

At the sound of his voice, so near, Lori started nervously and almost fell into the pool as she jerked around to see who it was.

"You!" she gasped as she quickly scrambled to her feet and hurried to smooth her long skirts. But her efforts were not quick enough, and Rand smiled widely as he caught a glimpse of her long, bare legs. "What are you doing here?" Lori demanded.

"I happen to have a room here. I might ask you the same question, little lady," he added in a serious tone, but his eyes were alive with mocking laughter.

"I have a room here, too," Lori replied with as much dignity as she could as she bent to pick up her shoes and stockings. "And I think I'll just retire there now—for some much needed privacy."

"How convenient for you, but don't rush off on my account. You seemed to be enjoying yourself and I'd hate to think that I'd robbed you of any pleasure. Especially since your straight shooting saved my life yesterday."

As she looked up, her eyes met his and their gazes locked in mental combat. Did he truly mean that or was he ridiculing her again? The starkness of the moonlight only seemed to enhance his good looks and Lori was mesmerized by him. He had been her hero as a young girl, and now he was here with her, alone, in the dark of the night.

"It did?" Her voice was tight and the words she uttered in such disbelief would, at any other time, have enraged her.

"You did," he agreed, and his deep voice flowed over her taut nerves like soothing honey. "And I wanted to thank you properly."

Rand suddenly knew he could not deny his need to kiss her. He wanted to taste of her sweetness, to hold her close and feel the fullness of her breasts pressed against him. With a gentle hand, he cupped the side of her face, and making no fast moves, he slowly dipped his head, his lips finding hers in a brief, soft caress . . . once . . . twice . . . before    claiming    her mouth completely for a devouring, possessive exchange.

Time ceased to exist for Lori as she was enveloped in

a strong embrace and held immobile against the hard wall of his chest. She knew she should fight him, that she should deny him the liberties he was taking with her, but there was something so devastatingly wonderful about being in his arms that she could neither think nor act. His passionate kiss left her heady and breathless, and when he finally released her, she could only look at him in dazed confusion.

Rand, too, was stunned by the intimacy of their kiss, but he quickly masked his feelings as he stepped back. Staring down at her, he was suddenly irritated by the force of his passion, and knowing there could be no future for them, he managed a wry grin, then said, "Thanks, little lady."

As his taunt cut through the romantic haze that had enveloped Lori, she returned to reality. He was not the longed-for prince of her dreams! He was Rand McAllister, the same lecher she'd seen kissing his stepmother only days after the woman had married his own father! He was a ruthless womanizer, and she'd been a fool to allow herself to be carried away.

"You're welcome, *Sheriff,*" Lori got out through gritted teeth, and with her head held high, she swept past him, shoes and stockings in hand.

Rand watched as she stalked rigidly across the courtyard. Despite his determination not to feel anything for her, he found himself admiring the sway of her hips and remembering the slender shapeliness of her long legs.

Lori was relieved when she made it back to her room without seeing anyone else and she shut and locked the door behind her in a symbolic gesture of defiance. As she was turning to her bed, she caught sight of herself in the mirror and she stared at her reflection in surprise. She looked so different! Her hair was flowing wildly about her shoulders, and her cheeks were flushed, whether from embarrassment, anger, or the as-yet-unforgotten pleasure she'd found in his embrace she wasn't sure. Nonetheless, her emotions were running wild and she knew she needed to bring herself under control. She despised Rand McAllister, and she must not let his one simple kiss affect her so!

Stripping off her clothing, she donned her night-gown and slipped beneath the covers of her bed, resolving not to think of him again. But even as she declared to herself that she would have nothing further to do with him, the memory of the feel of his hard body, the heated exploration of his lips, left her heart pounding. Not until the wee hours of the morning did sleep finally claim her.

# Chapter Five

"I see," Lori said slowly, frowning at the news the lawyer had just imparted to her. "Everything my father owns is tied up in the mine."

"I'm afraid so, Miss Spencer. Mr. Johnson your foreman at the mine hired me after your father's death to try to straighten out his affairs for you so you would have an accurate picture of your financial status when you returned. I've spent the last several weeks looking into his dealings."

"I appreciate all your efforts, Mr. Swartz," she replied. "It just comes as a bit of a shock to find out that all my father's wealth is on paper."

"I can well imagine, but your situation is not as desperate as it sounds. There is still the monthly stipend from your trust fund that he arranged to have paid to you in St. Louis. It was just his on-hand assets that were greatly strained by his venture into the new vein." The lawyer gave her a sympathetic look. "I suppose that's why he went to Taylor at the bank."

"I don't understand?"

"I see you haven't spoken with Mr. Taylor yet."

"No, but I do have an appointment with him later this afternoon. How was he involved with my father?"

"Your father was anxious to get as much of the new lode out as possible so he borrowed a considerable sum from the bank to cover the cost of the work."

"Oh." This was news to her for her father had never been one to borrow money. She decided he must have been extremely confident in the new strike to take such a risk. "Well, thank you for that bit of information."

"Of course," the older man nodded. "And if there's anything further I can help you with, please let me know."

"I will. There is one thing. I would appreciate it if you could arrange for my allowance to be paid into an account here in town. I'll be staying for a while and will be needing funds."

"I'll see to it right away."

As Lori left the lawyer's office, she found herself wondering at the arrangements her father had made with the bank's Mr. Taylor. Obviously, the assayer's report must have been good or they would never have loaned her father the money to develop the lode, and if Taylor was now interested in buying the Triple Cross, she was certain that the mine was capable of producing quality ore. Encouraged, she found herself looking forward to her meeting with the banker later that day.

Lydia was bored. There was no other term for it. Her days were stretching out in unending monotony, and even her trip to town and her lusty tryst with Josh had done nothing to ease the tedium.

Though it was near noon, she had not bothered to dress. Clad only in a silken dressing gown, she sat at the dining room table, sipping strong coffee and wondering what she was going to do with the rest of her life. She knew she couldn't go on this way indefinitely. She was young and vibrant and alive—why her body was

94

still as firm and lush as it had been when she'd first married Will—and the thought of spending six months in mourning left her totally distressed.

"Can I get you anything, *señora?*" Juana asked quietly as she entered the room. The *señora* had been inconsolable since her husband's death and, try as she might, Juana had not been able to cheer her. Even the trip to town yesterday had done nothing to lighten her spirits.

"The only thing I need right now is my stepson!" Lydia responded desperately. "Where is he? I sent him word of Will's death weeks ago and he hasn't bothered to come. Didn't he love his father? Doesn't he care that I've been left alone with this huge ranch to run?"

"Señor Rand will come, *señora,*" Juana assured her. She had known Rand since childhood, and despite the estrangement between him and his father, she knew of the true depth of his love for Will McAllister. As soon as it was humanly possible, she knew he would return. "This I can tell you."

"But when? How long must I suffer here alone?" she cried melodramatically. Lydia was playing the sorrowing widow convincingly so the servants would not be suspicious of her "need for comfort" when Rand finally did arrive. If her plans went as she hoped, Rand would be doing more with her than comforting her. He had been enamored of her once and she was certain, now that his father no longer stood between them, she could easily rekindle that flame. Rand had been a wonderful lover, and she could hardly wait to share passionate moments with him. Josh Taylor be damned. Rand was the man she wanted now.

"He travels the territory, *señora.* You know that," Juana reminded her gently. "He may not even have received your letter yet, but when he does he will come without delay."

"I hope so." Lydia sighed, rising from the table. "I'll be in my room, Juana, and I don't want to be disturbed."

"Yes, *señora,*" Juana watched her mistress disappear down the hall toward the master bedroom.

Rand pulled back on the reins as he topped the low rise that overlooked the ranch. Spread out before him was the Lazy Ace and he couldn't help but appreciate the magnitude of what his father had created out of the Arizona wilderness. Rand felt slightly humbled by this overview of his father's accomplishment, and he hoped that he would be capable of keeping the Lazy Ace prosperous. Urging his horse forward, he started down the slope toward his long-avoided reunion with Lydia. Knowing that he would be staying on for at least a few days, he rode directly to the stables and gave his horse to Leroy, the ranch hand there.

"Welcome back, Rand," the man's greeting was warm but tinged with sadness.

"Thanks, Leroy," he replied as he took his saddle-bags and rifle from his mount.

"Sorry about your pa. We all miss him. He was a good man."

"I appreciate it. Is Jack around?"

"He rode out this morning, but I expect he'll be back by sundown."

"When he returns, tell him I want to see him at the main house."

"Yes, sir."

"And when the horse has been rested, have someone plan on taking him back to town. He belongs to Sheriff McCrea."

"Yes, sir."

Rand's expression was grim as he started toward the

96

house, rifle in hand.

"Señor Rand!" Juana greeted him ecstatically as he came through the back door into the kitchen. "We have been waiting—and worrying! We did not know if you were dead or alive." Her tears flowed freely as she went to him and Rand quickly put his things aside in order to embrace her. "It's been so terrible!"

"I know. I couldn't believe the news myself. Lydia's letter didn't reach me until just a couple of days ago. I came as soon as I could."

"I told the *señora* you would come!" she gave him a teary smile. "You are a good man, Rand. I know you will take care of everything."

"I'll try, Juana," he promised, feeling the pain of his father's loss even more greatly now that he was back. "Tell me . . . what happened? The letter didn't go into detail, and all John McCrea could tell me when I stopped in town was that there had been a landslide and both father and George Spencer were killed in it."

"*Sí.*" She took his hand and led him to the table so they could sit. "Your father had gone to visit him. It was an accident and so tragic and the *señora* . . . she is so sad now. I have tried and tried to cheer her, but she is beside herself with grief. She will be so glad you are here! She needs you, Rand."

Girding himself to face Lydia he asked, "Where is she?"

"In her room, resting," Juana offered.

"I'll go to her," Rand declared reluctantly. "Have my room readied. I'll be staying."

"That's wonderful! I'll take care of your room myself right away," she promised. "Now, go to her. She's afraid that something has happened to you, too. It will do her good to see you and know that you are well."

Rand nodded as he started off toward the master bedroom. He hesitated only briefly at the door before knocking twice and softly calling her name.

Lydia had been lying down, the drapes drawn against the blinding brightness of the sun, when she heard the knock at her door. Annoyed that Juana was disobeying her order not to be disturbed, she called out in a waspish tone, "What is it? I thought I told you I wanted to be left alone!"

"Lydia?"

The sound of the deep voice, so well remembered, sent a surge of excitement through her, and Lydia flew from the bed and threw open the door, unmindful of her half-undressed state.

"Rand?" She sighed breathlessly as she stared up at him. "Oh, thank God, you've come." And in a perfect imitation of a swoon, she let herself go limp.

Reacting instantly, Rand took her in his arms, lest she fall.

"Lydia? Are you all right?" Lifting her slight form, he carried her a short distance and then laid her carefully upon the wide softness of the bed. Only as he put her down did he notice she was only wearing a silken wrap that did little to conceal her figure. Even after seven years, he appreciated her beauty, but he felt no desire and he quickly covered her with one of the sheets on the bed.

Lydia suppressed a smile at his action. He had noticed her! That was the first step in her plan, to make him aware of her as a desirable woman.

"I think so," she told him weakly as she took his hand and held tightly to it. "I was just so glad to see you. So much has happened."

His heart hardened as he remembered the ploy in the stable all those years ago, and he looked down at her skeptically.

Lydia accurately read his thoughts. "Rand, I know you must hate me after what I did the last time we

98

were together, but you must believe me when I tell you that I did it only because I cared so deeply for your father!" Her grip on his hand tightened in feigned desperation. "Please . . . I loved Will with all my heart and I was so afraid that you would tell him about us."

"You didn't know me very well if you thought I was capable of such an act," he replied tersely.

"Maybe not. We were different people then, but I've been a good wife to your father all these years. He meant everything to me." His money meant everything to me, she thought. "That's why his death is such a shock. I mean one day he was here and he was fine, and the next . . ." Lydia choked back a sob.

"Tell me about it," he coaxed, finding her performance convincing.

"Help me sit up first. I feel so ridiculous just lying here like this." She sighed and, as Rand leaned over her, clung to his shoulders, allowing him to lift her to a sitting position. After positioning several pillows behind her, she waited as he drew a chair up beside the bed and sat down. "Thank you. This is much better." Her smile was effectively tinged with melancholy, and as she straightened the sheet across her lap, she was very aware of the way the satiny gown clung to the curves of her breasts outlining their succulent sweetness. Lydia remembered how enamored he'd been with her all those years ago, and she wanted to arouse the same excitement in him.

Rand was beginning to feel compassion for Lydia as he waited for her to tell him of his father's accident. What had occurred between them had happened long ago, in another lifetime, almost; and it was true that she had made his father a good wife during the intervening years. Perhaps he was being too hard on her, letting his judgment be colored by her past deeds. His gaze swept over her, and though his expression was carefully controlled, he could not miss the full press of her bosom against the invitingly soft material of her wrapper.

"Go on," he urged.

"There's really not much to tell. He went to the Triple Cross Mine to visit George Spencer, and from what I understand, they were on their way back here when they were caught in a landslide in the mountains. They were both killed instantly." She shivered as she remembered the afternoon when the miners had brought Will's body to her. "Oh, Rand, it was terrible."

This time Rand took her hand, and Lydia knew another moment of triumph.

"It's over now, Lydia."

"I know, but I miss him so." She began to cry softly. "I had gone into town. I had been socializing with our friends and shopping and enjoying myself, and all the while he was . . . I should have been with him!"

Seeing her desperation, Rand sat beside her on the bed and took her into his arms, drawing her across his lap. "It'll take time, but the hurt will lessen. You mustn't feel guilty. It was an accident, Lydia. Father would have wanted you to go on with your life."

Lydia smiled to herself at Rand's words. She would go on with her life, and though Rand didn't know it yet, he was going to be a part of it.

She sat quietly as he held her, enjoying the feel of his hard strength. It had been a long time since she'd known the power of his driving possession, but she knew she would not have much longer to wait.

"Thank you, Rand," she murmured as she leaned against him.

"For what?" He was surprised by her words.

"For not hating me anymore. I know you did when you left, but I'd always hoped we could be friends." Lydia pulled slightly away to look up at him. "Especially since we're now co-owners of the Lazy Ace."

Again, she took him off guard by being so forthright, "Yes, well—"

"It's all right." She moved away from him, and as she settled back on the bed once more, he stood up and strode across to the window. "Your father loved you very much and he was very proud of you, in spite of what you may have thought during these last few years."

"And I loved him, Lydia," he told her gruffly as he pushed aside the drapes and stared out at the vastness of the ranch.

"I know. That's why I want us to get along, for the sake of your father's memory and for the sake of the Lazy Ace. Do you think after all this time you can bring yourself to understand and to forgive me?" Lydia felt she would have more control over Rand and their current situation if she brought the reason for their enmity out in the open.

Rand didn't know what he'd been expecting from Lydia, but it had not been this. Caught unprepared, he was momentarily at a loss as to how to handle her.

"You were a free woman and you made your choice. What happened, happened. I'm sure you had your reasons, but it's over. Let's leave it that way." He did not hear her get up from the bed, and he was surprised when he felt her hand on his arm and found her beside him, looking almost radiant.

"Thank you, Rand." Her voice was husky with meaning. "You'll never know how much this means to me."

Josh came forward to take Lori's hand as she entered his office. "Miss Spencer! How nice to see you. I'm only sorry we have to begin our acquaintance under such trying circumstances. My sympathies on your loss. It was a terrible tragedy for both families."

"Thank you, but what do you mean by 'both' families?" Lori found his statement puzzling.

"Why, yours and the McAllisters."

"The McAllisters? I don't understand."

"You didn't know that Will McAllister died in the same accident?"

"No." She was shocked by the news. No wonder Rand had been back in the area. "Hal made no mention of that in his letter."

"Perhaps he didn't want to add to your burdens . . . I'm sure it's been difficult enough for you just dealing with your father's death . . ."

"It hasn't been easy," she responded as he showed her to a chair.

"How was your trip?" Taylor inquired, politely changing the subject as he seated himself behind his desk.

"My trip was . . . shall we say, eventful?"

"Oh? I hadn't heard that there was any trouble. What happened?"

"My stagecoach was set upon by bandits on the trip from Maricopa. Luckily, with the help of the guard and another passenger we were able to fight off the holdup attempt, but there were a few tense moments."

"I can imagine," Josh agreed, thinking that she was certainly composed for someone who'd been through such a near brush with disaster. "But I'm glad to see that you've suffered no ill effects from it."

Lori forced her most gracious smile, even though she found his words annoying. Was she supposed to swoon over bandits and holdups? "I'm quite fine, I assure you." Having dismissed the episode, she hoped not too abruptly, she got to the point. "Now, in regard to your letter . . ."

Josh was surprised by her no-nonsense manner, and he wondered if she was going to be as easy to manipulate as he'd originally thought.

"Yes." He cleared his throat. "I take it you've had the opportunity to study my offer. Have you reached any conclusions?"

"Not as yet." She was unwilling to tell him the truth until she found out the exact details of her father's indebtedness to the bank. "I've sent word of my arrival to Mr. Johnson, the supervisor at the Triple Cross, and I'm not going to make any final decisions until I've spoken in depth with him."

"I see."

"I also learned through the lawyer who's handling my father's affairs that the bank holds a note on the mine."

"Yes. That is true. Your father came to me shortly before his death and arranged for a loan in the amount of twenty thousand dollars to help expedite the development of the new vein he'd discovered."

"I'd like to see a copy of the agreement," she said and when he held out a document, she read it carefully as he looked on. "These terms are a bit unusual, wouldn't you say, Mr. Taylor?" Lori asked pointedly as she studied the loan papers.

"This is what your father requested. Evidently he did not like being in debt to anyone. That seemed to be his primary concern when he set the payback date," Josh explained, now slightly uneasy for he realized this was no simpering miss, but an educated, intelligent young woman.

"That's very true. He would have wanted this amount paid back on time, if not earlier," Lori agreed, seemingly calm while her mind raced to find a way to come up with the twenty thousand dollars by September.

"My offer to buy the Triple Cross stands," he told her smoothly. "And as you know, the amount I am willing to pay would leave you comfortably well off after repayment of the debt."

"Yes, and I appreciate the generosity of your proposal. As soon as I've had a chance to meet with Hal, I'll contact you." She handed him the note and stood up. "Thank you for your time."

"Of course. I'm anxious to know your decision, so don't hesitate to call upon me."

"You'll be among the first to know, sir."

Lori's spirits were flagging as she returned to the hotel. Twenty thousand dollars! She had to come up with twenty thousand dollars within five months. Surely, she reasoned as she tried to calm herself, her father loved the mine so he would not have done something foolish. He certainly would not have borrowed that amount unless he'd been positive it could be paid back on time. Hoping that Hal would confirm her suspicions, she went on into the hotel dining room where Roger and Sally were waiting for her.

"Hello!" Roger stood as she approached the table, and he held the chair for her as she sat down. "How did the meeting go?"

"Well," Lori began, feeling weary now, "my father does owe the bank a substantial sum, and it's due and payable in September."

"So, did you tell Taylor you'd take him up on his offer to buy you out?" Sally asked.

When they had discussed this in St. Louis, Lori had been very tempted to take the money so she could remain there, but of course Sally didn't know that the night at the relay station, she'd decided she would not

104

be going back.

"No. I told him I hadn't reached a firm decision yet and that I would speak with him again after I meet with Hal Johnson."

"The mine supervisor?" Roger looked puzzled.

"Yes." Lori suddenly became very serious. "I am certain my father would not have gone into debt unless he was certain the money could be repaid. The Triple Cross is a working, profitable mine, and if Hal thinks I can make a go of it, I'm going to stay here and give it a try."

"What!" Roger was astounded, as was Sally. When last they'd talked, it had been decided that they would all be returning to St. Louis as soon as possible.

Lori sensed their stunned disapproval, and her expression was slightly .mutinous as she met their questioning gazes. "I know this is totally at odds with what I said before we left, but now that I'm back, I want to stay here. I love the West; I've always loved it. I just didn't know how much until now."

"But surely you don't want to work the mine?" Sally couldn't hide her shock. "What kind of work would that be for a woman?"

"Sally," Lori scolded, "I've worked in mines ever since I was old enough to carry a shovel. It's hard work, but familiar to me. My father taught me everything he knew, and that's why I feel certain I can handle it."

"Lori," Roger said levelly, "if it's the money you're worried about, I'll give it to you. Keep the mine as an investment, but there's no need for you to become involved in the everyday work, is there? Many mines operate successfully though their owners are in the East. Why not the Triple Cross? You can return to St. Louis with us as we'd planned and leave your Mr. Johnson in charge. You've said he's honorable and trustworthy and capable."

Lori understood their objections, but her mind was made up and they could not deter her from her purpose. "I appreciate your offer to help, Roger, but this is something I feel I must do. I owe it to my father—and to myself."

Though Roger loved Lori, he'd always had trouble understanding her stubborn independence. Other women he knew were delighted to let men handle things, deferring to their "superior intellect and judgment," but not Lori. She challenged him at every turn, and her astute observations and clear thinking kept life exciting. Now they were again at odds on an appropriate course of action, and Roger knew better than to argue with her. Lori knew her own mind. She would not be swayed once she'd decided to do something.

"If you've definitely made up your mind, I know I can't deter you," he remarked with a small smile. "But please think about my offer to pay off the debt. There is no reason for you not to accept my help."

"There is every reason," Lori countered, her pride coming to the fore. "I will not presume upon our friendship to finance my father's work."

Roger's heart sank when she used the word "friendship," but he responded calmly. "I understand your reasoning, but remember, if you do find that you need my help all you have to do is ask."

"I know." Lori's eyes were warm with gratitude. "And it's a good feeling to have two such close friends."

"We'll be glad to do whatever we can to help you," Sally promised.

"After I talk to Hal, I'll know more about what needs to be done. Until then, I appreciate your being here with me."

"I wouldn't want to be anywhere else," Roger said with heartfelt sincerity, and Lori couldn't help but feel a slight twinge of guilt for she was well aware that she was not in love with him.

"Miss Lorelei?" The gruff familiar voice hesitantly broke into their conversation.

"Hal!" Despite the stares of the onlookers in the restaurant, Lori flew into the waiting arms of Hal Johnson. "I'm so glad you're here!"

The white-haired man embraced the young woman as if she were most fragile, and his tanned, weather-beaten face revealed his devotion. "I came as soon as I got your note."

Lori gave him a beaming smile. "Thank you."

"I'm sorry about your father." He choked up as his eyes met hers in silent acknowledgment of their loss.

"I know." She touched his forearm in understanding. "We'll talk more later, but right now I want you to meet two friends who accompanied me on my trip. Hal Johnson, this is Sally Westlake and her cousin Roger Westlake. Sally, Roger, this is Hal."

The Westlakes greeted him, and Roger stood to shake his hand. "Will you join us?"

"Please, Hal. There's so much we need to discuss."

"Miss Lorelei . . ." Hal glanced about the crowded room. "Is there some place more private where we can talk?"

"We could go upstairs to my room," she offered, and he was quick to agree.

A short time later the four of them were ensconced in Lori's quarters at the hotel, deep in conversation.

"It's been difficult with your father gone, but we are still making the progress he'd hoped for," Hal was saying, his expression reflecting his earnest excitement about the new lode. "This is it, Miss Lorelei! The vein has shown no sign of weakening!" Suddenly his animation died. "I just wish George had lived to see it. He worked so hard for so long and now . . ."

Lori understood Hal's sentiments and quickly reassured him. "And now, *you and I* will see it through."

"You're not going to sell out?" Hal was amazed. Although he'd worked with George for years and had known Lori as a child, he'd been afraid that the time she'd spent back East had changed her. He had not expected her to want to continue with the Triple Cross. In fact, he had been expecting her to tell him that she was selling out.

Lori was startled by his words. "Sell the only connection I have to my father? Sell his dream? No, Hal. I won't do that. He loved the Triple Cross and I owe it to him to try to follow through with his plans."

"Miss Lorelei, that's the best news I've ever had!"

She smiled. "We can and will bring this to fruition, but I have to know the current status of everything involved in our operation. Do you know about the debt to Taylor at the bank?"

"I knew that George borrowed some money."

"Well, it's more than 'some'," Lori declared "We have to repay twenty thousand dollars by September. Can we do it?"

"The way things are going right now . . . yes." Hal answered thoughtfully. "But it will take a lot of hard work."

"I'm ready and willing to do whatever needs to be done." Lori's unfaltering response reflected her commitment. "We can leave for the mine in the morning, after I pay Mr. Taylor a visit."

"Yes, ma'am."

"Roger and Sally will be coming with us."

"That's fine, Miss Lorelei. There's plenty of room in your father's house for you two ladies and Roger can bunk with me."

"Good. We'll make some purchases before we go and

pick up any additional supplies you may need." She realized the clothing she'd brought was unsuitable for working at the Triple Cross. "Shall we plan on heading out some time before noon?"

"Whenever you're ready," Johnson agreed, then he stood up to go.

"Good night, Hal, and thanks for everything," Lori said softly as she walked with him to the door.

"Good night, Miss Lorelei." Hal Johnson smiled down at her affectionately, seeing a resemblance to her father in the steadfast honesty of Lori's gaze.

## Chapter Six

As the first tinge of sunlight brightened the horizon, Lydia came awake, happily anticipating the new day. It was the first time in months that she'd been excited about anything and she liked the feeling. Even before Will's death she'd grown weary of the tedium of ranch living, but now, with Rand's return, she could view the Lazy Ace from a different perspective. No longer would she look upon each day as twenty-four hours to be coped with; now she had a goal and that goal was within reach. Rand would be hers!

Slipping from beneath the covers, she called for her maid Isabel and then stripped off her gown and hurried to begin her toilette, knowing that she now had reason to take extra care with it. Mourning clothes or not, she was determined to look her best for Rand. The young Isabel was surprised by this sudden change in her mistress' behavior, but knowing that it was not her place to make any remark, she catered silently to the *señora*'s wishes, and almost an hour later, Lydia emerged from her room. Her cleverly applied makeup enhanced her pale beauty, and her hair, brushed out into a mass of silvery blond curls, tumbled down her back in studied disarray, making her appear very youthful. Even in the somber black, her loveliness was undeniable, and she entered the dining room feeling confident of her ability to seduce Rand back into her arms and her bed.

"Good morning, *señora.*" As was her custom Juana brought Lydia coffee after she'd taken a seat at the table.

"Good morning, Juana," Lydia replied coolly as she sipped the steaming brew. "Where is my stepson this morning?" she asked, as if this were an afterthought.

"Señor Rand rode out with Jack before sunup, *señora,*" Juana explained as she served her mistress her breakfast.

That news surprised Lydia, but she hid her reaction behind a veil of confusion. "Are there problems that I wasn't made aware of?"

"Not that I know of," Juana replied. "Will there be anything else for you this morning?"

"No . . . no, this is fine, Juana. Thank you."

Alone in the massive dining room, Lydia quelled her disappointment at not seeing Rand and she began to plot the best way to greet him upon his return. Certainly, she could not go running out to him like an eager lover. She must exercise caution, treat him as her partner in ownership of the ranch. The rest would follow in time.

Josh Taylor's handsome features were twisted by rage as he paced his office. Though he had suspected it might happen, he had never really believed it would until Lorelei Spencer had calmly informed him, only a short time before, that she was going to assume control of the Triple Cross and work it herself. He had tried to convince her a mere woman would not be able to run a mine, let alone make it pay, but she had dismissed his carefully cloaked discouragement without a thought. She was determined to make the Triple Cross a success, she'd told him so as she'd left his office, and she'd also assured him that the bank would have its money by September.

Stung by Lorelei's confident manner, Josh gritted his teeth, angry over his thwarted takeover. He knew that he would have to rely on Harley Oates again, for he was not going to give up his plan to have both the money and Lydia. Oates could slow the operation so the loan could not be repaid; then foreclosure would be automatic. He smiled thinly at the thought. He'd truly enjoy watching that arrogant little miss fail.

As Rand left Jack at the stables and started back toward the main house, he was pleased with what he'd learned that morning. Jack had updated him on the condition of the ranch, and the news had all been good. Satisfied that he could keep to his original plan—leave the Lazy Ace under Jack's supervision and return to his duties as deputy marshal, he was now set to offer to buy Lydia out.

Rand had thought of her often that morning and it had surprised him to discover that he no longer harbored any ill will toward her. He'd realized, after their frank discussion last night, that she had been in a desperate position when she'd thrown herself at him all those years ago. He'd been young and naïve at the time, and her betrayal in choosing his father over him had been a painful lesson. Because of Lydia, he would never again trust a woman, but it was time to let go of his bitterness. He would buy out her share of the Lazy Ace, at a profit to her, and then get on with his own life. Having determined his course of action, he entered the house to find Lydia awaiting him in the parlor. With

112

her was a nattily dressed man he'd never seen before.

"Rand . . ." She stood and came to meet him. "I'm so glad you're back. This is Mr. Richards, your father's attorney. He heard of your return, and he's come out to the ranch to go over the will with you and to give you the papers your father entrusted to him."

Rand shook the lawyer's hand. "Mr. Richards."

"It's nice to meet you, Mr. McAllister."

"Rand, please," he insisted as they sat down.

"I take it Mrs. McAllister has made you aware of the contents of your father's will and that you know you now own a sixty percent interest in the Lazy Ace with your stepmother owning the balance?"

"Yes. She included that information when she wrote to inform me of my father's death."

"Good. She assured me that she would explain the terms to you." He looked pleased and then he frowned. "But, in case you're wondering, that was not my primary reason for coming here today."

"Oh?" Rand looked at him questioningly as did Lydia.

"There's something else?"

"Yes. It has to do with the additional documents Will placed in my keeping some time ago." He took out a packet of official-looking papers from his inside coat pocket. "They were to be delivered to you personally, should anything happen to him."

Rand was puzzled as the attorney started to untie the string that bound the packet. "Have you gone over those?"

"I am aware of the contents, yes."

"And?"

"And there is only one that really has any bearing on your current situation," the lawyer stated as he unfolded the yellowed sheet of paper he'd withdrawn from the envelope. "According to this document drawn

113

up ten years ago, you are now the legal guardian of George Spencer's daughter, one Lorelei Spencer."

"What?" Rand quickly looked up at the attorney. "What are you talking about?"

"Evidently, George Spencer was alone in the world except for his child, and he wanted to make certain she would be cared for should anything happen to him. He and your father were close friends so they drew up an agreement whereby your father agreed to take custody should George die before Lorelei was twenty-one."

Rand stood up impatiently. "Are you telling me that I'm now responsible for some little child?"

Richards smiled wryly. "Lorelei Spencer is not a child. According to my calculations, she is now eighteen years old."

"Eighteen?" Lydia remembered only too well the unwelcome presence of Lorelei in the first days of her marriage to Will. Though she had seen the child on several occasions, she had always disliked her.

"Yes," Richards answered. Then he turned back to Rand. "And it is binding, for your father wrote in a special provision that should he not be able to carry out the responsibility, it would fall to you." He handed Rand the letter of agreement.

"But why?" Rand's exasperation was obvious as he read the document.

"George Spencer had no one else to turn to. You know the kind of life a gold miner lives. He loved his daughter above all else, and he wanted her to have someone she could turn to." He pointed to the document. "There are certain exclusions at the end."

Rand quickly read the last clauses. "So, I'm her guardian until she turns twenty-one or marries."

"Correct."

"Where is she? Does she know about this guardianship?" Lydia was irritated by this unexpected discovery.

114

The last thing she wanted was an involvement with that Spencer girl.

"I'm not sure, although there certainly must be a copy of this agreement with Mr. Spencer's papers. As far as I know, Miss Spencer is East at school."

"Fine," Lydia remarked with ill-concealed malice. "She can stay there. I'm sure there's enough money coming out of the Triple Cross to keep her comfortable."

"Indeed there is, but according to this paper, and it is legal and binding, Rand has complete control of all the monies."

"I do?" He scowled as he realized that a web of unforeseen complications was tying him more and more firmly to the Lazy Ace and that he might not get back to his duties for some time.

"Yes, you do," Richards affirmed. "And as your legal counsel, I think it's important that you get in contact with Miss Spencer as soon as possible to work out some kind of understanding."

"Yes, yes, of course," Rand agreed distractedly. He could barely remember Lorelei for it had been over seven years since he'd last seen her. She'd been a mere child then. No, he wanted as little to do with this as possible. "Contact her and make whatever arrangements you need to make."

"Fine, I will, and as soon as I learn anything, I'll notify you."

"Thank you." As Rand showed the lawyer out, he added, "I'll be waiting to hear from you."

When he'd gone, Lydia faced Rand. "I don't believe it."

"Neither do I," he replied grimly. "Lord." Wearily, he rubbed the back of his neck. "I don't even remember what Lorelei Spencer looks like."

"She was a pretty enough child, I suppose," Lydia

said coldly. "But I haven't seen her since she left for school years ago."

Rand nodded. Then he stalked to the small table that served as a bar and poured himself a bourbon, neat. "I can understand why George and Father drew up the agreement back then, but she's no longer a little girl."

"Don't worry, Rand." Lydia went over and stood beside him as he downed his drink. "Lorelei is probably so enamored of her life in the East that she wouldn't think of returning. You'll probably just have to set up some kind of allowance for her. And who knows, she might already be engaged to be married."

"I hope so. I don't need responsibility for some young girl tying me down here."

"What are you saying?" Lydia was shaken by his statement. "Are you planning on leaving the Lazy Ace?"

"I want to return to my job. I'm needed."

"But I need you here, Rand. This ranch is so big it'll be virtually impossible for me to run alone."

Rand glanced down at her and he quickly realized this would be a good time to discuss his plan to buy her out. "I've wanted to talk with you about the ranch and our future dealings together, Lydia. I might as well do it now."

Lydia felt the color drain from her face. "Of course. What is it that you wanted to say?"

"I want to buy out your share, Lydia." He was aware of her gasp of disbelief. "Before you say anything, understand that my price will be more than fair. You'll make a fine profit from my offer, and you won't have to worry about managing the Lazy Ace all by yourself."

"Rand! How can you even suggest that I sell?" She was outraged and totally unprepared for this. After last night, she'd thought things were better between them. "The Lazy Ace has been my home for the past seven years and I love it here!"

"I can understand your sentiments, but—"

"No, you can't understand, not if you expect me to sell my interest to you. I don't want to leave here, Rand. I can't. All my happiest memories are here." Desperate to find a ploy that would work, she resorted to the age-old feminine tactic of tears.

Frustrated, Rand stared down at her. His guardianship of Lorelei Spencer was complicating his plans and now Lydia was refusing to sell. "Lydia," he began, and she raised her tear-filled eyes to gaze up at him.

"You don't want me to stay here, do you Rand?" she asked in a breathless whisper. "Oh, Rand, please tell me that you don't want me to go."

"Lydia, I—"

"Please . . ." Reckless because of her sudden need to know that a spark of the old flame still existed between them, Lydia took a daring chance. With mesmerizing slowness, she leaned toward him, offering herself in helpless surrender.

Rand had no intention of kissing her, but it happened. One moment she'd been crying in heart-broken desolation; the next she was in his arms, kissing him and clinging to him with a passion he thought he'd forgotten. He indulged himself for only a moment before tearing her arms from his neck and moving away from her.

"Lydia"—his voice was hard—"there was no need for this desperate move seven years ago and there's no need for it now. If you think I'll throw you out of your home, you've misjudged me again."

Without another word he quit the room, leaving Lydia staring after him in stunned uncertainty. He had thought that she was prostituting herself to achieve her goal and the thought riled her. Didn't the fool realize she really wanted him?

As the heat of her anger cooled, she realized that she had made a serious tactical error. It didn't matter that she now truly desired him. He had judged her actions by her past behavior, and she could not allow that to happen again. In the future, she must be most careful about how she approached him and why.

Rand strode purposefully from the parlor wanting only to get away from Lydia. Despite the fact that most of his plans had gone awry, he felt more in control than he had been for some time. He had kissed Lydia—it was something he'd alternately dreaded and hoped for since he'd had to return home—and he'd discovered that she no longer had any power over him. Her kiss had been pleasant enough, but the explosive passion they'd once shared was dead. In fact, compared to the kiss he'd shared with the woman from the stage, Lydia's was sadly lacking. The thought of the fiery vixen named Lori brought a small smile to his lips, and he wondered if she was still in town . . . if he would ever see her again.

The jostling of the poorly sprung wagon left Sally and Lori feeling battered and bruised as Hal drove them over the rough mountainous terrain toward the Triple Cross. The young women couldn't help but envy Roger who had elected to ride Hal's horse rather than crowd onto the single seat of the buckboard. They'd been traveling since before noon, but now, as the sun dipped low in the west, they knew the end of their journey was near.

"I'm glad you suggested these clothes," Sally told Lori as she hung on to the edge of the buckboard seat for support.

"I know they're not fashionable, but where we're

going fashion is the last thing we'll need to worry about."

Both women had forsaken the usual cumbersome sunbonnets for Stetsons, and they'd traded their traveling gowns for practical split riding skirts, tailored blouses and boots. These outfits were far more comfortable in the stifling heat.

"I still can't believe you're really going to wear those breeches!" Sally couldn't help but laugh as she thought of the men's denim pants Lori had bought during their excursion to the store in Phoenix.

"Once we get to the mining camp, you'll understand my need for them," her friend assured her.

Roger glanced at her askance as he rode alongside the wagon. He wondered what the miners in the camp would think when they saw a woman as attractive as Lori wearing pants. "I suppose so Lori, but—"

She cut him off, not wanting to listen to any protests over her mode of dress. "Roger, don't worry."

There was work to be done and she would do it. The men at the mine were her employees. As such they would not dare show her any disrespect. "The pants are practical for working in the mine, that's all. You'd be far more outraged if I tried to go up and down the ladders in skirts." Her eyes twinkled as she imagined herself trying to make such a climb in one of her dresses.

"I see your point." He grimaced at the thought.

Lori smiled at him good-naturedly and let her gaze take in the change his new apparel had made in him. No longer wearing the duds of a greenhorn, Roger looked like a whole new man in the more practical Western wear. The denims he'd purchased fit him snugly, emphasizing the lean length of his legs, and the soft, white material of his shirt stretched tautly across the muscular width of his shoulders as he expertly handled Hal's spirited mount. His low-crowned white Stetson he'd purchased gave him a rakish look, and the new six-gun he was wearing low on his right hip already looked a part of him.

It pleased Lori to know that he could fit in so easily, and she hoped that her feelings for him would deepen during the time they'd have together at the mine for she could think of no man she liked more than Roger. Still, the fleeting remembrance of her response to Rand McAllister's passionate embrace taunted her though she tried to dismiss it. That moment of desire she'd felt in his arms must have been a fluke. Surely, if Roger kissed her in the moonlight, with a seductive pool of cool, splashing water nearby, she'd be breathless in his embrace, too!

"There it is! The Triple Cross," Hal suddenly exclaimed.

Nestled in the protective valley between two towering hillsides ahead of them lay the rock and mortar outbuildings of the mine. The tents that belonged to the miners were set up around the larger structures. To Roger and Sally, who were unfamiliar with mining life, the Triple Cross looked little better than some of the shanties they'd seen in St. Louis, but to Lori it was beautiful. Only Hal noticed her rapturous expression as she gazed upon her home for the first time in four years, and he slapped the reins impatiently on his team's backs, urging the beasts to pick up their pace.

Pulling up to a stop before the largest of the permanent houses, Hal turned to Lori. "Do you want to go on in alone?"

She smiled tightly. "Yes . . . Do you mind Sally?"

"Of course not," her friend quickly replied, knowing how heartbreaking it must be to return and face the ultimate loss—the death of a loved one.

120

Lori started for the door just as Roger reined in beside her. "Lori?"

"I'll be fine, Roger. Just give me a few minutes," she declared, and with a bravado that was rapidly diminishing, she entered her home and closed the door behind her.

Nothing has changed, she thought as she stared around the main room, noticing that everything seemed just as she'd left it years before. The furnishings were sparse, but out here there was little need for the trappings of town living. The rough-hewn table and chairs, the threadbare sofa, were all endearingly familiar to her, and a shudder shook her at the final realization that her father was, indeed, gone. Her vision blurred by tears, she wandered to the mantel over the wide stone fireplace and lovingly picked up a proudly displayed tintype. It was a picture she'd had taken in St. Louis. She'd sent it to her father the first year she was away. Stifling a sob of loneliness, she moved blindly through the rest of the house, pausing in each of the two separate bedrooms to let memories drift over her, then, her emotions once more in control, she returned to the main room and opened the door.

"Nothing has really changed." She gave Hal a tender sad smile.

"I know," he told her, his voice husky with feeling. "Your Pa wanted to keep things pretty much as they were when you left. He said it made him feel closer to you."

Lori sighed and glanced back inside, half expecting her father to be there awaiting her with open arms, but the reality of his death could not be avoided.

Several hours passed before they were all finally settled in, Sally and Lori sharing her home and Roger moving into the supervisor's house which Hal occupied.

"Tomorrow, I'll call a meeting of the miners," Hal

121

was saying as they shared dinner that night in the main house. "And I'll fill you in on all the details."

"How many men do we have working for us now?" she asked, eager to learn all she could about the operation.

"There are fifteen miners and a resident assayer," he explained. "Your father had hoped to hire more, but the cost of hauling the ore to the stamp mill was keeping him on a tight payroll. Still, we're making it. I think you'll be pleased."

"I already am, Hal. You've done a wonderful job, carrying on since Father's death, and I appreciate it."

Hal's expression was serious, "I love the Triple Cross, Miss Lorelei. These past few years have been hard ones, but I know she's finally going to pay off big!"

"I feel it, too, Hal," she told him confidently. "The Triple Cross is everything my father believed it to be. We're going to pay off the bank debt on time and make him proud."

"I'm sure he already is," Johnson responded, his admiration growing for this young woman, who was proving to be so like her strong-willed sire.

"I hope so," Lori replied, and her smile was bittersweet.

# Chapter Seven

"She's here already? Where? In town?" Rand glanced sharply at the attorney. Two days had passed since their initial interview regarding his guardianship of Lorelei Spencer, and Richards had just returned to the ranch with the news that the young woman was already back in Phoenix.

"No. It's my understanding that she's already moved out to the mine—The Triple Cross."

"You're telling us that this eighteen-year-old girl is living in a mining camp—unchaperoned?" Lydia's disbelief was evident.

"Yes," the lawyer responded with a grimace. "That's why I thought it was important I inform you right away. It's hardly the place for a young, unmarried woman, even if her father's foreman is still running the mine."

Rand shook his head in disgust. "I suppose the only thing I can do is get her and bring her back here to live."

"I'll go with you, Rand," Lydia offered quickly, thinking that the ride to the mine would give them some time away from the watchful eyes of the servants.

"No, I'll be able to travel faster alone," he answered, preoccupied. "And I'd better take that copy of the

123

agreement with me, just in case she has any doubts."

"Would you like me to accompany you?" Richards offered.

"I really don't see the need. I'm sure Hal Johnson will remember me, even if Lorelei doesn't, and hopefully we'll be able to find her copy of the letter while I'm there. That should provide irrefutable proof should she decide to oppose me. Once that's settled, I'm sure she'll be amenable to my dictates." Rand sounded confident. "Certainly living here on the Lazy Ace will be more appealing to a young woman than life in a mining camp."

"I'm certain of it," the attorney agreed.

As she listened to the two men discuss the prospect of Lorelei Spencer's moving into her home, Lydia had trouble controlling her ire. The child had been incorrigible during her visits to the ranch, refusing all of Lydia's attempts at friendship. She was not looking forward to seeing her again, nor to her presence at the ranch.

"I'll leave right after noon," Rand was saying. "That way I should arrive at the mine by sundown."

"Please keep me notified of any developments," Richards requested.

"Of course. I'll send word to you as soon as we get back."

"Fine. Good day."

After the lawyer had gone, Rand went to his room to pack the few things he needed for the overnight trip and Lydia followed him, approaching him worriedly. "I don't know if this is such a good idea, Rand."

"What do you mean?"

"I mean, this Lorelei Spencer is your responsibility yet you're having her move into my home while you plan on leaving to return to your job as a deputy marshal."

124

"It's my home, too. I do own sixty percent of it," he told her cuttingly. "And if I choose to have my ward live here, she'll live here."

Lydia stiffened at his attempt to put her in her place. "I was only pointing out that she is *your* ward, not mine, yet I'll probably end up being responsible for her!"

"It's not as if she's a child, Lydia," Rand replied. "She's just spent four years in school and would, no doubt, like to return back East to finish her education. Who knows? She might even be engaged to be married! That would solve our problems."

Lydia pondered that thought and smiled. "You're right, of course. I'm worrying needlessly."

"You are," he declared as he picked up his saddlebags and started from the room.

"Rand . . ."

"What?" Rand turned back to her impatiently.

"Do you know when you'll be back?"

"I shouldn't be gone more than a couple of days." He headed down the main hall, stopping only briefly to retrieve his rifle from the guncase.

"You'll be careful?"

"I'm always careful, Lydia."

Then, without another word, he was gone, leaving her hoping for his return but dreading Lorelei Spencer's presence.


Black threatening clouds stained the western horizon as darkness staked an early claim on the land, and when streaks of lightning erupted from the roiling dark clouds in the distance, the deep rumble of thunder reverberated through the valley.

Lori had always been fascinated by desert storms, and though they could be dangerous, she felt no fear as

125

she stood on the narrow front porch of her home watching this one approach. Instead, she was thankful for the much-needed rain that would increase their scant water supply.

"Hal says it's going to be a real downpour," Roger remarked as he crossed the dusty yard to join her on the small veranda. He had yet to become accustomed to the sight of her in the denim pants she'd donned for the first time that morning, and his gaze admiringly traced the slender curve of her hips as she stood there observing the storm.

"We don't get rain here very often, but when it does come, it can be torrential," she explained, unaware of his observation. "We need it, too."

"Where's Sally?" Roger asked, forcing himself to look away from her gently rounded bottom.

"She's inside. I don't think she likes thunderstorms." Lori grinned as she remembered her friend's reluctance to come out.

"No, she doesn't. She saw a tornado once as a child, and she's been terrified of high winds ever since," he answered distractedly as he fought down the urge to take Lori in his arms.

"How's your work going?" she asked. Roger had volunteered to help the foreman with the paperwork so he'd had little time to socialize in the two days since they'd arrived at the mine.

"We should have it all straightened out in another day or so." He glanced around, hoping to find that they were alone so he could take advantage of this moment.

"Good," she responded enthusiastically, and Roger was just about to kiss her when Hal's voice cut through the semidarkness.

"Roger!"

Roger cursed the foreman's intrusion under his breath. "I'd better go see what he wants. He was talking about working late tonight," he told her resignedly.

"Well, good night, Roger," she said softly, and though Roger was tempted to kiss her anyway despite the audience, he refrained.

"Good night, Lori. I'll see you first thing in the morning." He headed off toward Hal's quarters and then stopped for a minute. "Lori, don't stay out in this too long."

"Don't worry. I'll be fine." She waved him on, unconcerned.

When the fierce winds that always preceded thunderstorms swept through the camp in vicious swirls full of blinding dust and grit, Lori took refuge inside with Sally. She patiently made every effort to reassure her friend as they waited out the storm. It was almost midnight before the worst of it had passed over and Sally was finally able to fall asleep. Lori, keyed up by the excitement of the tempest, grabbed her hat and a slicker, and stepped out onto the porch to enjoy the serenity of the night.

The soft, mellow cadence of the lessening rain entranced her, and after stuffing her hair protectively up under her hat and pulling on the slicker, she wandered from the porch, unmindful of the, now, gently falling rain. Finding the coolness of the drizzle exhilarating, she paused by the corral, then climbed up on the rail to get a better view of the clouds as they raced onward, their electric fury still illuminating the darkened land.

Max, the miner standing guard that night, saw her approach and came out from the relative dryness of the stable, shotgun in hand, to greet her. "Evenin', Miss Lorelei."

"Good evening, Max. Why, you're soaked! What happened?"

"One of the horses decided to make a dash for it

127

when the rains first started and I had to bring him in," the older man explained.

"Do you want to go change? I can stay here while you're gone and keep an eye on everything."

"I don't know, ma'am." Max was miserable in his soaked clothes, but he was leery of turning over his guard duty to a female, owner or not.

"Go on." She smiled at him. "I'll wait right here."

"If you're sure?"

"I'm sure. I'm the owner, remember? Now, give me the gun and go ahead. I'll be here when you get back. Besides, no man or beast would be out on a night like this. I assure you, nothing's going to happen."

"I'll only be a minute, ma'am. Thanks." He handed her the gun and then hurried off.

Lori watched him go, impressed by the fact that he obviously took his duty very seriously. Holding the shotgun in a relaxed way, she moved easily around the corral until her view of the valley was unrestricted. The storm was still wreaking havoc on the countryside, its brilliant lightning flashes sending erratic splashes across the land, and during one of these she saw him—a lone rider, close, and heading in their direction. It was unusual for a man to travel through a storm of such magnitude so a prickle of fear ran down her back. Who was he and why was he coming to the mine?

Lori glanced around, hoping to find that Max was still within shouting distance or that someone else was stirring, but the camp was silent and dark, save for the golden light of the single lamp she'd left burning in the parlor. She knew she should go for help, that she should awaken Hal and Roger, but there was no time. The rider was too near. If he did intend any malice . . . Girding herself and expecting Max to return momentarily, she tightened her clasp on the gun and boldly stepped forward to block his entrance into the camp.

Rand was disgusted. Since he'd returned to the Lazy Ace he'd run into one complication after another, and here he was in the drizzling rain in the dark of night, riding up to a mining camp. It was possible someone just might take a potshot at him. Miners were a particularly nervous bunch. They didn't take kindly to strangers at any time, let alone this long after sunset.

He'd considered stopping for the night, but he'd already been an hour's ride from the mine when the storm had struck so he could see no reason to delay his arrival until morning. The sooner this was over and done with, the better.

"Hold it right there, mister," a rather high-pitched voice called out over the rumblings of the distant storm.

The flare of a thunderbolt revealed a slicker-clad figure—it looked like a teenage boy—blocking the trail, and the youth's shotgun was leveled at Rand's chest. Knowing how ominous his arrival must seem to the boy who was obviously standing guard, Rand remained calm and started to dismount, wanting only to approach him, unthreateningly, on foot.

"I said hold it!"

The blast of the shotgun erupted as he started to swing down from his mount and though the shot was wide Rand was infuriated. The idiot! Why the hell was he shooting at him! In a lightning move, Rand launched himself forward from the saddle, knocking the gun from the youth's grip before he could get off another round and tumbling him to the ground. The momentum of his assault sent them rolling down the slight, rocky incline, and when a boulder stopped their erratic descent with bone-jarring suddenness, Rand found himself flat on his back, the guard sprawled on top of him. Struggling for breath, he threw off the youth's slight weight and then rolled to pin him, arms

129

spread-eagled, to the ground. It was only then that he knew. . . .

"What the hell!?" Rand rasped, feeling, not the angular boniness of a young boy, but the softness of a woman's body beneath him. In the blackness of the night, he could barely make out the pale features of the female trapped beneath him, and it was not until a jagged bolt of lightning split the sky, providing a moment of stark brightness, that he recognized the burnished tangle of curls and the wide, beautiful eyes. "You!?" he snorted in disbelief, too shocked to even think about loosening his punishing hold on her.

Wanting only to cow the intruder and to alert the others in camp to her dilemma, Lori had deliberately missed when she'd fired the shotgun at him. She had expected the man to remain in the saddle until help came and she'd been totally unprepared when he'd attacked. The force of his body and the subsequent tumble down the hillside had knocked her breath from her, leaving her unable to move and fearful for her very life. Who was this man! As her wits returned, and her ability to breathe, lightning lit up the heavens and she stared up into Rand McAllister's face, totally incredulous.

"What are you doing here?" she demanded hoarsely as she tried to pull free of his restraining grip, but her struggles only made her more aware that his lower body was pressed intimately to hers. Her slicker, twisted beneath her, did not shield her quaking limbs from his dominating form.

The feel of her, soft and helpless as she squirmed against his overpowering weight, evoked unbidden desire in Rand, and Lori went perfectly still as she felt the heat of his sudden need straining against her denim-clad thigh. Again the storm's flare flooded the blackness, and it was then that he realized that her

130

breasts were exposed, the fierceness of their scuffle having ripped the buttons from her blouse and rent the soft material.

His breathing, strained before, now became labored as he stared down at the creamy beauty of her bared bosom. Like a man possessed, he slowly released his grip on one of her hands and moved to cup one tender orb, his thumb sensuously tracing an arousing pattern over the tautness of its already hardened crest.

Lori had never known a man's touch before, and she gasped at the sensations that jolted through her as he explored, with tantalizingly practiced caresses, the fullness of her delicate flesh.

"Please . . . you mustn't," she protested, fearful of the powerful feelings pulsing through the depths of her, but she could not suppress a groan of ecstatic agony when he lowered his head to kiss the firm sensitive nub. "No . . ." she moaned. Whether she was denying him access to her body or denying her reaction to the exquisite poignancy of his lips upon her, she did not know, and at that point, as he suckled her breast, she was almost beyond caring. Twisting violently in a desperate attempt to get away from the fiery excitement of his touch, she bucked against him, and her sudden contact with his hardness sent a pleasurable shock through her.

Rand could not resist taking what she seemed, despite her protests, to be so eagerly offering, and he lifted her hips, holding her tightly to him as his mouth claimed hers in a deep, heart-stopping exchange. Caught up in the rapture of her nearness, he became a man possessed, wanting only union with this vixen who'd been haunting his thoughts since last they'd kissed.

Lori's conscience was screaming *no*, but her body seemed to have a will of its own as it responded

131

hungrily to Rand's every move. Desire was blossoming in the sweet heat of her, and for the first time she knew the spiraling passion of a woman's need. Without conscious thought, she looped her arms about his neck, drawing him closer, and at this encouragement, Rand slipped a hand between them to gently explore her hunger. His touch ignited previously unexplored fires within Lori and a shudder of expectancy shook her as she began to move instinctively against his questing caress. There was no thought, only feeling and when she could bear the ecstasy of his arousing exploration no longer, her throbbing need exploded, rocketing her to the pinnacle of pleasure and awakening in her a knowledge of the depth of her own passion.

As Max's call drifted through the night, Lori blanched in sudden realization of what had just happened.

"Oh, my God," she whispered in sickening acknowledgment of her actions. Then she scrambled away from Rand, to stand and stare down at him in outrage and fearful understanding.

Rand, too, had come crashing back to reality, but he hid his frustration at the interruption by getting easily to his feet. Wanting to protect her from embarrassment, he moved to help her straighten out her slicker, but Lori would have none of it and she viciously slapped his hands away.

"Don't." Moving unsteadily away from him, she shivered uncontrollably as the force of her need drained from her, leaving her weak-kneed and wondering at her own lack of control.

In a low, controlled voice that revealed none of the confusion he was feeling at this change in her, he told her quickly, "Cover yourself with your slicker, then, but let me do the talking."

Numbly she adjusted the slicker about her to hide the

132

damage to her shirt, and knowing she had to respond to the guard lest he grow alarmed by her disappearance, she called out.

"I'm down here, Max!" Her voice was tremulous, and furious with herself over her own behavior, she cast a murderous glare in Rand's direction and then started to trudge up the incline. The footing was treacherous and she cursed soundly as she slipped. Rand, following behind, caught her as she fell, but she jerked free of him as if his touch burned. "Stay away from me!" she hissed, and her fury was rewarded with a chuckle.

"Miss Lorelei?"

Max was nearer now and when Rand recognized, at last, the name he was calling he felt suddenly chilled. Lori was Lorelei? The realization astounded him. This was Lorelei Spencer. But he had no time for further thought; the man named Max appeared at the top of the hill.

"Miss Lorelei, I was getting worried. What happened to you? What are you doing down there?" Max was instantly alert as he hurried to her aid. "And who's that with you?" He drew his six-gun as he spotted the dark form of a man coming after her up the hill.

"It's all right, Max. Really," Lori tried to sound convincing as she came to stand beside him.

"What happened?" The guard was worried, and though he couldn't make out much in the concealing darkness, he sensed that something unusual had taken place.

"I'm Rand McAllister. Will McAllister's son," Rand declared as he topped the rise and joined them. "I just rode into camp."

"What are you doing riding in at this time of night?" Max's tone was hard with suspicion, even though he'd met Will McAllister on many occasions. "And what were you two doing down there, Miss Lorelei?"

But before Lori could speak, Rand explained coolly, "I got caught up in the storm about an hour's ride out, and wet as I was, I decided to just come on in." Lori could imagine his mocking smile as he continued. "Miss Lorelei here saw me coming and came out to meet me, but there was a crack of lightning and my horse spooked. When he reared up, she tried to get out of his way, but she lost her footing and fell. That was when the gun went off. It's mighty slippery tonight. I was just helping her back up the hill, when we heard your call."

"You fired a shot?" Max swung around to face her.

"Didn't you hear it?" she was surprised.

"No," he told her in consternation. "With all that thunder, I guess I didn't recognize it. Miss Lorelei, if I'd known you were in any kind of trouble, I would have come right away."

"She knows that, Max," Rand went on, not giving her a chance to respond. "She suffered no lasting damage and as she said, she's just fine."

Lori was seething. The arrogant ass! How dare he tell such boldface lies! She could have shot him right off his horse's back if she'd had a mind to, and she intended to make him aware of that fact at the first opportunity!

To think that only moments before she'd been in his arms allowing him to . . . Lori was grateful that the darkness hid her embarrassed blush. How could she have allowed him to touch her that way? And what was worse, she'd enjoyed it—reveled in it, even. It infuriated her to think that his touch could effect her so. Surely, she reasoned, it was just his vast experience with women that had taught him how to arouse her. She did not desire him. She couldn't. She knew what kind of man he really was.

"Well, if you're not hurt, Miss Lorelei, I'll go back

on watch."

"Yes, Max. You do that. Everything's fine," she lied. Then she watched in silence as the guard disappeared into the darkness, leaving them alone in the ebony stillness.

"Is everything fine?" Rand taunted.

"You know how fine everything is, you lout!" Lori snarled in low tones. "How dare you manhandle me!"

"Manhandle?" he retorted, and there was a tinge of amusement in his voice. "I've heard it called many things before, but not manhandled."

"It's most apropos, if you ask me!" she told him heatedly. "First you attack me and then you . . . you . . . From now on, Rand McAllister, you just keep away from me."

Rand firmly believed that she had loved every minute of their embrace, and he couldn't understand why she was being so contrary now. Never before had a woman responded to him as fully as she had. Indeed, he felt a tightening in his loins at the remembrance of her surprising passion.

"If you're sure that's what you want . . ." He let the sentence hang with maddening insinuation. "Of course a few minutes ago, if I'd tried to get away from you, you'd probably have begged me to stay."

"Oh you!" The rawness of Lori's emotions led to her next action, and she was a bit stunned after she slapped him viciously. "I'd never beg you for anything, Rand McAllister!!"

Rand stiffened at the blow, but did nothing. He had not thought she would react so violently to his gibe. Now, realizing that he'd pushed her too far, his eyes narrowed as he stared down at her in silent consideration before speaking.

"I came here for a reason," he said slowly.

His abrupt shift in focus left her slightly bewildered,

and it stifled the flare of temper that had possessed her. She had expected anything from him, but this calm statement. The rain had ceased, but neither noticed as they faced off against one another.

"What reason?" she challenged.

"I have personal business with one Lorelei Spencer. I take it you are Lorelei Spencer?"

"Of course I am," she snapped, her nerves on edge. She wanted only to get away from him. "And whatever it is you've got to say to me can just wait until tomorrow morning."

"This is important," Rand said, his tone serious, but knowing that at the moment they were hardly in a position or in the mood to discuss any future dealings between them, he assented. "But if you prefer to wait until tomorrow, we can discuss it then."

"I do," Lori answered with finality for she knew, upset as she was, she was in no condition to match wits with this man. "You can bed down in the stable. Good night, Mr. McAllister."

"Good night, Miss Spencer," Rand replied sardonically as he watched her stalk away. He couldn't help but wonder what her reaction would be when, in the light of the new day, she discovered that he was now her legal guardian.

Leading his horse into the stable, he unsaddled the mount and, after rubbing it down, fashioned himself a makeshift bed in a dry, protected corner of the darkened building. Though his clothing was damp, he took little notice as he pondered the happenings of the night. Lori . . . the copper-tressed female who'd been in his thoughts since his first encounter with her on the stage. In reality, she was Lorelei Spencer, the daughter of his father's closest friend and, now, his ward.

Scowling at the thought, Rand tossed restlessly on his uncomfortable pallet. Even though she was a full-grown woman, he was responsible for her until she married or turned twenty-one. Again he frowned. She was under his care, yet he had attacked her as if she were a man, had knocked her to the ground, scuffled with her down a muddy hillside, and had nearly made love to her right out in the open in the middle of the mining camp.

Rand was filled with self-reproach as he thought about his actions. Why had Lorelei had such an effect upon him? No other woman had aroused him to the point that he forgot everything but the need to possess her. Only Lydia had come close to exerting such control over him, but his own naïveté had made that possible. He'd learned enough about women and himself during the intervening years to know that whatever existed between Lorelei and him, it was potent and special—and something to be avoided at all costs. Beautiful and desirable though she was, he did not want any romantic or sensual involvement with her. Being her guardian precluded that, anyway. He would keep his distance from her and maintain a hands-off relationship.

She could remain at the ranch with Lydia while he returned to his job, he decided. That was the perfect solution. Lydia would introduce her to the right men, and maybe, by the time he returned for a dutiful visit, she would be married off to some nice, upstanding young fellow. Rand was totally pleased with his reasoning until he allowed himself to envision Lori with another man, wrapped in his arms, making love. That possibility filled him with rage, and he was surprised by his reaction. What the hell was the matter with him! Rolling over, he closed his eyes and tried to force Lorelei from his mind. Still, he could not banish the tantalizing memory of her creamy flesh. Stifling a groan and fighting down his natural response to such

137

thoughts, Rand lay awake throughout the night.

Lori had sensed his eyes upon her as she'd hurried back inside the house, and bolting the door behind her, she snatched up the lamp and made her way quickly to her bedroom. There, when she came face to face with herself in her mirror, she stared at her reflection with a mixture of humor and horror. She was drenched. Her hair, usually sweetly clean, was soggy. Clumped with mud, it hung about her face in scraggy strands. A streak of dirt darkened her cheek, and mud caked her wrinkled slicker.

She pulled off the offending garment and spread it out over a chair. Then, as she was moving to her wash stand, she caught sight of herself in the looking glass again and this time she gasped in surprise. Her blouse was torn from neck to waist and her breasts were completely bared, their paleness marred now by dirty smudges that looked suspiciously like imprints of Rand's hand.

That last thought shattered her composure and she rushed to pour a bowl of clean water. Tearing off the remnants of her shirt she threw it on the floor and then proceeded to scrub herself vigorously with a washcloth and soap until she felt every trace of his touch had been erased. Stripping off the rest of her clothing she completed her bath, and after shampooing her hair, she donned a long, plain nightgown and slipped beneath the covers of the bed.

Only then did she allow herself a moment to think, to wonder about Rand McAllister's presence there. What did he want? He had said he'd come for a personal reason, that it had to do with her. Lori shivered in anticipation of their encounter in the morning and she hoped fervently that she would be able to maintain her composure when she faced him in the light of day. All she had to do, she kept telling herself, was to remember the scene between him and his stepmother in the Lazy Ace's stable years ago. That would allow her to keep his attractiveness in perspective. It would help her to overcome whatever perverse attraction she was feeling for him.

Even so, the events of the evening troubled her. There could be no denying the fact that she had responded wantonly to his touch, and now, lying safely in her bed, just the thought of the passion he'd aroused in her filled her with an unfamiliar, feverish yearning.

Never before had she experienced such feelings. She wondered if, in a more intimate embrace, Roger could evoke the same response from her. It was a possibility that merited consideration, she decided. Then, closing her eyes, she tried to sleep. But it wasn't until the wee hours of the morning that she slipped into slumber.

*Chapter Eight*

Lori lay quietly staring out the window at the rapidly brightening sky. Her few hours of sleep had left her feeling somewhat refreshed, and she knew she would be much more capable of dealing with Rand now that she felt more in control.

He had overwhelmed her last night. Their encounter had been outrageous from beginning to end, and she knew she would have to make certain that they stayed far apart from now on. Whatever it was that Rand had to discuss with her, they would discuss it in the presence of others, then quickly conclude their business so he could be on his way, for she knew she would not be able to relax until he'd gone.

Too anxious about the upcoming confrontation to remain in bed any longer, she started to rise, but the motion brought a pained groan from her. Every muscle in her body seemed to ache. Knowing it was Rand's tackle and their subsequent tumble down the hill that were making her feel so battered this morning, she mumbled uncomplimentary things about him as she got up gingerly from her bed.

The sight of her ruined blouse and mud-covered pants, discarded haphazardly on the floor, strengthened

140

her determination to get Rand out of her life, and in spite of the fact that her sore muscles protested her every movement, she made short order of pulling on clean clothes and tugging on her boots. Resolved to have this meeting over and done with, she headed from her room, hoping to find that Roger, Sally, and Hal were up and about so they could sit in on her discussion with Rand.

Despite having lain awake all night, Rand had waited until sunup to get cleaned up. Now shaved, washed and wearing the set of extra clothing he'd brought along, he strode out into the main yard and took his first good look at his surroundings. Already the small settlement was coming to life. Miners were emerging from their dwellings to begin the workday, and Rand concluded as he observed these goings-on that this was no place for a young, unmarried woman to live alone. Convinced that his plan for her to live at the Lazy Ace was the only reasonable answer, he started off in the direction of the house Lorelei had entered last night.

"Rand? Rand McAllister?" As Hal and Roger emerged from their quarters they recognized Rand immediately and though they were surprised by his unexpected presence here at the Triple Cross, they went forward to greet him.

"Hal, good to see you. Roger." Rand shook the older man's hand and then Roger's as they joined him. He couldn't help but wonder about Roger's presence here and about his relationship with Lorelei. On the stage, Roger had seemed very possessive of her, and though Rand had dismissed it at the time, seeing Westlake here led him to believe that the man might have a place in her life. For some reason that possibility troubled him.

"Marshal," Roger said by way of greeting.

141

"Call me Rand, please," McAllister invited, and Roger smiled in acknowledgment.

"Rand, I'm sorry about your father. We all are up here. He was a good man."

"Thanks, Hal."

"Rand's father was killed in the same accident that killed Miss Lorelei's father," Johnson explained quickly to Roger. Then he turned to Rand. "Did you just ride in?"

"No, as a matter of fact I made it in last night during the storm, but it was so late the guard suggested I bed down in the stable."

"It's not exactly the most comfortable place to spend the night, but I've slept in worse places." Hal chuckled. "So what brings you to the Triple Cross?"

"I've got some business to discuss with Lorelei."

"Does she know you're here?"

"Yes. We spoke briefly last night and agreed to meet this morning."

"I'm glad to see that you're up Mr. McAllister," Lori remarked, keeping her tone very businesslike. "Hal, I see you know Mr. McAllister?"

Rand watched her as she walked toward them and he found the sight of her in her slim-fitting riding skirt, white blouse, and boots most appealing. It was obvious that she'd taken the time to wash her hair for it hung down her back in a silken, fiery cascade of curls that seemed to cry out for his caress. Meeting her cool gaze, he sent her a mocking look because she'd refused to call him by his first name.

"Sure, Miss Lorelei. Rand and I are old friends. I've known him for years." Hal clapped Rand heartily on the shoulder.

"Wonderful," she said dryly, trying to keep from staring at Rand; he looked so handsome in the light of day that she had to fight down a surge of excitement at

142

the remembrance of his passionate embrace. "Mr. McAllister tells me he has some important business to discuss with me, and since you and Roger are familiar with the current status of the Triple Cross, I'm hoping you'll have time to join us, that is, if Mr. McAllister doesn't mind?" Lori looked at Rand, one eyebrow raised questioningly.

Rand had no objection to her including the other men, but he did wonder why she felt it was necessary.

"I don't mind. What I have to say to you will be public information soon anyway, but please, Lorelei, call me Rand. We've known each other for some time now and I see no need for such formality between us," he chided.

Inwardly she balked at taking him up on his request for she felt calling him by his first name would establish a certain intimacy between them. Instead, she avoided the issue entirely, saying, "Why don't we go inside now and find out what this is all about?" She stood aside so the men could walk past her into the house; then she invited them to make themselves comfortable. "Have a seat at the table."

Lori had already told Sally about Rand's arrival at the mine and about the reason he'd given for his presence, so Sally was not surprised when he entered, accompanied by the others.

"Marshal McAllister, how good to see you again!" Her welcome was warm and sincere, and Lori had to refrain from shaking her head in disbelief at her friend's attitude. She had always thought Sally a good judge of character.

"Ma'am." Rand smiled at the young woman with genuine affection.

"My name is Sally and I'd appreciate it if you'd use it."

"Of course, Sally. I'd like that, and please call

143

me Rand."

Sally beamed and moved to the cookstove. "Can I get anyone a cup of coffee?"

"Please," all three men answered, so she busied herself with serving them as Lori sat down at the table opposite Rand.

"Now," Lori challenged, feeling quite brave because she was not alone with him. "What kind of business is it you have with me?"

Rand took the carefully folded document from his shirt pocket. "This is an agreement drawn up by your father and mine some years ago. My father's attorney brought it to my attention several days ago and according to him, it is still binding in every sense."

"An agreement?" she frowned. "My father never told me that he'd made any deals with your father."

"It's not a 'business deal' per se, Lorelei," Rand explained patiently as he handed it to her. "Please, read it."

Lori took the document and scanned it. Her expression was guarded when she looked up at him, "Father had this drawn up years ago and I can understand his purpose at the time, but surely your lawyer doesn't interpret this as binding now?"

"I'm afraid he does. In the eyes of the law you are my ward, Lorelei." He said it flatly, revealing to her just how distasteful he, too, found their situation.

At his declaration there was a moment of stunned silence in the room before Lori declared indignantly, "This is asinine! I refuse!"

"I wish it was that simple, but I'm afraid it's not. Richards tells me that until you turn twenty-one or marry, I'm fully responsible for you and all your property."

Lori bit back a candidly frank retort as she glared at him, "Look, I'm sorry about your father's death—he

144

was a nice man and I liked him very much—but please, don't feel that you owe me any favors. I don't want you to be responsible for me. Feel free to go on about your life as you normally would. I'll just stay here and take care of myself and the mine."

"I'm afraid I can't allow that."

"What do you mean *'you can't allow that'?"* she was incredulous.

"I mean this mining camp is no place for an unmarried woman to live alone, so I'm taking you back to live at the Lazy Ace where my stepmother Lydia will serve as an appropriate chaperone until the conditions in the agreement are met."

Lori got to her feet so violently that she almost overturned her chair. Barely in control of her temper, she faced him, her hands on her hips, her breasts heaving, and her eyes sparkling with an inner fire. "I will not go anywhere with you, Rand McAllister, let alone to live with you and *Lydia* at your ranch! I came home to the Triple Cross and I plan to stay at the Triple Cross."

"Lorelei, be reasonable." Rand had not expected this at all.

"Reasonable!" she spit out. "You be reasonable! You show up here out of the clear blue telling me you're my legal guardian for the next three years or until I marry! That's reasonable? That's ridiculous. Maybe when I was eight years old this arrangement would have been appropriate, but I don't need a guardian now. Especially not you! You go back to your ranch and *you* live with Lydia. I have no intention of doing so!"

"You will if I say you will!" he countered, her obstinacy beginning to irritate him. But even as he struggled to maintain his calm and deal rationally with her, he could not help admiring the way her emerald

145

eyes flashed defiantly, the way her blouse molded the soft outline of her breasts. At this last train of thought Rand grew even more irritable. He had vowed that he would not get involved with her. She was his ward; he was her guardian. She would follow his dictates because he knew what was best for her.

"You'll have to drag me bodily out of here, and I'll scream and fight you every inch of the way!" Lori declared. Just who did he think he was? She wanted absolutely nothing more to do with him; last night had taught her that. He had no claim on her, and if he thought she was going to allow him to control her life, he had another think coming.

"Let me see that." Roger suddenly broke in, reaching for the paper. He read it through thoroughly and frowned. "It does appear to be authentic, Lori, but if it is, your father should have a copy of it. Do you know where he kept his personal papers?"

Lori was shaking with anger, and it took her a moment to gather her wits. "Yes. He kept them in a small box in the bottom desk drawer. Hal did you give those papers to Mr. Swartz?"

"No, Miss Lorelei. I didn't even know they were there," Hal told her.

Racing to the desk in the bedroom her father had used, Lori threw open the bottom drawer. Relieved to see that nothing had been disturbed, she took the small locked box from its place of safekeeping and returned to where the others awaited her. Her fingers were trembling as she unlocked the box and carefully sorted through the papers in it. Her eyes widened in shock when she found her father's copy of the very same document.

"No." She gasped, and when she looked up at Rand, her expression was one of desperate determination. "I won't go with you. You can't make me!"

146

"Lorelei, you don't understand." Rand was feeling frustrated now. "It's not my intention to ruin your life. If anything, I feel this move to the ranch will be beneficial for you. Being properly chaperoned, your reputation will be guarded, and there will be opportunities for you to socialize."

"You're the one who doesn't understand, Rand McAllister," Lori said testily. "If I'd wanted to be properly chaperoned, to have a pleasant social life, I'd have stayed in St. Louis. I came back here to help Hal work the Triple Cross. We're just about to make my father's dream come true. The vein we're working is richer than anything I've ever seen before and I have absolutely no intention of leaving. If you're so worried about being my guardian and protecting my property, you can just move in here and keep watch over me and the Triple Cross!"

Rand had not heard of the mine's new strike. Now he could understand her reluctance to leave, if indeed, things were going as well as she said. "Hal"—he turned to the mine's supervisor—"what she's saying about the mine—is it true?"

"Every word, Rand. That's what makes George's death even more tragic. We're working on the purest vein I've ever seen. If it holds, our fortunes are assured, but we've got trouble on one count."

Lori glared at Hal, not wanting Rand to find out any more about her business, but the older man ignored her.

"Trouble? What kind of trouble?" McAllister asked, becoming more interested in the mine.

"It's not serious—yet—but right before he died, George got a loan from the bank in town. He needed it to cover the cost of expanding our operation, so we could make the most of the lode."

"And?"

147

"And he was so certain of our success that he set the payback time as six months. The balance, plus interest, is due the first of September."

"That should be no problem for you if the ore is as pure as you say."

"True, but without George . . . well, things just aren't running as smoothly as they should. The paper work is piling up, and though Miss Lorelei and her friends are pitching in, it's going to take a lot of hard work to meet that deadline."

Again Rand wondered about Lori's relationship with Roger and Sally. Obviously they were not visiting relatives, for if she had any living, he wouldn't be in his present situation. Regarding Lorelei thoughtfully for a long moment, he noticed that the tenseness of her stance had not relaxed. She looked like a gorgeous avenging Valkyrie, and he felt a stirring of desire, which he quickly denied. "Since I'm now responsible, not only for you, but also for the protection of your assets, I guess the best solution *would be* for me to move in here."

Even as he said it, Rand wondered why he'd arrived at this decision, whether it had anything to do with his feeling for Lorelei. He wasn't sure and he refused to dwell on it. Certainly this guardianship added another entanglement to his already complicated affairs, but living at the mine was far preferable to sharing the ranchhouse with Lydia.

In a few weeks, if things were going well and real progress was being made, Lorelei might mellow and agree to live at the ranch, and once he got her settled in there, he could resume his normal life. Until then though, he would have to wire Marshal Duke and request additional leave, a request he was sure would not be denied.

Lori felt relief at his announcement, but she

remained wary. She was glad that she would not be forced to leave the Triple Cross, that she could continue her father's work, but the knowledge that Rand would be living at the mine was threatening. The effect Rand had on her senses was devastating, and she knew she would have to remain cool and aloof around him, thereby discouraging any encounters like the one they'd had the preceding night. Guardian or not, she wanted as little contact with Rand McAllister as possible.

"Thank you," she said with quiet disdain. Then she seated herself. "I'm glad you can appreciate the significance of my remaining at the Triple Cross."

"I can," Rand remarked casually. "And, since I'm now officially in charge here, I'd like to take a look at the operation." He was familiar with the basics of mining and was interested in learning all he could about the Triple Cross since he was going to be directing its future.

Lori stifled a groan. She had not thought that he would want to involve himself so completely; the prospect of having to clear every decision through him grated on her.

"We can show you around today, if you want," Hal offered. "Miss Lorelei?"

"Yes . . . yes, of course. I suppose it will be necessary for you to know what's going on."

Her attitude was a bit smug so Rand gave her a derisive half-smile. "I'd appreciate it.


"What's goin' on?" Harley Oates asked his companion Rocky Barnes later the same morning as they watched Hal lead a stranger into the mining office.

"I'm not sure, but I heard some of the men sayin' earlier that Will McAllister's son had somehow gotten control of the mine."

"What?" Harley was shocked. He wondered if Taylor had heard the news. The last word he'd received from Josh had been a quick message delivered secretly the day of Lorelei Spencer's return to the Triple Cross. In the tersely worded communiqué, Josh had admonished him to continue to create as much undetectable havoc as he could in order to slow the operation down because the stubborn young owner had refused to sell to him. So far, Harley had had little opportunity to rig any accidents, but now that another person was involved, he knew he would have to act quickly.

"I don't know the whole story. They were just sayin' that McAllister is now in charge, that he's movin' in with Hal and that Roger fellow and he's plannin' to stay."

"Wonder if he knows anything about mining?"

Rocky shrugged expressively, "I guess it don't matter as long as Hal's around. Him comin' around sure ain't no worse than some rich Eastern company buyin' us up, I guess. C'mon Harley, we gotta get to work."

And Harley quickly followed Rocky to the lift on which they descended into the mine's cool enveloping darkness.

"Our biggest expense is the freight to the stamp mill," Hal explained as he went over the basic facts and figures for Rand's benefit, Lori and Roger looking on. "In fact, that was the primary reason why George took out the loan; he wanted to build his own mill right here on the site. Construction has started, but it will be at least another few weeks before it's completed and until that time we have to ship the ore."

"The stamp mill sounds like a good investment if the vein is as rich as your assay reports indicate."

"It is," Lori told him solemnly. "As soon as you've finished here, we'll take you below so you can see it for yourself."

They spent the better part of an hour going over the expenses involved in the running of the Triple Cross before heading for the mine itself. Oil lamps in hand, they started toward the main shaft with Hal leading the way.

Strategically located candles provided an eerie illumination in the main tunnel as they stepped off the lift, and though Rand found the chill penetrating, Lori seemed exhilarated as she boldly led the way toward the crosscut that would take them to the drift where the new lode had been discovered.

"Watch your step. Tools are often lying about, and the ore cars can be treacherous. The main ore shoot is at the end of this tunnel." She nodded as they passed a station where several miners were gathered.

"Good mornin', Miss Lorelei," they greeted her.

"Good morning, men," she answered, paying little attention to their half-dressed state. The temperature at the lower levels of the mine far exceeded that in the tunnel, and when the miners worked in such close confines, they often stripped down to their trousers and brogues.

Rand, however, found her nonchalance toward the men's partial nudity annoying. Didn't she realize she shouldn't expose herself to such sights? But he soon banished that thought. Lorelei was no ordinary woman. She was the owner of the Triple Cross, and the fact that her workers accepted her set her apart. There had been nothing suggestive about the miners' greetings. In fact, they had been courteous and respectful. Rand didn't know how she'd done it, but

Lori had already won the hearts and the cooperation of her men.

"We store supplies there," she was saying as she gestured back toward the combination station and lounge where the workers had been congregated. Then she continued down the tunnel, turning off at an angle on the crosscut. "And up ahead is the winze that leads down to the new drift. That's where the new vein was discovered," Lori told him proudly.

Harley and Rocky were busy shoveling ore into a waiting car when he saw the Spencer girl, along with Hal and the others, come toward them. Oates had not expected to see Lori in the mine today, and he suppressed a smile at the thought of what might happen if she lingered here too long. In his eagerness to help Taylor and without Rocky's knowledge, Harley had already weakened one of the structural supports at the far end of the newly blasted tunnel, and he knew it would not hold for long. Harley would never knowingly plot anyone's demise, but he knew Taylor would be pleased if the girl and the new guy who was taking over were lost in a cave-in.

"That must be McAllister," he muttered under his breath, nodding toward Rand.

"Yep," Rocky agreed, subtly eying the newcomer. Both miners paused in their efforts to speak to the group. "That's where the blasting was last night, so keep a sharp eye out," Rocky said.

Acknowledging his warning, the group went on their way, while Rocky and Harley started to push the filled ore car to the lift site.

Cam Larsen, the resident assayer, was busy taking ore samples at the end of the recently opened area when they came upon him.

"Cam."

"Miss Lorelei! I didn't know that you'd be down this

morning." The bespectacled young man greeted Lori with enthusiasm. "But I'm glad you came. The blasting last night uncovered more ore of the same quality, and although I can't be sure until I test it, the lode seems to show no inclination of dying on us—so far."

"Cam, that's wonderful!" Lori was thrilled at the news, for always, in the back of her mind, was the worry that a blast would reveal that the vein was a fluke and would not hold. Suddenly remembering Rand's presence, she introduced him. "By the way, this is Rand McAllister, Will McAllister's son. He's going to be helping out here at the mine for a while. Rand, this is Cam Larsen."

"Glad to meet you, McAllister." Cam shook his hand. "I was just about to go back up to the station to make my tests." Cam started to gather his map and measure, along with the ore samples. "Be glad to have you come along and see the results for yourself firsthand."

"Fine," Lori replied, and eager to know the findings, she and the others followed him through the narrow newly timbered opening.

It happened so quickly that no one was sure exactly how the accident occurred. At one moment the timbers were holding, the next, they had collapsed. The ensuing cave-in half buried Hal who was caught by an onslaught of rock and wood. Lorelei and Rand were trapped in the pitch darkness of the now completely blocked tunnel. Roger and Cam had dived ahead as the groaning supports gave way, and after the choking cloud of dust had cleared, they relit the candles that had been extinguished by the crash and rushed back, desperate and worried.

"Lori!" Roger's cry was agonized as he stared in horror at Hal who lay unconscious among the rocks, the sealed tunnel behind him. "My God, she's buried in there with McAllister!" Unwilling to believe that she had not survived, he worked feverishly, along with the assayer, to free the supervisor.

"Don't worry, we'll get 'em out," Cam gasped out as he pushed stones and broken supports aside to get a hold on Hal.

Roger was not aware of the continued creaking of the still-remaining timbers, and Cam didn't speak until they'd finally pulled Hal free.

"We've got to get out of here. It's not safe."

"I can't leave!" Roger argued, continuing to scrape, with his bare hands, at the dirt, rock, and boulders. "Lori's in there and she may be hurt!"

"I know that!" Cam shouted, grabbing him by an arm to restrain him. "But let's get Hal out of here and get some help. The rest of the tunnel may go. We won't be any good to her or McAllister if we're dead, too! Come on! I need your help with Hal."

Common sense told Roger that the assayer was right, but he hesitated. "I can't just leave her."

"We have to! We need jacks and more timbers. There's no way we can dig through this alone. Now, help me!"

Forcing himself to deal with the reality of the situation, Roger assented, and he and Cam carried Hal back down the drift toward the winze.

# Chapter Nine

Lori had just started to follow Rand back down the tunnel when the overhead support suddenly splintered and collapsed, striking Rand a glancing blow.

The falling beam stunned him, and he staggered from the force of it. "Lorelei, stay back!"

"Rand!" she screamed, in horror as a cloud of choking dust enveloped them. The last thing she saw as timbers and rocks came crashing down, blocking their only escape route and enshrouding them in the suffocating blackness, was Rand lunging in her direction in an attempt to protect her from almost certain death.

There was no time to think. Rand threw himself at Lori, forcefully shoving her back into the newly dug out tunnel, out of harm's way. They landed in an awkward heap with Rand above her, his body a protective shield against the falling debris.

It was over almost as quickly as it had begun. The thunderous roar of the cave-in ceased abruptly, and the silence that engulfed them was so complete it seemed almost tangible.

For a moment, Lorelei could not move. Frozen by fear, she lay immobile, her mind racing, trying to understand that she was safe. After what seemed an eternity, her terror began to ebb, and she realized that Rand was not moving and he seemed almost a dead weight upon her.

"Rand?" Lori finally gasped, her voice hoarse, and when he didn't respond, she pushed ineffectually at his broad shoulders. "Rand?"

When there was no response, Lori began to tremble. She conjured up visions of Rand dead or dying and all because he'd tried to save her. Suddenly she became aware of something warm and sticky dampening her neck near where his head rested heavily on her shoulder, and her panic became real as she realized that it must be blood.

"Rand . . . Oh, God, don't let him be dead!" Her voice was a terrified whisper for she remembered the beam striking him. She pushed with all her might to dislodge his considerable weight, and finally managed to wriggle from beneath him, in the process shifting him onto his side.

Blinded by the darkness, Lori let her hands rest on his chest, praying that she would be able to find a heartbeat. She almost cried out in relief when she felt the heavy thud of his heart beneath her palm; then she quickly sought to find his wound, gently exploring his neck and scalp until she located the gash on the side of his head. Sitting back, she pulled her shirt free of her waistband and started to tear a strip of cloth from it to use as a bandage for his head.

While she did so, Rand regained consciousness, and his first thought was of Lorelei. Was she dead? Injured? Imagining the worst, he tried to get up, to find her. "Lorelei!"

"Oh, Rand! Thank God!" Unthinking, she reached out to him, and was swept into a clutching embrace.

"You weren't injured?" His voice was gravelly as he

156

held her close in the pitch-darkness, his fear eased by the knowledge that she was indeed still alive and presumably in one piece.

"No. I'm fine," she told him, drawing strength from his nearness. Feeling protected in his arms, she almost allowed herself to relax against him. "I was so worried about you."

"You were?" he caught the deep feeling in her voice, and he was amazed by this previously undiscovered softness in her. At the same time, he found it disconcerting and intriguing. Until now, she had been prickly with him, yet she had just admitted that she cared what happened to him.

"Of course," she said, then stopped for she suddenly realized how intimate their conversation had become. The remembrance of who she was, and just who he was, injected reality back into their situation. Anxious to mitigate the revealing import of her words, she replied tartly. "Who wouldn't be? I thought I was trapped in the dark with a dead man!" With a nervous jerk, she freed herself from his arms and moved slightly away from him. The cool, dampness of the air chilled her, and she almost regretted leaving the warm security of his embrace.

Put off by her harsh denial of any real feeling for him, Rand shrugged away his original impression, but he couldn't resist saying, "Lucky for us I managed to get us both out of the way."

"Yes, it was," Lori admitted despite her reluctance. "And I'm grateful for your quick action."

Shifting to a more comfortable position, he asked, "What about the others?"

"I don't know." Aware of the tremor in her voice, Lori became aggravated by her own weakness. "There's been no sound—no light. I hope they made it."

157

Rand tried to sound encouraging, "They were several steps ahead of me, so with any luck, they were already clear when the timber failed."

"Roger's got to be safe!"

Rand was annoyed by her obvious distress, and unbidden, a thought came to him: she must love him.

"I'm sure he is," he stated flatly.

"I hope you're right." Her tone was soft.

Rand didn't know why, but he wished he could see her at that moment, just to read the expression in her eyes. Irritated with himself for even caring what she thought, he tried to get to his feet, intending to dig them out, but the sudden shift in his position aggravated the throbbing in his head. With a muffled groan, he sat back down, gingerly touching the wound.

"Your head." Lori moved closer to kneel beside him.

"Is fine," he growled, lying.

"How can it be fine, if it's bleeding?"

"Just how do you know that my head is bleeding?"

"While you were unconscious, I checked you to see how badly you were injured. I remembered the timber hitting you." It made Lori nervous to admit that she'd touched him of her own free will.

"How long was I out?" Rand wondered.

"Not long, a few minutes maybe." The sound of ripping material accompanied her words.

"What are you doing?"

"Trying to make a bandage for your head, but it's a bit difficult in the dark. Let me see if I can find one of the candles that were in the wall before the collapse."

"Be careful," he warned sternly. "One bump against a loosened upright and the rest of the tunnel could give way."

"I know that," she answered, resenting his ordering her around. "You just stay still."

Rand wanted to be the one searching for the light,

but he knew she was right in directing him to remain where he was for he was feeling dizzy.

On hands and knees, Lori began to work her way around the darkness of their living tomb.

"How much room do we have?"

"Not much. Another three or four feet toward the back wall, maybe. Here!"

"What?"

"I found a candle and its holder. Just a second. There should be matches somewhere nearby. It's customary to try to keep them handy in case of situations like this."

Time passed slowly as Lori felt her way along the dirt floor strewn with rocks, and just as she was about to give up, she found the small container of matches. Without a word, she struck one and she watched thankfully as the blue-yellow flame sputtered to life. Then, with an economy of movement, she lit the candle. Shielding it with her hand from any air currents that might be stirring, she turned slowly to Rand.

Though she had known he was bleeding, the sight of his blood-streaked face sent a shudder through her. "Oh, Rand."

In the flickering light of the candle, he could see how pale she was and how her hand was shaking. He feared that she had lied to him about being all right, that he had injured her when he'd knocked her down. Disregarding his own weakness, he went to her and would have taken her in his arms had the candle not been between them, "Lorelei, are you sure that I didn't hurt you in any way?"

"Hurt me?" His question confused Lori; he was the one who was hurt. "No, I'm fine, really. Why?"

"You look so shaken and pale."

She forced a smile. "It's just that you're covered with blood."

"I am?" Rand knew his head injury was painful, but he had not realized just how bloody the wound actually was. He glanced down at his blood-stained shirt in surprise.

"Yes. Let me see if I can find the hole this candleholder fell out of." Getting to her feet, she moved away from him, her eyes scouring the wall for the niche of the holder. "There, that should give us light for at least a few hours."

Feeling slightly more in control, she went back to Rand and picked up the strip of material she'd torn from her blouse. "Sit down and hold still for me while I see if I can get the bleeding stopped." Kneeling beside him again, she pressed the cloth to the gash and, with gentle hands, effectively staunched the flow of blood.

Forced to remain perfectly quiet while she leaned near to apply steady pressure to his wound, Rand tried not to think about her closeness or how her blouse was now ripped up to her midriff, exposing an expanse of creamy, silken skin to his gaze. He swallowed and forced himself to look elsewhere. It seemed a long time before she removed the cloth and sat back on her heels to examine the cut.

"The bleeding has stopped." She was pleased that it was under control. "I'll try to fashion another bandage and I'll—"

"No, don't. Leave it. There's no need as long as the bleeding's stopped." He spoke sharply. In truth, he didn't want her to tear more strips of material from her blouse, for he feared that he wouldn't be able to keep his desire for her under control if, no matter how innocently, any more of her body was revealed to him.

Lori was puzzled, but said nothing. It made sense to her to wrap the wound so it would stay fairly clean, but she supposed he probably had a good reason for not wanting it done.

Aware of how gruesome he must look, Rand stripped off his own shirt, then used it to wipe the blood off his face and neck.

Lori watched in silence, surprised to find herself fascinated by the sight of his bare, hair-roughened chest. She wanted to touch that broad, tightly muscled span. She had seen innumerable men without shirts in the course of working in the mine, but she had never experienced a reaction like this. Why did Rand McAllister arouse such feelings in her?

"How's that? Any better?" Rand asked, as he rubbed ineffectually at his face and neck.

Lost in her thought, Lori blinked at his question. "What?"

"Did I get all the blood off?"

"Most of it," she responded blandly.

"Here." He thrust the wadded up shirt at her. "Finish for me. There's no way I can tell."

Knowing she couldn't refuse without revealing her own confusing emotions, she took the proffered garment and moved closer to rub away the dirt and the drying gore. As clinically as she could, she wiped at the remaining streaks of blood until his face and throat were reasonably clean.

As she fought down her desire to reach out and caress the lean hardness of his cheek, her eyes accidentally met Rand's and their gazes locked. She had no time to prepare herself for the soul-challenging, mental combat that ensued. The moment was electric. Lori could neither move nor speak as his dark fathomless eyes probed her, and she knew with a breathless certainty that he could read the feelings she was trying so hard to deny.

Rand did recognize the barely controlled desire reflected in her eyes, and he knew a moment of primitive triumph. All thoughts of denying his passion

161

for her disappeared as quickly as wisps of fog before a strong wind. He wanted her, and he knew now that she wanted him.

Borne on by emotions more powerful than any he'd ever experienced, he reached out, and taking the rumpled shirt from her numb fingers, he gently stroked the side of her neck where his blood had stained her delicate skin. Lori gasped at the touch of the cloth on her sensitive flesh, and she instinctively arched into his caress, her eyes fluttering closed and her nipples hardening invitingly against the soft material of her blouse. Rand dropped his shirt and framed her face with his hands.

In the dimness of the candlelight he bent to kiss her with exquisite care. Never before had they been like this. Their first kiss had been more of a teasing torment than a loving exchange, and their near mating the night before had been as tempestuous as the storm that had been exploding around them. No . . . this was different and he wanted to cherish every instant.

Gone was any awareness of right and wrong . . . of guardian and ward . . . of Roger and her very real concern for him. At this moment in time, they were man and woman, alone. He wanted to touch her and be touched by her; to experience moments of ecstasy, to take her to the heights of her passion. Rand wanted to pierce her responsive sweetness with his thrusting gift of love, to know the full splendor of joining with her silken, hungry flesh.

Lori sensed she was drowning in a vortex of desire as he leaned nearer to kiss her, and she tensed as their lips met in tentative exploration of the fragile wonder of their need. With the last thread of sanity she possessed, she held a part of herself back for fear that any moment she would be lost forever to the power of the attraction she felt for him. And, when his mouth suddenly slanted possessively across hers, demanding an answering response, she was, indeed, lost. She surrendered willingly to the burning desire that had been building within her from the first moment she'd seen him on the stagecoach.

Lori wanted him. She no longer cared about what had happened in the past; she only knew that she wanted this man with a feverish need that defied reason. It made no sense to her that his kiss and touch could awaken such a maelstrom of emotion; Lori was now driven by the force of her as yet unexplored passion to know all of him. He had taken her to the brink of ecstasy the night before and now her body was responding to his with the same abandon.

Of their own volition, it seemed, her arms wound about his neck, and Rand, encouraged by that sign of surrender, pulled her across his lap and began to unbottom her blouse, stripping it from her. Lori lay quietly in his arms as he traced teasing, arousing patterns over her tingling breasts. Then, when he moved to press hungry kisses to their budding, aching peaks, she moaned out in her need and began to move restlessly in his arms.

"I know, love," he growled, his voice heavy with passion. "I know."

Beyond the brink of thought, Rand shifted her weight to the ground and followed her down, taking care not to lie too heavily upon her. Lori was pliant and willing, and when he moved over her, she welcomed him without constraint. Deep in the recesses of her womanly core a flame of yearning was burning, and when he fit his body intimately to hers, she surged upward in wild, rapturous surprise. The soft swells of her breasts were crushed to his rock-hard chest, and the heat of his need was a brand against her. The thrust of her hips had felt so good that Lori began to move against him in a regular rhythm, although innocent of what was to come.

This naïve urging on her part broke the little control Rand was still exerting over himself. Deftly he reached between them and unbuttoned her skirt, then, shifting briefly away from her intoxicating nearness, he slipped the garment from her along with the rest of her clothing, baring to his gaze for the first time the glory of her gently rounded hips and long, slender legs.

"Lorelei . . . you're far more beautiful than I'd ever imagined," Rand told her, the undeniable hunger in his feverish gaze telling her that he wanted her beyond all else.

Lori's initial timidity faded at these words, and her lips curved in a smile of satisfaction for she had pleased her man. "You make me feel beautiful." Her voice was so sultry she hardly recognized it as her own.

"I want you, Lorelei, more than I've ever wanted any woman." Rand moved between her legs and bent to kiss her, his lips claiming hers in a passionate exchange.

In the distant recesses of her mind, she knew that there was something in his last remark that she should think about, but his lips and hands were doing wonderful things to her. There was no time for thought, only time for pleasure, as wave upon wave of heart-stopping rapture swept over her, peaking in a crash of climactic abandon that left her sobbing and helpless beneath him.

The knowledge that he'd satisfied her strengthened Rand's desire, and freeing himself of his trousers, he guided the proof of his need to the hidden sweetness of her womanhood. Completely pliant now, Lori lay quiescent as he pressed into her, breaching her virginal flesh and, in one smooth thrust, claiming her. Lori had not considered that there might be pain involved, and she suddenly gasped and tensed against this intrusion into her body.

"Easy, sweet." Rand held his riotous emotions in check as he waited for her moment of shock to pass. "Relax and let me love you. I promise it will never hurt again."

"Oh, yes. Please, Rand."

He began to move within her, soon reviving her desire. He had been delighted to discover she was a virgin, that he was her first and only lover, and he was enraptured by her unconditional response to his lovemaking for she held nothing back.

The tight velvet clasp of her body sent sensations of exquisite agony through Rand as he thrust deeply into her damp, welcoming heat until ecstasy shuddered through him as he convulsed in sweet release. The bliss of completely possessing her left him sated in her arms, and for some moments they lay together in silent rapture, too spent to speak.


"We'll need jacks and timbers," Cam told the men who'd gathered at the entrance of the mine to organize a rescue effort. "I don't know how bad the rest of the drift is, but the part we blasted last night near the end of the shift has totally collapsed. That's where Miss Lorelei and McAllister are trapped."

"Are you sure they're still alive?" someone asked, and Cam and Roger turned baleful glares in the man's direction.

"We are not going to assume the worst."

"How's Hal? Is he going to make it?" another man called out. The miners had seen Cam and Roger carrying the injured supervisor from the mine and they were all concerned about him.

"Yes. He's conscious now and able to move. He's going to be sore for a while, but he'll pull through,"

Cam responded. "It's the others we've got to help."

"Let's get going then!" a miner shouted, and an approving murmur swelled through the gathering.

Since they had been working in the drift before the cave-in and were familiar with the new tunnel, Harley and Rocky led the group as they started back down with lanterns, jacks, and new timbers.

Sally had been staying with Hal, but not knowing what was happening was driving her to distraction so she left him resting quietly and rushed out to try to locate Roger and find out what was going on.

She hurried to her cousin's side.

"Sally? Is Hal worse?" he asked.

"No. He's resting right now. I just want to find out what you are going to do." Her dark eyes were wide with concern.

"We're going to go back in and try to dig them out, but from what I understand, it's not as simple as it sounds. If it collapsed once, it might do it again, so each step of the way has to be reinforced with new beams."

"And that takes time?"

"Yes, ma'am," Cam answered respectfully as he joined them. Turning to Roger, he asked, "You coming?"

"You know I am," Westlake answered determinedly, and giving Sally a quick hug, he followed Cam toward the lift.

"Roger!"

"What?"

"Do you think they're alive?" She had not wanted to ask the question.

Roger's expression was hard as he faced her. "Lori has to be, Sally. If anything's happened to her . . ." Unable to express his thought, he turned away and joined Cam on the lift.

Sally watched until they had disappeared down the

166

shaft, and then slowly, with a prayer on her lips for Lori's and Rand's safety, she started back toward the house.

Her passion spent, Lori was reproaching herself, wondering how could she have been so weak willed as to have given herself to Rand with such abandon. She didn't love him! He was everything she disliked in a man; he was arrogant, demanding, and overconfident . . . yet she had given him her most precious gift—her virginity.

Circumstances had stripped her of her resolve to stay away from him, she reasoned. They had just survived an almost fatal cave-in, and they had needed each other. Satisfied with her logical assessment of what had just happened, she discounted her own unbridled response and moved away from Rand, needing to put a distance between them.

He, too, was realizing the mistake he'd made in losing control of his passions. Regardless of how much he'd wanted Lorelei or how much she'd wanted him, taking her innocence had been a grave error. Though their joining had been as near to perfect as anything he'd ever experienced, he knew there could be no repetition of it. The desperate situation had made him lose control, and he'd vowed silently that it would not happen again. When Lori stirred and left his embrace, he made no protest but began to straighten his own clothing without even glancing in her direction.

Had Rand encouraged her to stay with him, Lori might have thrown all of her rationalizations to the wind and returned to him, but his lack of acknowledgment of what had just passed between them only reinforced her resolve. He was a man who took what he wanted when he wanted, and since she had offered no resistance, he'd made love to her. She felt bitter because of her own willingness so, snatching up her clothes, she began to dress, feeling far too vulnerable in the nude.

"Lorelei," Rand said calmly, "what happened between us just now was a mistake and it will not be repeated."

Lori's glance was sharp as she looked at him, but despite her conviction that she wanted nothing to do with him, her heart twisted painfully in her breast at his words. She forced herself to meet his gaze coolly, all the while wondering how he could be so aloof after what they'd just shared. She had just known him intimately, and she was angered by his seemingly casual attitude toward their union.

"Thank you for that assurance," Lori managed to say. "I'm certain what just happened here, unfortunate though it was, was a result of our current situation; however, do I have your word that in the future you will not take advantage of our legal relationship?"

Lori knew she was on shaky ground, for she could not deny that she had desired Rand and certainly she had not resisted him in any way. Still, resenting his cool dismissal, she wanted to challenge his composure. She didn't want him to feel as if he were in total control of her, able to dictate terms.

Her no-holds-barred remark shocked Rand and he frowned angrily, wondering what she thought of him if she suspected he'd use his guardianship to gain access to her bed.

"You can rest assured that I will not take advantage of my guardianship to abuse you," he bit out caustically, then added snidely, "It is not my custom to make love to unwilling women."

A deep flush stained Lori's cheeks, but remembering Lydia, she quickly retorted, "And there haven't been many unwilling ones, have there?"

Rand thought she sounded almost jealous, but unable to imagine why, he shrugged off the thought as ridiculous.

"I can hardly say I'm inexperienced, Lorelei," he stated arrogantly. "A man seldom reaches my age without gaining some knowledge of the world and its ways."

"So I understand," she answered slowly, wondering what it was he'd learned from Lydia all those years ago.

"Lorelei, this is hardly a suitable conversation for us to be having. What happened between us, we've both admitted, was a mistake and it will not be repeated. Our primary concern right now, should be getting out of here." He directed his attention toward the completely blocked exit. "We've only got another few hours of light from the candle, so we'd better do what we can, while we can."

Knowing he was right on that score, Lori climbed as high up as she could on the mound of dirt and rocks and began scraping at the top, trying to dig through. Rand watched her work for only a moment before pitching in to do his share, and they struggled together in silence, shoving the debris aside as quickly as they could in their quest for freedom and survival.

# Chapter Ten

Lydia was surprised to see a lone horseman coming up the road toward the house. Unable to recognize the rider yet, she went out to meet him, hoping Rand was returning. She was disappointed when she recognized the man as John McCrea, the sheriff from Phoenix, but she did not let her feelings show. Instead, she welcomed him warmly.

"John, good to see you."

The sheriff dismounted and followed her into the cool shade of the ranch house. "Nice to see you, Mrs. McAllister."

"What brings you out our way? Not trouble, I hope," Lydia inquired with studied casualness.

"I've come to see Rand. I've got some important news for him. Is he around?"

"I'm sorry, John, he isn't right now, but I do expect him back by tomorrow. Can I help you in any way?" she led him into the parlor and then asked Juana to bring them drinks.

"I have a telegram that I think he might be interested in. The Benton boys . . ." He paused. "Are you familiar with them?"

"Only vaguely. Aren't they the ones Rand helped to

put in prison some years back?"

"Yes, ma'am. Anyway, I got word from the territorial office that they've escaped and have not yet been recaptured."

"Oh, no!" Lydia's dismay was real for she feared Rand would be called back to duty.

"Yes, ma'am, and as I remember, they swore to get Rand."

Her eyes grew wide with fright at the thought of two deadly villains gunning for Rand. "Do you think they might be coming here?"

"I don't know, Mrs. McAllister; it's hard to say with those two. They might have fled the territory." John hoped his very real concern was hidden. It wouldn't do to upset this lady. After all, there was no proof that the Bentons were anywhere near Phoenix. "Still, I thought I'd best let Rand know about it, seeing as how he was involved with them in the past."

Relieved that Rand wasn't being called back to duty and that the outlaws were not known to be in the area, Lydia relaxed a bit. Still . . . "Just how dangerous are these men—the Bentons?"

John knew there was no way to soften the blow. "They're killers, ma'am. They should have been hung years ago instead of sent off to prison, but it's too late to worry about that now. We just have to be prepared in case they do show up," he advised.

"Do you think there's a chance they've left the territory?" Lydia asked.

"I hope so, ma'am. The less civilized folks have to deal with their kind, the better." He accepted the cool drink that the servant offered, and after a few minutes of small talk, he prepared to leave. "Will you see that Rand gets my message as soon as possible?"

"I most certainly will," she promised.

"I'd appreciate it. If he has any questions or needs

any more information, just have him get in touch with me in town."

"I'll do that, Sheriff McCrea."

"I have another request, too," John went on.

"Oh?"

"Ellen and I are having a party on Saturday night, and we want you and Rand to come, if you can manage to get into town."

"Why, thank you," Lydia was delighted at the thought of attending a social gathering with Rand. "I'll be sure to mention it to him when I see him."

"That'll be just fine. I hope to be seeing you both then." John started from the room.

"I'll look forward to coming."

Lydia was smiling as she closed the door after watching the lawman ride off. The hours since Rand's departure had passed with dreadful slowness, and the thought of having a good excuse to go up to the Triple Cross to seek him out pleased her. She'd make the trip under the pretense of delivering the sheriff's message, and while she was at the mine she'd manage to get a good look at Miss Lorelei Spencer. Ordering Juana to pack a small bag for her, she rushed to her room to change into her riding clothes, eager to be on her way.

Stripped to the waist, his muscles taut and straining with each load of rock and dirt he lifted into the ore car, Roger paused in his efforts only long enough to wipe the sweat from his eyes. After seeing the injured Hal safely from the mine and placing him in Sally's care, he and Cam, along with a full crew of miners, had returned to begin the rescue. They had been slaving in the mine's close, dimly lighted depths for hours now; yet it seemed to Roger that they had made little progress. Car after car of debris had been carted from the bowels of the mine, and new timbers had been added as reinforcement, yet they seemed no nearer to rescuing Lorelei and Rand. Still, he had hope, for in clearing the passage, they'd uncovered no bodies.

"How you holding up?" Cam asked as he came to stand beside Roger. He knew Westlake had little experience in mining, but he also knew the man would not be deterred from helping in the rescue attempt.

"I'll make it," Roger answered flatly as he began to shovel again.

"According to my charts"—the assayer started to unroll the map he'd made earlier of the newly blasted tunnel, and Roger quickly threw his shovel aside to look it over—"there's at least another five feet between us and the point at which we last saw them."

"How long?"

"To dig them out?" Cam frowned. "A day . . . day and a half at the rate we're going. 'Course if we blast, use small strategically placed charges, it could cut down our rescue time. We might be able to get them out by tonight."

"No!" Roger's fear was real. "You can't be seriously considering blasting after what's happened in here."

Cam shrugged. "We've doubled the reinforcement of the entire drift. There won't be any more cave-ins behind us."

"I don't care about what's behind us. As unstable as this area is, we would be risking their lives if we try to blast."

"But if they're injured or trapped in the debris they might not live until tomorrow."

Cam had voiced the possibility that had been haunting Roger, and he recoiled at the thought of Lori . . . dead. "That's the chance we'll have to take, Cam. We'll keep digging, it's the only option we have." Solemnly he returned to his work.

\*      \*      \*

Lori's hands were bleeding and sore, and her entire body ached as she sat down wearily in the dirt, her eyes fastened on the sputtering, dying light of their only candle.

"It's almost out," she said emotionlessly.

Rand paused in his attempt to loosen a good-sized boulder near the top of the mound, and he glanced in her direction just as the candle went out. Muttering a curse, he wiped his battered hands ineffectually against his torn, filthy pants, then half-climbed, half-crawled down the hill of debris.

"Lorelei?"

"To your right," she offered numbly.

Rand worked his way to her, sitting down close beside her yet taking care to avoid touching her. They had spoken little during the hours since their confrontation and that had suited him just fine. Survival had to be their goal right now; he could not afford to let her distract him from that purpose. At this point, nothing else mattered except getting out.

Lori could feel the warmth emanating from his body as he joined her on the ground, and she couldn't suppress a shiver at his nearness.

"I guess there's nothing left to do, but wait," she remarked, breaking the heavy silence. "They'll be here as quickly as they can. I know they will."

Rand knew she was right. The miners, no doubt, would work around the clock until they rescued them. The only thing that worried Rand was the extensiveness of the cave-in. Were they trapped behind only a few feet of rock or had the rest of the tunnel collapsed? If it had, and he prayed to God it hadn't, then no matter how hard the miner's worked, he doubted that he and Lorelei would be alive when the rescue crew broke through. Pushing that morbid thought away, Rand leaned back against the wall and tried to relax.

Lori was not naïve where mine accidents were concerned, and she, too, was worrying about how much of the tunnel had collapsed. No food . . . no water. She knew they could last a few days here in the dark, but beyond that . . . Lori had never given much thought to dying, but in the suffocating blackness, exhausted in both mind and body, she felt an overpowering sense of weakness, and though she tried, she could not smother the small, desperate sob that escaped her.

"Lorelei?" Rand was puzzled by her cry. She had always seemed so strong that he'd never expected her to break down.

"It's nothing," Lori choked out, trying to disguise her vulnerability for Rand was the last person she wanted to know of her lapse in self-control.

"Lorelei." This time his tone was understanding, and as gently as he could, he reached out and drew her to him.

Lori tensed at the unexpected tenderness of his gesture.

"I'm not going to make love to you, Lorelei. I'm just going to hold you." Rand was exasperated by her skittishness.

"All right," she agreed, sniffing loudly and fighting down the uneasiness she felt as she rested her head on his shoulder and closed her eyes against the blinding blackness.

Rand took care to hold her only comfortingly, and he was surprised when, within minutes, Lori seemed to have fallen asleep. Though he knew this was hardly the time to remember the passion they had known just a few hours ago, his mind evoked the memory of her body joined to his. He bit back a groan of protest as his body responded to his thoughts, and he only hoped that Lori didn't realize the effect she was having upon

175

him. Sweat beaded his forehead, but this time it was not from exertion. He gritted his teeth against the desire pounding through his veins. Annoyed by his body's betrayal, Rand wondered why Lorelei, of all women, could create such havoc within him. Refusing to give in to his lusty craving for her, he leaned his head back wearily against the wall and tried to focus on something else . . . the mine . . . his job . . . the Lazy Ace—anything, except the silken rapture of her presence as she lay trustingly in his arms.

Jack accompanied Lydia on the trip to the mine, and they rode up to the Triple Cross just before sundown. Despite the massive rescue effort underway, guards had been posted, and a burly miner, shotgun in hand, blocked their path as they drew near the stables.

"What's your business here?" the guard demanded, eying them skeptically.

"I'm Jack Barlow and this is Lydia McAllister. We've got an important message for Rand. Is he here?"

The miner thought better of telling them of the tunnel's collapse so he said, "Ride on through. The first house is the one you want."

"Thanks," Jack answered, kneeing his mount forward. Lydia followed suit.

Sally had just started from the house to check on Roger and the progress being made in the mine when she noticed two riders heading her way. Watching their approach with open curiosity, she was unable to imagine who the attractive woman could be, Lorelei had made no mention of having women friends in the area.

Lydia had very vivid memories of Lorelei Spencer so one look at the dark-haired beauty standing before the house told her this was not the chit who had visited the

176

Lazy Ace with her father years ago. Wondering who this could be, she kept her probing gaze carefully guarded as she reined in.

"Good evening." Sally's smile was real as she greeted them.

"Evenin', ma'am," Jack replied respectfully, thinking her a most attractive young woman. "As I told the guard, I'm Jack Barlow and this is Lydia McAllister. We've come to see Rand. Is he here?"

The stricken look on Sally's face alarmed Lydia and she hurriedly asked, "Is something wrong, miss?"

It had been a shock for Sally to discover that this young, attractive woman was Rand's stepmother, but she realized there was no way to keep the truth from her. "Yes. I'm afraid so."

"Oh, God." Immediately thinking the worst, Lydia paled. "Rand's not dead, is he?"

"Oh, no! At least we hope not! There was a cave-in this morning and—"

"Jack . . ." Lydia turned terrified eyes on her foreman, and Jack quickly dismounted to help her from her horse.

"Please come in the house and I'll explain everything to you." Sally was concerned that the woman might faint. "I'm Sally Westlake, by the way," she declared as she ushered them inside.

"You must tell me what's going on!" Lydia demanded as Jack guided her with a supportive arm to the sofa. "Where's Rand?"

Sally quickly explained. "As I was saying, there was a collapse in the newest tunnel this morning. I'm sorry to have to tell you this, but Rand is trapped and so is Lori. The assayer and my brother Roger made it out unharmed, and the mine supervisor was only slightly injured; but Lori and Rand were walking a few feet behind them when the cave-in occurred. The miners

177

have been down there trying to dig them out since it happened."

"Oh, Jack." Lydia clasped his hand. Her upset was very real, yet she reacted as Rand's father's wife. "I don't think I could bear to lose Rand, too."

"Why don't you two wait here while I go see if I can find out anything?" Sally offered, planning to check in on Hal at his house while she was gone.

"Thank you," Lydia responded worriedly. She wanted Rand. His kiss had stirred feelings she'd long thought dead and she could not bear the thought of anything happening to him. True, he had not been exactly receptive toward her, but with time she felt certain he would come around. After all, the love they'd shared so long ago had been consuming so she was confident that they could rekindle the desire that had been such a dominant part of their relationship. Sitting back, she gave Jack a weak smile.

"Don't worry, Lydia. Rand's going to come out of this just fine."

"I hope so, Jack," she murmured and she meant it.


Lori had awakened to find herself in Rand's arms, nestled comfortably against him, but, embarrassed to think that she could relax so completely in his embrace, she'd jerked nervously away from him.

Rand had finally managed to fall asleep, but when Lorelei tore herself away from him, he was jarred back to reality with an abruptness that left him annoyed and frustrated. "For God's sake! What the hell's the matter?" he thundered.

"I'm sorry . . . I—" she apologized quickly, chagrined.

"You what!"

"Nothing," Lori snapped, refusing to explain that

178

coming awake in his arms had disturbed her. Obviously, she knew now that she could trust him to some degree, that he would keep his word about not trying to make love to her again, but she didn't want to reveal her childish reaction to his nearness. "I had a bad dream, that's all."

Rand grunted in reply, and unfolding his long, cramped limbs, he stood up.

"What are you going to do?" she asked, sensing his movements.

"I don't know. I can't stand doing nothing, but I'm afraid if we start digging in the dark, we won't be able to gauge the danger. One wrong move could bring the rest of the tunnel down on us," Rand rubbed the back of his neck wearily.

"I know. If they don't start breaking through to us soon, we'll have to take that chance though."

He nodded in the darkness. "I just wish we knew what was going on on the other side."

"If my calculations are correct, we should break through by morning," Cam told Roger as they stood together at the station in the upper tunnel of the mine. "That is, if the whole tunnel didn't go—"

"I can't even consider that—not now." Roger shook his head. He'd been working nonstop and was just taking his first real break.

"Either way, we'll have our answer then," Cam stated, and Roger nodded his acceptance of that fact.

"Mr. Westlake?" a miner paused on his way past the station.

"What is it?" Roger was instantly alert.

"It's Miss Westlake, sir. She's waiting above to talk to you."

"Thanks." He turned back to Cam. "I'd better go see

179

what Sally wants. There might have been a change in Hal's condition."

"Sure."

"I'll be right back," Roger hurried to the lift and ascended to find Sally waiting anxiously for him. "What's wrong? Has Hal worsened?"

"No, he's doing fine, but Lydia McAllister has come here to see Rand. When I told her what had happened, she got very upset, so I had her wait at the house while I came to check with you. Have you made a break-through yet?"

"No," he replied. "But according to Cam we should know whether they're dead or alive by morning."

Sally gazed sympathetically at her cousin, reading in his exhausted expression all the agony and anxiety he was feeling. "Don't worry, Roger. She'll be alive."

"I hope you're right, Sally. I don't know what I'd do if—"

"I don't even want you thinking such thoughts!" she told him feverishly. "Why don't you come back to the house with me and speak with Rand's stepmother? I'm sure she'll be reassured if you talk to her, and I'll fix you something to eat while you're there."

"I don't want to be away for very long."

"I'll hurry. I promise." She gave him a reassuring smile and then led the way back to the house.

Lydia looked up quickly as a sweat-streaked, unshaven, half-dressed man entered the house, closely followed by Sally. Coming to her feet, she started toward him, anxious to learn of Rand.

"I'm Lydia McAllister, Rand's stepmother." She said as Roger approached.

"Ma'am." Roger was stunned. He had expected Rand's stepmother to be an older woman, but Lydia McAllister, he ventured to guess, was no more than thirty and she was most beautiful. "I'm Roger Westlake."

"Mr. Westlake . . ."

"Roger, please."

"Roger." She gave a nervous smile, and they were both glad the formalities were over. "Have you found Rand yet? Is he safe?"

"We haven't made any breakthroughs yet, Mrs. McAllister, but we'll know more by morning."

"Please, call me Lydia," she told him distractedly. "So you have no news."

"No, ma'am," he answered. "But we do know Lori's and Rand's position before the collapse of the support beam."

Lydia nodded slowly at his words for she was envisioning Rand lying dead beneath tons of rubble. "Is there truly any hope?" The question seemed torn from her.

Roger's tired expression turned fierce. "There is always hope, and I won't entertain any other possibility until we have proof of the worst."

"Is there anything we can do to help?" Jack spoke up for the first time. "I'm Jack Barlow, by the way, foreman from the Lazy Ace."

"No, I'm sorry. There's really nothing more to be done. It's all a waiting game now," Roger told them as he sat at the table and began to wolf down the plate of hot stew Sally had just set out for him.

"You and your wife both seem very familiar with the mine and its operation," Lydia ventured. "Have you been associated with the Triple Cross for very long?"

"Wife?" Sally and Roger exchanged confused looks.

Sally couldn't help but smile at her assumption. "Roger and I aren't married, Lydia," she explained quickly. "We're cousins."

181

"And we really know very little about the mine for we just arrived here with Lori," Roger went on.

"You traveled with Lorelei?" Lydia inquired.

Sensing her unspoken question, he added, "As soon as I can arrange it, Lori and I will be married, and after what I've gone through today, I hope she won't keep me waiting much longer!"

That news pleased Lydia. If Lorelei married, Rand's guardianship would no longer apply. The prospect of having him alone with her at the Lazy Ace thrilled her and she prayed that he had not been injured by the mine disaster.

"Do you know if cave-ins are common? I know so very little about gold mining."

"I'm just learning myself," Roger began. "But from what I've heard from the men, safety has always been a key issue at the Triple Cross. This is evidently the first real problem they've had. I hope it's their last."

"You don't suppose . . ." Lydia paused, suddenly remembering McCrea's warning about the Bentons.

"What?"

"Are there any men working here by the name of Benton?"

Roger frowned, "No. I've met them all and I don't recall anyone by that name. Why?"

Lydia was relieved, "I guess it's not really relevant, but the message I had for Rand was from the Phoenix sheriff. He came out to the ranch to tell Rand that two men he'd sent to prison several years ago had escaped. The sheriff seemed to think that they might come gunning for Rand; he wanted him to be aware of the situation."

"And you thought they might have tracked him to the mine and set up the accident?"

She nodded. "The sheriff said the Bentons were killers. I'm just glad this really was an accident."

"It couldn't have been anything else," Roger said firmly. "I was there with them when it happened. It's just luck that I wasn't the one trapped with Lori. I had just preceded them from the area when the timber snapped. No one else was near except for two miners—Rocky Madden and Harley Oates—and they've been with the Triple Cross for years." Finishing off his food, he pushed the plate across the table toward Sally and stood up. "I've got to get back. If there is any word at all, good or bad, I'll send a message up to you right away."

"Thanks, Roger." Sally stood on tiptoe to kiss his grimy, beard-stubbled cheek, then she watched worriedly as he headed from the room. "Be careful."

"I will."

Once he'd gone, Sally turned to her unexpected company. "Would you care for something to eat? I imagine it was a long ride for you."

"That's very kind of you, but I can't possibly think about food at a time like this," Lydia demurred, but Jack accepted gratefully and sat down at the table.

"Thank you, ma'am," he told Sally graciously, admiring her trim figure and the glossy darkness of her hair.

"I'm Sally and I'd be pleased to have you call me by my first name," she invited.

"Sally . . . that's a right pretty name. It suits you."

Sally blushed becomingly, "Why thank you, sir."

"Jack. My name's Jack." As he smiled at her, he wondered what a woman as pretty as Sally was doing way out here in the desert.

The long hours of the night passed at a snail's pace, for Lori and Rand sat in the pitch darkness awaiting some sign that rescue was imminent. The precariousness of their situation had become more evident with the passage of time, and they were now in a period of black silence. They had made several attempts at conversation, but Lori, having regained her equilibrium where Rand was concerned, refused to be drawn out. No matter how considerate he was being, she knew the kind of man he really was and she was not going to allow him to have any power over her. It was bad enough that he was her guardian; it would not do to give him insight into her emotions. In spite of what had passed between them, when they left this dungeon she was going to treat him exactly as she had been treating him before their intimacy.

Rand found the incarceration maddening. He was unused to enforced inactivity, and the long hours of helpless idleness were taking their toll. With each passing moment, he was becoming more and more apprehensive about the likelihood of rescue and he knew that they would soon have to take matters into their own hands, or go mad with the waiting. Unable to play the victim any longer, Rand rose and slowly felt his way along the base of the debris.

"Rand?"

"I'm going to start to clear some more of this out of here. Why don't you move farther back so I don't have to worry about you?"

"You don't have to worry about me. No one asked you to!" Lori declared pointedly.

"Your father did," he countered.

"Well, I'm sure my father had no idea of what he was letting me in for when he drew up that misguided directive." She bridled at the mention of that ridiculous document. "Why, if it hadn't been for you, we wouldn't be trapped in here right now!" Lori knew she was deliberately baiting him. The collapse could have happened at anytime, but the long hours of tense waiting had taken their toll and she didn't care.

"Are you always going to be this contrary?" he shot back, tired of her shrewishness. They were stuck with each other until she turned twenty-one and he didn't understand why she couldn't just accept it.

"I have no intention of just sitting here while you do all the work," Lori informed him levelly. "I'm as capable as you are of digging us out of here."

"Fine!" Rand exploded. "Since you're so capable, get started, and maybe, just maybe, between the two of us we'll find a way out of this hellhole!"

Cursing under his breath, he maneuvered himself to the top of the mound and began to claw at the unseen rocks and dirt that blocked their escape. Blindly, Lori scrambled up after him. Then, silently and side by side, they worked with frenzied desperation, knowing that time was running out.

# Chapter Eleven

Neither Rand nor Lorelei had any idea of how long they'd been digging for they had been concentrating solely on the fact that each handful of jagged rock and dirt they pushed aside brought them closer to salvation. The staleness of the air made their breathing ragged, and sweat poured from their bodies as they labored ceaselessly. Thirst and hunger were their constant companions now, but they ignored the aching pangs that gnawed at them for they realized it would do no good to dwell on them. Time was of the essence. They had to get out, and soon.

"I hear something!" Lori panted as she paused. "Rand! Listen!" Sitting back, she waited until the sound of drilling on rock came to them again. "They're coming! I knew they would!"

"Thank God!"

As time had worn on, Rand had become more and more skeptical of their chances of being rescued. He had not shared his misgivings with Lorelei, but had turned his anger and his frustration at their circumstances into direct action, throwing aside the stones and grit with a furious, continual motion. Now, as the sound of the drill came to them, joy surged through him, and he reached out in the dark for Lori and hugged her to him.

His move had been instinctive. In fact, knowing how explosive his reaction to her was, he had never wanted to touch her again, but suddenly she was in his arms and he could not prevent the kiss that seemed so natural.

Lori had gone into his arms automatically. They were being saved! Any minute light would pour through some man-made opening in the blockage and they would be freed from the darkness of their living tomb! Thrilled, she hugged Rand spontaneously in return and it was in that moment of contact that she realized what had happened between them earlier had been no fluke. The feel of his hard body pressed so tightly to hers sent her blood racing, and despite her resolve, she offered no resistance to his kiss.

Ecstasy flooded them both as their lips met and parted to taste of one another's sweetness. Wrapped in each other's arms, they strained together, their hands restlessly seeking, igniting fires that they had denied. Keeping his word not to make love to her again was proving more difficult than Rand had imagined, and only by sheer force of will did he tear himself from Lorelei and move away.

"We'd better start digging again."

His tone was controlled, giving Lori no clue of the turmoil within him, but at his apparent indifference Lori plummeted from the heights of joy and remained unmoving for an instant as she realized that their kiss had been nothing more than a celebration of rescue to him. Bitter over her own riotous feelings for Rand, she turned back to her task.

"Yes. You're right. The more we help, the sooner we get out of here. Do you think we should shout?"

"Not yet," Rand replied in clipped tones. "We'll wait

until they're closer; I doubt they could hear us over the drill right now."

Knowing he was right, Lori kept scraping away at the top of the debris, eagerly anticipating the moment light would burst through and illuminate their dark prison.

Roger had slept for only a few hours during the long night and, as the sun edged higher in the Eastern sky, he was back in the tunnel, working with the same intensity he'd displayed on the previous day. The miners had been drilling continuously since sunup, only pausing to allow some of the rock to be shoveled into the waiting cars. During one of these breaks Roger heard the faint sound of Rand's and Lori's shouts.

"Dear God! It's them!" he bellowed. "Cam! They're alive!"

Cam had been standing back as the workers loaded the cars, but at Roger's call, he rushed forward to take charge of the next phase of their drilling efforts.

"Send word up to Sally and the others," Roger told one of the men, and the miner raced off to do his bidding. "What's safest, Cam?"

"We'll continue the way we've been going. We can't afford any mistakes, not now."

Shouting at the tops of their voices, Cam and Roger called out encouragement to Lori and Rand, and he ordered them to stay back from the area of drilling if they could.

"They heard us!" Lori cried when she heard someone call her name, and tears of joy stung her eyes.

"And they also told us to get back," Rand said, his voice sounding calm and unaffected. "Do you need any help down?"

"No!" Lori answered almost too quickly. "I'm fine."

Scrambling down the pile, they moved to the back of the tunnel, and taking care not to touch one another, they waited for the breakthrough.

Since Hal was resting in her room, Sally had offered Lydia the use of Lori's, and she'd accepted gratefully for the tension and worry of the day had left her exhausted. Still, once she'd changed into her night-clothes and tried to rest, sleep would not come. She'd been haunted by memories of Rand when he'd been her lover, and it had been near dawn when she'd given up on the idea of getting any real rest.

Now, dressed once again in her riding clothes, she was sitting at the small table, sipping coffee and looking distractedly out the window as she considered the bleak day ahead. As she did so she saw a miner emerge from the lift and race in the direction of the house. Getting to her feet, she hurried to the door.

"There's a miner coming! Something's happened! I know it!"

Sally hurriedly followed her outside. She had passed the night catnapping in a chair for fear of missing any news so she ran eagerly from the house hoping to learn what was happening.

"Miss Westlake, ma'am, they're alive!" the man called excitedly.

"Thank heavens!" Sally glanced toward the main shaft. "Are they coming up?"

"No, ma'am. We haven't got through to 'em yet, but we heard 'em hollerin'! Mr. Westlake said to come tell you, 'cause he knew you'd be wantin' to know."

"Oh, thank you." Tears of relief coursed, unheeded, down her cheeks.

"I'm going below," Lydia declared.

"That's not a good idea, if you don't mind me sayin'

so, ma'am," the miner began.

"I do mind," Lydia snapped, hurrying on toward the lift. "I must see Rand, be there when he comes out."

"Lydia"—Sally tried to stop her—"maybe the miner is right. It's really no place for a woman."

"Lorelei is down there, isn't she?"

"Well, yes, but—"

"Don't try to stop me, Sally. I mean to be there when they break through." Disregarding both of them, she rushed onward to the lift. "Take me down there now!" Lydia ordered imperiously and the man at the shaft complied.

Sally watched in dismay as the headstrong woman disappeared into the lift and was lowered away. Had she not been responsible for Hal, Sally would have gone after Lydia, but she knew she should go and tell the injured foreman the good news. Returning to the house, she knocked softly on the bedroom door, and at Hal's gruff call to enter, she went in to tell him of the imminent rescue.

Lydia reached the main tunnel, and spotting two miners at the station, she approached them with cool authority, "Take me to the rescue site."

"But, ma'am—" they started to protest, knowing that Cam and Mr. Westlake would not approve of a woman down there.

"I said, take me to them. I am Lydia McAllister and I have every right to be here. Unless you want to risk losing your jobs, you'll lead me to them."

Her haughty attitude intimidated the men and meekly they led her through the maze to the site.

"Roger! Have you broken through yet?" Lydia asked excitedly as she came down the tunnel toward him.

"Lydia! What the . . . You shouldn't be down here;

190

it's dangerous!" He was irritated by her interruption.

"I don't care about danger—only about Rand. How soon will you have them out?"

"I'm not sure. Hopefully, it won't be too much longer, but Lydia, I want you to get out of here. I can't be worried about your safety while we're working."

"I'll stay out of your way, but I am not leaving. I intend to be waiting right here when Rand is freed!" She was adamant.

Roger hadn't the time or patience to deal with her. Short of having her carried from the mine, he knew there was little he could do. "Stay back, then," he ordered tersely, his displeasure obvious as he set back to work.

It happened suddenly. One moment Lori and Rand were smothered in the heavy darkness, and the next a tiny patch of life-giving light streamed into their enclosure.

"Lori?" Roger called out. "Sweetheart, are you all right?"

Racing forward, she scrambled up the incline to claw at and enlarge the opening. "Roger. Oh, Roger, darling, thank you."

Rand had started to follow her, but the sound of her calling the other man darling infuriated him and he held back.

"Lorelei Spencer," Roger said teasingly. "After what we've just been through, we are not going to postpone our marriage any longer!"

"Roger . . ."

"Are you injured in any way?" he went on.

"No. I'm fine. Rand is, too. Please hurry!"

"We will, love. Just get back," he called out to her. "We're going to get you out of there right now."

Returning to the relative safety of her position near Rand, Lori waited for the last of the rescue work to be done, completely unaware of the effect her conversation with Roger had had on him. The shock of Roger's remarks about their marriage plans had left Rand enraged and even more cynical about women. Since his early experience with Lydia, he had avoided entanglements for he'd long suspected that women were all alike. Lydia had made love to him, while plotting to marry his father. Lorelei was promised to Roger, yet she had made love to him!

All along he had suspected a depth of feeling between Lorelei and Roger, but it had never seemed a reality. Now that he knew they were involved with each other, he was furious with himself for imagining, even for a moment, that things could have been different.

The loud blast of the drill began again once Roger was certain that she'd moved away and within minutes, the hole had been widened to allow them to crawl out.

"Lori! Rand! Can you climb out now?" Cam called.

"We'll try," Rand replied, and he gestured casually for Lori to go first.

In a timeless moment their eyes met across the semi-darkness, and Lori hesitated for just an instant, staring at him with wide, frightened eyes. Rand seemed so strong and virile as he stood there that passion for him pulsed through her. Torn between the desire to go into his arms and remain with him forever and the need to run from him as quickly as she could to save herself from what she was certain was unending heartache, she stood poised and achingly unable to decide.

Rand read the fear in her gaze but mistook the reason for it, thinking she was afraid that he would tell Roger of their lovemaking. He remarked in a low, sneering voice, "You don't have to worry. I won't tell your boyfriend what happened here, Lorelei. As far as I'm concerned, nothing happened. Now, go on! He's waiting!"

His easy dismissal of something so important seared her soul with the burning brand of reality and she turned from him quickly, stifling a sob as she scrambled from the place of their entombment and launched herself into Roger's waiting arms.

"Roger!" she cried, throwing her arms about his neck and accepting his kiss with an enthusiasm she did not feel.

"Lori . . . oh, Lori . . . I was so worried," he managed to get out after their kiss had ended, and it was then he saw Rand climbing carefully out of the inner chamber. He started to speak, but before he could say anything, Lydia rushed forward to embrace Rand, kissing him in an altogether unmotherly fashion, her arms tight about his neck, her breasts pressed fully against his chest, her mouth warm and devouring upon his. For once, Rand was glad to see her, and determined to wipe all memories of Lorelei from his mind, he returned her welcome with obvious enthusiasm.

"Oh, Rand! We've been so worried. We thought you might be dead," Lydia gushed when their kiss had ended. Using this moment to press her advantage before everyone, she clasped his hand possessively to her bosom and gazed up at him adoringly.

Lydia was talking endlessly, but Lori was aware of nothing save the heartrending sight of Rand kissing her. From the moment the older woman had appeared, it had been almost as if Lori had been reliving a bad dream, and the sight of Lydia in Rand's arms now made her shiver in revulsion. Nothing had changed. Nothing. No doubt, from the way they were kissing, they were still lovers. His father's death had only made things easier for them. Why else would Lydia be here now? And why else would Rand have kissed her so ardently in front of everyone?

"Roger," Lori said in a husky whisper as waves of

nausea filled her, "please . . ."

Thinking that she was weak and about to faint from the horror of her ordeal, Roger swept her up into his strong embrace and carried her quickly from the site.

Rand had given the impression that he was listening to Lydia's prattle, but in reality he'd been watching Lori from beneath half-lowered lids and when she had seemed to collapse into Roger's arms, he'd almost gone to her. Only his iron-willed self-control kept him at Lydia's side as he watched Roger rush from the tunnel. Lorelei did not want him. She'd made that perfectly clear. She had only used him in those moments of fear and distress, and he berated himself for the passion he'd felt for her.

"Let's get out of here," he said, suddenly needing to be out in the open, away from all the dark reminders of the past twenty-four hours.

"Yes, of course. You must be exhausted after all that time penned up," Lydia sympathized, feeling quite pleased that he'd returned her kiss so heatedly.

"I am, Lydia, and there's nothing I want more right now than to get outside. What time is it? What day?"

"You've been trapped almost a full day," Cam told him.

"Cam, I appreciate everything you and Roger did to get us out. Thank you."

"You're welcome, Rand," Cam clasped his hand in friendship. "Now go on up. Get some food in you and enjoy the sunshine. We've got a lot more restoring to do down here before we can get back to mining."

Rand thanked the miners and then headed toward the lift, barely conscious of Lydia's presence at his side.

"I'm so glad that I came here to the mine," she was saying as they rode the lift to the surface. "Why, if I hadn't, I wouldn't have found out about your misfortune for days. Thank heaven you're all right. I

194

don't know what I would have done if you'd been hurt or killed. I couldn't have borne losing both Will and you."

"Lydia, I'm fine as you can see," he said curtly.

"But your head!" she exclaimed as the lift emerged topside into the brightness of the new day.

Rand lifted a weary hand to touch the dry, matted blood that marked the injury he'd received during the cave-in. "It must look worse than it really is," he said offhandedly as he stepped from the lift and walked out into the sunlight for the first time in a full day. Though his eyes were sensitive to the vivid glare of the sun, he reveled in his freedom, and he stood in silence, his eyes closed, appreciating the warmth of the sun and the fresh clean scent of the desert air.

"Rand? Are you feeling well?" Lydia questioned.

"I'm fine, Lydia," he replied harshly.

"Rand!" Sally called delightedly as she came forth from the house, and he started toward her. "I am so happy to see you!"

"I'm happy to see you, too," he answered, a warm smile breaking forth. This was the one woman he felt he could trust. She was so totally open and so unaffected that he knew instinctively she was incapable of deceit.

Sally touched his arm affectionately as she came to stand before him, "I've got food almost ready. Why don't you wash up and come get something to eat? I had one of the men put your things in Hal's house," she told him.

"I'll do that," he agreed, and without a word to Lydia he moved off to get cleaned up.

"Come on inside, Lydia. I'm sure you must be hungry, too."

"Yes. Now that the danger is over, I think I could eat something," she said as she walked along with Sally, but even as she kept up a trivial conversation with the other woman, her eyes were on Rand who was striding toward the supervisor's home.

Lori was tense and exhausted as she lay on her bed, her face turned toward the window. Sunlight . . . how beautiful it was. She knew she would never take the light of day for granted again.

Roger had carried her all the way to her bedroom, and though he knew it was improper for him to be there, he could not bring himself to leave her except for a short period of time when she washed and changed clothes. In all the time he'd known Lori, he had never thought of her as anything but a strong, determined woman, but she had looked so pale and frightened when she'd climbed out of the tunnel that he'd wanted to hold her in his arms forever and protect her with his life, if necessary.

"Lori . . ." he began hoarsely. "Lori, I can't tell you how worried we all were about you."

"I know, Roger," she answered, giving him a small smile. She wanted to rejoice in her rescue, but she had been so devastated by Rand's mocking dismissal of what had happened between them and by the passionate embrace he'd shared with his stepmother that her heart was leaden in her breast.

"Damn it, Lori!" Roger was near to bursting with love for her, yet he found no answering emotion in her. "I love you! This disaster only made me realize how much."

"You are so sweet," she told him, but her words only increased his frustration.

"I don't want you to think of me as sweet, Lori," he stated emphatically, and sitting down beside her and dragging her into his arms, he kissed her passionately. During all the time of their courtship in St. Louis,

Roger had held himself in restraint. What he'd felt for Lori was different from anything he'd known before, but he'd not wanted to risk frightening her with the power of his desire. However, enough was enough. He'd been without a woman for months now, and his control over himself was slipping.

His kiss took Lori by surprise. She had never thought of Roger as a particularly passionate man, though she'd certainly heard enough rumors about his roguish ways back in St. Louis before he'd started courting her. To be swept into such a possessive, urgent embrace both startled and pleased her. Here was a man who would cherish her, care for her, and though she had to admit that his touch was not nearly as exciting as Rand's, it was not unpleasant either.

Looping her arms willingly about his neck, she returned his kiss eagerly, wanting to arouse within herself the same thrilling sensations she'd experienced with Rand. To her disappointment, the flame of desire that a simple touch from Rand could spark to life did not flare within her. She experienced only a warm, comfortable feeling of protection and tenderness in Roger's arms. Even as he boldly sought the softness of her breasts beneath the clean blouse she'd donned, no sense of driving need was awakened within her. Though she surrendered to his caress without protest, she realized that she would never feel ecstasy with Roger as she had with Rand, and that acknowledgment left her feeling very empty.

The door, which had been partially closed, opened unexpectedly, and Sally, who was coming to tell them their food was ready, caught them in a most intimate position. Rand, who'd already washed, changed clothes, and returned to the main house, was standing back from the bedroom door, but when Sally opened it, he glanced up and saw Lori clasped in Roger's arms,

197

the other man's hand resting familiarly on her breast. Abruptly he turned away and went to join Lydia, Jack, and Hal who were already sitting at the table. Deliberately, he took the seat next to Lydia.

"Hal, it's good to see you up and about," he told the foreman sincerely, all the while trying not to think about what Lori had been doing in the bedroom with Roger. He had no doubt, now that he'd initiated her into the joys a man and woman could share, that she was eager to experience them with her fiancé. A burning rage engulfed him at the thought of her being taken by the other man, and he tore his thoughts away from her with a vengeance.

"It's good to be up and about. One day in bed was enough. I'm sore as hell, but that's not going to stop me. We're going to have this mine producing again as soon as Cam and I can get that drift cleaned out and reinforced."

"That's good news."

"I'm just sorry I couldn't help rescue you."

"Doesn't matter." Rand smiled. "All that matters is we got out, and in one piece." Glancing at Lydia, who seemed to be hanging on his every word, he asked, "You haven't told me yet what it was that brought you out to the Triple Cross, Lydia."

"Sheriff McCrea paid me a visit early yesterday," she began.

"And?" Rand looked questioningly from Lydia to Jack.

"And the Benton boys have escaped."

"How?" he demanded, his eyes narrowing at the thought of those killers once again terrorizing the countryside.

"I don't know all the details. He just knew they'd vowed to get even with you someday so he wanted to warn you that they were on the loose."

Rand was tense, "I'd better get back to town and find out exactly what's going on. How soon do you think you'll be resuming regular work here?"

"Good three or four days," Hal answered, having already discussed it with Cam.

"That'll give me time to make the trip." Rand nodded.

"Trip?" Roger asked, as he and Lori came to sit at the table.

"I've got to go into Phoenix to see the sheriff." Rand's gaze roamed dispassionately over Lori, noting the becoming flush to her cheeks and thinking it was from Roger's heated caresses.

"Has there been some trouble?"

"Not yet. Just some old unfinished business, that's all," Rand shrugged off his interest.

"I'll be glad to help, if there's anything I can do," Roger told him.

"It might not be a bad idea for you two to go with him," Hal suddenly put in. "Supplies are running low. Miss Lorelei knows what we need. Besides, she could probably use a few days away from here right now."

Lori had felt a moment of relief at the thought of Rand being away for a while. She needed time away from him in order to get control of her emotions and her life. Hal's suggestion that she and Roger accompany him to town caught her off guard and she began to argue. "I don't think—"

Roger, however, cut her off. "That's a good idea. We'll ride out with you, Rand."

Lori bristled at Roger's take-charge manner, and Rand was thoroughly disgusted. The last thing he wanted to do was spend time with Lori. The farther away he was from her, the better; and, the sooner she married Roger, the happier he'd be, for once she was married, he'd no longer be responsible for her or her money.

"Jack and I were planning to head back to the Lazy Ace tomorrow," Lydia added, hoping to spend more time with Rand. "Why don't we all ride together?"

"Sounds fine," Roger agreed. "Sally? Would you like to go, too?"

Sally, who had been anxious for some news about Brady Barclay, eagerly agreed. "I'd like that."

"All right," Rand assented, knowing there was no graceful way to get out of it. "We'll ride out in the morning."

"You're sure you won't need me here, Hal?" Lori had one last hope.

"No, Miss Lorelei. Things will run just fine without you for a few days. You deserve a trip to town."

Lori knew she should put her foot down and refuse to go, but she didn't want anyone wondering why. Giving in quietly, she silently fumed at the thought of being thrown together with Rand for the entire ride into Phoenix. Thank goodness, Roger and Sally would be along.

## Chapter Twelve

"Are you sure you're gonna be able to make it?" Riley worried as he watched Brady Barclay swing slowly up into the saddle.

"I'm sure, Riley," Barclay stated firmly. "I've been sitting out here far too long already. Ten days of lying around seems a lifetime."

"I know what you mean, but you had good reason to be takin' it easy, young fella. That wound of yours came real close to killin' you."

"I was lucky, but I also have you to thank for your help—you and my elusive angel of mercy." He smiled slightly at the memory of the young, dark-haired female passenger on the stagecoach.

"She was a pretty one," the stationmaster remarked. Over the past few days, they had spoken many times of the young woman who'd helped to nurse him, and he definitely agreed with Brady's assessment of her. "Think you'll see her again?"

"I tell you, Riley, if she's still in town I'm going to find her. All we know about her is that her name was Sally, right?"

"That's it, but as good lookin' as she was, she won't have gone unnoticed. If she's still around, somebody will know where."

Brady nodded and then his expression grew solemn. "I'll send word if I come up with anything on the holdup. I don't intend to let those bastards get away with almost putting me six feet under!"

"I'll be lookin' forward to hearin' that you've tracked 'em down, Brady."

"I'm going to check in with Sheriff McCrea and see what he and McAllister turned up. Maybe they've got something I can go on and, if not, I'll find them on my own."

"You just be careful."

"I will, Riley, and thanks again for everything."

"You're welcome. Take care." The stationmaster raised a hand in farewell as the Wells Fargo guard put his heels to his mount and started off in the direction of town.

"I appreciate your agreeing to accompany me to the ranch on your way to town," Lydia cooed sweetly to Rand as the group headed for the Lazy Ace that morning. "I know it's out of your way."

"With the Bentons on the loose, we can't be too careful," Rand told her grimly as he rode at her side.

Rand didn't doubt for a moment that the Bentons were gunning for him. They had sworn to have revenge on him, and savage animals that they were, he knew that sooner or later they were going to show up. When or where, he had no idea, but he planned to learn everything he could about their last-known whereabouts so he could be ready.

"Are they really that serious about getting even with you?" Jack asked, breaking into his troubled thoughts.

"They're dead serious," Rand answered flatly, remembering Moran's death, the bloody shootout, and the Bentons' vows to get even.

"But why?" Roger, who was riding slightly behind the others with Lori and Sally, was curious.

"It's been years ago, but I killed their brother and a couple of members of their gang in a shootout. The ones I killed were trying to free the Bentons from custody. They're not the type to forgive and forget. I'm sure they're out there somewhere, looking for me."

"How can you be so cool about it?" Sally asked nervously. She liked Rand and the thought of someone actually wanting to kill him frightened her.

Rand slanted her a crooked smile. "I'm not cool. This is all a part of my job. I've learned the only way to deal with these situations is to be prepared for them all the time."

Lydia did not care for the note of concern she'd heard in the young woman's voice or for the tender smile Rand had given her. Eying Sally coldly, she tried to judge her worth as a rival and she wondered if Rand would find her attractive? The girl was pretty enough, but she was so . . . so bland, so sweet. Surely, Rand found her own blond beauty more stimulating.

As she started to turn back, Lydia noticed that Rand had cast a quick, sidelong glance in Lorelei's direction and she pondered his relationship with her. Rand's ward . . . The thought rankled, and Lydia let her critical gaze sweep over Lori. The young woman's appearance today was certainly vastly improved since yesterday. Then, the chit had been pale and withdrawn and Lydia had dismissed her as unimportant; but today she seemed more alive, more vibrant. Her red-gold hair was tied neatly back in a long, single braid and her cheeks were flushed with a rosy glow that emphasized her creamy complexion and highlighted her wide, sparkling eyes. In that moment, Lydia knew that she did not like one thing about Lorelei Spencer. She never had and she never would. Years ago, the child had been a spoiled, stubborn brat; it seemed to Lydia that she had not changed. She hoped Lorelei would marry Roger and get out of Rand's life.

Sitting straighter in the saddle, Lydia thrust her breasts forward, hoping to draw Rand's attention to herself. Since their passionate kiss in the mine, she had been trying to arrange a time when they could be alone together so she could press her advantage, but during the past day she had not been allowed even the briefest private contact with him. Perhaps when they got to the ranch . . . His concession to go there had given her hope. He had said that it was dangerous and that they had to be careful. Surely that indicated that he did feel something for her, if he didn't care, he certainly wouldn't worry about her safety. She would play upon that angle and hope he would fall prey to her charms.

Rand rode in silence. He had slept little during the past night, despite being tired from his ordeal, and he was having to force himself to focus on their surroundings. Never before had he had difficulty staying alert in such situations, and he was aggravated with himself for not being able to devote his full attention to watching for any possible signs of trouble.

Worry about the Bentons was not distracting him. He almost wished it were. It was Lorelei's quiet presence—she rode with Roger behind him—that was disturbing him and making it impossible for him to concentrate. Over and over in his mind he replayed the sight of her kissing Roger, of Roger's hand possessively fondling her breast, and he couldn't stop himself from wondering if she'd made love to the other man that night after everyone had gone. Rand knew for a fact that Roger had retired late for he hadn't returned to Hal's home until well after midnight. Rand suspected he'd been with Lorelei all that time, sharing her bed and

204

tasting of her passion. His hands clenched into fists at his vision of Lorelei and Roger entwined in a lover's embrace and his horse shied suddenly at the change in tension on the reins. Much as he hated her for being the woman she was, Rand could not stop the desire he felt for her. Dragging his thoughts away from Lorelei and her lover-soon-to-be-husband, he scanned the horizon in search of anything out of the ordinary.

Roger, though he was putting on a good show of normalcy this morning, was not happy as he rode between Sally and Lori. The strain he had just been through had revealed to him how deeply he cared for Lori, but somehow things had not turned out the way he'd hoped they would. He had expected that Lori would come to her senses about the danger of actively working in the mine, that she would agree to marry him right away, return to St. Louis, and allow qualified men to run the Triple Cross for her. But she had remained fiercely resolved to stay and personally make the mine work. Her independence had always been hard for him to deal with, but yesterday's revelation had forced him to seriously consider his feelings for her.

True, that afternoon she had not protested when he'd sought to touch her, allowing him far more liberties than ever before, and Roger was reasonably certain that he could have taken her completely in that moment of weakness had Sally not interrupted them. But he was glad now that he hadn't had the opportunity for Lori had not professed to love him and had made no mention of accepting his proposal. As much as he cared for her, Roger knew he could not continue to come second in her life, behind the mine. His feelings for her had been ravaged by her decision to stay. When he'd tried to argue the point last night, she'd sent him away, angrily accusing him of trying to dominate her and run her life. Perhaps, he thought, when they got to town and were able to enjoy each other for a day or two away from the looming presence of the Triple Cross, she might come to understand that his only concern was for her safety. He wanted her alive and well and by his side for the rest of their lives.

Lori could not remember ever being so miserable. Nothing seemed to be going right.

Rand . . . She glanced up at his wide, powerful back as he rode, easy in the saddle, ahead of her with the charming Lydia by his side, and she knew a moment of real fury, most of which was directed at herself. How could she have been so weak during their time in the tunnel that she'd allowed him to make love to her? And why, of all the men she'd ever known, was he the only one who could arouse her so with just a touch or a kiss? Again and again that question taunted her and she knew she had no answer.

She had tried to achieve that same level of excitement with Roger yesterday when she'd kissed him and allowed him to caress her intimately for the first time, but it had not been the same. There had been no flash of passion, no uncontrollable fire of desire to cause her to lose her head and surrender to Roger's ardent embrace. She was relieved now that Sally had come into the room; it would not have been right to use Roger as a substitute for Rand. She had only been playing a game, and a dangerous one at that—one in which she ultimately would have been the loser.

Lori knew she did not love Roger. No one had ever explained to her what true love was really like, but she sensed that what she felt for Roger was friendship and not undying passion. It saddened her to realize that, but she felt wiser for the knowledge.

What troubled her most were the feelings that Rand aroused in her whenever he was near. Even as she consciously denied any love for the man, her body craved his touch, and the sight of him, riding so casually beside Lydia, seared her with a flame that she refused to admit was jealousy.

Lori knew Rand had retired early the night before. Indeed, she had been tormented throughout the long dark hours by the possibility that he'd had a rendezvous with Lydia in the privacy of the desert, that he had made love to her. Now as she watched Lydia playing up to Rand, she wondered if they'd been together.

Lori knew Rand couldn't possibly care anything about her, not when he'd dismissed their lovemaking in the tunnel so easily, vowing that as far as he was concerned nothing had happened between them. Obviously, he was the rogue she'd always thought him, and she supposed she should count herself lucky that he'd not revealed all, or threatened to do so. She hoped fervently that there would be no lasting repercussions from their encounter. Suppressing a shudder, she considered for the first time that she might be pregnant with Rand's child, but she quickly put that thought from her mind, determined not to even think of that possibility unless nature forced her to.

Keeping up a pretense of enjoying this trip that she hadn't even wanted to go on, she struck up a conversation with Sally, hoping that some small talk would help to pass the time and would clear her mind of thoughts of Rand in an intimate embrace with Lydia.


John McCrea came to his feet as Brady entered the office. "Good to see you, Barclay! I'm glad you're up and about!"

"So am I, John," the big blond man responded as he

took the seat opposite the sheriff's desk. The ride had been more taxing than he'd expected, and he sighed deeply as he settled back in the chair.

John sat back down and met his gaze, "I take it you want to know everything we were able to find out?"

"Everything," Brady stated firmly. "I intend to find those bastards and when I do—"

"I understand your desire for justice, but I'm afraid there's very little I can tell you. We couldn't identify the man we found back on the trail, so we buried him out there. Our trip to the scene was really useless."

"And there have been no more attempted holdups in the area?"

"None that I've heard of. Have you been by the Wells Fargo Office yet?"

"Yes. I stopped there first. They've given me time off with pay until they think I'm fully recovered, but I have no intention of sitting around Phoenix. Those lowlifes who tried to kill me are out there somewhere, and I'm going to find them. The company's offering a decent reward, so maybe I can collect it."

"If I hear anything more, I'll be sure to let you know, although at this late date I doubt that anything new will turn up."

"I'll be staying at the Phoenix Hotel, should you need me for anything."

"I'll be in touch. Oh, Barclay, the missus and I are having a party Saturday night. Be pleased to have you come."

"I'd like that." Brady accepted quickly, thinking how long it had been since he'd been to a party. "What's the occasion?"

"No occasion." McCrea smiled. "Just wanted to do a little socializing with the folks from town. I've invited the McAllisters, too, and I'm hoping they'll come. You know Rand, don't you? He was my deputy several years back before he took the job with the government."

"I know I'll be there now. I didn't get a chance to thank him for saving my life before he left Riley's. If it hadn't been for McAllister taking charge like he did during the robbery, I wouldn't be talking to you right now."

"He's a good man," John agreed. "We'll see you Saturday then."

"Right," Brady started to leave, then turned back. "You wouldn't happen to know who the other passengers on the stage that day were, would you?"

"No, not offhand. I know there were two women and a man. One of the women shot the bandit, but I have no idea who they were. Why?"

"Oh, nothing important." Embarrassed, Brady hastened from the office, saying, "I'll be seeing you."


As he lay on the bed in the room over the Sidewinder Saloon, Cody Benton tilted the bottle of tequila to his lips and swallowed thirstily, paying little attention when the liquor dribbled down his chin. "You know, Pat"—his speech slurred, he set the bottle aside and wiped at his chin with the back of his forearm—"I'm gettin' real bored with this here town. Why don't we get out of here, head up to Prescott or maybe down to Tucson?"

"You're forgettin' our reason for being here, stupid," Pat Benton snarled, not turning from the window or taking his eyes from the street below.

"I ain't forgettin' nuthin'!" Cody retorted. "I'm just tired of sittin' here."

"I know. This ain't exactly fun, but you know what that man said last night in the saloon. McAllister's back in the area."

*"In the area,* don't mean here!"

209

"Patience, Cody," Pat said slowly. "I'm sure McAllister's been told we're on the loose, and if I know him, he's gonna come lookin' for us."

"That's the point! If we want to get him, we're gonna have to surprise him. I don't want him surprisin' us!"

"You worry too much. We're gonna sit tight right here in Phoenix until we hear something more about good ol' Marshal McAllister."

"What about money?"

"What about it?"

"You know for a fact that we're runnin' short."

Pat shrugged. "Maybe we can pick up some odd jobs around town. Who knows? Money always has a way of takin' care of itself and with Angelo around to help out, we'll be just fine for another week or so."

Cody glared at his brother, but said nothing. Instead he tilted the bottle of liquor and drank some more. In all their years together, he'd never defied his older brother and he knew he would not do so now. They would wait and perhaps soon they'd have some news about McAllister so they could go after him.


As Lydia led the way into the ranch house, she was feeling quite satisfied with herself. Rand had agreed to spend the balance of the day on the Lazy Ace in order to take care of any problems that had arisen during his absence. He wouldn't go into town until the following day. That gave her an entire night in the privacy of their home to try to work her wiles on him. Almost giddy at the thought that she might have Rand in her bed that very night, she directed the two young women and Roger to make themselves comfortable in the parlor while she went to order refreshments for them. Rand and Jack had not stopped at the house, but had gone on to see to any pressing ranch business.

"Are you sure we won't be inconveniencing you, Lydia?" Sally asked when Lydia returned to the parlor.

"No, not at all. We have plenty of room, and it will be good to have some company. It's been very lonely here since my husband died," she told them graciously.

"It was truly a tragedy that two such wonderful men as your husband and Lori's father died so suddenly."

"Indeed," Lydia responded brittlely. "It has not been easy for me, that's why I am so thankful for Rand's return. We may be co-owners of the ranch, but it takes a strong man to run the Lazy Ace. I'm sure, Lorelei, you appreciate having someone as capable as Hal to operate the mine for you." She glanced at Lori who sat beside Roger on the sofa.

"I do appreciate Hal, but I plan to run the Triple Cross myself, Lydia," Lori answered, stung by the comparison to her.

"I don't understand?" Lydia glanced at her sharply, wondering how Lorelei was going to take charge of the mine while she resided at the ranch.

"I guess Rand hasn't told you yet." Lori was surprised to discover that Rand hadn't revealed his plans to his lover.

"Told me what?"

"Since he's my guardian and completely responsible for my welfare and for my inheritance, he's planning to move in at the mine to oversee the operation," Lorelei explained. She noticed that for a fleeting moment the older woman seemed stricken.

Lydia's mind was racing. Why would Rand have agreed to such a thing? "But Rand wanted you to move in here with us at the ranch."

"He did mention that, but I refused."

"You what?" None of this was making any sense.

"I need to be at the mine, not trapped here on the

211

ranch. I know I could have a social life here, but I don't care about that. And I won't be unchaperoned." Lori was anticipating Lydia's next argument. "That's why Rand is moving in at the mine."

"You're telling me that he has bowed to your wishes in this matter?" Lydia was amazed. "I thought *you* were the ward and by law were required to be submissive to him?"

Anger flared through Lori at this reference to her situation. "Lydia, I do not need a guardian. I have been on my own for some time now, and it came as quite a surprise to find that someone else was supposed to be running my life. It's just a perverse quirk of fate that I have been saddled with Rand."

The young woman's vehement reaction to having Rand as her custodian satisfied Lydia. She now felt there was no danger of an attraction between them, and remembering Roger's declared intention to marry Lori as quickly as he could, she went on. "Well, this farce will be over soon then, for he feels the same way."

A shaft of pain knifed through Lori's heart, and though she'd already acknowledged to herself that Rand did not care about her, hearing it stated aloud by Lydia hurt. Three years did not seem soon to Lori. "How can this be over soon?"

"By your marriage, of course," Lydia declared confidently as she took a glass of lemonade from the servant who'd brought their refreshments.

"I beg your pardon?" Lori frowned.

"Well, Roger has told me that you two are going to be married as quickly as he can arrange it." Lydia glanced questioningly at Roger.

"The wedding is not as imminent as you were led to believe, Lydia," Lori answered smoothly, not wanting this woman to know any of her personal business. "We have not yet set a date."

"Oh." Lydia hid her disappointment at the news. "Well, the sooner the wedding takes place, the sooner this awkward situation will end. You must admit, dear, that it is quite unconventional for you to live at the Triple Cross with your fiancé in residence without proper chaperonage. It would be just dreadful if your reputation was ruined by thoughtless disregard for society's mores. I suppose, that's why Rand has taken this guardianship so seriously."

Having heard this line of argument from Rand earlier, Lori sighed. "Rand and I have come to an understanding regarding my desire to stay at the mine, and that's precisely why he's agreed to take up residence there." Even as she said it, she felt deceitful for if anyone found out what had already happened, her reputation would be in shreds, because of her chaperone not because of her fiancé.

"I see." Lydia's reply was stilted for her earlier joy at the prospect of living alone with Rand at the ranch had faded. He would be leaving, and soon. Needing time to think, she finished her cooling drink and stood up. "If you like, I can show you to your rooms now."

"That will be fine," Sally replied, and they all followed Lydia from the parlor.


It was near dusk when Rand finally finished taking care of ranch business and returned to the main house. After directing the servants to bring a bath to his room, he went straight to his quarters for he was eager to wash away the day's grit. In short order a tub of steaming water was set out for him and, after dismissing the maid, he stripped off his work stained clothing and stepped into the hot, soothing water. He had just gotten comfortable when there was a knock at the door.

"What is it?"

"Rand, it's me . . . Lydia. I need to speak with you."

He noticed the slight impatience in her tone, but started to tell her he couldn't talk with her at the moment. "I'll talk with you later, Lydia. I can't—"

"Rand, this can't wait." Thinking that he might be putting her off, she brazenly opened the door and walked into his bedroom.

"Lydia," he said sternly, irritated by her boldness. "As I started to tell you, I am taking a bath and am not in any position to discuss anything."

Lydia swallowed nervously. Although there was nothing she wanted more than to climb into that tub of water and make passionate love with him, she knew she dared not touch the hard masculine beauty of his body now so she forced her gaze away from his broad, bare chest and shoulders.

"It is important, and I was afraid if I waited we wouldn't have the privacy necessary to discuss this issue before you left with the others in the morning."

"If you'll give me time to finish bathing, I'll meet you in father's study."

"Yes, that would be much better," she replied, and fighting to control her raging need for him, she left the room.

In less than half an hour, shaved and dressed, Rand entered the study where he found Lydia anxiously awaiting him, her expression grave.

"I take it this is serious?" he asked as he entered the room.

"Yes. I think it is," she responded, quickly moving to close the door behind Rand so that they were enclosed in the small room.

If Rand placed any import on this, he did not reveal it as he casually sat in one of the high-backed wing chairs situated before his father's massive desk, stretching his long legs out before him. "Well?" he glanced back at Lydia who still stood by the door, her fathomless eyes upon him.

"While you were gone, I had occasion to visit with our guests—your ward and her friends."

"And?" Rand wanted her to get to the point.

"And I was summarily informed by Lorelei that you plan to move to the Triple Cross and take up permanent residence there. Oh, Rand . . . is that true?" There was a strategically arranged catch in her voice.

"Given the situation I find myself in and the options available to me, yes, I have decided to move in there."

"But why, when you know how desperately I need you here?" She walked toward him, her hands outstretched in supplication.

"I'm sure you and Jack can handle the day-to-day business of the ranch. I plan to come down every week or so just in case you need me, and you can always send for me if there's an emergency."

*I'll always need you!* her mind screamed, but she managed to answer with reasonable calmness. "I don't understand how you can do this to me."

"I'm not doing anything to you, Lydia. I'm assuming my responsibility as Lorelei's guardian. When we discussed this before I left, you said yourself that it was highly irregular for a young woman to live up there alone, unchaperoned. The Triple Cross is working a very productive vein, and Lorelei feels it's essential that she remain on site; so it follows I will have to take up residence there."

"That's ridiculous! A mining camp is no place for a female to live. Why don't you just force her to come here? Then you can visit the mine every week or so."

"She refuses to leave and Hal can use my help." Rand was not swayed by her arguments, yet he couldn't

215

help wondering why he felt a driving need to persist in the arrangement now that he knew what kind of woman Lorelei really was. He finally acknowledged that he'd agreed to stay at the Triple Cross because he wanted to be near her. She intrigued him and attracted him, and though it annoyed him to admit it, he still wanted her. Nonetheless, he felt confident that, given time, he would be able to conquer his powerful desire for Lorelei, just as he had overcome his passion for Lydia.

"Surely you know so little about mining, you don't have to be there constantly. Tell the chit to come here to live and be done with it! You're her guardian! Besides, she's been nothing but a troublemaker in all the time I've known her!"

"What do you mean?" Rand looked up quickly, curious as to why Lorelei might have given Lydia any trouble in the past.

"She was always a spiteful child. Try as I might, she never made any attempt to warm up to me, even though they visited here regularly during the first years of my marriage to your father. It seemed she went out of her way to be obnoxious to me," Lydia said angrily, remembering Lori's distant coldness. "She certainly liked your father well enough, though."

"Maybe she was jealous," Rand remarked insightfully.

"Of me and your father?"

He shrugged. "Who knows? She was just a child at the time. Anyway, there is no connection between that situation and this one. Lorelei is needed at the mine, so I will be moving in at the Triple Cross."

"And what about your job?"

"When I get to town tomorrow, I'll send a request to Marshal Duke for more leave time."

"And if he won't give it to you," Lydia asked, "what

216

will you do then?"

"I'll worry about that when the time comes," Rand had not given much thought to that possibility, and he refused to consider it now.

"Rand, I thought this ranch meant something to you. It's your father's legacy, yet you're acting as if this girl is more important."

"That's ridiculous, Lydia. It's because of my father that I'm involved with Lorelei. I'm only trying to do what he would have thought right. She needs my help."

"And I need you, Rand." Lydia raised tear-filled eyes to his. "More than you'll ever know." This last was spoken in a broken-hearted whisper.

Touched by the sincerity of her words, Rand stood up and went to her, taking her by the shoulders in a gentle grip. "Lydia, I know the past month has been difficult for you, but I also know that you're a strong woman. Everything is going to be fine. You'll see."

Releasing a shuddering sigh, she leaned forward to let herself be enfolded by his strong arms, and closing her eyes for just a moment, she rested her head on his chest, pretending this was a lover's embrace rather than a comforting one. "I hope so, Rand."


Lori's mood was pensive as she entered the parlor. Since her conversation with Lydia earlier that day, she'd been seriously thinking about accepting Roger's proposal. Though she wasn't in love with him, she knew they could be happy together, and certainly the marriage would end her forced involvement with Rand. Lori was beginning to think it would be worth it to marry without love just to be rid of Rand.

"Good evening, Juana," she said to the servant who was in the adjoining room preparing the table for the evening meal.

"Miss Lorelei." Juana's smile flashed widely as she responded. "It is good to have you here at the Lazy Ace again."

"Thank you, it's nice to be back." Lori tried to sound sincere, but she was finding that her stopover was stirring up too many memories, bittersweet ones of her father and Will, painful ones of Rand and Lydia.

"Miss Lorelei, Rand is in the study. He was late getting back this evening, and I have not had the chance to tell him that we're dining an hour earlier. Would you mind telling him for me? The *señora* seemed to think that, since you're leaving so early in the morning, everyone might want to retire early."

"Of course, I don't mind." Lori agreed immediately for she was fond of Juana and did not mind helping out.

As she started down the hall toward the study, Lori was still pondering the wisdom of marrying Roger to end Rand's influence over her, and upon reaching the study, distracted by her thoughts, she knocked only once before opening the door to relay the message.

"Rand, Juana said that—" The sight that greeted her left her weak with disgust. Before her stood Rand and Lydia, wrapped in each other's arms, and Lydia looked shocked and guilty. "Oh, dear Lord!" Lori gasped. "Not again!" And without another word she rushed away, ignoring Rand's urgent call for her to return.

Though it was dark outside, Lori raced away from the ranch house and didn't stop until she'd reached the stables. Thankful that there was no one in attendance, she dropped down upon a pile of fresh hay and buried her face in her hands, denying herself the right to cry. What did it matter that Rand was his stepmother's lover? What did it matter that only a day ago he had made love to her and now he was in Lydia's arms? She hated him, didn't she? He was a cold, unfeeling bastard

218

who had used her, so why did it hurt so to see him with Lydia?

A firm resolve grew within her heart. She would be done with Rand McAllister just as quickly as possible. She would marry Roger and bar Rand from her life, forever. But even as she made that decision, her mind taunted her with the knowledge that Rand wouldn't care—that he would be glad to be rid of her.

Rand watched in dismay as Lorelei ran from the study, and he wondered what she'd meant by "Not again." Driven to go after her and explain, he extricated himself from Lydia's arms and started for the door.

"Rand? Where are you going?"

"After Lorelei!" he snapped.

"Whatever for?" Lydia drawled, glad that the younger woman had seen them together.

"To explain to her just exactly what it was she saw here."

"Why are you worried about it? For heaven's sake, Rand, she certainly overreacted to the whole thing. You were only giving me comfort and support. It was hardly a compromising situation."

"I know that Lydia, but Lorelei doesn't. I want her to understand."

"Fine, but frankly I think you're acting like a damned fool. Perhaps this girl does mean more to you than the ranch does or than I do." Her eyes narrowed at the thought.

"Don't be ridiculous. I'll be back." He rushed from the room in hot pursuit of Lorelei, leaving Lydia to wonder at his motive.

Remembering Lori's love of their horses, Rand headed first for the stables, and he was greatly relieved to come upon her there, feeding a handful of hay to one of the stallions. "Lorelei?"

Though Lori had heard him coming, she still flinched at the sound of his voice. "What do you want?" She did not bother to turn around and face him.

Rand heard the hardness in her tone and he knew she had already convinced herself that he and Lydia were involved. "Lorelei," he began, his voice stern, "what you saw in the study was—"

"Was disgusting, Rand. Once was bad enough, but twice . . . Of course, it doesn't make any difference now, does it? I mean your father's dead, so that makes everything all right, doesn't it?!" Lori had not intended to reveal what she knew, but her anger and hurt were so overpowering she could not suppress this accusation. Wheeling around, she glared at him, her eyes flashing, her copper hair magnificent as it cascaded about her shoulders in a red-gold cape of curls.

Rand was, at once, totally surprised by her hostility yet caught up in the glory of her beauty. "Lorelei, I can assure you that I have no idea what you're talking about."

"I'll tell you what I'm talking about," she continued vengefully. "I'm talking about you and Lydia! I know all about you two. I have for years!"

"What do you know?"

Lorelei gave him an accusing look. "Look Rand, I know that you and Lydia are lovers. I saw you myself seven years ago. Right here in this very stable, as a matter of fact."

"What?"

"You heard me. It was the morning you were leaving, right after Lydia and your father had been married. I saw you kissing her—your father's wife—right here in this stable. I thought the two of you were loathesome then and I still think so. Only now it's not adultery, is it? I mean, how convenient for you! Will's dead!"

Rand grabbed her by the shoulders and gave her a

hard shake. "You don't know what you're talking about!"

"I saw it all! How can you even try to deny it?" She glared up at him.

"I'm not denying that you saw a kiss between Lydia and me, but that's all you saw, because nothing else happened."

"I wouldn't know. I was so disgusted that I ran away. Until then I had thought you were someone special, but I was wrong."

Her words touched his heart, and he blinked as he stared down at her. He remembered Lydia's complaints about Lori's behavior toward her, and his own remark that she might have been jealous. It all fit. Lorelei had been jealous, but not of his father—of him.

"Lorelei," he began slowly, wanting to be convincing.

"Don't, Rand!" she seethed, wanting to free herself of him for all eternity. "Just let me go and leave me alone. Go back to your 'grieving' stepmother." Lori was panting now, her fury nearly spent, her breasts heaving with each breath she drew. But knowing that she had to get away, she tried to get out of his punishing grip. Twisting quickly, she sought to break free, but he stopped her easily, trapping her tightly against his chest.

"You're going to listen to me!" he said steadily, but as he spoke he suddenly became aware of the soft crush of her body. "Lorelei . . ." Her name was a groan as his desire for her erupted, filling him with an overwhelming need to kiss her and caress her, to force her to submit to his will.

"No!" Lori saw passion flare in his eyes, and she fought even harder to get away, losing the battle as one of his hands snaked up to entwine her hair and hold her head still while he lowered his mouth to hers.

"Lorelei . . ."

It was a bruising kiss; a kiss that did not coax but demanded, and after only a moment of resistance, her will fled and she surrendered to the compelling need that throbbed to life deep within her. Her hands clutched his shoulders as his free hand moved to her breasts, fondling them through the thin fabric of her blouse, and she moaned in excitement as a spiraling coil of anticipation awoke in her.

Why did this excruciating ecstasy overwhelm her everytime Rand touched her? Lori knew she should stop him, she knew he didn't love her, but reality and reason were lost to her at that moment. She knew only that she wanted Rand and her hunger would not be appeased by less than total oneness. His touch was her heaven—and her hell.

Her knees buckled as his lips left hers to explore the sweetness of her throat, and Rand, feeling her weakness, lifted her slight weight and lowered them both to the fresh, sweet-smelling hay. A portion of his mind warned him that they could be discovered at any moment, but he was beyond caring. With unsteady fingers, he unfastened the buttons on her blouse and then lifted her breasts from the confines of her lacy chemise. His lips seared her satiny flesh and his hands were never still as he sought to please her.

Enraptured, Lori held his head to her as she moved sinuously beneath him, reveling in the throbbing passion that his knowing kisses aroused.

Rand had to have her. Brushing aside her skirt, he sought and found the dark, hot sweetness that was Lorelei, stroking and probing her warmth until she was mindless in her need for him.

"Rand . . . oh, Rand," she gasped his name as he moved over her, possessing her body in one hard, smooth stroke.

"Easy, love," he murmured, the anger he'd felt

222

moments before fading as the joy of their joining overtook him. He wanted to please her, to love her, to give her ultimate pleasure; and he began to move slowly and steadily within her.

Unthinking, guided only by her need to be one with him, Lori matched his rhythm, her hands tracing patterns of fire over his back and hips as they urged him ever deeper into her welcoming heat. Hardness melded with softness, tender flesh yielded willingly to thrusting maleness until a shattering, pulsing delight claimed Lori. As rapture flooded through her, she cried out and clung to Rand, helpless in the grip of her excitement.

Knowing that he'd brought her to the pinnacle of desire drove him over the edge, and as his self-control dissolved, he joined her on love's peak.

Replete, they lay together, limbs entwined, caught up in the hazy remnant of their passion. Their mouths met time and again, blending in gentle exploration, until a horse nearby stirred restlessly and brought them back to full awareness of their surroundings.

Rand stiffened as he realized what he'd just done, and then he jerked away from her and stood up, straightening his clothes. He knew he should say something, but he was so filled with self-reproach that he couldn't speak. His original intention to explain his situation with Lydia had been forgotten the moment he'd touched her; his promise not to make love to her had been lost in the haze of desire. Schooling his features into an aloof mask that hid his anger at himself, he glanced down at her, silently cursing himself for breaking his vow.

Stiffly, he told her, "Lorelei, I'm sorry. I didn't mean for this to happen. I will not let it happen again."

Lori stared up at Rand, her expression contemptuous. How could he stand there looking so cool and composed after what had just occurred between them?

He had come to her from Lydia's arms, made wild, passionate love to her, and now he was apologizing? Did he think every woman was his for the taking?

"I hate you, Rand McAllister!" Her hands shook with anger as she tried to adjust her blouse and her skirt. Then, getting to her feet, she faced him unflinchingly. "I have for a long time—since that day seven years ago—but you just made me realize how much. You seem to think you can do whatever you want, that it doesn't matter who you hurt! We may be stuck with each other right now because of this guardianship, but that won't last forever. I want you to stay away from me from now on." Lori turned stiffly away and left the stable with as much dignity as she could muster.

"I'll be glad to leave you alone." He sneered after her. "For I want as little to do with you as you want with me. Perhaps the faster you marry your lover the better. Then I can be relieved of the tiresome burden this arrangement has become." As he watched her disappear into the darkness, he wondered how things had gotten so out of control. Why did Lorelei ravage his self-control? Why did his desire for her torment him? Unable to answer these questions, he, too, started back to the house, knowing that Lydia would be awaiting them and not wanting her to learn of their brief moment of passion.

# Chapter Thirteen

"I don't know what could be keeping them," Lydia remarked to Sally and Roger, her puzzlement real. It had been over half an hour since Rand had gone after Lori, and she found herself in the awkward position of trying to explain their absence. "I suppose—"

"Lorelei and I have been in the stables," Rand's authoritative voice cut across the room as he entered, his stride confident, his manner seemingly relaxed.

Lydia flashed him a tight smile of gratitude for explaining his and Lori's mysterious tardiness, but when she searched his expression for some sign of what had happened, she found no clue. Annoyed, she asked pointedly, "And where is Lorelei now? We're awaiting dinner."

"She's gone to her room to freshen up. I'm sure she'll be right with us," he replied smoothly, giving no indication that anything was amiss. "Lorelei always had a fondness for our horses," Rand continued, "and she was interested in seeing some of the new bloodlines that have been introduced since her last visit."

"I see," Lydia responded, pleased that Sally and Roger accepted Rand's explanation without question. Now that her fear of an embarrassing scene had been put to rest, she could hardly wait until later, when she would have an opportunity to speak with Rand privately and find out exactly what had transpired for she didn't understand Lorelei's reaction at finding Rand comforting her. Surely, there had been nothing lurid about his holding her for a moment, yet Lorelei had acted as if she'd caught them in bed, making love. It didn't bother her that the chit might suspect Rand of being her lover; in fact, Lydia found the idea highly titillating. But because Lorelei had reacted so violently, she wondered if there was more between Lori and Rand than she'd been led to believe.

"Sorry I'm so late." Lori greeted them breathlessly as she entered the room, but she looked completely at ease. She had heard Rand's quick response to Lydia's probing question as she'd come down the hall, and despite her reluctance to admit there was anything good about him, she was glad he'd had the presence of mind enough to think up such a logical excuse for their delay.

"Shall we start dinner then?" Lydia suggested as her gaze locked with Lori's. She noted the current of tension underlying Lorelei's outward composure, and her suspicions increased. Wondering exactly what had gone on out in the privacy of the stable, she swung her gaze back to Rand. "Rand?"

Playing the part of the head of the house, he took Lydia's arm and escorted her in to dinner, leaving the others to follow. Roger stepped to Lori's side, glad of the chance to engage her in a social situation, away from the roughness of the mine.

The food served was delicious, and the meal passed pleasantly enough. Totally unaware that anything was amiss, Roger and Sally took great interest in the ranch, questioning both Rand and Lydia about the operation of such a huge spread.

Lorelei, though she indulged in witty repartee during the meal, was miserable. Over and over she worried that Rand had told Lydia everything; yet she instinctively felt that he had not, for the look the older woman had given her when she'd returned had been one of probing interest, not one of hatred. Lori had no doubt that Lydia would have been furious if she'd learned that Rand had made love to her. Not that it had been lovemaking, she amended silently. There had been no love involved in what they'd done. It had been only a sensual encounter. Guilt was assailing her now, for no matter how much she wanted to deny it, she had not fought Rand. Indeed, she had surrendered to him and had even encouraged him in the heat of their joining. A pink flush stained her cheeks at that remembrance, and she looked up nervously, to find Rand's eyes upon her.

Rand had been regarding Lorelei casually as he carried on his part of the conversation. While his expression remained untroubled, his thoughts were confused and the sight of her faint blush puzzled him. He'd never known a woman as complex and maddening as Lori. What was she thinking? Was she remembering the feel of his caresses, the way he had driven powerfully into her, taking them both to the height of desire? He felt a tightening in his loins and swore silently as her eyes glinted coldly, reflecting all to clearly her true feeling for him.

Turning his attention back to the conversation, he found himself regretting more bitterly than ever his decision to live at the Triple Cross, for no matter how he might try to avoid Lorelei, they would be in daily contact. Her nearness drove him to recklessness, and he knew the only way to keep his desire under control was to remain away from her as much as possible. Somehow he would find a way to do it.

"Rand?" Lydia's piqued tone cut through his

disquieting thoughts and he glanced over at her quickly.

"I'm sorry, what were you saying, Lydia?"

"With all the excitement at the mine, I had completely forgotten another of John McCrea's messages."

"There was something else?" He became concerned.

"Yes, but nothing bad." She smiled pleasantly. "The McCreas are having a party on Saturday night, and John made a point of saying that he'd like us to come. I'm sure everyone is included in the invitation." Lydia glanced benevolently at the others.

"That sounds fine. What do you say?" Rand looked at Lori, then Sally and Roger. "Do you mind spending an extra day in town?"

Lori bristled at the thought of an additional day away from the Triple Cross. "If you want to remain in town for a party, we can find our way back without you."

"Lori," Roger contradicted patiently, "there's no reason to rush our return. One day certainly isn't going to make any difference. You know Hal said it was going to take awhile to get that tunnel back in working condition; there won't be any ore shipments to worry about."

Realizing that further argument would only make her look petty, Lori yielded. "You're right, I suppose."

"Then we're all going? It's settled?" Lydia asked cheerfully. She was happily anticipating the social outing, her first since Will's death, and wondering exactly what she should wear.

Lori longed to point out to Lydia that the proper period of mourning was, at the very least, six months, but she said nothing.

"We can all go into town tomorrow, then," Lydia was saying. "Do you have something appropriate

228

to wear?"

"I'm afraid Lori and I only have riding clothes with us," Sally admitted, ruefully thinking of all the fashionable dresses she'd left back at the mine in her trunk.

"That's a shame," Lydia responded. "And you're both much taller than I am so it wouldn't do for you to borrow any of my things. Perhaps there will be something already made up you can buy in town."

"I'm sure we'll make out just fine," Sally agreed. She was excited by the thought that she might discover something about the condition of Brady Barclay while they were in town.

Lori, Sally, and Roger did not linger over dinner, but retired from the dining room early so they could get a full night's rest in preparation for the journey to town the next day. When Rand started to follow them from the room, however, Lydia stopped him by placing a hand on his arm.

"I need to talk with you," she told him in hushed tones, wanting total privacy for the moment.

"Of course." Rand had known that she would be curious about what had happened with Lorelei.

"A brandy?" Lydia offered, moving into the seclusion of the parlor.

"No, but I will take a whiskey," he replied, and he accepted a tumbler of the golden liquid as she came to sit beside him on the sofa. "Thanks."

"So," Lydia began, keeping her tone carefully detached. "What was Lorelei's problem?"

Rand took a deep drink from the glass before answering. "It seems Lorelei thinks we're lovers."

"What!" She tried to sound suitably outraged, but actually she was pleased, for she now understood the tension she'd sensed in Lorelei.

"You remember, of course, our indelicate scene in

the stable right after you married father?"

"It's a time I'd like to forget," Lydia snapped.

"Well, it seems we had an audience we didn't know about."

"Who?"

"Lorelei saw us that morning and concluded the worst."

"That certainly explains her attitude toward me during her visits. She must have thought we were lovers while I was married to Will."

"Indeed, and she thinks we are still involved, even now," Rand went on.

"Did you tell her how ridiculous that is?" Lydia went on the offensive. "I loved your father!"

"I tried to make her listen, but she's convinced she's right." He shrugged. "I suppose that's why she refused to move in here at the ranch."

"She has caused nothing but trouble all her life, and we'll be well rid of her. I just hope she marries Roger soon, so you won't have to concern yourself with her. It will be difficult enough for you to divide your time between your work and the ranch after your leave is up without worrying about Lorelei and her precious mine."

"Have they set a date for their wedding?" Rand wasn't sure that he wanted to know the answer.

"No," she answered in disgust. "In fact, this afternoon she remarked that the wedding would definitely not be in the near future, and I sensed that Roger was disappointed by her statement. I'm certain he loves her. I just wish she'd marry him and be done with it!"

"I do, too," Rand answered mechanically, but he wondered how he would feel if Lorelei really did wed Roger. "But until she does, I am responsible for her, and no matter how much she professes to hate the arrangement, she's still going to have to answer to me for everything."

"Let's just hope this doesn't drag on for the full three years. What will you do with her if she hasn't married by the time you have to return to duty? And if she doesn't marry him right away, how long do you think Roger will stay to help her?"

"I don't know, but that's something I'll have to consider. Perhaps I'll have a talk with Roger while we're in town, try to find out exactly what his plans are." Finishing his drink, he set it aside. "Now, I'm going to bed and I suggest you do the same, since we'll be riding out shortly after sunup."

"Good night, Rand." Lydia used her most seductive tone, but he seemed preoccupied and did not notice.

"Good night," he replied as he left the room.


Lorelei tossed restlessly as her nightmare tightened its hold upon her, the passionate dream arousing her even in her sleep. She was with Rand—loving him— and in her dream, he was tender and considerate and he cared about her. Then her vision changed, and she pictured Rand and Lydia clasped in a lovers' embrace, moving together in the age-old rhythm of mating.

Though she was sound asleep, Lori cried out as emotions roiled inside her, calling out Rand's name. Then she abruptly awakened. Disoriented, she sat up and then began to shiver as she finally recognized what she was feeling for Rand. God help her, she loved him.

Her claims of hating him had been only childish denials of the truth. She had loved him since her earliest years, and she loved him still. The knowledge did not give her any pleasure for he'd made it plain that he didn't care about her, that he considered her a burden, and that he would be glad to be done with the arrangement their fathers had imposed upon them.

Forcing her thoughts away from Rand, she tried to envision what her life would be like if she went through with her plan to marry Roger. It would be a pleasant enough existence, Lori was sure, for he did love her, and though her feelings for him were a far cry from her blinding obsession with Rand, Lori was certain that, given time, she could come to love Roger in a comfortable sort of way. If she went through with the marriage, she would do her best to make their life together a happy, contented one, but . . .

She had not yet mentioned to Roger that she'd had a change of heart, and she knew she would soon have to tell him of her decision to marry him. The only thing that restrained her was the possibility that she was pregnant with Rand's child. If that was the case, and she hoped it was not, she would not enter into marriage while burdened with another man's child. In the meantime she must wait until nature had taken its course.

Lying back down, she turned on her side and hugged her pillow to her breast as she once again courted sleep, hoping that this time her rest would be undisturbed.

Rand had lain awake for hours in the comfort of his bed, his thoughts tortured by the memory of the condemning words Lorelei had spoken in the stable. She hated him, but she certainly had derived pleasure from his touch. She was a paradox . . . one moment a spitfire accusing him of committing adultery with Lydia, the next a willing lover surrendering to his embrace and giving herself to him with abandon. He had never known fulfillment as sweet, yet there had been only lust involved in their coming together . . . or had that been all?

She had claimed in her fury that she'd once thought

him special, but seeing him with Lydia had changed that. He had been touched by her naïve disclosure. Had he been the object of her affections when she'd been just a young girl? Rand frowned into the darkness as he tried to remember what she had looked like seven years ago, but he could conjure up no image of Lorelei. He had paid scant attention to her then for he'd been too wrapped up in his own misery after discovering that Lydia had married his father.

Shrugging away the remembrance of that difficult time in his life, Rand turned his thoughts to Lorelei. He wanted her physically, that he could not deny, but he knew he could have no future with her for she was just like Lydia—making love with him, while planning to marry another man. Why else would Westlake have followed her here? There must have been some kind of understanding between them.

With a touch of bitterness he didn't fully understand, Rand wondered how many times she'd given herself to Roger since she'd learned the joys of lovemaking. It angered him to even consider that, and getting up from his bed, he pulled on his pants and strode barefoot from his quarters to get another glass of whiskey. He hoped a drink would dull his senses and give him surcease from thoughts of Lorelei in Roger's arms.

It was past midnight, but Josh Taylor, dressed in nondescript dark clothing, sat at a table near the rear of the Sidewinder Saloon. He was conversing with Harley Oates.

"I'm glad you could meet me," Oates told the banker as he downed another glass of beer. "'Cause I got to get back to the mine by midmorning."

"Why?"

"No one knows I'm gone. I snuck off jes' at

233

sundown," he confided. "There's been a lot of action goin' on up there—action you're gonna like!"

Josh smiled thinly. "Like what?"

"Like a cave-in on the new drift. It was testin' out real fine and they was makin' good progress 'til one of the support beams gave way."

"Was anyone hurt?"

"Not really, but it took us a full day to dig 'em out."

"Dig who out?"

"The Spencer girl and some fella named McAllister. Hal was injured, but he's already back on the job. Still, we're gonna lose at least a week of work because of the collapse."

"McAllister?" Josh's eyes narrowed.

"Yep, Rand McAllister. Some of the men were sayin' that he's takin' control of the mine. I dunno for sure, but he was pretty interested in the operation, went down there with the assayer and Miss Lorelei and poked around."

"How would McAllister come to be in charge of the Triple Cross?" Josh wondered out loud.

"Rumor has it through his father, but that's all I know," Oates offered. "Anyways, he and the girl were jes' fine after we dug 'em out and they're probably here in town already, 'cause they were comin' here for supplies. That's why I got to be extra careful, ya know what I mean?"

"I understand." Taylor motioned for the barkeep to bring his hireling another beer. "You'd better head on back as soon as you finish this next drink."

"Didn't I do good for ya?" Oates was obviously proud of his handiwork in slowing down progress at the mine.

"You're doing fine so far, but until I have title to the Triple Cross, I won't be satisfied." Taylor's expression hardened. "Do you know what I mean?"

Harley nodded nervously as he gulped the cool brew. "Yes, sir. I'll keep ya posted on everything that happens. I'll get word to ya somehow when the shipments start up again."

"How long until the new stamp mill starts operation?"

"A couple of weeks, why?"

"Nothing," Josh replied distractedly, for another plan of action was forming in his devious mind. "You get on back now while I try to find out exactly what connection Rand McAllister has to the mine."

"Yes, sir." Draining the last of his beer from the glass, Oates hurried away, leaving Josh to plot further mayhem.

On the other side of the room, Angelo glanced quickly at Cody. "Did you hear that?"

"I only heard parts of it . . . but the parts I heard were very interesting," the killer replied. "I think we'd better find Pat and fast."

"Right, *amigo*. This could be what we've been waiting for."

Slowly, so as not to draw attention to themselves, they got up from their secluded table and left the bar, heading directly up the stairway to the second floor. Their movements were casual until they reached their room and then they burst inside, anxious to relay their news to Pat.

"Pat! We done found out where McAllister is, or at least we think so."

Pat had been dozing on the bed, but at their unexpected entrance, he quickly sat up, turning on them with cocked gun in hand. "What the hell!" he snarled, slowly lowering his pistol.

"Sorry, Pat." Cody apologized shamefacedly, realizing how close he just came to meeting his maker. "But

Angelo and I were jes' downstairs in the bar and we heard two men talkin'."

"And?"

"And, Pat," Angelo continued, "they were talkin' about McAllister."

Pat Benton's eyes lit with a fierce inner zeal. "What'd they say?"

"Somethin' about him bein' at a mine called the Triple Cross. Ever heard of it?"

"I ain't yet, but I'm gonna find out everything I can about it, startin' right now." Pat headed for the door. "Show me which men were doin' the talkin' downstairs."

They followed him out into the hall and down the stairway, but when they reached the saloon, they discovered that the man who had been sitting at the table discussing McAllister's whereabouts was no longer there.

"Damn!" Cody swore violently. "He's done gone!"

"Now don't get all riled up," Pat said with viperish coolness as he headed for the bar. "We still got the name of the mine. All we gotta do is find out where it is."

Cody and Angelo exchanged confident glances as they sidled up to the bar with Pat. If McAllister was at the mine called the Triple Cross, he was a dead man.

# Chapter Fourteen

Lorelei stood at the window that overlooked the courtyard of Gardiner's Hotel, staring down at the pool of water below and remembering with vivid clarity the night when Rand had first kissed her. It had been less than two weeks since he'd thanked her by that pool for saving his life during the stage robbery, but so much had happened since then it seemed the kiss had happened in another lifetime.

Things certainly have changed, she thought. In the beginning, she'd seen him as a mocking, arrogant cowboy and she'd hoped she would never have to see him again. Now . . . Now, Rand was her guardian, and he was also the man she loved. That knowledge, when it had finally come to her during the previous night, had shaken her to her very depths and she'd been struggling with it ever since, trying to come to grips with the futility of feeling such an emotion for him.

Though Lori had thought it would be difficult to keep her love hidden, now that she recognized it for what it was, she'd been amazed at how easy she'd found it to ignore Rand, especially since he had been so coldly indifferent to her during their limited dealings throughout the course of the day. She had not known what to expect from him after their explosive encounter the night before, but judging from his steely-eyed look and distant manner, he'd evidently meant what he said. He wanted as little to do with her as possible and had barely spoken to her during their journey to town. Devoting his attention to Lydia, he'd ridden at her side and engaged her in easy conversation for the entire length of the trek.

A knock at the door interrupted Lori's thoughts and she hurried to answer it, glad to have respite from her memories.

"Yes? Who is it?"

"It's me, Lori," Sally called out happily. "Are you ready to go shopping?"

"I suppose." Her answer was less than enthusiastic as she opened the door to admit her friend.

"You really don't want to go to the party, do you?"

Sighing, Lori gave Sally a small, tight smile. "I'm worried about the mine, that's all. There's so little time, and the delay because of the cave-in puts much more pressure on us."

"I understand," her friend replied. "But it's like Roger said, our spending one extra day in town isn't going to affect the Triple Cross at all. So, why don't you relax and enjoy this party? I'm sure you'll know a lot of the people there, won't you?"

"It's been years since I've spent any time here, but I should know some of them," Lori agreed.

"And maybe you can help me find out how the guard from the stagecoach is doing." It was the first time Sally had mentioned the man since they'd arrived in Phoenix, and Lori shot her a questioning look.

"You mean Brady Barclay?" At her friend's telltale blush, Lori grinned. "Why Sally Westlake, I suspect you may have more than a nurse's interest in the man."

"I liked him, Lori. He was different from the other

238

men I've known, but as far as a romantic interest . . . I'm not sure." Sally was self-conscious about her feelings. "I just know that I've been concerned about him ever since we left the relay station."

"Why didn't you say something sooner? We could have sent a message to town to find out how he was doing."

"I didn't want to be *that* obvious!" Sally protested with an embarrassed groan. "I just want to make sure he recovered."

"I'm sure we'll be able to find out something without tipping our hand. After all, we were involved in the holdup." Lori was already thinking of men who might know the wounded guard's condition.

"You're right." Sally sounded more confident than she felt. "Shall we go? Lydia told me that there are several stores on Washington Street where we might be able to find something to wear."


Rand strode the length of Washington Street with John as the sheriff made his rounds.

"Are you going to come to our get-together tomorrow night?" McCrea asked.

"Yes, and thanks for the invitation. Lydia is particularly glad to be able to visit with her friends."

"It's been a difficult time for her, I'm sure. Widowed twice and without any children. She's such a young woman to have gone through so much."

"She's been handling it pretty well from what I can tell. I know she wants me to stay and help her run the ranch, but things have gotten so complicated."

"How so? Your job and this news about the Bentons?"

"That, yes, but I guess you haven't heard about the agreement Will drew with George Spencer."

"No, not a word, although as close as they were, it doesn't surprise me that they had worked something out between them. What is it?"

"Well, George was worried about his daughter being alone in the world, so my father agreed to take custody of her, should anything happen to George."

"And?"

"Though she's eighteen, she's now officially my ward until she turns twenty-one or marries."

"Yours?" John turned quickly to stare at Rand.

"Mine," the younger man answered bitterly. "Not only am I responsible for her welfare, I'm in complete charge of her inheritance—the Triple Cross."

John emitted a low, stunned whistle. "You certainly do have your work cut out for you. What are you going to do about your job?"

"I've already wired Marshal Duke for additional leave time. I hope he won't have any objections."

"He'll understand." The sheriff nodded. "So you have the Lazy Ace to worry about, and you've also got a paying gold mine to supervise. How did the Spencer girl react to your taking over? I know she's been back East and is probably pretty citified."

"Not Lorelei," Rand told him ruefully.

"No?"

"No. She was already living out at the Triple Cross when I found out about all of this."

"That mine is no place for a lady, not alone!"

"I know. That's why I've agreed to move in up there."

"You're going to be living at the mine?" John was incredulous. "Why didn't you just have the girl move in with Lydia at the ranch?"

"Because Lorelei refused to leave, and after speaking with the mine supervisor and the resident assayer, I know she was right. The lode they've discovered looks more than promising, and now that George is dead,

240

they need all the help they can get."

"What about the ranch and Lydia?"

"Jack Barlow will take charge, and I plan to check on things every other week or so."

"You have got your share of problems," McCrea declared. "And now with the Bentons loose—"

"What's the latest? Have they been spotted anywhere?"

"No one's seen them since they broke out, and I can't decide if that's good or bad. Either they've left the territory or they're hiding out somewhere—"

"Waiting for me," Rand finished his sentence. "I know they want me. They didn't leave any doubt in my mind that they'd come after me if they got the chance. I've been cautious and I haven't noticed anything unusual."

"Well, don't let your guard down. I'll keep you posted on everything I hear—possible sightings, robberies and the like."

"Have there been any more attempts to rob the stageline?"

"None," John answered as they stopped before his office. "There's a sizable reward for information on the bandits who attacked you. Hell, it might have been the damned Bentons for all we know."

"You're right. If we'd been able to identify the dead man, we might have gotten a line on who was behind the whole thing, but as it is—"

"We're stymied unless they strike again." McCrea opened the office door and both men entered, grumbling in frustration.

"He's out at the moment, Mrs. McAllister, but he's due back any time now. Would you care to wait?" The bank clerk was very attentive to the lovely widow.

"Yes, thank you."

"Go right on in then, and make yourself comfortable."

"You're most kind."

"Can I bring you anything?"

"No, I'd like to be alone, if you don't mind?"

"Not at all, Mrs. McAllister. Just call if there's anything I can do for you," he offered solicitously.

"I will. Thank you." Lydia's eyes were alight as she swept into Josh's private office and closed the door securely behind her.

Since she'd kissed Rand at the mine, she'd been burning for a man's touch, and knowing that it was too soon to press her advantage with Rand, she was going to settle for Josh. Not that Josh wasn't a good lover, he was; he just wasn't Rand. Still, the thrill of surprising Josh here at the bank, offered much in the way of forbidden excitement, so deliberately she took off her black bonnet and pulled the pins from her lustrous pale hair, letting it fall in shining curls about her slim shoulders. Moving to the wide window, she drew the heavy drapes against the revealing brightness of the day and then sat down in a chair to slip off her shoes. With shaking fingers, she worked at the buttons of her bodice, eager to strip off the depressing black gown and be ready for Josh when he returned. How surprised he would be to find her nude in his office!

A feline smile curved her perfect lips as she stood up and slid the hated dress from her body, then tossed it aside. Afire with desire now, she pushed the straps of her chemise from her shoulders, allowing it to fall unheeded to her waist and thereby revealing the glory of her breasts, throbbing now with the need of a man's hungry caress. Stifled by the rest of her clothing, Lydia shed her remaining garments quickly, and feeling gloriously free, she moved away from the door so her

242

lover wouldn't see her when he entered and betray their mutual passion to the employees working out front.

Josh was troubled as he strode back toward the bank. His meeting with Harley Oakes the night before had alerted him to the newly established connection between Rand McAllister and the Spencer girl, so using his position as a bank officer as an excuse, he'd paid a visit to Swartz, the lawyer who'd been handling Lorelei's affairs. Swartz had informed him that Richards, McAllister's attorney, had been in touch with him and he'd then proceeded to explain the unsettling details regarding Rand McAllister's guardianship of Lorelei.

This news had greatly disturbed Josh, but he had not revealed any of his anxiety to the lawyer. He'd dealt with the matter coolly as if it were bank business; however, when he'd left the attorney's office his expression had become thunderous. Damn! What else could go wrong? First, that stubborn girl had refused to sell, and now she had Rand McAllister supporting her endeavor to make the mine a success.

He was in no frame of mind to deal with his employees as he entered the bank, and he waved off a clerk's attempt to speak with him, striding into his office and slamming the door shut. It took Josh a moment to realize that something was different. When he noticed the drawn drapes and the semidarkness of the room, he wondered who dared to enter his inner sanctum in his absence. He was ready to storm out of the room and demand an explanation when Lydia's sultry voice called out to him from a shadowy corner of the room.

"My, my," she taunted. "You certainly seem on edge, darling. Perhaps I can ease your tension?"

Josh swung in her direction both startled and pleased to find her waiting for him. "Lydia . . . I'm

243

so . . ." The sight of her as she crossed the room struck him speechless. She was totally naked! His breath caught in his throat, and he groped behind him, finding the lock and turning it soundlessly, without taking his eyes from the beauty of her pale body. "My God, Lydia, you're—"

"Yes, darling. I am." She chuckled throatily as she wound her arms about his neck in a serpentine clasp. "And I've been waiting here, just for you. Have you missed me, Josh?"

"Lydia, you can't know how much," he gasped as she brought her body against his and rubbed sinuously against him.

"I can feel how much, Josh—now, show me!" she demanded as she drew his head down to hers for a flaming kiss.

Beyond all reason now, Josh tore at his own clothing, driven to penetrate her teasing hotness. Lifting her and bringing her legs about his waist, he thrust avidly into her as his lips sought the burgeoning fullness of her breasts. Release came to Lydia quickly, for her need had been great, and she bit her lips to keep from crying out as passion throbbed through her in ever-widening circles.

Though Josh knew that Lydia had reached her peak, he was still far from his own so he continued to drive forcefully into her, feeling a certain power in knowing that he could take her to the pinnacle of pleasure so easily. Determined to take her with him when he ascended the heights, he pressed heated, arousing kisses on her throat and bosom, reawakening her temporarily sated desire.

Lydia had been so hungry for Rand that she was not surprised to find herself responding again to Josh's expert touch, and she eagerly joined him in wanton play, imagining all the while that Rand was holding her and touching her and giving her ecstatic pleasure.

Thrilled by her excitement, Josh reached his own peak and emptied himself within Lydia, his breathing strained, his heart beating wildly in his chest. For some moments they remained unmoving in the center of the room, clasped in each other's arms; then Josh released her legs and let her slowly slide down his body. His mouth sought hers in a deep exchange, and when the kiss ended he looked down at her. She was smiling up at him, a satisfied expression on her face.

"Was this a business call, Mrs. McAllister?" he asked, his eyes aglow with the love he felt for her.

"Definitely, sir. I came to discuss my dead husband's estate," she answered archly. "And I asked your clerk not to disturb me while I awaited your return."

"A good thought, my love," he growled. "I would have hated to have had my clerk walk in and find you naked in my office."

She lifted a delicate brow in amusement as she tried to envision the scene. "What do you think he would have done?"

"He probably wouldn't have been able to control himself, and he would have ravished you himself," Josh remarked. "I don't know a man who could resist you, Lydia. You're the most seductive, gorgeous woman I've ever known."

A flash of bitterness shot through her as she thought of Rand and the ease with which he ignored her sensuality.

"Your body is perfect . . . your skin is alabaster, so smooth." He ran a cherishing hand over her breasts and thighs. "Every inch of you is responsive and exciting, and I can't wait until we can be together like this all the time."

His mention of a permanent relationship grated on Lydia's nerves, but she said nothing. Until she had

245

some sign from Rand that he was warming toward her, she would continue to use Josh to assuage the hunger she could not control.

"I'd better dress," she said huskily, moving slightly away. Josh, she knew, could be insatiable, and she didn't want to risk spending too much time in his office alone with him. "And so had you."

He silently pulled on his own clothing while he watched Lydia don her chemise and pull on her stockings. "Love, I'm ready for you again," he remarked.

As her eyes caressed the evidence of his desire, she answered lightly, "Pity we don't have more time."

"What about tonight?"

"No. That's impossible. Rand has come to town with me, along with the Spencer girl and two of her friends. We're all to attend the party at the McCreas'."

"Ah. I'll be there. Perhaps we can find a way to be together. I just heard about the unusual situation of Rand's guardianship." Josh watched her with studied calm as he probed for more information.

"Oh?" Lydia was surprised.

"As the officer of the bank holding the loan on the mine, I'm entitled to know any and all pertinent details, and I daresay, Rand McAllister's taking charge is a pertinent detail. How is your stepson going to manage it?"

For a moment Lydia forgot to disguise her feelings. "The fool is going to live at the mine!"

"He's what?" Josh was watching her closely.

"He's leaving me all alone at the ranch, while he runs off to play nursemaid to that eighteen-year-old witch! I pleaded with him to bring her back to the ranch to live with the both of us, but Lorelei insists on being in charge of her father's mine and, so far, Rand has supported her."

246

"That's ridiculous!" Josh certainly didn't want Rand to get too involved in the operation of the Triple Cross.

"I know." Lydia sneered. "I've tried to convince him that I need him more than she does, but he's firmly convinced that the mine is about to pay off big, and soon. Until Lorelei decides to marry that Eastern boyfriend of hers, I'm forced to run the ranch with very little help from Rand."

"What does Lorelei's marrying have to do with the situation?"

"If she marries, Rand is relieved of his role as guardian."

"Oh, and is the girl serious about this other man?"

"Who knows? When I questioned her about it the other day, she denied having set a date, so I would guess she's never given Roger a definite answer."

"Darling," Josh said silkily, "don't be concerned. If my plans come to fruition, you will no longer have to worry about the Lazy Ace or McAllister."

Buttoning the last button on her bodice, Lydia looked up at him questioningly. "When are you going to tell me about these plans of yours?"

"I can't just yet, but rest assured, when all is said and done, I will be rich and able to give you everything you've ever wanted." He took her in his arms and kissed her feverishly.

Lydia accepted Josh's embrace and returned his kiss with practiced enthusiasm; yet as she melted against him, she was thinking that the one thing she wanted more than anything else he would never be able to give her. She wanted Rand McAllister back in her bed.

After Josh had shown her from his office moments later, he sat pensively behind his desk, his thoughts centered on Harley Oates. He hoped that the miner would be able to prevent that vein from being developed in time to pay back the loan. If not, all his

247

plans would come to naught, and he could not let that happen. He wanted Lydia too much.

Cody, Pat, and Angelo hunkered down quickly as the armed guard at the mining camp's entrance glanced in their direction.

"What do ya think, Pat?" Cody asked excitedly. They'd had no trouble getting directions to the Triple Cross, so they'd ridden out from town at first light. It was well past noon now, and they had been hiding on the rocky mountainside overlooking the mine for several hours already, trying to catch sight of McAllister.

"I dunno." Pat frowned as he watched the normal workday activity at the mine. "Ain't seen hide nor hair of him yet, but that don't mean nothin'."

"We gonna stay here and wait or what?"

"I think we'd better go into the camp and find out exactly where McAllister is." Pat's obsidian gaze slid to Angelo. "And only one of us won't be shot on sight. How much do you know about mining, Angelo?"

"A little."

"Enough to get hired on at the Triple Cross?"

"I think so." He nodded.

"Well, go get yourself a job, Angelo. Me and Cody's gonna stay right here while you ride in there and find out everything you can about our friend the marshal. You got it?"

"*Sí, Pat*. As soon as I know something, I will sneak up here and tell you," Angelo was already making his way toward his horse.

"Pat, don't you think them minin' folks might think it a bit odd, him just ridin' into camp and askin' fer a job?" Cody asked.

"Naw. Happens all the time. Miners generally don't stay too long in one place. They'll probably be glad for the extra help."

Cody nodded, relieved that his brother knew so much. "Good."

"We'll be waitin', Angelo. Don't forget."

"*Sí, compadre.*" Eager to avenge the death of his friend Juan, he mounted his horse.


When Rand returned to the hotel, he was surprised to find Roger just on his way out.

"Did you get all your business taken care of?" Roger asked as he met him in the lobby.

"Just got finished. I was going to check on the women and then find a quiet corner and enjoy a beer. Join me?" He'd been wanting to speak with Westlake alone since the previous night, and this seemed the perfect opportunity.

"Sounds fine, and you don't have to worry about the women. Lydia left a message that she had a meeting with the banker and after that she was going to visit friends. Lori and Sally have gone shopping."

"Let's go then. The Gold Nugget is right across the street." The two men left the hotel and they were soon settled in at the bar. Cool glasses of beer in hand, they occupied a table near the front window.

"Tell me about yourself." Rand gave Roger a friendly smile, hoping to draw him out and learn more of his intentions regarding Lorelei.

Roger regarded Rand levelly as he took a sip of his beer, "You know Sally and I are from St. Louis. Our family has lived there for years. I was working with my father in his law practice before deciding to accompany Lorelei and Sally."

"So, you're a lawyer?" Rand was impressed. "How long have you been practicing?"

"About five years. I find it challenging."

Rand nodded in complete understanding, for he felt the same way about his own profession. "How did you meet Lorelei?"

Roger grinned. "She was Sally's best friend, so my cousin brought her along on a family outing one Sunday. I always dreaded those get-togethers, but that Sunday I was glad I went. It was love at first sight for me, but I've had to convince Lori." Punctuating his last words with a heavy sigh, he drained his glass and directed the bartender to bring two more beers. "She's different from any woman I've ever known."

"I know." Rand finished off his own drink and gratefully accepted another from the barkeep. It had been a long hot afternoon and the cool beer was going down smoothly. "She can be downright maddening at times."

"This guardianship has really created problems for you, hasn't it?" Roger asked.

Rand nodded, his smile derisive. "That's an understatement. I only came back because of my father's death. I wanted to settle things as quickly as possible out at the ranch so I could return to my duties."

"And then came Lorelei." Roger returned his smile.

"Right. I hadn't seen or even heard of her in seven years, but suddenly I was responsible for her well-being and for her inheritance. It wouldn't be such a complex situation had she agreed to move in at the Lazy Ace, but she's determined to stay at the mine and work it as her father did."

"I know. Her independence frustrates me at every turn."

"Are you planning to marry her soon?" Rand had been waiting for the chance to bring that up, but he now found himself dreading Roger's answer.

"That was my intention when I agreed to travel with them. Originally Lori planned to settle things here and

250

then return to St. Louis with us, but now . . ." His expression revealed his perplexity. "I don't know. I pressed her to marry me right after the cave-in. God, I was so worried about her!"

Rand was momentarily disgusted with Lorelei because she'd betrayed Roger, yet he knew he was equally to blame. "And?"

"And she avoided giving me a definite answer. I don't know how much longer I can stay in limbo like this." Roger stared blankly at his empty glass for a moment before beckoning the bartender to bring another round. "The only thing I could think of the whole time we were digging you out was how I was going to spirit her away from all this and keep her safe and protected back home." Disheartened, Roger looked up at Rand. "But that's not what she wants. She loves this country, and that mine. I don't think she'd ever agree to live in the city again, now that she's in control of her own future."

"And you wouldn't be happy settling here?" Rand prodded.

"If Lori loved me and agreed to marry me, I'd be happy anywhere, but as it is . . ."

Rand felt a peculiar stirring within him at Roger's words. *If Lori loved me* . . . Had she never told him she loved him? "Surely she must love you."

"I wish I knew," Roger muttered, well into his third beer. "Sometimes she acts like she does, but at other times . . . She keeps me on tenterhooks with her mercurial moods."

"I know what you mean." Rand recalled his own run-ins with Lori, her quicksilver temperament; he remembered how quickly her fiery protests had turned to fiery response.

"I know she needs my help at the mine, but I don't know if she needs me. That's what I have to find out."

251

He looked glum. "This is the first time in my life that I've had to pursue a woman, and I'm not at all sure that I'm fond of the chase. A bit of elusiveness is attractive in a female, but, damn, Lori's pushing it to the limit with me."

"Perhaps she really doesn't know her own mind," Rand offered by way of explanation.

"I'd like to think that was it, but I've been courting her for quite a while now"—Westlake paused as he remembered Lori's heated embrace the day of the rescue—"and it's a rare occasion when she gives me reason to hope."

So, Rand mused as Roger spoke, Lorelei was not officially promised to the man. He did love her and did want to marry her, but she had never given a positive answer to his proposal. Rand's whole perception of the situation was changing due to this conversation, and he was aware that his feeling for Lorelei was altering in a subtle way.

Obviously, from the tone of Roger's conversation, there had been little, if any, intimacy between him and Lori. Though Rand vividly remembered their embrace, he knew now it has been only that—an embrace. She had not shared passion with Roger. That realization left Rand feeling strangely pleased, and he stifled the urge to smile, turning instead to order two more beers.

The knowledge that marriage was not in Lori's immediate future did not relieve Rand of his resentment of his tedious role as guardian, but it certainly eased the bitterness he'd been feeling toward his ward. He no longer thought she had betrayed her fiancé. *Lorelei was not like Lydia.* The discovery jarred him, and Rand knew a moment of confusion as he tried to understand exactly what he was feeling for Lori now that he knew the truth: Lorelei had not been using him; what had

252

happened between them had been spontaneous and natural.

"I'm hoping the party tomorrow night will take Lori's mind off the Triple Cross for a while and get it onto other things." Roger smiled good-naturedly as he glanced up at Rand, unaware of the other man's thoughts.

"I'm sure it will help," Rand said noncommittally. Then he accepted the fresh beer from the bartender and drank deeply.

## Chapter Fifteen

In the darkness of the predawn hours, Angelo stole silently up into the rocky outcropping where he knew his *compadres* were camped.

"Cody? Pat?" he whispered, pausing to listen for their response.

"Here," came Pat's husky answer, and Angelo moved to join them beneath the sizable overhang under which they were crouched.

"Where is he?" Cody demanded excitedly for he was eager to see the marshal pay for killing his brother.

"He ain't there."

"What!"

"Not right now, he ain't. Seems he's gone into town to get supplies, but they're expectin' him back sometime today," he told them hurriedly, wanting to return to the quarters he'd been given before his absence from camp was discovered.

"How'd he come to be involved with this here mine?" Pat asked, cunningly.

"I don't know the whole story yet, but rumor has it he's runnin' the place."

"What about his job as marshal?"

"There ain't been a word said 'bout that. I'll know

more once he shows up. You got a plan yet as to what we're gonna do once he gets here?

Pat's eyes glowed with an inner intensity. "I been watchin' and plannin' real careful. I got a good idea, but I'm not sayin' a word until I see how things are goin'. When the time is right, we'll take him."

"I gotta get back." Angelo started away. "If I learn anything tomorrow I'll come back and let you know."

"We'll be here."


Though the first rays of the morning sun were staining the eastern horizon with pale shades of pink and yellow, Lorelei had not yet managed to fall asleep. She knew she shouldn't let it bother her that Rand had not dined with them. In truth, she would have considered his absence a blessing except that Lydia had not joined them either. She had immediately envisioned the pair making love in the privacy of one of their hotel rooms.

Lorelei had tried to tell herself that it didn't really matter what Rand did for he meant nothing to her, but, when she'd heard Lydia return to her room, accompanied by Rand, just after midnight, any doubts she'd harbored about their relationship had been negated.

She'd spent the balance of the night fighting the feelings of misery that threatened to engulf her. Though logic dictated that she should not love Rand, she could not control her emotions. It was Lydia he loved, and Lori had no reason to think that that would change. She knew he didn't care about her for he'd made it plain that he thought his guardianship a burden.

Padding barefoot to the window, she stared across the courtyard at the slowly brightening sky, anxious

255

about how she was going to deal with the love she felt for him. She knew marrying Roger would get Rand out of her life, but it would not help her to forget him, now that she'd tasted desire. Lori shivered as she remembered all too well the ecstasy Rand's caresses had aroused in her, and she agonized over the possibility of wedding Roger, wondering if she could ever experience with him the same rapturous joy she'd known with Rand. No matter how happy Roger could make her it might never be enough, not after Rand.

Restless and unable to sleep as the night wore on, Rand had finally wandered out into the courtyard as dawn drew near, to linger by the side of the pool where he and Lorelei had shared their first kiss. The night just ending had been exceedingly dull, and he knew he had no one to blame for that but himself. Wanting to avoid Lorelei, he had not joined the others for dinner but had sent Roger on ahead while he remained at the Gold Nugget, drinking and playing poker until almost midnight. He had been surprised when, upon returning to the hotel, he'd met Lydia who was returning from her visit with the Harpers. After escorting her safely to her room, he had retired to his own, intending to get a good night's sleep, but that had not happened. Instead, he'd been caught up in thoughts about what Roger had told him, and he'd become increasingly restive until, in desperation, he'd fled to the patio area in search of peace.

Out of the corner of his eye as he stood in the deep half-shadows of the fading night, Rand caught a movement at one of the windows. He pivoted slowly, glancing upward to see what it was that had drawn his attention. Then he saw Lorelei, bathed in the first rosy glow of the morning sun, her glorious hair streaming about her shoulders, her lush body shielded from his probing gaze by a gossamer gown that, though not revealing, hinted seductively at the womanly curves it covered.

His breath caught in his throat and he remained unmoving as he stared up at her, enchanted by her untamed beauty. God, how he wanted her! His reaction to her presence was immediate and strong, but he fought down his surging desire. Only by remembering their parting scene in the stable and her vehement declaration of hatred was he able to bring his passion for her under control. Rand was glad when she stepped away from the window a few moments later, for he was able to leave the courtyard undetected. The less she knew about his need for her, the better.

Checking her reflection in the small mirror over the wash stand in her hotel room, Lori smoothed the skirt of the dress she'd bought that afternoon and nodded approvingly. Emerald in color, with a modestly cut square bodice and slightly flared skirt, the gown fit her superbly, accentuating the creaminess of her skin and the coppery brilliance of her hair, which she wore up and away from her face. Pleased that she'd been able to find a suitable gown on such short notice, she felt confident that she looked her best. She turned away from the mirror as a soft knock sounded at the door.

"Yes?"

"It's me, Sally. Let me in so I can see how gorgeous you look."

Lori smiled as she opened the door to admit her friend. "I want to see your new gown, too," she said, studying Sally who swept into the room wearing the deep rose-colored dress she'd purchased that afternoon. Its stunning color emphasized the young woman's dark beauty, and Lori remarked, "That shade of rose becomes you. Maybe your Wells Fargo guard will be at the party tonight!"

"Lori!" Sally blushed prettily. "It would be nice to know that he'd recovered, but . . . Thank you for the compliment," she returned. "I've never worn anything quite this bright before, but I think I like it. You look wonderful! Green is certainly your color. Roger won't leave your side all night!"

Lori's smile of pleasure was forced. Dear Roger . . . so kind . . . so attentive . . . Before she could respond another knock came at the door.

"Lori? Is Sally with you? I tried her room and there was no answer." It was Roger's voice.

"Yes, she's here, and we're both ready."

Roger's eyes lingered appreciatively on Lori's soft curves as she stepped from the room. "You look lovely, Lori, Sally."

Both young women thanked him for the compliment, and Lori added with a smile, "You're looking rather dashing yourself."

"Thank you." Roger grinned. He felt more like himself now that he'd donned dress clothes.

They started down the hall, heading toward the stairs that led to the lobby where they had arranged to meet Rand and Lydia.

When they'd descended, it took all of Lori's will power not to remark on Lydia's attire for she had forsaken her mourning clothes after little more than a month and had donned a pale lavender gown with a bodice that displayed her bosom.

As she glanced quickly away from Lydia, Lori's gaze was caught and held by Rand's. He stood attentively at his stepmother's side. The white shirt he wore with his dark jacket and pants served to emphasize his darkly tanned features, and Lori found herself momentarily

258

mesmerized by his dark-eyed, inscrutable regard. Only when Lydia touched his arm and made some remark did he turn away from Lori and flash Lydia a warm, seemingly intimate, smile.

"We're ready, if you are," Roger was saying as he escorted Sally and Lori to where Rand and Lydia stood.

"Of course," Lydia told him. "Sally, you look very pretty this evening."

"Why, thank you, Lydia." The young woman accepted the compliment graciously, but she was slightly nonplused because Lydia had forsaken her mourning attire so soon so she hesitated to return the compliment, even though the older woman looked marvelous.

"Shall we go?" Rand suggested, and Lydia took his arm possessively as they left the hotel.

It was only a short walk to the McCrea home, and the party was in full swing when they arrived, the sounds of the music and revelry greeting them as they started up the front walk.

"Rand! Lydia!" John welcomed them warmly. "Come in."

"Thank you, John." As they were ushered inside, Rand made the introductions. "This is Lorelei Spencer, George Spencer's daughter, and these are the friends who accompanied her from St. Louis, Sally and Roger Westlake."

"It's nice to meet you and Miss Spencer."

"Lorelei, please." Lori smiled at the friendly woman.

"Lorelei, then. I'm so sorry about your father," Ellen McCrea said with heartfelt sincerity.

"Thank you, Mrs. McCrea."

"Please, you must call me Ellen, and this is my husband John, we're so glad you could join us this evening."

"Sally and I appreciate your including us in your invitation," Roger put in.

"We wouldn't have it any other way. Any friend of Rand's is welcome in our home," John declared. "Come meet our guests."

Though the McCrea affair was a far cry from the society balls Lori had attended in the East, it lacked nothing in the way of food, drink, or dancing. The McCreas had moved the furniture from their parlor and had hired several local musicians to provide music, and the guests already in attendance were indulging in a little lighthearted fun.

Josh Taylor was standing across the room as he saw Lydia enter on Rand's arm and a surge of hatred seared through him as he noticed Lydia's enraptured expression every time she spoke to her escort. He had hoped there was nothing to her preoccupation with her stepson, but as he watched her smile glowingly up at Rand, Josh knew he had competition for her affection. Determined that she would be his no matter what, he started toward the pair.

"Lydia! Rand! How delightful to see you both!" he lied smoothly.

"Good evening, Taylor," Rand responded evenly. "You know Lorelei Spencer, of course, and her friends, Sally and Roger Westlake of St. Louis."

"Lorelei," Josh said cordially. Then he turned to the others. "How do you do?"

Roger and Sally nodded.

"Hello, Josh." Lydia gave him her best smile.

"May I presume to ask you to dance, Lydia?" Josh made his request as the music started up again.

Though she had longed to be in Rand's arms, Lydia did not hesitate to reply, "I'd be delighted, Josh. Thank you. Rand, I'll speak with you later."

When they had danced out into the middle of the

room, out of earshot, Josh muttered, "I can't tell you how pleasant it is to see that you've openly given up mourning for Will. You look beautiful tonight, Lydia."

"Thank you, darling. You know how I detested wearing those widow's weeds." Lydia shivered in disgust. "I suppose I'm lucky that we're not back East where social convention is so rigidly followed, but then I'm not nearly as scandalous as the widow Jones. Why she remarried only two weeks after her husband's untimely death!" She chuckled.

"Indeed," he agreed letting his gaze feast upon the tempting swell of bosom revealed by Lydia's low-cut gown. Remembering that just yesterday she'd been writhing in his arms, naked, his desire for her flamed to life and he said huskily, "We shall have to arrange a moment alone, later."

"I don't know if that will be possible." Lydia hesitated, wanting to spend every moment she could with Rand.

"Perhaps later, in your room," Josh pressed. "I know the others are situated near you, but somehow we'll manage."

Lydia did not argue the point. She glanced across the room to where Rand, Lorelei, Roger and Sally stood in conversation with their hostess.

"Rand told us all about being named your guardian. You're so lucky to have him," Ellen was telling Lorelei, while Rand looked decidedly uncomfortable at being publicly praised. "He's such a good man. John and I have always been very fond of him."

Not wanting to get into a discussion of Rand McAllister's finer points, Lori gave him a challenging look. "I hadn't seen Rand for over seven years, but he seems to be the same man I remember from my childhood."

Though his expression didn't change, inwardly

Rand flinched at the hidden meaning in her words.

"There aren't many like him," Ellen told her proudly, and Lori thought, Thank God.

"Would you like to dance?" Roger asked as the musicians struck up another tune, and he whisked Lori out onto the floor.

"Roger's your husband?" Ellen asked Sally.

"Oh, no. Roger's my cousin, but I hope he will soon be Lori's husband."

"Oh, how nice. Are they engaged?"

"Not yet, but I'm sure they will soon." Sally sighed romantically as she watched the attractive pair dance around the room. "They make such a handsome couple. Don't you think so, Rand?"

"They certainly do," he responded flatly, having glanced quickly in their direction. "Would you care to dance, Sally?"

"I'd love to, Rand." She smiled enchantingly at him.

"Ellen, if you'll excuse us?"

"Of course. Enjoy yourselves!"

Rand regarded Sally critically as he drew her out onto the floor. She was a gentle, lovely woman, and he wondered why her sweet presence didn't stir him as the tempestuous Lorelei's did. He gathered her in his arms, and they swept about the room, delightfully in tune to the music and each other.

"Perhaps Sally has finally met the man of her dreams." Roger nodded in the direction of Rand and Sally, and when Lori saw her friend in Rand's arms jealousy, unbidden, stirred within her.

"Rand?" Lori was surprised.

"Why not? McAllister's not a bad sort. I like him. So would you if he hadn't been named your guardian," Roger said sagely.

Lori shrugged noncommittally, "Maybe, but it goes against my grain to have someone who doesn't even know me trying to run my life."

"I think he's been very accommodating." Roger defended Rand for he'd come to like and respect him. "He could easily have forced the issue and made you live at the ranch with Lydia, you know."

Lori's expression was mutinous as she countered, "He could have tried. You know how I feel about leaving the Triple Cross. I won't do it."

"I know it," Roger's tone was less than enthusiastic. "Sometimes I just wish you weren't so determined, Lori. After I almost lost you in the cave-in—"

Her heart softened, but not her resolve. "I'm sorry I can't be what you want me to be, Roger. I truly am."

He didn't say any more, and the subject hung unsettled between them.

Meanwhile, Rand, making a concerted effort not to watch Lorelei dancing with Roger, escorted Sally to the refreshment table. "Punch?"

"Please." She gratefully accepted the cup he offered, smiling a greeting at Lydia who was approaching them.

"Are you having a good time, Sally?" Lydia asked, but her gaze lingered on Rand.

"Yes. Everyone is very friendly. I'm glad you asked us to come with you," Sally responded.

"Lydia? Would you care for a cup of punch?"

"Please, Rand." Lydia smiled seductively at him.

The three of them stood quietly together, enjoying the punch and making small talk, until the music started. Then Lydia turned casually to Rand. "Would you mind dancing with your stepmother?"

"Of course not," he replied gallantly, and setting their glasses aside, he squired her about the floor.

Though she was dancing with Roger, Lori watched surreptitiously as Rand swept Lydia out onto the floor, and she couldn't help but notice the possessive way the other woman touched him or that she gazed up at him in a way that was intimate. Lori's heart contracted painfully as she realized just how cruel fate had been to her. From now on she would be in almost constant contact with Rand, not because of any desire on Rand's part to be with her. He'd told her in no uncertain terms how he felt about their relationship, and she'd believed him. She knew she would have to fight her feelings while trying to maintain some kind of civil behavior toward him. That was not going to be easy, but if he continued to ignore her as completely as he had the last two days, it wouldn't be impossible. Turning away from the disturbing sight of the two of them, she laughed lightly at something Roger had said and pretended to be enjoying herself.

Lydia was in paradise as she rested her hand on Rand's broad shoulder and her flesh tingled at the touch of his strong hand at her waist. She would have loved to lure him out onto the McCreas' dimly lighted patio, share a few heated caresses beneath that romantic sliver of a moon! How she longed to share his bed again, and know his powerful, driving possession!

"You're a wonderful dancer, Rand." Lydia's voice was husky with desire, and he looked down at her sharply.

"So are you," he replied distantly.

"We do well together, you and I," she continued, her hand moving in a slight sensual rhythm on his shoulder as her eyes darkened with remembered passion, but he stiffened at her words. "Don't you remember how it used to be between us?"

"Yes, Lydia, I remember quite clearly, and I also remember that you married my father the moment I left town," he said sharply.

"I thought we'd agreed to put the past behind us and begin anew?"

"You were the one who brought it up, Lydia, not

me," Rand answered indifferently.

"That's true. I did, but only the good part—the part where we couldn't get enough of each other every night we met."

Her tone left no doubt as to the direction of her thoughts, and Rand became eager for the dance to end. He wanted nothing to do with Lydia. He'd been unable to get her to sell out her part of the Lazy Ace, but he had no intention of becoming involved with her.

It occurred to him then that Lorelei was the only woman he wanted and that she would never be his. He scanned the room, and when he saw her with Roger, laughing in seeming delight, his jaw tightened in frustration. Did she really care so much for Westlake that she was going to dance every dance with him?

As Lydia followed the direction of Rand's gaze, she felt the bite of the green-eyed monster. "Worried about Lorelei are you? Is there more to your relationship than guardian and ward?"

"What makes you think that?" he drawled protectively, as he gave her a mocking look.

"Your expression when you look at her and she doesn't know you're watching," she retorted perceptively, remembering when Rand used to look at her that way.

"You're wrong, Lydia. There is nothing between Lorelei and me except antagonism. I've already told you what she thinks about the two of us."

"I may be wrong about you and Lorelei, but is she so far from wrong about us, Rand?" Having broached the subject, she breathlessly awaited his reply.

"What do you mean?"

"I mean, would it be such a terrible thing for us to be lovers again?"

Rand stiffened. "You are my father's widow, Lydia. There will never be any more to our 'relationship' than that."

"But why? Will is dead and we're very much alive." She let her voice drop so there was no mistaking her meaning. "And I know you can't have forgotten how well we go on together in bed."

"You're wrong, Lydia," he ground out tautly. "I have forgotten. I made it a point to forget when I discovered you'd married my father. Now he's dead, but that doesn't mean we will revive what once existed between us. Any feelings I had for you are as dead as he is."

She gasped at his bluntness, and when the music stopped, he strode quickly away from her without a word or a glance, disappearing across the center hall into the den where the men had gathered to gamble and drink.

Cursing herself for rushing him, Lydia tried to maintain a calm exterior as she joined some of her friends.

As nonchalantly as she could, when Roger had gone from her side to get them both a cooling drink, Lorelei searched the crowded room for Rand. She noticed Lydia talking with a small gathering of ladies by the refreshment table, but finding no sign of him anywhere, she felt oddly let down at the realization that he was not nearby.

"Lori!" Sally's nervous whisper interrupted her thoughts, and she turned to her friend with a questioning look.

"What is it? Is something wrong?"

"No . . . he's here!" Sally clasped her hand excitedly. "He just walked in!"

"Who just walked in?" Lori pressed.

"Brady Barclay—and he looks fine. He's over there." She nodded toward the center hall where Brady was conversing with John and Ellen.

Lori's smile was wide. "So he is. Come on, we'll go

266

talk to him."

"No! We can't just walk up to him." Sally held back.

"I don't believe you! Are you the same female who dragged me to all your soireés in St. Louis and practically forced me to dance with all those men I didn't know?"

"I knew them," Sally argued defensively.

"But I didn't, and that didn't stop you!"

"That was different," Sally hedged.

"I fail to see how!" Lori was grinning. "Come along. He looks decidedly uncomfortable. Maybe he doesn't know anyone here, and if he doesn't, he might be eternally grateful if we make the first move."

Stifling a groan, Sally let herself be guided across the room to where Brady stood with their host and hostess.

"Ellen, Sally and I never had the chance to be properly introduced to Mr. Barclay, but we'd both like to thank him for his bravery during the holdup attempt on our stage from Maricopa," Lori stated matter-of-factly her boldness covering Sally's sudden lack of nerve.

"You haven't been introduced. Well, we'll correct that right now. Lorelei Spencer and Sally Westlake, this is Brady Barclay. Brady, Lorelei and Sally." Ellen made the introductions easily.

"How do you do, Mr. Barclay."

"Brady, please, ladies, and may I call you Lorelei and Sally?" Brady ventured, unable to believe his luck. He'd been hoping to learn something about his elusive angel and he couldn't believe that she was actually here.

"Please do," they responded.

"Why don't we get something to drink?" Ellen encouraged as she led the way to the refreshments.

"So, Brady, how are you doing?" Lori asked as she smiled up at him. "Even though the doctor seemed certain you'd recover, we were worried about you when we left the relay station."

"I'm fine," Brady answered. "In a couple of weeks I'll be back on the job."

"Aren't you afraid that you might be robbed again?" Sally was obviously concerned.

The young man's friendly gaze suddenly hardened. "If they do try again, the outcome is going to be different."

For the first time Sally realized what a formidable opponent Brady could be, and she felt respect for him as a man though she feared for his safety.

"Do you think they will make another attempt?" Ellen knew John had been unable to track down this unknown gang and she wondered if Brady had any idea who they might be.

"I don't know," he told her honestly. "I hope not. I hope they're long gone from the territory, but if they aren't, I wouldn't doubt that they'd give it another try when their money runs low."

"Brady. Glad to see you're up and about." Roger greeted the guard as he intercepted them and handed Lori the cup of punch he'd gotten for her.

"Thanks. You were on the stage, weren't you?" He and Roger shook hands.

"Yes. I'm Roger Westlake."

Brady's heart sank. *Damn! Sally was married.* "Nice to meet you," he said. The music was starting up again, so forgetting about the refreshment table, Brady turned quickly to Lori and asked her to dance.

She accepted gracefully, knowing there was no tactful way she could direct his attention to her friend, and, setting her cup aside, went into his arms.

Sally was crushed. Brady had chosen Lori over her! Though she managed to control her expression so it revealed none of her heartbreak, her high spirits died and she was glad when Ellen left to greet some late arrivals leaving her alone with Roger.

"Sally? Is something troubling you?" He noticed how quiet she'd suddenly become.

"No." She gave him her brightest smile, though she watched Lori and Brady out of the corner of her eye. "Dance with me?"

"Only if you promise to watch yourself and not tromp all over my feet!" His eyes twinkled as he remembered when he'd been recruited years ago to help with her dancing lessons.

"I never tromped on you!" she countered, as he led her out onto the dance floor. "You were the one who stepped on me, and intentionally."

He lifted his shoulders in helpless acknowledgment. "The last thing I wanted to do was spend my time dancing with my cousin! So, I thought if I appeared clumsy and oafish, our mothers would let me off the hook."

"You did a good job." Sally grinned.

"At appearing clumsy or teaching you to dance?"

"You decide," she countered as they moved about the floor in perfect harmony.

"Either you learned how to skillfully avoid my tromping feet or you're an excellent dancer."

"If I was angry with you I'd say the first, but I do believe that between your efforts and those of Monsieur Xaupi, I turned out quite well."

"I do believe you did," Roger laughed good-naturedly. "Now, why don't you tell me why it upsets you that Lori is dancing with the Wells Fargo guard?"

Sally glanced up at him sharply. "You know me far too well."

"I should. Now, explain." He was grinning at her discomfiture.

Sally sighed. "I find Brady very . . ."

"Attractive?" Roger's smile widened.

"Yes."

"So?"

"So, he asked Lori to dance." Sally sounded more spiteful than she intended.

"Do you think Lori is interested in him?" Roger looked quickly in the other couple's direction, suddenly seeing Brady as a competitor.

"No, not at all."

"How can you be so sure?"

"Because, I've already told Lori how I felt. She knows I'm interested in Brady, but she couldn't very well turn him down and then say 'Why don't you dance with Sally?'"

"I see your point." He nodded in agreement. "What shall we do?"

"I guess nothing," Sally admitted defeatedly.

"Don't be so quick to give up," Roger chided. "You were the belle of the ball at home. Go after him, if he's the one you want."

"That's your philosophy of life, isn't it?"

"You'd better believe it. Things don't happen unless you make them happen," he answered. "If you want Brady Barclay, then give it your best try. I mean, things can't get any worse than they are now, right?"

Sally took a deep breath and glanced over at Brady. "No, things can't get any worse, and you're absolutely correct. I've been acting like a ninny ever since he walked into the room."

"You have?" Roger chuckled. "Could this be love?"

"Shush," she scolded without anger. "I don't know what this is, but I'm going to follow your advice and see what happens. Now, when this dance is over, I want you to claim Lori."

"The sacrifices I make for you," Roger teased.

"I'm sure you'll survive."

"It'll be a hardship, but I'll manage."

Meanwhile, in the study, Rand drained the mellow bourbon from his tumbler as he watched the card game in progress. Josh Taylor had taken the betting to the limit and the other gamblers were folding, not wanting to risk more heavy losses than those they'd already suffered at his hands. When his last opponent had conceded, Josh victoriously raked in the money, and after pocketing it, he joined Rand for a drink.

"You aren't a gambler, Rand?" Josh asked as he took a deep swallow of the potent brew.

"Only when the occasion calls for it."

"It's a wise man who knows the odds and plays them well," the banker remarked, but Rand didn't bother to reply. "How are things going for you? I understand that you'll be staying on for a while."

"It looks that way."

"Will you be living at the ranch or the Triple Cross?" Though Josh knew the answer, he didn't want Rand to suspect him of being too well informed.

"The way things are working out, I'll be living at the mine for the time being."

"You won't be staying at the Lazy Ace?" Josh tried to sound surprised.

"No. Jack Barlow will be running the ranch for me while I concentrate on the Triple Cross."

"I find this news reassuring. You know, of course, that I hold the loan on the mine. I can't tell you how good it is to know that someone like you is going to be in charge. Lorelei is knowledgeable to a certain extent, but she is, after all, only a woman."

Rand found the man's remarks highly irritating, but he didn't quite understand why. "Lorelei is most capable, and she will be taking an active part in the running of the Triple Cross," he retorted.

"I'm sure George taught her well, but some situations call for a man, if you know what I mean. Do you

271

plan on remaining there long?"

"As her guardian, I am responsible for her inheritance until she marries or turns twenty-one."

"I see." Josh paused, affecting thoughtful consideration. "I feel much more comfortable about the fate of the loan now that I know you're involved. I can't tell you how nervous I was when Lorelei returned and informed me that she was going to run the mine. I've got a lot of money invested in the Triple Cross, and that news left me a bit unnerved. Why, I even offered to buy her out, but she refused."

Rand understood the banker's distress. "She's a determined young woman, but I think that very quality will help her succeed."

"I certainly hope you're right. This is too important a venture to risk through incompetence, no matter how well intended."

"You don't have to worry, you'll have your money in plenty of time," Rand was becoming annoyed. "Now, if you'll excuse me, I think I'll return to the dancing."

"Of course, good to talk with you." As Josh watched Rand walk away, his eyes narrowed with hatred. He was not going to let McAllister ruin his plans to take over the Triple Cross and win Lydia.

Rand surveyed the dancers with a casualness that belied the tension in the pit of his stomach. Noting that Lorelei was dancing with the guard from the stagecoach and she appeared to have a wonderful time, he fought down an overwhelming need he felt to tear her from the arms of Barclay. He knew he did not have the right, guardian though he might be.

Letting his gaze roam slowly about the room, Rand noted that Sally and Roger were dancing, and Lydia was standing alone near the double doors that led out to the McCrea's small courtyard. Not wanting to return to the study where Taylor lingered, yet unwilling to encourage Lydia's desire to revive their relationship, he made his way to John's side and joined him in conversation with several of the townfolk. All the while, however, he kept a nearly undetectable, yet steadfast, watch on Lorelei.

Lydia noticed Rand's return to the parlor, and thinking that he'd come back to talk with her, she was thoroughly disappointed when he walked over to John. From beneath lowered lashes, she observed with interest the direction of Rand's gaze as he socialized with the small group, and a blazing fury grew within her when it became clear that he had eyes only for the red-haired witch!

What she'd suspected from the beginning had to be true! He did feel something for that little vixen! Lydia glanced over at the younger woman, studying her with a critical regard. What could he possibly see in her? She was tall, much taller than herself, and that hair . . . Lydia grimaced with distaste for she found Lorelei's natural hair color brazen. How could Rand find such a woman attractive?

Stymied, she became coldly calculating. Rand had lied to her about his feeling for Lorelei. That was now obvious, but he'd already admitted that Lorelei had no use for him and Lydia intended to see that that state of affairs didn't change. Lorelei suspected she was Rand's lover, so she would play up that angle. If she couldn't have Rand, nobody would. Turning away to get herself a drink, she began to plot the best way to keep Lorelei and Rand apart.

As the music ended, Brady led Lori back to the side of the dance floor, engaging her in easy conversation. He thought her a most attractive woman and he regretted that he didn't feel more for her than just a mild interest. However, he'd dreamed too long of his elusive angel. Now reality had ruined the dream. Sally

Westlake was already taken, and as much as he regretted that, he understood. It seemed logical that, lovely as she was, some other man would have claimed her. Since he had not had an opportunity to thank her for her tender care while he'd been recovering, he looked about the parlor for her as he spoke with Lori.

"Are you looking for someone?" Lori asked, hoping against hope that it was Sally he was looking for.

"No, no one in particular." He shrugged, not wanting to reveal his innermost thoughts.

"Oh, here are Sally and Roger," she said quickly as she saw them approaching.

"Really?" Brady brightened considerably and Lori sensed more in his response than a passing interest.

"I've never seen you two dance before," Lori remarked as the Westlakes drew near.

"We did quite well, don't you think?" Roger quipped.

"You seemed very adept," Lori agreed.

Knowing that Sally wanted to be alone with Brady, Roger invited Lori to dance and she accepted quickly, allowing him to sweep her away as the music began again.

"Perfect timing." She smiled as they moved away.

"I hope so," he answered. "I've never known Sally to be this interested in anyone, so I thought I'd better help things along a little."

"She really does care for Brady."

"It's hard to explain love, I guess. There's no way of knowing when it will strike."

"You make it sound like a dreaded disease or, worse yet, a snake!" Lori laughed.

"It can be painful, Lori." Roger's mood was suddenly less than light-hearted, and somewhat nervously he suggested, "Why don't we go out onto the patio? It's getting warm in here." Without waiting for

274

her consent, he maneuvered them quickly out into the moonlight.

Alone, they walked in silence across the tiled courtyard to the small fountain that splashed in its center.

"Lori . . ." Roger's tone was husky with emotion as he pulled her into his arms and kissed her.

She wanted to respond, wanted to feel the excitement she knew with Rand, but no driving emotion surged through her, no dazzling, breathtaking need banished all thoughts of resistance from her mind. Roger was kissing her, and that was pleasant and nice and . . . Suddenly Lori became furious with herself.

"Roger . . . no." She pushed him away just as he tried to deepen the embrace.

"No?" He looked down at her, his frustration evident. "I don't understand just what it is you want from me, Lori."

"Roger, I—"

"You what?" he demanded icily, his usual good nature deserting him. "The day you were rescued, you seemed so glad to see me. You gave me hope that we might have a future together, but, Lori, I'm beginning to think accompanying you to Arizona was a big mistake. I'm at a point where I don't really believe we have any basis for a marriage. Perhaps following you here was a flight of fancy on my part."

"Roger—"

He cut her off. "No. Don't say a word. I think it's best if I leave the party now. I'm sure Rand will see you back to the hotel." He left her then, departing without returning to the house.

Lori stood unmoving in the center of the patio, stunned by what had just passed. She had never known Roger to lose his temper, and she was shaken by the change that had come over him.

When Rand had seen Roger and Lori go outside, jealousy seared his soul. As casually as he could, he made his way toward the door, avoiding Lydia, and he stepped out into the darkness just as Roger kissed Lori. He then saw Roger stalk away from her, and when she started back toward the house several minutes later, he stepped out from the shadows to block her path.

"Rand! What are you doing here?" Lori was shocked and dismayed to find herself with him in the moonlit garden. All night he'd ignored her, and in the face of his indifference, she had managed to maintain an outward calm, but not . . . What was he doing out here in the garden, alone?

Rand shrugged. "I saw my ward go out into the night with a man, unchaperoned, and I thought I'd better keep an eye on things."

"Of all the arrogant, high-handed—"

"Now, now. You're a lady, remember?" Rand's grin was deceptively lazy. "And I *am* your guardian."

Lori was seething. It was embarrassing that he'd witnessed the kiss she'd shared with Roger and their subsequent argument, but his proclamation of guardianship was more than she could stand.

"Roger's a good man, Lorelei," Rand went on, gesturing easily in the direction Westlake had taken. "You're a fool to let him get away like that. Unless, that is, you've just been using him all this time."

"Mind your own business," she snapped.

"Your business is my business," he countered. "I'm responsible for you. Have you forgotten?"

"I wish I could forget! You are only interested in Roger because you wish me to marry so you can be relieved of your 'duties'! Well, I've told you before, I don't need you and—"

Rand's control snapped at her cutting words, and he took her by the arms, crushing her to his chest as his

276

lips found hers.

Time stood still as his mouth plundered hers, ravaging its sweetness and leaving no doubt as to his possession of her. They stood clasped in a desperate embrace, each fighting the power of the emotions that threatened to engulf them and sweep them away from all contact with reality. Only Sally's call put an end to the madness that erupted when they touched, for hearing it, Lori broke away from Rand, then stared up at him with wide, almost frightened, eyes.

"Sally! Rand and I are over here," she responded quickly.

Within moments Sally joined them, Brady at her side. "Have you seen Roger? I am looking for him."

"He left the party, Sally." Lori wanted to explain further, but Rand's and Brady's presence prevented her from revealing what had happened. "He said he'd see us at the hotel."

"Oh." Sally frowned and Brady tensed at this news.

"Lori and I were just about to go back inside and enjoy our first dance together." Rand took Lori's arm, and when she attempted to pull free, he exerted enough pressure to prevent her from doing so.

"We'll join you," Brady said.

Realizing that she must follow Rand's lead, Lori allowed him to escort her back into the parlor, where she almost groaned aloud for a waltz had just begun. Rand's expression was wooden as he drew her into his arms, and as they moved onto the dance floor, Lori held herself stiffly away from him.

"You look scared to death," he snarled under his breath. "Do you want everyone to wonder exactly what went on out there in the garden? You go out with one man and you come back in with another? Smile, damn it! Act like you're having a wonderful time."

"I don't need you to tell me how to act!" Lori argued,

277

but even as she spoke, she knew that he was right. Forcing herself to relax as they waltzed about the room, she found herself responding to the lilting music and to the joy of being held in his arms. It was a magical moment, and when the music came to an end, she blinked up at Rand in stunned surprise. How could she have forgotten herself so completely, and in front of all these people?

"Thank you for the dance," Rand remarked with an off-handedness that hurt, and Lori could manage only a brittle smile before she walked away from him.

"You're welcome."

Brady and Sally had been partners in the waltz, and when it ended, he'd asked her if she'd like something to drink."

"No, thank you, but I would love to sit down and rest for a few minutes."

He agreed, and they found two seats in an uncrowded corner of the room. "I've been wanting to thank you for all you did for me at the relay station."

"There's no need for thanks," Sally demurred sweetly. "I was glad to be able to help."

Brady fell silent, wondering what to talk about next. He questioned his own foolishness in staying with Sally for she was a married woman, but somehow he couldn't bring himself to leave her, especially now that her husband had gone off and left her alone at the party. He thought it quite odd that she hadn't been upset when Roger had gone out onto the patio with Lorelei, and he wasn't quite sure what to make of the entire situation. If he were married, he wouldn't be so nonchalant if his wife went outside with another man, especially if his wife was Sally. Why, he'd protect her and cherish her and never let her out of his sight. . . .

"Brady, is something wrong?" Sally had noticed his sudden fierce expression and she wondered at the cause.

"What?" He'd been so immersed in his thoughts that he'd momentarily forgotten where he was. "Oh, yes. Everything's fine."

"You're sure? You looked so worried."

Brady was embarrassed. "No, I wasn't worried. I was concerned about Roger going off and leaving you like this. Would you like me to escort you home when the party is over? I hate to think of you making the trip back to your hotel alone."

"That's very kind of you." She smiled sweetly. "I'd like that, although I didn't come just with Roger. Lori and Rand were with us and Rand's stepmother, Lydia."

"Oh."

"But I would enjoy your company on the walk back," Sally said quickly, emboldened by his offer.

"Well, good." He was perplexed by her encouragement. "But won't Roger mind?"

"Roger?" Sally frowned. "No. I doubt it. Why should he?"

"Well, if you were married to me, I certainly wouldn't go off and leave you alone at a party and then let another man escort you home!"

Sally's smile was bright for she finally understood his confusion. He thought Roger was her husband. That was probably the reason he'd asked Lori to dance first! Filled with a light-hearted joy, she asked, "You wouldn't?"

"Look, I've spoken out of turn." Discomfited by his revealing outburst, Brady suddenly wanted to get away. Standing, he said quickly, "I think maybe I'd better be going."

The realization that he was about to walk out of her life forever motivated Sally to act and she reached to him. "Brady, Roger is my cousin, not my husband."

"What?" The news totally stunned him.

"I'm not married, nor have I ever been."

"You and Roger—"

"Are not married."

Brady grinned sheepishly as he slowly sank back down onto his chair, "But I thought—"

"I know. Lydia thought the same thing when we were first introduced. I'm sorry I didn't make it clear to you earlier that Roger and I are not husband and wife."

"You're cousins?"

Sally nodded, her eyes aglow as she watched his expression change.

"Would you like to dance again, Miss Westlake?"

"I'd love to, Brady. Thank you." Her smile was an enraptured one.

# *Chapter Sixteen*

Lydia had been curious when she'd watched Rand disappear into the courtyard earlier and furtively she'd followed him. She had taken care to keep out of sight so that Rand had no knowledge of her presence, and she'd been livid when her clandestine surveillance had yielded far more than she'd ever hoped to discover. Her suspicions had been confirmed. She knew now that it was Lorelei Rand wanted, and despite what he had told her about the girl's supposed dislike for him, Lydia could tell that Lorelei wanted Rand.

Angrily Lydia had wondered if Rand had already introduced the chit to the joys of his lovemaking, and after watching them dance together when they'd come back inside, she'd decided that he had. The way they had moved together and the expression on Lorelei's face as she'd practically floated about the room in Rand's arms had left no doubt in Lydia's mind that they had known one another intimately.

The realization that Rand would never be hers again filled Lydia with a terrible desire to hurt him and Lorelei. No longer did she care about driving a wedge between them in the hope that Rand would come back to her. If she couldn't have his love, she didn't want

Lorelei to have him. Somehow, she would find a way to wreak vengeance upon them both.

Roger sat at a secluded table in the back of the Gold Nugget Saloon concentrating solely on getting drunk. Though beer was his usual fare, tonight he had needed something more potent so he'd ordered a full bottle of the barkeep's best bourbon to aid him in his quest for forgetfulness. Tilting the now half-full bottle to the rim of his tumbler, he refilled his glass and then slowly set the bottle aside. With measured movements, he lifted the tumbler to his lips and took a deep drink, enjoying the burning sensation as the bourbon seared its way to his stomach.

Enveloped in a liquor-induced, semilogical haze, Roger was pensive as he considered his situation. After another large swallow from his glass, he was pleased to note that his emotions did not seem quite so distressingly powerful as they had half an hour ago, and he smiled in appreciation of the bourbon's potent effect. The pain that had tormented him since he'd left Lori at the party had driven him to the saloon and he was glad that he'd dulled it.

Roger stared blankly about the raucous, crowded bar as he tried to decide what course of action he should take. He had diligently avoided coming to a decision for some time, but he now realized, regretfully, that there was no point in staying on here any longer. He had his own life to live, and he could no longer justify remaining with Lori when it was painfully obvious that she had little real need for him. She liked him, he knew that, but she did not love him, and Roger wanted her love.

As frustration welled up anew inside him, Roger was tempted to smash his glass against the wall, but having no desire to draw unwanted attention to himself, he simply refilled it.

Accept it, Roger silently lectured himself. For the first time in your life, you've lost, and you don't know why. He loved Lori more than he'd ever loved any woman, yet that hadn't been enough for her. He'd left a flourishing law practice to accompany her here to settle her father's estate, and he'd been patient in helping her with the mine. He'd professed his love, and he'd probably done it so often his behavior must have bordered on the ludicrous as far as Lori was concerned for she never had returned the emotion.

He had loved in vain, Roger concluded bitterly, and unrequited love bred cynicism even in the most stout-hearted of men. Something that had never existed in the first place, except in his own mind, was over, and the sooner he acknowledged it the better. Tomorrow after they returned to the mine, he would speak with Lori and tell her everything—that he loved her, that he wanted her, but that he had a life of his own so he could no longer sit idly by and wait for her to make a decision. He was going home to resume his law practice, and if she ever decided that she wanted him, she would know where to find him.

Roger raised his glass in a silent toast to himself. Then he drained the contents. Taking the bottle with him, Roger stood up and slowly made his way from the saloon, his decision made.

It was late as he staggered down the hotel's dimly lighted hallway and paused unsteadily before the door to his room, trying to get out the key and let himself in. For some reason, which at that moment he could not fathom, the key would not fit properly into the lock so he maneuvered down the hall to Sally's room and knocked loudly on the door, seeking to enlist her help.

"Who is it?" was her frightened response.

283

"It's me. Open up," he called out, and Sally quickly unlocked her door. Grabbing him by the arm before he woke everyone in the hotel, she dragged him inside.

"Roger! Where have you been? I've been worried about you! You left the party hours ago, and you weren't in your room." Sally stood before him, dressed in a long, sedate dressing gown, her hands on her hips, her usually gentle temper aroused by his strange behavior.

"Ah, Sal, I wish Lori felt as you do," he muttered downheartedly.

"I'm sure she does," Sally began, but he cut her off coldly.

"I don't believe it for a minute, Sal." Roger sat down wearily on the edge of her bed. "She doesn't care about me. I realized that tonight and it's hard to accept, you know?"

Sally moved to stand beside him, then touched his shoulder in gentle understanding. "Surely, you're wrong. Lori loves you. You're going to be married, aren't you?"

He looked up at her, his gaze focusing sharply on her concerned features. "No, Sal. We aren't."

"You're talking gibberish and you're very drunk, Roger Westlake." She tried to chide him out of his black mood, but Roger had, at last, accepted the truth and he knew his cousin should be made aware of it.

"I know I'm drunk, but I also know exactly how things stand between Lori and me. She doesn't love me. She never has, and I can't fault her for that."

"I don't understand."

"It's not difficult." He tilted the bottle of whiskey to his lips and drank deeply. "I should never have followed her here. She doesn't love me, Sally. She's never told me that she did and she's never accepted my proposal, though, God knows, I offered to marry her

284

often enough."

"She hasn't?" Sally was completely surprised. "I thought you had an understanding."

"We had an understanding, all right," Roger remarked sardonically. "I understood from the beginning that she didn't love me. Oh sure, she liked me well enough, but love . . . Well, anyway, being a suave man about town, I was confident that I could win her." He shrugged. "I freely admit that I was wrong. We don't always get what we want in life, Sal."

"Roger . . ." Sally sat down beside him and slipped an arm about his broad shoulders. "I'm sorry. I didn't know."

"I can't stay here any longer," he went on, swigging again from the near-empty bottle. "I'm going to tell Lori tomorrow that it's time I headed home."

She nodded slowly, her own thoughts in turmoil. She and Brady had just passed a wonderful evening together and she felt as if she were on the brink of some wonderful discovery with him and now . . . "I'll go with you."

Roger glanced at her, confused. "Are you sure? What about Barclay? I thought maybe he was the one for you."

Sally turned away. "I don't know for sure. We did get along really well tonight, after he discovered you were my cousin and not my husband, that is." She smiled at him over her shoulder.

"Ah." Roger nodded sagely. "That explains a lot."

"I know, but it doesn't matter. If you're going, then I should go with you."

"I don't see that, Sal," he argued. "I'm sure Lori needs you. She has no one else to talk to, and you are her best friend."

"Still, my parents—"

"I'll explain everything to them. With Rand and

285

Lydia acting as chaperones, there's no reason for you to leave. I've made this decision based on my needs. My choice shouldn't influence you. Besides, when you do come back home, you might just bring a fiancé with you." He smiled, but his smile wavered and disappeared as he remembered his own dreams of just a month ago.

Sally's heart ached for her cousin, but she knew there was nothing she could do to ease the pain he was feeling. "Come on. Let's get you to your room."

"Yeah," he muttered, getting to his feet. "I think I need to lie down for a while."

"I'm sure you do," she suppressed a smile as she imagined the headache he was going to have in the morning. Then, placing a helping arm about his waist, she guided him from her room, not noticing that Lydia's door was just closing as they stepped out into the hall.

Lydia stared up at Josh excitedly as they stood stock-still just inside the door to her room. "That was close!" she whispered.

"I agree." He smiled widely as he stepped closer to her. "But perhaps getting caught together would be worth it."

"What do you mean?"

"I mean, if our love affair was open knowledge, it would be in our best interest to marry right away, especially since you've officially given up mourning your dear departed." He drew her into his arms and Lydia went willingly.

"I suppose you're right, but I'd rather people didn't think I'd been coerced into marrying."

"Darling"—Josh's voice was deep with emotion—"I would never coerce you into anything. I want you to come willingly to my bed."

"Oh, Josh." She sighed, feigning passion, but she

was thinking of vengeance against Rand and Lorelei, not of lovemaking. However, she knew she had to act the part of the wanton, eager lover to keep Josh enamored of her. He had promised her wealth and security as soon as his mysterious plans came to fruition, and she was not about to throw away that chance for happiness now that she'd lost Rand. Moving from Josh's arms, she slipped off her dressing gown and led him to her bed, drawing him down with her onto its wide softness. "Love me, Josh. Please love me."

Josh needed no further encouragement, and he responded with hot-blooded ardor to her passionate request, pressing heated kisses upon her throat and bared bosom. Lydia arched against him, urging him on. She wanted to please him, to arouse him, to make him her sensual slave; and her frenetic movements did just that, spiraling Josh's excitement to a fever pitch. He rolled away from her only long enough to shed his own clothing, and when he returned to her heated embrace, Lydia caressed him brazenly, teasing him to the heights with her expertise. Then he came to her, and she took him deep within her body. They mated in a heated frenzy and they reached the pinnacle together, their peaking excitement bursting upon them in shattering splendor. Finally, their passion spent, they lay in one another's arms, replete.

Later, when they finally stirred, Josh shifted so he lay at Lydia's side. Bracing himself upon one elbow, he stared down at her blond beauty.

"I never tire of looking at you, Lydia. You're perfect in every way," he said huskily as he leaned over to kiss her lightly.

"You make me feel beautiful, Josh." She smiled at him. "I can't wait until we can be together like this always." It was the first time she'd brought up the subject of a lasting relationship and Josh was delighted.

"It won't be long, love. By September everything should be settled."

"September?" she frowned, wondering what September had to do with anything.

Josh would have liked to confide his plan to Lydia for she was, after all, the woman he loved, but a niggling suspicion that she harbored some feeling for Rand kept him from doing so.

"In September I will have all the money we'll ever need, my love, and then we can be together."

"Why do we have to wait? What is this great secret of yours that delays our happiness. I want us to be together now."

"But what about McAllister?" The accusing words were out before Josh realized it.

"Rand? What about him?" Lydia asked innocently.

"Just yesterday in my office you were angry because he was going to leave you all alone at the ranch. That made me wonder about your feelings for him and for me, and then tonight at the party . . ." Josh's gaze hardened as he remembered the way Lydia had looked at Rand.

"What about tonight at the party?"

"You looked at him as if you wanted him, Lydia," Josh stated bluntly.

She was surprised that he could read her so well, but she had no intention of letting him know just how close he'd come to the truth.

Reaching up, she caressed his chest and then pulled his head down for a kiss. "I'm glad I fooled you, Josh, for if I can fool the man I love, then no one else will guess the truth."

"Guess what?" He moved away from her, not quite sure he should believe her.

"That I hate Rand McAllister with all my heart and I

wish he'd never come back," she hissed, her vehemence taking Josh by surprise.

"What?" He was astonished.

"I despise the man. He's treated me abominably ever since I married his father, and things have only gotten worse. When he first got back, he wanted me off the Lazy Ace! He even tried to buy me out!" Lydia pretended to be outraged, and she did not mention that Rand's offer for her share of the ranch had been more than generous. "That ranch has been my home. I didn't want to leave it." She added slyly, "At least not until I can be with you, Josh."

"Lydia . . ." He wished he could take her away from all her heartache.

"And that's not all. Despite my opposition, he threatened to bring that disgusting Lorelei Spencer to the ranch to live! Thank heaven, she refused."

"Why didn't you tell me all of this before?"

"I didn't want to trouble you with my problems. I thought I could handle everything, but now I find myself completely under his control. He owns sixty percent of the ranch so I must abide by his decisions."

"My darling, you should have told me how you felt about Rand and Lorelei."

"Why? What difference would it have made? As things are now, neither of us has the resources to live as we should. I suppose we'll have to wait until your plan works out."

"My plan, my love, is directly related to your stepson and his ward."

"What?" She was astonished. She had hoped to enlist his aid in dealing with Rand, and she was caught off guard by discovering that Josh's covert plan involved him.

"Now that I know how you feel, I can tell you everything."

"What you're planning has to do with the Lazy Ace?"

"No, Lydia. I've no interest in ranching. I'm after the real thing—gold—and I mean to acquire it by gaining title of the Triple Cross Mine in September."

"Lorelei's mine . . ." She was enthralled at the prospect of that girl losing everything.

"Indeed. You see I made a good-size loan to George Spencer some time ago and there's a six-month payback on it. Lorelei Spencer has to pay up by September or forfeit ownership." His smile had a feral quality about it.

"How utterly delightful." Lydia pulled Josh down for a kiss. "How clever you are! How in the world are you going about it?"

"I have my ways. I don't intend for anyone to be injured, but I'll slow down the work at the mine so it will be impossible for them to meet her deadline."

"Did you arrange George's and Will's deaths?" Lydia asked quickly.

"No. That little concidence was pure luck." He kissed her shoulder and then looked up to meet her gaze. "But you must admit that fate was on my side that day. As a result of that 'accident,' I have you and I'm almost certain to have the mine." Josh paused and then frowned as he thought of Rand. "My only worry right now is Rand McAllister."

"Because of his interest in the mine?"

"Yes. I spoke with him briefly tonight, and although he revealed very little, he does seem intent on making it work."

"I'm certain of that." Lydia sneered. "And all because of that stupid Spencer girl. Can you imagine him leaving his job temporarily to go live at the mine?"

"Do you really care what Rand does?" Josh asked astutely.

"No." Her tone was deadly. "In fact, lately I've been

wishing the damned Benton brothers would get him."

"The Benton brothers?"

"I guess you haven't heard."

"Heard what?"

"Several years ago, Rand put them away, but they've just escaped from prison. According to John McCrea, they've sworn revenge on Rand and are gunning for him."

Again Josh smiled as he thought of now nicely everything would turn out if Rand met with an untimely demise. "It certainly would be tragic if they managed to catch up with him, wouldn't it?"

"What are you thinking?"

"Oh, nothing definite, but if the Bentons killed Rand, you'd have sole ownership of the ranch and Lorelei Spencer would be in dire straits. Of course, we'd still have to wait until September to claim the mine, but—"

"Unless Lorelei happened to meet the same fate as Rand," Lydia crowed excitedly. "Do you realize that if she and Rand both fell into the hands of the Bentons, I'd inherit the mine as well as the ranch?"

Josh's eyes glittered at the prospect. "I wonder . . ."

"The Bentons, we have to locate them. Do you have any contacts who might know where they're hiding out?"

"A few." Josh smiled coldly as he pulled her into his embrace. "My dear, very soon we are going to be rich."


Rand lay upon his bed in the hotel room, his arms crossed behind his head, staring into the darkness. The heat was oppressive and despite the fact that he'd shed his shirt, the room was stifling.

Still, the sweltering heat wasn't all that bothered Rand as he lay there. Thoughts of Lorelei had been plaguing him since he'd seen her to her room at the end of the evening, and he wondered what was he going to do about her. He had managed to ignore her until he'd seen her in Roger's arms, but when he'd watched them embrace, he'd experienced a driving need to claim her as his own. Even knowing how she truly felt about him had not tempered the force of his desire, and if Sally hadn't interrupted them when she did, he might have thrown caution to the winds and made love to Lorelei right there on the patio.

*Made love to her?* He focused on that thought. Was this love? This maddening need to have her for his own, this crazy jealousy that possessed him every time he saw her with another man? His feeling for Lydia had been strong years ago, but it was negligible compared to the emotions Lori aroused.

With stark clarity, Rand suddenly knew he loved Lorelei Spencer. She was fiercely independent and could be totally frustrating at times, but when she surrendered to him, he found bliss and beauty in their union. The joy of her love was something that he'd never experienced before, and he could never live without it.

Rand slowly realized that he was going to have to overcome Lorelei's hatred of him. It would not be easy, he would take one step at a time. He knew he'd gone out of his way to be cruel tonight when he'd taunted her about Roger and then kissed her against her will, but all that was going to change. No longer would he force his attentions on her. They would be together at the mine from now on so it would be next to impossible for her to avoid him. He would first work to convince her that there was nothing between himself and Lydia, and that accomplished, he'd begin to build some kind of relationship with her.

292

Rand thought briefly of Roger, but having witnessed the other man's argument with Lorelei in the courtyard, he knew there was little chance she would marry him. He was certain that Lorelei did not love Roger, and now that he was sure Roger had no claim to her affections, he intended to win her himself.

Everything suddenly seemed so clear, so simple, that Rand felt relaxed, and closing his eyes, he was soon asleep.

Lori lay awake feeling quite ashamed of herself. Rand had been cruel, but he'd also been right when he'd accused her of using Roger. Much as she hated to admit it, it was true. Roger was a dear friend and she respected him, but she had led him on, letting him hope that at some time in the future she might come to return his love. She had been wrong to do it, and regardless of how difficult it was going to be, at the first opportunity she would tell him the truth about her feelings. It pained her to think that she was going to say things that would hurt Roger, but Lori felt it was now necessary to be forthright.

Silently, she chided herself for thinking she could have married Roger just to be rid of Rand. Regardless of their situation as guardian and ward, she would not have been able to forget the thrill of Rand's kisses, the enthralling joy of his lovemaking. It would have been a major mistake to have entered into such a marriage and she was glad that she had not done so. Despite the fact that Roger did love her, she would not have been doing him a favor marrying him when she secretly loved another.

Her decision to be honest with Roger would not help her as far as Rand was concerned, but it would certainly lessen the guilt she was feeling over Roger's unfaltering devotion and her inability to respond to him. Curling on her side, she tried to relax, and when sleep did come the memory of her waltz with Rand floated into her thoughts. Lori sighed, her lips curving in rapturous remembrance.

# Chapter Seventeen

"Well? Where did ya go?" Cody asked as Pat slipped back into their camp near dawn. "I was gettin' worried."

"I've been down by the mine takin' a look around. You know there ain't no way we're gonna be able to get McAllister with all them people around. I was tryin' to find a place where I think we can take him without drawin' any attention."

"And? Did you find anything?"

"I think so. Pat settled in beside his brother. "You know that new building they're puttin' up?"

Cody nodded.

"Well, it's away from the main buildings, so if we can surprise him, I think we can get him out of there without anybody seein' us."

"Good," Cody answered, his eagerness obvious. "I can't wait to get my hands on that bastard. I'm gonna make him pay for what he done to Matt and to us."

"We're both gonna enjoy that." Pat's smile reflected his grim determination to even the score with Rand.

Harley Oates was becoming frustrated. He'd hoped

the cave-in would close down the mine for quite a while, but Hal and Cam had had the miners work round-the-clock shifts, and the newly dug drift had been cleaned out and reinforced in record time. Last night the crew boss had announced that at dawn they would once again begin to work the rich, new vein.

Harley knew that Taylor would be furious when he learned that the mine was back in operation. He would want more "accidents," but Harley hadn't been able to think of something that would seem plausible. If too many things happened in a short period of time, Harley did not doubt that someone would get suspicious, and he had no desire to get caught sabotaging a mine. When a traitor was found in their midst, miners' justice was swift and deadly. Harley did not want to repay his debt to Taylor with his life. He owed the man, but not that much.

Moving to the doorway of his tent, he stared out across the predawn darkness, trying to come up with an idea, and it was then, when he noticed the skeletal silhouette of the stamp mill against the slowly brightening sky, that a thought came to him. What better way to force the mine into default than to destroy the stamp mill before it could even begin to operate. The owners would lose everything they'd invested in it, and they'd be forced to keep paying to ship the ore overland to the other mill. Pleased that he'd thought of this approach, Harley began to consider the means by which he could arrange to destroy that structure.

Lori smiled wanly at Sally as her friend made another effort to strike up a conversation. The ride from town had been long and tedious, for both Rand and Roger had been distant and unwilling to talk, preferring, for some reason, to make the long trek in comparative silence.

Lori had not expected such a reaction from Roger. She had known him for so long that she'd expected his natural good humor to reassert itself, and she was dismayed to find that he'd had very little to say to her that morning when they'd saddled up and left town. Sally had been quick to confide to Lori that Roger had had too much to drink the night before and was now suffering the aftermath of his foolishness, but knowing there was much more to his solemn mood than a hangover, Lori girded herself for the confrontation she anticipated once they'd reached the mine.

Rand's detached manner did not surprise her, although his refusal to accept Lydia's offer to stay at the Lazy Ace did. She had thought that he would be eager to spend one last night with his lover before moving in at the Triple Cross, but she was glad that he'd refused. That meant she wouldn't have to argue the point and, if necessary, continue on alone. She really felt she'd been away from the mine far too long already.

"At last." Lori breathed a heavy sigh of relief as she caught sight of the Triple Cross.

"It's certainly been a long ride." Sally, too, was feeling weary after her seemingly endless hours in the saddle.

Neither man chose to comment as they rode into camp, and Rand didn't even bother to stop in front of Lori's home but continued on to join Hal and Cam who were standing together near the mine entrance. Roger, however, reined in with Sally and Lori.

"Lori . . ." he said determinedly.

"Yes?" She had already dismounted, so she glanced back up at him questioningly.

"I'd like to speak with you in private for a few

minutes, if you don't mind."

His words, so formal and carefully chosen, chilled her and she nodded slowly. "Of course. Do you want to come in now?"

"Fine," Roger agreed, swinging down from his horse.

"I'll go see how Hal is doing," Sally put in quickly, and she headed off toward the mine entrance as Roger followed Lori inside.

Roger closed the door behind them, but he remained standing. He wanted only to say what he had to say and then make his arrangements to depart.

"Lori, I've been giving serious consideration to the conversation we had last night and there are a few things I have to say."

"I need to talk with you, too, Roger, I—"

"Please. Don't interrupt me. Not now." His dark-eyed gaze pierced her, committing to memory the beauty of her features and the tumbling wind-tousled glory of her hair. "I've done a lot of thinking, Lori, and I've come to some conclusions. I'm leaving here. I'll be packing tonight and at first light, I'll be heading back into town."

"Roger!" Lori was stunned and saddened.

"No, don't say anything, Lori. This is the way it has to be," he couldn't stop himself from walking toward her and almost against his will, he reached out and rested both of his hands on her slender shoulders as he gazed down at her fondly. "I know you don't love me." When she would have protested, he shook his head to silence her and gave her a wry smile. "It's all right. It took me long enough to realize it. I should have known better, but I'd never been involved with anyone like you before, and I kept thinking that things would change . . . that somehow you would come to love me. I was wrong. I've discovered that you can't make someone love you. It either happens or it doesn't. Love is not something you can turn on or off at your discretion." Roger brushed a soft kiss on her cheek before moving slightly away from her. "You're a gorgeous, wonderful woman, Lorelei Spencer and I still love you with all my heart, but I can't stay here any longer. I left my practice—my entire life—behind. I've got to go back."

"Roger, I'm so sorry," her eyes were brimming with unshed tears. Everything he'd just said was true; she knew it.

"There's nothing to be sorry about, Lori." He shrugged as he started for the door. "But if you ever need me, all you have to do is send word." Roger paused and then turned back to her, his hand on the doorknob. "Remember that."

"Thank you," she whispered. "I will, Roger. I'll remember it always."

He nodded slowly before he departed, silently closing the door behind him.

Sally saw him leave and she hurried to his side as he strode purposefully toward the quarters he was sharing with Hal and Rand. "Roger, how did it go? Did she change your mind?" she asked hopefully.

Though Roger smiled, his eyes reflected the sadness and pain within his heart. "No, Sal. She didn't even try."

"Oh, Roger." Sally sounded so miserable that he slipped a comforting arm around her waist.

"Hey, we're both better off this way. I've told her exactly how I feel, and I know exactly how she feels. I also told her if she ever needed me all she had to do was let me know."

"You're a good man, Roger. The woman who marries you is going to be one lucky girl."

"Right," he drawled. "All I have to do is find her, and right now that's something I don't even want to consider."

"You'll find her one day, when you least expect to," Sally promised him, but he shook his head in denial.

"Frankly, I think I've had enough of 'love' to last me a lifetime. I'm heading home first thing in the morning, and when I get there I'm going to develop the most successful law practice St. Louis has ever seen."

"Good for you." She smiled up at him as they reached the supervisor's house. "Need any help with your packing?"

"No. I'll manage. Why don't you go see how Lori is? I didn't give her much of a chance to say anything, but then there wasn't really anything to say, was there?"

"I will, and we'll talk more later."

Sally found Lori sitting on her bed staring out the window when she returned to the house. "Feel like talking?" she asked quietly.

Lori's welcoming smile was strained as she faced her friend, but Sally ventured to sit beside her. "How's Roger?"

"He'll be fine, don't worry."

"I never wanted to hurt him, Sally, but I'm afraid I've done just that," Lori told her softly.

"I know you didn't want to hurt him, and he knows that. We just can't make some things happen, no matter how good our intentions are."

Lori nodded, "Roger is so sweet and I do care about him . . ."

"But that's no basis for a lifelong commitment, which is what Roger wanted."

Again Lori nodded. Then she asked the question she'd been dreading, "Will you be going with him?"

"No. I'm staying."

"You are?" Lori's excitement was real, and her relief

300

was tremendous. She had not acknowledged it to herself, but the thought of living alone at the mine with Rand had unnerved her. "That's wonderful. I was afraid you would want to leave when Roger did."

"No. We discussed it, and I must admit, I did offer to go with him, but he wanted me to stay. He thinks a lot of Rand, and he feels that we're adequately chaperoned. He's promised to explain the situation to my parents so they won't be concerned."

"Roger likes Rand?" Lori didn't know why this surprised her.

"Very much and he trusts him, too," she added. "Didn't you think they liked each other?"

"I don't know. Everything is so confusing." Lori nervously rose and went to stand by the window. She looked toward the mine's entrance, where Rand was still meeting with Hal and Cam.

"Somehow, I think there's something you haven't told me." Sally's gaze followed Lori's. "Do you want to talk about it?"

"I'm not sure." Lori hedged for she was fearful of putting into words all the emotions that were tormenting her. Though she was relieved that Roger had decided to leave, the prospect of his departure only focused her attention on what she was feeling for Rand.

"You know you can trust me," her friend prodded. "Is Rand the one you love? Is that why you're so upset?"

Lori spun about, ready to deny her feelings, but Sally knew her far too well and her protest faltered. "I . . ."

"You've fallen in love with him, haven't you?"

"Yes," she admitted grudgingly. "Yes, I'm afraid I have, and my love for him is as hopeless as Roger's for me!"

"But why? Rand is—"

"Rand is the most deceitful man I've ever known!"

301

"Lori, you're wrong."

"You just don't know the whole story, Sally," Lori countered.

"Then why don't you tell me the whole story, right now. It might help you to talk about it." She patted the bed beside her and reluctantly Lori sat back down.

"As you know Rand's father and my father were the best of friends."

"Obviously or they wouldn't have drawn up the agreement."

"Anyway, Father and I used to visit the Lazy Ace when I was little, and Rand was always there. He was much older than I, and so handsome."

"You loved him even then, didn't you?"

"I suppose I did in a childish sort of way." Lori took a deep breath. "I idolized him, you know? I thought he was perfect, and the fact that he paid absolutely no attention to me only intensified what I was feeling."

"Sometimes I think our childhood feelings are much more fierce than anything we experience as adults," Sally remarked thoughtfully. "I guess it's because we're experiencing them for the first time."

"I know. And then . . ."

"Something happened?"

"Yes. That was seven years ago, but I remember the whole thing as if it occurred yesterday."

"What?"

"I discovered that Rand McAllister was an idol with feet of clay. I'll hate him forever for what he did!"

"What in the world did he do?" Sally could not imagine Rand doing anything really horrible.

"We'd gone to the ranch for a visit and to congratulate Will on his marriage to Lydia. Will was crazy about his wife and she was very beautiful then."

"She still is," Sally pointed out.

"I know." Lori's tone was bitter. "Will and Lydia

302

seemed happy together. I thought they truly loved each other, and I thought that was wonderful. Rand arrived while we were there. He'd come under the pretense of congratulating Will on his marriage, but in reality . . ."

Sally was hanging on her every word. "Yes?"

"In reality," Lori spat out. "He was Lydia's lover."

"Don't be ridiculous."

When Sally spurned this revelation disdainfully, Lori's eyes flashed angrily. "I'm not being ridiculous! I saw them!"

"You saw them making love?" Sally was stunned for this seemed so out of character for Rand. She was quite fond of the man and would never have suspected him of committing adultery with his own stepmother.

Lori nodded. "In the stable, the morning he was leaving. I went down to visit the horses and they were there—kissing! I was so shocked all I could do was run away. I hate him, Sally, and I still do!"

"But one kiss does not make them lovers," her friend reasoned, although she found an embrace in the seclusion of the stables rather incriminating.

"You didn't see the kiss." Lori's tight expression did not change. "And why in the world would he have been kissing his own stepmother?"

"You'd have to ask him, but it seems to me, you might have been condemning him for years without knowing all the facts."

"Hardly." Lori sneered, for she was certain she had not come to the wrong conclusion. "They're lovers now. I accidentally caught them in a compromising position when we stopped at the ranch on our way to town."

"I don't believe it." Sally shook her head in denial. "What kind of 'compromising position'?"

"Juana wanted me to tell Rand that we would be dining early so she told me he was in the study. I

303

knocked and opened the door, and there they were, wrapped in each other's arms. Lydia looked very guilty."

"Maybe he was just hugging her. I mean the woman just lost her husband."

"That's what he wanted me to believe, but I know too much about the two of them to believe that."

"He tried to explain the situation to you?" Sally was surprised by this revelation.

"Yes, he came after me and told me nothing was going on."

"Rand did care enough to try to explain, Lori. I don't know many men who would have bothered, guardian or not."

"Well . . ." She hesitated, realizing the truth of Sally's argument and remembering the passion she and Rand had shared in the aftermath of their disagreement.

"If you hate him so much, how can you say you love him?" her friend went on.

All the anger and fight went out of Lori then. "That's why I'm so confused. I don't understand it myself."

"Frankly, Lori, I don't think you hate him at all, and I don't think you ever did." When Lori gave her a puzzled look, she went on. "You were young and impressionable. I can just imagine how terrible for you it was to see Rand kissing Lydia, but that is all you saw—a kiss, nothing more."

"Even so, what was he doing kissing her!"

"I don't know. I'm sure it shocked you at the time, but you don't know for a fact that anything else ever happened between them."

"No."

"You know I'm right, admit it."

"Maybe." Lori refused to give in. She had believed in Rand's involvement with Lydia for far too long to dismiss it so quickly. "Still, I heard them in the hall at the hotel, late that first night—the night they didn't have dinner with us. He went to her room with her."

"They didn't dine with us, but that doesn't mean they made love."

Lori had no more evidence against the pair except their kiss at the mine during the rescue, and she was sure Sally would have some logical explanation for that. "I suppose you're right."

"I know I am. For heaven's sake, if they were lovers why in the world would he agree to live up here at the mine, far away from her? I really think you're wrong about this, Lori."

"I may be, but that doesn't change the fact that Rand wants nothing to do with me. He already told me he'd like to get out of this guardianship, that I am a burden to him. Why, he was even hoping that I'd marry Roger, just so he'd be free of me."

"That may be true, but can you blame the man? You've done nothing but upset his life since he's taken responsibility for you. You argue with him over every decision, and in regard to his urging you to marry Roger, why with us staying here with you, no doubt he thought you two were engaged. It would be a natural assumption on his part."

"Do you really think so?" Lori suddenly began to realize what Rand must have been feeling when they'd made love. He'd thought she'd been betraying her fiancé. No wonder he'd been so sarcastic and bitter. Was there hope that he might, indeed, care for her? As quickly as her spirits lifted, they fell again. No, she could not allow herself to pretend that he might be harboring some deep emotion for her. What existed between them was only blatant physical desire, nothing more.

"Probably, and I think he's going to be surprised

when he finds out that Roger is leaving."

"Surprised and disappointed," Lori said crossly, remembering Rand's derisive taunt about letting Roger get away.

Sally patted her hand. "It doesn't matter. What matters is that you learn to trust him. He's not the awful person you've thought him all this time. I liked him when I met him."

"I know." Lori smiled slightly as she recalled her annoyance at Sally's open acceptance of Rand.

"He's a good man, just as Ellen McCrea said he was. Give him a chance. He seems determined to help you with the mine and that should count for something."

"But what about Lydia?"

"What about her? She's not a part of your life. You won't have to deal with her on any regular basis."

"But she is a part of Rand's life." Lori looked miserable as she fought to overcome her previous attitudes. "I can't help but remember the way he kissed her when we were rescued from the cave-in, the sight of them holding each other in the study."

"You're going to have to stop imagining the worst if you expect to have any peace of mind," Sally declared. "If you continue to dwell on these things, you're only going to make yourself unhappy. I'll tell you something—Roger's philosophy on life—if you want something, go after it. The worst that can happen is that you won't get it, but it's better to try and fail than to sit around thinking about doing something and never making the effort."

Confusion flickered across Lori's lovely features.

"If you do love Rand, then you have to try to win his love. If you continue in the path you've chosen, you'll only create a breach between you two, one that will never heal." She paused. "Now, why don't we get something to eat? It's been a long hard day, and the sooner I get cleaned up and go to bed, the better.

I'm exhausted."

"When is Roger riding out, did he say?"

"First thing in the morning, I think," Sally answered softly.

"I want to be up to say good-bye."

"I know he'll be glad to see you before he goes. Now, how about some food?"


After clambering over the rocky terrain, Angelo raced into Pat and Cody's camp.

"He's here!" he told them excitedly. "He just got back."

"Good. Now all we have to do is find a way to lure him out to the stamp mill some time after dark," Pat remarked thoughtfully.

"The stamp mill? What ya got planned? You gonna kill him there?"

"No, but we've got to get him away from the main camp before we make our move. I don't want him dyin' too easy on us." Pat leered. "Follow him for a day or two, Angelo, and figure out what his routine is. Once we know exactly what he's doin', we'll be able to decoy him to the mill when it's deserted. How late do the men work on it?"

"Usually they quit right about sundown," Angelo replied.

"Well, that's when we want McAllister to wander over there, after everybody's gone. You find a way to get him there and then Cody and I will take care of the rest."

"I'll let you know as soon as I can figure something out."

"Right."


It was time to leave. Roger solemnly gazed around

the room that had been his since his arrival at the Triple Cross several weeks before. The wagon that would take him into town was ready to roll, so, suppressing the frustrated anger that threatened to erupt, he quickly grabbed up his baggage and strode out of the house to where Lori and the others waited to see him off.

He did not want to see Lori before he left, but knowing that there was no way to avoid doing so, he braced himself for his last moments with the woman he loved. He even managed a smile as he tossed his things in the back of the buckboard and then turned to speak with her.

"It's time." He glanced expectantly toward the driver who was waiting for him to join him in the driver's seat.

"Have a safe trip, Roger," Sally said quickly for she sensed the terrible awkwardness of the moment.

"Thanks. I will." He gently kissed his cousin on the cheek. "Rand, Hal, Cam . . . it's been good knowing you. If you're ever in St. Louis, please look me up." They shook hands all around. "Lori . . ." Roger's heart caught in his throat as he gazed down at her. This morning she looked more beautiful than ever, and he had to force himself to maintain a nonchalant attitude for he really wanted to sweep her into his arms and run off with her. "I'm glad things are working out so well here, and remember what I told you last night. If you ever need me, all you have to do is let me know. I'll be there for you, always." His smile was tender and his eyes spoke volumes.

"Thank you, Roger," Lori said slowly, her eyes meeting his and reading there his own understanding that what they'd had was finished.

Not willing to succumb to maudlin moments, he kissed her just as he had Sally and then climbed aboard.

"Tell Mother and Father hello for me," Sally called

as the driver slapped the reins against the horses' backs and the wagon started to move out.

"I will. Be careful, both of you."

"We will. Bye."

Roger lifted a hand in farewell and then directed his attention toward the road ahead. It led back to his life in the city—a life that seemed barren and joyless without Lori.

Rand watched the wagon drive off with mixed feelings. He'd liked Roger and was certain they could have become good friends had things been different, but under the circumstances, he was glad to see him go. Roger had made no secret of his love for Lorelei, or of his desire to marry her, and it was a relief to Rand that Lori had not encouraged him to stay. Now that Roger was completely out of the picture, Rand knew he would be better able to deal with his feelings for her. At least he wouldn't be suffering from pangs of guilt or remorse because of Roger.

As Rand glanced at Lorelei, he noticed that tears were collecting in her eyes and he longed to kiss them away, to tell her that everything would be all right. But he knew it was too soon to begin to actively pursue her. Her hatred for him was fierce and deep, and Rand was well aware that at the moment even a comment might unleash Lori's caustic tongue. Luckily, one of the miners called out to them from the mine entrance, breaking the strain, and Rand moved quickly away to see what he wanted, leaving Hal and Cam to follow after him.

"I'm going to miss him a lot." Lori looked at Sally.

"I'm sure he's going to miss you, too, but you both know this is for the best," Sally counseled. They returned to the house, each lost in her own thoughts.

The sun was hot so Roger went into the stage office to await the arrival of the coach from Prescott. That

309

would take him on to Maricopa where he would board the train heading East. He ruefully remembered his excitement upon arriving in Phoenix, and for a moment he deeply regretted leaving. He had grown attached to this rough and tumble land, and he wished that things had worked out differently. Nonetheless, Roger was certain that he was doing the right thing in going home. Staying here would serve no purpose. It would merely frustrate him further and make Lori feel more guilty than she already did for not returning his feelings. It was best that he go.

"Roger?" Brady's deep voice interrupted Roger's thoughts, and he turned to greet the other man as he entered the office.

"Brady, good to see you." They shook hands.

"Going somewhere?" Brady asked lightly as he noticed the luggage nearby, though he honestly did not expect an affirmative answer to his question.

"As a matter of fact, I am. I'm leaving on the afternoon stage for Maricopa," Roger replied.

"What?" Shocked, Brady glanced quickly around for some sign of Sally, fearful that she would be leaving with her cousin. Though he hadn't seen her since the party the other night, he'd hoped to be able to visit her at the Triple Cross soon, but if she was leaving and going back East with Roger . . .

"It's time I got back to my life in St. Louis."

"I see. Well, have a safe trip." Nervously expecting Sally to appear at any moment, Brady finally just blurted out. "Is Sally going with you?"

Roger immediately understood the man's tense manner, and he smiled at him understandingly. "No, my cousin has decided to stay on for a while. She's living with Lori out at the mine. You might want to pay her a visit," he added, hoping Brady would take the hint.

"As soon as I get time, I may do just that," the big blonde man replied. "She's a lovely woman, your cousin."

"That she is and I'm sure she'd be pleased to see you again. She's spoken quite highly of you."

"That's good to know." Brady was breathing easier now that he knew Sally was not leaving.

They shook hands and parted company then, Roger hoping that his carefully chosen words would encourage Brady to pursue Sally for he wanted her to have the happiness he had not attained.

## Chapter Eighteen

Several days passed uneventfully after Roger's departure. Rand and Lori were both working in and about the mine, yet despite the close quarters, she managed to distance herself and had little direct contact with him during the course of the workday. Much to her satisfaction, they were in proximity only during the evening meal which they shared with Sally and Hal at the main house. At these times, Lori was grateful for Sally's presence, and she gladly let her friend carry the bulk of the conversation. Though she had listened to Sally's counsel regarding Rand, she was still finding it difficult to reverse her attitude toward him after so many years of despising him.

"I have to make a trip to the Lazy Ace sometime early next week," Rand was saying as he finished eating, his eyes on Lorelei for he wondered what her reaction to his announcement would be. He had taken great care to pretend indifference to her since they'd returned to the Triple Cross—he hoped to win her over slowly—but it hadn't been easy for him. Lately, all he could think about was how wonderful she'd felt in his arms and how much he wanted to make love to her, and it had become a real struggle to control the powerful desire he was feeling.

Rand wished there was some simple way to prove to Lorelei that nothing existed between him and Lydia. He'd told her the truth in the stable, but she'd refused to believe him, so he had no reason to think anything he would say now would change her mind.

"Will you be gone long?" Sally inquired politely, for she'd sensed a sudden tension in Lori, who was sitting next to her.

"No. I want to check with Jack to see if there have been any problems at the ranch and to find out if the Bentons have been sighted. I should only be gone overnight."

"One night is certainly long enough." Lori's tart remark was prompted by the surge of jealousy she experienced at the thought of Rand at the Lazy Ace with Lydia.

"Be sure to give Lydia our best when you go." Sally spoke up quickly to cover Lori's sharpness.

"I'm sure he will," Lori snapped.

"I won't be leaving until Monday, but you're both more than welcome to ride along with me when I go." He met Lori's gaze mockingly, refusing to let her know how much her suspicions disturbed him.

"Why, I—"

Sally was ready to accept, but Lori broke in.

"No. Thank you. Sally and I will be staying here. We have a lot of work to do." Lori was not going to put herself in a position in which she'd see him with Lydia, not if she could help it.

"Perhaps, Sally would like to answer for herself?" Rand ignored Lori's quick refusal and turned his most charming smile on her friend. "Sally? I'd certainly enjoy your company."

"Why, yes, Rand. I think I'd like that," Sally responded cheerfully.

Lori became agitated. How dare her friend agree to go with Rand? But irritated as she was, Lori knew why Sally had done it. She liked Rand, trusted him. She hadn't believed what Lori had told her. Lori was greatly annoyed, but she was careful to disguise that.

"Well, if you'll excuse me," Rand said politely as he stood up. "I'm going to make my rounds and then retire early."

"I'll join you," Hal said as he got to his feet. "I've a few things to check before tonight's blasting."

"Of course," Sally replied easily.

"Dinner was wonderful as usual. Thank you." Rand smiled at Sally and pointedly paid little attention to Lorelei.

"I'm glad you liked it. We'll see you tomorrow," Sally included Lori in the conversation, knowing that her friend would not speak up.

"Good night."

When the men had gone, Sally turned to Lori, her aggravation great.

"Why in the world were you so sarcastic to Rand?" she asked as she set about clearing the table.

"I didn't realize that I was." Lori sniffed as she picked up several dishes and carried them to the sink. "I only said—"

"I know what 'you only said'," Sally declared sharply. "Luckily Hal didn't read the double meaning in your words, but after our heart-to-heart talk the other night, I'm too aware of what you're feeling to believe you didn't mean anything by that remark, Lori." She paused and faced her friend, her hands on her hips. "It was almost as if you were trying to goad Rand into an argument over his 'supposed' relationship with Lydia."

Lori's expression became stubborn and she didn't reply.

"Think about it, Lori. Would Rand have invited

us—you—to come along on the trip, if he was planning to spend the night making love to Lydia?"

"Well . . ."

"You know darn good and well that he wouldn't want you, or me, anywhere near if he was going to have a rendezvous with a woman," she stated emphatically. "Especially when he knows your suspicions, and that woman is Lydia."

Lori knew Sally was right, but it irked her to admit it so she remained silent.

"What does the man have to do to prove to you that there's nothing between him and Lydia?"

"That isn't pertinent," Lori finally replied. "I told you already, Rand doesn't care about me one way or the other. He's forced to deal with me because of the agreement, not because he cares about me."

"I think you're wrong."

"What are you talking about?"

"I think Rand cares about you, more than you know."

"Don't be ridiculous."

"I'm not. I've been thinking about this ever since we talked. Why else would he have tried to explain what had happened when you saw him holding Lydia at the ranch that day? And why else would he take an extended leave from a job he loves to stay here and work your mine? He's not a miner, he's a federal marshal, Lori."

"He's only doing it because he has to," she retorted hotly.

"Rand is a grown man, Lori. He doesn't have to do anything he doesn't want to do," Sally persisted. "He asked for and was granted a leave so he could help you, not Lydia, and I think you owe him an apology."

"For what?"

Sally was amazed that her well-founded arguments

had fallen on deaf ears, and she found her friend's mulish attitude exasperating. "Because he's trying his best to help you, yet you only make things more difficult for him." Without another word, she turned her back on Lori and went to her room, closing the door with emphasis.

Lori was feeling decidedly guilty. Sally was right about Rand's being willing to help her, and regardless of whether he was doing it out of duty or because he wanted to, she knew she'd been wrong to be so sarcastic to him. She had no concrete proof of his involvement with Lydia and she had to acknowledge that she might have been wrong in suspecting him of the worst all these years. Lori knew it would not be easy, but she would go to him and apologize; then, maybe, just maybe, they could come to some kind of understanding. Girding herself to face Rand, she went outside.

Pat and Cody crept ever nearer to the deserted stamp mill as darkness settled over the land.

"Be quiet and keep down," Pat whispered to his brother.

"Angelo said that McAllister makes his rounds late," Cody argued. He thought they were moving into position by the mill too early in the evening.

"I know, but we can't be sure when he'll show up so I'd rather be here than miss the chance to grab him. Wouldn't you?"

"You're right."

"Good. Now, stay right here while I find a good place on the far side to hide. When Angelo gets McAllister up here, he's gonna take him by surprise and knock him out. All we gotta do is carry him off. Nobody'll be the wiser until morning. Got it?"

"Yeah. I got it and I'm ready." Cody caressed the

handle of his gun and smiled wickedly.

"Don't be stupid. We don't want gunplay unless it's absolutely necessary. The main thing is to do this as quietly as possible."

Reluctantly, Cody nodded. Then he watched his brother move stealthily into position.


Harley was ready and waiting as night came. For the past several days he'd been sneaking explosives from the mine's supplies and he now had enough to do substantial damage to the mill. Quietly, so as not to attract any notice, he made his way from his tent, and after retrieving his hidden cache of dynamite and blasting caps, he headed for the now-abandoned stamp mill. Furtively, he placed the dangerous materials in the weakest structural areas; then he retreated to safety.


Angelo had gone to his quarters under the pretense of retiring for the night, but he was keeping a close watch for McAllister. He knew that Pat and Cody were already in position. Now he had to figure out a way to lure the lawman to the mill so the others could capture him. When he spotted Rand and Hal leave the owner's house, he watched them carefully and struggled to hear what they were saying so he might better plan his actions.


Rand and Hal crossed the yard together, deep in conversation.

"I don't know how serious this problem is, Rand, but it's time I mentioned it to you. There have been some discrepancies in our explosive inventory over the last few days."

Rand frowned. "Discrepancies?"

"A small quantity of blasting caps and dynamite are unaccounted for," Hal explained.

"Why would anybody want to steal explosives?" The thought of sabotage crossed his mind, but he disregarded it. The workers at the Triple Cross seemed dedicated to their work.

"I don't know." Hal shook his head. "I'm going down to do a final check of the supply levels at the stations and I'll report back to you if there's any shortage."

"Fine. I always check the explosives' shed during my rounds and I'll check the stock there, too."

"Good. I'll meet up with you later," Hal started off toward the mine entrance as Rand headed for the hut where additional explosives were stored.

Lorelei had just stepped outside, eager for a breath of cool night air before she tracked Rand down to offer her apology. She was not looking forward to the upcoming confrontation and was hesitating as long as she could before facing him.

As she surveyed the area, she noticed that the door to the explosives' shed was ajar and that a light was shining within. Wondering who would have business in the hut at this time of night, she immediately went to investigate. Pushing the shed door fully open, she surprised Rand who was diligently studying the inventory sheets.

"Rand? Is something wrong?"

Startled by Lorelei's unexpected presence, he turned quickly toward her, his sudden move surprising her. She was overwhelmed to find herself face to face with him in the narrow shed, and when she stepped backward, wanting to put space between them, she awkwardly lost her balance.

Rand's reaction was instinctive. Seeing her distress, he reached out to help her regain her balance. When his hands gripped her upper arms firmly, the contact was electric, and their eyes locked in sensuous combat.

Rand inhaled sharply as he struggled to keep a tight rein on his riotous emotions. He wanted to pull her into his arms and kiss her into submission as he'd done before, but he knew, if there was to be a future for them, he could no longer force her to admit her desire for him. She had to come to him of her own free will. Aggravated with himself for being tempted by her nearness and needing to put her from him, he released her abruptly.

"Did you want something?" he asked, his voice sounding harsh even to him.

Lori was dazed by the power of his touch. Just the feel of his hands upon her had left her breathless and aching for him. But when his expression had turned stony and remote and he'd let go of her so quickly, she'd realized her response was one-sided. No matter what Sally preached, Rand truly did not care for her— not the way she wanted him to. There was no way, feeling as bereft as she did, that she could apologize for her attitude toward Lydia at that moment.

"I saw the light and wondered if something was wrong," she said, moving as far away from him as she could in the cramped space of the shed.

Rand watched her nervously sidle away from him. He found her obvious dislike of him annoying. "Damn it, Lorelei, I'm not some monster who's going to abuse you," he snarled, turning his back on her.

She bridled at his words. "I wish I could believe that!"

"Believe it! I regret what's happened between us more than you'll ever know!"

Rand meant that he was sorry that she believed he was

involved with Lydia, but Lori placed a different meaning on his words. She thought he regretted their previous lovemaking, and she rushed from the hut, devastated.

He almost went after her, but common sense held him back. Cursing under his breath, he quickly completed his inventory and then threw the sheaf of papers down in disgust. He then extinguished the light, and he was locking the shed door when the new man, Angelo, approached him.

"*Señor* . . ." Angelo had just the proper amount of respect in his voice.

"Yes? What is it?"

Having overheard part of the conversation between Rand and Hal about the missing explosives, Angelo decided to use that ploy to get McAllister to the mill. "I accidentally overheard some of your conversation with the boss," he confessed, then paused to await Rand's reaction.

"Oh?" Rand eyed him skeptically.

"And I'm not sure if it's important or not, but I thought I saw someone over by the mill right after sundown when everybody else was settlin' in for the night. He was carryin' somethin' with him."

"Can you show me where the man was?" Rand was instantly alert.

"About where he was." Amazed at the ease with which he'd enticed McAllister to follow him, Angelo led the way to the secluded construction site.

"Did you happen to recognize who it was?" Rand was instantly alert.

"No. It was too dark," Angelo answered obliquely as they moved into the erected shell of the building, out of sight of the camp. "I think he went over there." Angelo pointed in the general direction of the place where Pat would be hiding, and as Rand started past him the outlaw drew the gun he'd hidden in his waistband and hit Rand from behind, knocking him out.

Then it happened. Harley had planned his next destructive act carefully, picking a time when the mill was usually deserted so no one would be injured and then making sure that the fuses were long enough so he could be safely away before the explosion took place. However, when he'd seen Rand approaching with the new man Angelo, he'd become excited for he knew Taylor would be greatly pleased if something 'accidental' happened to McAllister. As soon as the two men stepped inside the structure, Harley lit the fuses.

The explosion rocked the entire camp, rousing everyone. Pat and Cody had just started down from their hiding place to get Rand when the unexpected detonation caught them by surprise. Diving for cover, they'd stared at the nearly demolished structure in mute disbelief. Though revenge on McAllister fate had denied them, they felt certain as they surveyed the area that there was no way he could have survived the blast.

"Pat! I can see Angelo! Over here!" Cody called out. "And he's still alive!"

"He ain't gonna last for long! Forget him, there's no time! We gotta get out of here and fast!" Pat scurried to his brother's side and they both fled the scene.

Harley managed to blend in with the others as everyone raced toward the mill.

Lorelei had returned to the house and had just started to undress when the explosion occurred. Tugging her clothing back on, she ran in the direction of the blast, Sally following her. The sight that greeted them left them both stunned.

"Oh, my God! What could have happened?" Sally stood, motionless, at Lori's side.

"I don't know. Sabotage maybe, but who? And why?" Lori left her friend behind as she boldly raced

321

ahead to join the men. Spotting Hal rushing toward her from the mine's entrance, she went to him. "Hal! Do you have any idea what caused it? Was anybody in there?"

"I don't know, Miss Lorelei. I've been down in the mine checking on the blasting supplies."

"Blasting supplies? Why?"

"Well, as I was telling Rand earlier, there's been a shortage of them for the past several days." Hal regarded the ruined stamp mill wtih heartbroken digust. "Where is Rand? Maybe he knows something."

They looked around quickly, hoping to spot him, but there was no sign of him anywhere. Suddenly, the cries of the miners drew their attention.

"There's a man trapped in here!" Someone yelled from amidst the wreckage, and Lori hurried toward the ruined structure, Hal at her side.

"It's Angelo, the new man," another voice called out. "And he's still alive."

The miners worked feverishly to free him, and once they'd managed to work his crushed form free of the heavy timbers, they carried him clear of the site.

"Pat . . ." Angelo muttered, unaware of his surroundings. "Where's Pat? He was supposed to meet me here with Cody."

"What's he saying?" Lori asked as she knelt beside the dying man.

"He's callin' for somebody named Pat and Cody. Whoever they are."

"Take him to the supervisor's house and see what can be done for him," she directed.

"Ma'am, there ain't no point now. He's gone," a miner declared.

Lori stared blankly down at the dead man, trying to imagine who would have wanted to destroy the stamp mill.

Unaware that Angelo's deceitful blow had saved him from certain death beneath the crashing weight of the massive overhead supports, Rand had regained consciousness to find himself trapped face down beneath a heavy timber. Trying to come to grips with his situation, he lay immobile for a moment assessing the extent of his injuries, and he was surprised to find that nothing seemed broken.

When he heard the miners working above him, clearing the wreckage away, he'd shouted as loudly as he could to alert them to his presence.

"Help! I'm here!" his voice, though raspy from the shock, was loud enough to be heard and he was reassured when he heard their response.

"I just heard something over there!"

"Start digging!"

Men swarmed around to shift the lumber away, and they were amazed to discover Rand, pinioned beneath several of the huge support timbers.

"It's McAllister, Hal!" they called out to the supervisor. "He's alive!"

"Get him out of there!"

"Rand!" Lori gasped and then watched in frightened expectation as the miners dug through the rubble to free Rand. "Hal, what was Rand doing in the mill at this time of night?" She clutched the older man's arm as he joined her.

"I don't know, Miss Lorelei, but I hope to God he's all right." Hal slipped a supporting arm about her waist as she swayed weakly against him, her knees threatening to buckle.

Rand . . . injured, maybe dying . . . The thought terrified Lorelei and she refused to consider it. She'd just spoken to him, just argued with him. He couldn't die! Not like this! Not now, when she hadn't even had the chance to tell him that she loved him and

323

needed him!

Sally came to stand with Hal and Lori as the workers continued desperately to free Rand. "There's someone still trapped?" She turned worried eyes on Hal and then Lori.

"It's Rand, Sally," Lori answered with difficulty. "They say he's still alive, but so was Angelo when they first pulled him out."

Sally stifled a sob of despair provoked by the thought of Rand buried beneath the debris.

"Why was he at the mill, Hal? Do you have any idea?" Lori asked as she regained some semblance of control.

"I don't know, Miss Lorelei. He was supposed to meet with me after he went over that inventory. I can't imagine what he was doing at the mill."

"Hal"—Lori looked up at him gravely—"do you think someone deliberately sabotaged the mill?"

"I hate to consider it, but what else could it be?" he replied in frustration.

"Who would want to do a thing like that?" Sally was dumbstruck by the revelation.

"Someone who doesn't want us to succeed," Hal answered tersely. "But I don't know who that could be. There's no one who would profit if we fail."

Lori's head was swimming at the thought that someone would be trying to prevent her making a success of the mine and would be desperate enough to destroy the stamp mill.

"We got him!" The loud excited call came from the wreckage.

Lori rushed from Hal and Sally, and climbed over the ruins to where the miners were lifting the last beam to free Rand.

"Stand back, Miss Lorelei. If this support slips, it could be dangerous," one of the men ordered.

For once in her life, Lori did as she was told, but she remained hovering on the edge of the rescue scene, fearful that Rand would be dead when they finally managed to pull him out. When at last she saw the men lift Rand bodily from the wreckage, she ran to them.

"Is he alive?" she asked emotionally as she broke through the cluster of miners.

"I'm fine, Lorelei," Rand replied as the miners helped him to his feet and Lori stared at him in amazement, not even bothering to hide the depth of feeling she was experiencing.

"Oh, Rand," she sobbed, and she couldn't stop herself from going to him. She had to touch him, hold him, make sure she wasn't dreaming.

Her unexpected display of emotion took him by surprise and though he held her close as they walked toward Hal and Sally together, he was unable to resist taunting her for her fickleness. "Can it be that you actually care what happens to me, Lorelei? A little while ago you couldn't stand my touch."

"You!" she stiffened, suddenly aware of just how much she'd revealed to him, and she jerked away from his comforting grasp. "I wish the damned beam had squashed you!"

"I'm sure you do, my dear," he drawled, angered by her refusal to admit she felt something for him and by his own stupidity in chiding her for her outburst. "You'd have been completely rid of me then. Why, if I didn't know better, I'd say you'd planned this little 'explosive encounter' yourself!"

Before Lori could reply, Sally and Hal reached them.

"Oh, Rand. The other man was dead and Lori and I were so afraid for you," Sally said quickly.

"You were?" he cast a questioning look at Lori, but she turned away from his gaze.

"Yes!" Sally went on. "Lori especially. I've never

325

seen her so upset as when they found you buried under all that rubble."

Lori was furious with her friend for telling Rand of her feelings, but he glanced from Lorelei, back to where he'd been buried alive and said in slow deliberate tones, "I was lucky, but what I want to know is how and why this happened. You say Angelo is dead?"

"Yes," Lori replied tersely. "I was with him when he died."

Rand frowned, "He came up to me when I was leaving the explosives shed. He said that he'd overhead our conversation, Hal, and that he thought I might be interested to know that he'd seen someone over by the mill, a man who was carrying something."

"So you went with him to check it out?"

Rand nodded slowly as he rubbed at the back of his neck. "I wonder . . ."

"What?" Lori asked impulsively as she sensed his confusion.

"I don't remember anything about the explosion. Surely, I'd have heard something before the timbers hit me."

"What are you trying to say?"

"I don't know." He looked up at Hal, puzzled. "I've got a welt on the back of my head, and the last thing I remember is walking past Angelo after he pointed out where he thought he'd seen the unidentified man lurking."

"Angelo did say something before he died," Lori offered quickly.

"What?" Rand's question was sharp as he turned to her.

"It doesn't make much sense really, there's nobody here by these names, but he was calling out for Pat and Cody."

Rand's expression became so cold Lori almost

326

shivered beneath his icy regard. "The Bentons . . . Angelo must have been working with the Bentons."

"Those are the Bentons' names?" Sally asked in horror.

"It must have been a setup, and it looks like Angelo paid for it with his life."

"What are you saying?" Hal was completely lost.

"I'm saying the Bentons are blood-thirsty murderers. They had Angelo lure me to a deserted spot, intending to kill me and Angelo."

"They'd kill one of their own?"

"Angelo wasn't important to them. They really wanted me and I'll bet they're pretty sure they killed me," Rand swung around to survey the surrounding hillsides. "I'm going to have to get to town as quickly as I can to let John know about this."

"So you don't think it was sabotage at all?" Lori wondered.

"No. We've known all along that the Bentons were out there somewhere looking for me and now we know they've found me."

"But if they think you're dead, won't they just go away?" Sally asked.

"I'm afraid not," Rand answered grimly. "And I'm going after them at first light."

"You can't!" Lori protested.

"I have to. If I don't put them back behind bars, they're going to start a reign of terror the likes of which the territory has never seen." His gaze darkened as he realized Lori was again concerned for him, but this time he was wise enough not to remark on it. "I want you and Sally to move in at the ranch tomorrow. And, Hal, I want you to make sure that they stay there. See to it, will you?"

"I will," the supervisor quickly assured him.

Lori started to argue, but Rand's steely-eyed expression halted her protest.

"It's going to be too dangerous for you here once they find out I wasn't killed in the explosion. At the Lazy Ace, I'll know you're safe." His tone brooked no argument.

"We'll go, Rand." Sally reassured him.

"Good. I don't want to be worrying about your safety while I'm gone. I just hope it won't take too long to corner them." His eyes narrowed at that thought. "Let's go back to the house. I want to start packing now."

# Chapter Nineteen

"I don't know why Rand thinks it will be dangerous for us to stay here at the mine," Lori complained to Sally as she moved about her room, gathering the clothes she would take with her to the Lazy Ace the next day.

Sally shrugged. "I'm sure he has his reasons, Lori, and we'd better do as he says. Obviously, the Bentons are killers who wouldn't hesitate to eliminate anyone who got in their way."

"But if Rand's gone from here, why would they bother to come back?"

"Hopefully, they wouldn't, but he wants us out of here, just in case."

"I suppose you're right."

"I told you he cares about you," Sally pointed out. "If he knows you're safe at the ranch, he'll be able to concentrate on catching the Bentons."

"I hope he's careful. If they're as ruthless as he says they are—"

"Why don't you go tell him how you're feeling? He certainly didn't hesitate to let us know he is deeply concerned about our safety," Sally suggested, and when Lori didn't immediately agree, she probed. "You did talk with him earlier, didn't you?"

"Well, I tried to," Lori hedged. "But somehow everytime we're together, we end up arguing."

"And you argued with him again, after dinner?" Sally was dismayed by her friend's obstinate attitude toward Rand.

"I hadn't meant to, but one thing led to another . . ." She let her words drift off as she remembered his comment that he regretted what had happened between them.

"Why don't you go to him now?" Sally urged. "You know he's going to ride out in the morning after the Bentons. There's no telling how long he'll be gone or what's going to happen while he's away."

Lori wasn't sure what to do. The fear she'd felt when she'd thought him dead or injured beneath the weight of the fallen mill had only reaffirmed the depth of her love for him, nonetheless his words rang hollowly in her memory.

"What if I bare my soul to him and he truly doesn't care about me."

"I've never known you to be a coward, Lorelei Spencer." Sally tried to goad her friend to action. "What's the worst that could happen? You'll tell him to be careful and he'll say he will and that will be that. Right?"

Lori sighed, confused by the situation. "I do love him, Sally. When I thought he was dead—"

"I know, I saw it on your face, and I think it's time you told him." Sally sensed that Lori was wavering. "Lori, even though it's not something you want to think about, when Rand goes after the Bentons, he may not come back. Do you want him to leave without knowing how you feel about him?" She waited a moment before saying, "Now, go on. Talk to him while you've got the chance."

Impulsively, Lori hugged Sally and started from the room. "I will."

Hal and Rand stood together in the main room of Hal's house, deep in conversation.

"There's no point in worrying about rebuilding the mill right now, Hal," Rand was saying. "We've got to get enough gold out of the mine to repay the loan by September. We'll worry about the mill after we've paid back the banker."

"It's going to be close," Hal worried. "I hadn't anticipated paying the additional freight expenses after next month, because I'd assumed our own mill would be operational by then."

"I understand, but do your best. If worse comes to worst, we can ask for an extension from the bank or I can use my own funds."

"Lorelei wouldn't like that," Hal told him quickly, and Rand gave the mining boss an understanding smile.

"I certainly wouldn't tell her, would you?"

"I see your point."

"Good. Take care of things while I'm away and make sure Lorelei stays at the ranch."

"I'll do my best." Hal's grin was rueful. "But she can be plenty persuasive when she wants to be."

"I know. She's a wonderful woman, but she needs a strong guiding hand."

"Like yours?" Hal asked insightfully.

Rand gave the older man a measured look.

"I didn't mean to speak out of turn." As Hal quickly started to apologize, Rand waved the remark off. "But you two would make quite a team."

"I don't know, Hal," Rand said thoughtfully. "She's one hell of a woman, but she fights me every inch of the way."

"Her daddy was a proud one and I'm sure it rubs

Miss Lorelei the wrong way to be under anyone's domination. You're a better man than most, but it wouldn't matter who it was. George raised her to be independent and think for herself. She's not the type to keep quiet if something is bothering her."

"I know, Hal, believe me, I know." Rand gave him a ghost of a smile. "Maybe when I get back we'll be able to work out something."

"I hope so."

A soft knock at the door interrupted them and Hal went to answer it. "Miss Lorelei! Come on in. Is there anything I can do for you?"

"Actually, Hal, I came to see Rand." She glanced somewhat nervously in the younger man's direction.

"In that case, I'll go down and check on the progress in cleaning up the mill. I'll be back later."

"Fine."

When the door closed, Lori faced Rand awkwardly, not quite sure how to begin.

"Do you need something?" Rand finally asked as he tore his hungry gaze away from her and busied himself with packing his saddlebags. He was aching to draw her into his embrace and tell her that he loved her, but he knew better than to make the attempt. No doubt she was here only to voice her opinion of his order she go to the ranch to live.

Rand seemed so aloof and indifferent that Lori was suddenly unsure about how to approach him, and in desperation, she groped for something to break the silence and gain his attention.

"I just don't see why you think I have to leave the mine," she began, sounding more argumentative than she'd wanted to.

Rand looked up at her, his expression hard as he acknowledged to himself that he'd been correct about her motive in coming to see him.

"I am not accustomed to explaining my decisions to anyone, Lorelei, but in your case I'll make an exception. I want you away from here because I want to be sure that you're out of harm's way, should the Bentons decide to return," he answered with exaggerated patience.

"But why would the Bentons come back here if they think you're already dead? And when they do find out you're alive, they're going to know you're not here, so why do I have to leave?"

Rand drew a deep steadying breath and started slowly across the room toward her. What he was going to say, he was only going to say once, and he wanted her to absorb the import of his words.

Coming to stand before her, he reached out with a gentle hand and touched her cheek. "Lorelei, I want you to stay at the ranch because that's the safest place for you. I want to know that you're where the Bentons won't be able to get to you."

"What do you mean? Why would the Bentons want me?" His tender caress was mesmerizing and she could only stare up at him as the sweetness of his gesture sent tingles of love's recognition through her body.

"Because they'll know, soon enough, that by hurting you, they could hurt me." The words were difficult for him to say.

Lori was stunned. "Do you mean that?" she whispered breathlessly, her eyes widening as she realized the import of his words.

Rand had hesitated to tell her of his feelings, but he knew that he might not come back from his showdown with the Bentons and he wanted her to know of his love before he left. He bent to her and kissed her.

He'd fought his love for her for as long as he could, telling himself that she hated him and would despise him forever, but it no longer mattered if she rejected

333

him. He had to tell her. He had to let her know before he left. Whatever happened—well, he would handle that later.

Lori was stunned. This kiss was nothing like the embraces they'd shared before. Their previous encounters had always been sensual and desperate and explosive. But this one was totally different and she didn't understand quite why. His kiss was cherishing, not demanding, and she found herself responding to it with fervor. She had no thought of resisting him for she wanted this as much as he did.

Surprised by her willing surrender to his embrace, Rand drew back to stare at her. She smiled as she boldly slipped her arms around his neck to pull him back down to her.

Just before she pressed her lips to his, she told him huskily, "I can't fight the feelings I have for you anymore, Rand. I've tried, but they're too strong . . . I love you." It was not an easy profession for Lori to make, especially since he hadn't really voiced his devotion, and she knew a brief instant of fear as she awaited his reaction to her words. Would he laugh and carelessly deride her gift of love? Or had he meant what he'd implied?

"Ah, Lorelei." He groaned and crushed her to his chest as his mouth took hers in a passionate exchange. "I love you. God knows I do."

Thoughts of Lydia threatened her moment of happiness at his declaration and she pulled slightly away to look up at him, perplexed. "But what about—"

"Shhh . . ." Rand knew what she was thinking, and silencing her with a deep kiss, he told her, "What I told you was the truth, Lorelei. I was not involved with my stepmother. I've never lied to you and I never will."

"Oh, Rand." She sighed rapturously as she melted against him, believing him at last in this moment of total honesty.

They did not bother with words, time was too short. They only knew that they needed one another more than they'd ever needed anything in their lives and they came together in the pureness of their newly discovered love.

Tenderly and with infinite care, Rand swung her up into his arms and carried her into the privacy of his bedroom. They shared a kiss as he crossed to the narrow bed, and after he'd placed her upon it he closed and locked the door. Lori felt suddenly chilled, as if a vital part of her being was missing. She watched him with hungry eyes as he strode back to her, then she lifted her arms to him, welcoming him to her embrace.

Rand stared down at Lorelei in enthralled disbelief. A few minutes before, he'd felt certain that they were going to end up sparring and fighting as they always did, and he'd deeply regretted that they would be parting that way. Now, all that had changed. She loved him. She'd actually told him of her love and he'd admitted his feelings to her. She was everything he'd ever wanted in a woman. She was fire and passion and beauty—and she was his. He felt a burst of male pride at the thought, and when he stretched out beside her on the bed, he pulled her to him and kissed her fervently.

As she read the passion in his regard, Lori knew a thrill of excitement at the knowledge that he loved her. How could it have happened? How could she have won his love yet not even known what he was feeling until now? Sally had been right all along. Rand had cared, but their doubts had kept them apart. Her suspicions about Lydia, his about Roger. But all that was settled now. They were together and nothing else mattered.

Eagerly she returned his kiss, reveling in the joy of being close to him. How perfectly they fit together and how secure she felt in his warm, encompassing embrace! No harm would ever come to her while she was with Rand. He was her love . . . her life. She had loved him even as a child.

Lori gasped in delight as he unbuttoned her blouse and slipped a hand beneath it to caress her silken flesh. Then she arched toward him, offering full access to her aching breasts. His touch was ecstasy and she moved against him invitingly, wanting him to know of the power of her need.

"Easy, love." Rand pressed her hips to his, letting her know that his desire matched hers, but that he was in no hurry to appease his growing hunger for her. "We've all the time in the world. I want to kiss and touch all of you."

Lori shivered as she imagined him doing just that, and she worked at opening the buttons of his shirt, wanting to feel the heat of his hair-roughened chest against her bared breasts.

"Love me, Rand. Please, love me."

"I do, Lorelei." His eyes caught and held hers, and she saw the depth of his previously hidden devotion.

Gently, Rand rolled her beneath him, domininating her in the age-old way, and Lori smiled as she surrendered willingly to his maleness. He bent to her then, pressing heated kisses to her throat and shoulders before moving lower to savor the full, succulent sweetness of her bosom. Lori moaned as his lips explored her satiny mounds, and when he drew one taut peak into his mouth, she clasped his head to her, thrilling at the hot, wet warmth of his touch. The fire that had flamed to life deep within her at his first kiss, raged out of control as he continued his arousing play, and Lori became a mindless creature of desire, attuned only to Rand, wanting only Rand, needing only Rand for fulfillment.

Her passion blossomed as his lips and hands

continued to work their exquisite magic upon her, and she responded fully, eager to know his complete possession once again. Rand broke away from her only long enough for them to shed their clothing; then they came together again, desperate in their desire to meld.

Ecstasy was theirs as he took her with a penetration that was sure and true. Rand's thrusting gift of love filled Lori with rapture and they soared to the heights together, each seeking to give the other the ultimate pleasure. It came upon them swiftly, sweeping them away to blissful oblivion where nothing existed except the glory of their joining; then they slowly returned to reality, holding each other close.

"When we were together before, it was exciting, but I never dreamed it could be like this." Lori's voice was filled with wonder. "It was perfect, Rand. You were perfect." She kissed him.

"We were perfect, love. Together." He rose above her, supporting his weight on his elbows. "I've never known joy so sweet. I just wish we had more time."

"Time? For what?" Her tone sultry, she stretched languidly beneath his welcome weight.

"Time for this . . ." Rand sought the fullness of her breasts. "And for this . . ." One hand slipped lower in an arousing quest.

Lori was stunned to feel desire surge through her again, and she brought his lips up to hers, kissing him hungrily. "We don't have time?" Lori never wanted this closeness to end.

With a shudder, Rand moved away from her to sit on the side of the bed, his expression strained as he fought to bring his raging desire under control. "Not now, not when we could be interrupted at any minute," he explained with a tender half-smile.

"I forgot." And, indeed, Lori had. She'd forgotten everything when Rand had kissed her, and she was sorry that reality was intruding on their few precious moments together.

"We'll be married as soon as I take care of the Bentons," he stated matter-of-factly as he stood up and began to dress.

Lori blinked in stunned surprise. "Married?"

Rand's grin was sardonic. "I should have dragged you off to a preacher as soon as they dug us out of that mine after our first time together, but—"

"But you thought I was going to marry Roger?"

He nodded.

"Sally suspected as much, but Roger and I never came to a definite understanding."

"I thought you were engaged to him, and although I liked Roger, the thought that you belonged to him nearly drove me wild. I could never share you, never." He came to stand by the bed, and Lori knelt before him on its softness, looping her arms around his neck.

"You'll never have to, Rand. There's no other man. You've had my heart since I was eleven."

"I'm glad." Rand's mouth slanted across hers in a possessive caress. Then, despite his desire for her, he forced himself to release her. "Hal could return at any time," he told her apologetically.

"I know. We were taking a chance."

"It doesn't matter. I didn't want to leave you without setting everything straight between us," Rand declared.

"I felt the same way. I didn't really come here to argue with you about going to the Lazy Ace. I came here to tell you to be careful and to tell you how I felt. I was afraid to do that, you know." She was candid about her fear of being open with him.

Rand smiled at her. "If we'd been honest with each other from the start, we could have saved so much time."

"Time that we could have put to better uses than

fighting." Lori returned his smile.

"I wish it didn't have to be this way, but I have to see to it that the Bentons are put away for good this time."

"I understand," she agreed solemnly. "And you will be careful?"

"Especially so, now that you'll be waiting for me."

"Good." Lori got up from the bed and started to pull on her clothes.

"You never did agree to marry me." He embraced her.

"You never did ask," Lori teased.

"I didn't?" He frowned as he buttoned his shirt.

"No. In your usual domineering way, you simply declared that we'd wed," Lori pointed out and she enjoyed his look of discomfort at her revelation. "But you already know my answer, Rand. It's yes. Yes, I'll marry you as soon as you get back."

Rand drew a deep breath, his eyes aglow with love as he kissed her. "I'll do my best to hurry."

"Just don't take any chances," Lori warned, not wanting him to be distracted from his duty. Now that they finally understood each other, she certainly didn't want to risk losing him.

"I won't and you shouldn't. Stay put at the Lazy Ace until I come for you, understand? I need to know that you're safe." His tone was so imperious Lori couldn't prevent the gurgle of laughter that erupted from her.

"Why are you laughing?" Rand demanded.

"Because you're ordering me around again. I wonder if it's possible for you to change?"

He came to stand before her and helped her finish buttoning her blouse. "Bear with me. I haven't been answerable to anyone since I was a youth, and for the past seven years I've been used to having my orders followed without question." His grin was boyish, full of acknowledged guilt. "It's a habit that'll be hard to break."

"It may take time, but we've got the rest of our lives." Lori's expression grew serious as she thought of the danger he would soon be facing. "I promise I won't return to the mine until you can go with me, Rand."

"That's all I ask." He kissed her softly. "As long as I know you're all right, I'll be able to deal with the Bentons more efficiently. I'll come back to you as quickly as I can."

"Will you ride as far as the ranch with us this morning?"

"I don't want to take any chances." He nodded. "I'll see you safely there and then I'll go on to town."

"Good. I didn't want to say good-bye here."

"I don't want to say good-bye, ever." His expression was fierce as they embraced.

"We don't have to worry about that." Lori tried to sound cheerful as they reluctantly went to the door. "I'm sure you'll catch up with the Bentons in no time."

"Right." Rand didn't want to consider the possibility that it might take weeks, even months, to corner the vicious pair.

"I'd better get back," Lori said as she led the way from the bedroom. "When do you want to ride out in the morning?"

"At first light."

"Sally and I will be ready." She gazed up at him adoringly, and after one last heated embrace, she left him.

Rand watched as she closed the door behind her and he felt a sudden sense of misgiving. He loved Lorelei. He wanted to spend the rest of his life with her, but he wondered just how long his life was going to be.

# Chapter Twenty

The pink and gold streaks of dawn brightened the horizon as Lydia sighed and rolled over to face Josh. "This has been delightful, darling, but you really should go."

Josh's arm snaked out to pull her to him. "There's plenty of time, Lydia. Come here." His mouth descended with purposeful intent, claiming hers in a passionate, devouring kiss. "I'll never get enough of you—never," he claimed as he moved onto her quickly and thrust deeply within her.

"Josh!" Lydia was surprised by his ardency, but she didn't try to fight it. Josh had always been a good lover, and she needed him now. This was her first trip to town since the party at the McCreas', and Josh had secretly come to her hotel room for a night of erotic pleasure. Their lovemaking uninhibited, they both soon peaked and collapsed, sated by their hurried, yet satisfying, joining.

"I love you, Lydia," Josh swore as he withdrew from her and rose to dress. "As soon as I can take care of our 'problem,' we'll be married and leave this town."

"Have you made any progress in locating the Bentons?" she asked hopefully.

"None," Josh answered with considerable bitterness. "But I'm not about to stop trying. As soon as I can arrange something, I'll let you know."

"Good. Keep me informed," Lydia told him calculatingly.

"I have no secrets from you, Lydia." Josh glanced out the window and then back at her. "But I had better make my exit before I ruin your reputation."

She flashed him a heated smile. "We wouldn't want that to happen, not when everything is going so well."

"When are you coming back to town?"

"I don't know, but I'll send word. I'd hate to miss a business appointment with you, Mr. Taylor."

Josh smiled knowingly. "I do enjoy the privacy of my office on those occasions." He went to her and kissed her quickly. "I'll be in touch."

When he had gone, Lydia lay back in the comfort of the wide bed and smiled. Soon, very soon, she would have it all!

In that den of iniquity called the Sidewinder Saloon, Cody and Pat drank down their tumblers of bourbon and then clapped each other on the back as they guffawed over their success. They'd done it! Everything hadn't gone exactly as planned, but McAllister was dead and that was all that counted. The explosion had been a surprise. They still wondered what had caused it, but that really didn't matter. And Angelo's death didn't lessen their satisfaction. That was the breaks.

"I still woulda liked to have gotten my hands on him." Cody shook his head ruefully as he poured himself another drink. "He went too easy—too fast."

"I know," Pat sympathized, thinking of all the tortures he'd planned to inflict on McAllister. "But so what? He's dead and we're free. That's enough to make this one helluva celebration! The only thing we got to worry about is money. What we have'll last a couple of days, but after that we're gonna hafta go to work."

Cody smiled evilly. "And this town looks like easy pickins'."

Pat returned his smile. "It sure does."


Rand didn't sleep at all that night for his mind was filled with thoughts of Lorelei and worries about the Bentons. Anxious to begin his pursuit of the deadly pair and wondering if they'd been nearby when the explosion had occurred the night before, he headed for the mill at the first sign of day.

Expert tracker that he was, it didn't take Rand long to locate the killers' trail near, but after following it for some distance, he lost it in the rock terrain.

It angered him to know that the Bentons had been stalking him and he'd been unaware of it. He vowed to himself that he would never give them another chance to get him. No longer would he be the hunted; from now on, they would be the prey.

Lori had managed to get a little sleep, but not much. The knowledge of Rand's love filled her with an inner joy she'd never known before, and she could hardly wait to see him again, to reaffirm the wonder of his devotion. He loved her! She almost laughed aloud in delight as she scrambled out of bed shortly before sunup to get ready.

Once she'd dressed and awakened Sally, Lori hurried out to meet Rand, only to have Hal tell her that he'd ridden out a littler earlier and that he wasn't sure where he'd gone. Worried and fearful for his safety, she anxiously awaited his return and when she spotted Rand riding back into camp, she knew a moment of profound relief.

"Where did you go?" she called as he rode up to her. "I was worried when Hal told me you'd gone out alone."

Rand was still amazed by the transformation in Lorelei. No longer was she defensive and argumentative. Now she was all woman and he definitely liked the change. She'd been concerned about him and she hadn't been afraid to admit it. She loved him. He smiled as he swung down from the saddle to take her into his arms for a reassuring hug.

"I was just checking out a few things at the mill," he told her, affecting more confidence than he was really feeling.

Lori sighed deeply as she was enfolded in his strong embrace, closing her eyes for a moment to enjoy the closeness.

"Did you find anything?" she finally asked.

"I found what must be the Bentons' trail away from the mill, but I lost it in the rocks."

"You mean they were actually here last night?" Lori's eyes grew wide with fright.

"It looks that way." His arms tightened around her.

"Oh," Lori suppressed a shiver at the realization of how close the outlaws had actually been.

"Are you and Sally ready to ride out?" Rand knew what she was thinking and he wanted to redirect her thoughts.

"Yes. I'll get her." Though Lori wanted to stay in his arms forever, she reluctantly moved away from him.

"I'll go say good-bye to Hal and Cam while you get her."

"Fine." Bestowing a sweet smile on him, she disappeared into the house in search of her friend.

It was almost noon when they reached the Lazy Ace. Juana greeted them happily.

"Rand! It is so good to see you! Come in, come in!"

She ushered them into the coolness of the ranch house. "You are staying for a while?"

"No, Juana. I've got to be leaving for town very shortly, but Lorelei and Sally will be staying on. Is Lydia here?"

"No, the *señora* has gone to town, but I expect her back today." The servant was surprised by the news that the two young women would be moving in, and she wondered what Lydia's reaction would be to their presence. "Is something wrong?"

"The Bentons are in the area so it's no longer safe for Lorelei and Sally to remain at the Triple Cross. Is Jack around?" Eager to be on his way, Rand wanted to meet with the foreman as soon as possible.

"He was out in the stables just a short time ago. Shall I send one of the boys for him?"

"No. I'll find him myself." Preoccupied, Rand started from the room.

"Rand?" Lorelei's soft call intruded into his thoughts and he looked up quickly. "Will you come back to the house before you leave for town?"

"Yes," he replied. "I'll be back to say good-bye before I go."

Lori's smile wavered at the thought of his leaving. "I'll be waiting," she said, and she watched him stride purposefully from the room.

While Rand was gone, Juana showed Lori and Sally to their rooms and told them to come back to the parlor for refreshments after they'd settled in.

"I'm so glad things have worked out for you two," Sally remarked to Lori as they returned to the sitting room to partake of the cool lemonade awaiting them.

"I can't believe everything worked out so well. He loves me, Sally, and all that time I thought he loved Lydia." Lori's expression was rapturous as she thought of the closeness she'd shared with Rand the night before. Though she was not looking forward to living with Lydia, she no longer feared her as a rival. Rand was hers alone! They would be married soon.

"I'm just happy that you've cleared up all the misunderstandings between you," she said.

"Me, too. Rand is as wonderful as Ellen McCrea said, maybe better."

"I am, am I?" His deep voice cut through Lori's romantic haze and he chuckled as Lori flushed.

"Yes, you are." No longer afraid to tell him her feelings, she went to him and kissed him deeply.

When they drew back, he asked seriously, "Lorelei, I know how you feel about Lydia and I was hoping that she would be here, so you could see for youself that there is nothing between us."

"It doesn't matter," she answered firmly. "None of that matters anymore, Rand. I love you."

He crushed her to him, unmindful of Sally's presence. "And I love you."

Sally politely left the room to allow the lovers privacy, but they weren't even aware of her departure. Finally, knowing that another moment in her arms would distract him from his purpose, Rand ended the kiss and moved slightly away from her.

"I've got to go," he said gruffly. "Jack understands the danger the Bentons pose, and he will do his best to protect you."

Tears stung her eyes, but Lori fought to hold them back. "Please, be careful." Her words were heartfelt, but despite her effort to maintain a calm façade, they revealed the very real anguish she was feeling at being separated from him so soon after they'd discovered their love for each other.

"I will." He kissed her cheek softly. "I'll be back as soon as I can."

Lori nodded, unable to speak, and he left her,

standing alone in the center of the parlor. This was the remembrance of her he would carry in his heart—her hair tumbled about her shoulders in fiery disarray, her eyes wide and dark with unspoken emotion, her lips reddened from his passionate kisses—and Rand knew he would be back.

John was just coming out of his office when he spied Rand riding in his direction. It surprised him to find Rand back in town so soon and he waited near the door as his friend dismounted and tied up at the hitching rail.

"Rand! I didn't expect you in town yet. Something wrong?"

"The Bentons are in the area."

"Have you seen them?" They stepped back inside the sheriff's office to talk in private.

"They made an attempt on my life last night up at the mine," Rand declared. "And for the time being, I'm sure they think they've succeeded in killing me."

"What happened?"

"They planted a man at the Triple Cross, and he lured me out to the new stamp mill that was being constructed. When we got there, it blew."

John was startled. "How do you know it was them?"

"Angelo, their man, was critically injured in the explosion, and he was calling for them before he died. The only thing I can figure is that they double-crossed him, just to get me. This morning I found some tracks that led away from the mill, but I lost them up in the rocks."

"We'd better head out in that direction and see what we can pick up."

"I've moved Lorelei and Sally out to the ranch to keep them safe, and I warned Jack that there might

347

be trouble."

"Still?"

"They think I'm dead now, but when they find out that I'm alive, they'll come back. If we move fast, we've got the element of surprise on our side."

"Got any ideas where they might be?"

"Hard to say. Last night, they were probably holed up somewhere celebrating, but once they get done with that they're liable to strike anywhere and anytime."

"The faster we move the better. I think I'll look up Barclay and see if he wants to ride along as a deputy. We can always use an extra gun."

Rand nodded. "Lydia's in town, so while you go for Barclay, I'll speak with her to explain what's going on. Why don't we meet here in half an hour?"

"Fine."

Lydia had visited friends that morning, but she was in her hotel room, packing for her return home, when Rand knocked at the door. She thought it was the wrangler from the ranch who'd accompanied her to town and she called out to him to enter, planning to give him her bags to take to the wagon.

"That's a very dangerous thing to do, Lydia," Rand told her as he opened the unlocked door and walked in.

Lydia was completely taken by surprise at finding Rand in her room. For a moment she hoped he had come just to see her, and despite her declared hatred for him, her gaze lingered on his broad-shouldered manly form. She couldn't help but remember how exciting it had been to make love with him.

"Oh? Why is that?" she asked archly.

"Because it might not always be someone as safe as me," he replied.

"Are you safe, Rand?" Lydia took a step toward him, intrigued by his appearance in her room.

"Lydia"—Rand's tone suddenly became cold—"I've

348

come here with news, not to initiate an assignation."

She halted her approach, her eyes narrowing as she listened to his declaration. "I had hardly thought so. You made yourself perfectly clear at the McCreas' party." She affected disdain, as if seducing him was not on her mind. "What is it that's so important it dragged you away from your mine?" She turned back to her packing.

"I've just taken Lorelei and Sally to the Lazy Ace to stay. They'll be there with you for a time."

"Why?" Lydia kept her expression impassive as she glanced up at him.

"The Bentons are in the area. They've already tried to kill me once and—"

"What!" Lydia did not try to hide her horrified surprise.

"They made the attempt last night up at the mine, but I was lucky enough to escape unharmed."

"What happened?"

"There was an explosion. The man who was killed in it implicated the Benton gang, and knowing how they operate, I didn't want the women to be at risk."

"Why would the women be in danger? You mean, you think they'll try again?"

"Once they find out they didn't succeed, they'll be back. That's why I took Lorelei and Sally to the ranch. I want them out of the line of fire. It'll be safer there."

"Where are you going to be? At the mine?"

"No. I'm going after the Bentons. I'll be heading out shortly with John McCrea and Brady Barclay."

"So you're dumping your little ward and her friend at the ranch and you expect me to take care of them? Well, who's going to protect me? They could come after me, you know; we are related." Lydia was furious for she found the thought of living with the other women thoroughly distressing.

349

Rand bristled at her tone and her remarks. "You'll all be safe at the ranch. And you'd be wise to remember, Lydia, that I own sixty percent of the Lazy Ace and I'm more than willing to buy you out at any time. As it is," he went on coolly, "you don't have to concern yourself over Lorelei being my ward for much longer."

"Why?" She knew a brief instant of hope before his next statement shattered it.

"Because she will soon be the mistress of the Lazy Ace."

Lydia gazed at him in disbelief.

"Lorelei has agreed to marry me. We'll be wed as soon as the Bentons are captured. You'd do well to make her welcome, Lydia. The ranch will soon be her permanent home."

She stiffened at his words. So, the rotten little bitch had won his heart completely, had she? As her jealousy and anger mingled, Lydia had to fight to keep from revealing her more vicious reactions to Rand.

"Congratulations."

"Thank you." He mistook her fury for surprise.

"I suppose that's why Lorelei was so upset when she saw us together in the study. She must have been jealous."

Rand didn't bother to go into it. "That doesn't matter now. I've explained everything to her and she understands how things are between us."

"That's good," Lydia replied easily, hoping to convince him that she was concerned about any awkwardness a misunderstanding would create while both women were living at the ranch, but in truth she was wondering just how much Rand had told his precious fiancée about the relationship he'd had seven years ago with her.

"While I'm away," Rand went on, "Jack will be taking care of everything. I spoke with him earlier

350

today. He's aware of the danger and will take precautions to insure everyone's safety."

"How long do you think you'll be away? Do you know where the Bentons have gone?" Lydia asked, anxious now to gather any information she could pass on to Josh.

"Hopefully not too long, but we don't have anything certain to go on. I know where they started from, so we're going to begin there. We'll try to pick up their trail and then figure out where they headed after they left the mine." Rand shrugged. "The Bentons think I'm dead, so we can surprise them if we can catch up with them before they learn the truth."

"Be careful," she said slowly, all the while hoping that the Bentons would find him first.

"I intend to." He started for the door. "I'll be back just as soon as I've got the Bentons behind bars."

Lydia nodded as he left the room. Then, from the window, she watched the small posse ride off before she hurried to the bank to tell Josh the news.


Blackie Jones slugged down another beer as he listened attentively to the conversation of the two drunks at the table nearby. Ever since he'd received word that there was big money being offered, and not by the law, for information on the Benton brothers, he'd been keeping his eyes and ears open. He was not averse to making an easy buck and he was reasonably sure he'd found an opportunity to do so. For well over an hour now, he'd been casually lingering at the bar near the two scurrilous-looking strangers, and he was pretty sure that they were the two outlaws. They'd been calling each other Pat and Cody, and according to the wanted posters, those were the first names of the Bentons. Thinking that he had pretty much to go on, he paid the barkeep and headed out to make contact with the interested party.

As Josh pondered what Lydia had told him, he wondered if the Bentons had caused the explosion or if Harley had been responsible for it.

"Damn!" he said agitatedly. "If the Bentons have been in the area, why in the hell haven't I heard something?"

"Who knows?" She shrugged. "Maybe they've been hiding out up near the mine, waiting for a chance to get Rand. It doesn't matter now, anyway. What matters is they're nearby and we've got to get word to them!"

"I know, I know." Josh rubbed wearily at the back of his neck. "You say Lorelei is living at the ranch?"

"Right. She'll be staying there until Rand gets back."

He nodded. "Then if we can locate the Bentons and fill them in on everything we know—"

"In that case they wouldn't know much," Lydia said sarcastically, frustrated by their current inability to act.

"No, but they would have one vital piece of information."

"Such as?"

"Such as the location of Rand's dearly beloved."

Lydia's eyes brightened at the prospect. "You mean we should use Lorelei?"

"Of course. You do want to get rid of her too, don't you?"

She nodded eagerly at the thought.

"Then, we'll arrange something . . . I don't know . . . maybe a kidnapping. Anyway, once the Bentons get their hands on her, they can use her as bait to draw Rand out. We'll leave the rest up to them. It's not really important what they do as long as Rand and Lorelei end up dead."

"I agree completely. Then we, my darling, will be the proud owners of the Triple Cross and the Lazy Ace." She smiled widely as she silently tallied her future worth.

"Indeed, we shall." His greedy smile matched hers as their eyes met in silent understanding.

"I'll be returning to the ranch this afternoon. Send word to me as soon as you know something."

"I will."


"Mr. Taylor?"

Josh looked up from the contracts he was going over. "What is it, Wright?" he asked irritably.

The clerk stepped into the inner office and handed Josh a sealed missive. "Sir, a note was just delivered for you."

Josh took the envelope and then waved the clerk from the office. "That'll be all."

"Yes, sir."

When Josh was certain that the other man had closed the door as he exited the room, he slit open the envelope and quickly read the single page within. A malevolent glint lit his gaze as he devoured the news, and he quickly stood up, shoving the letter into his pocket as he strode from his office.

"I'll be out for about an hour," he informed Wright as he walked quickly from the bank and headed in the direction of the Gold Nugget.

It was early afternoon and relatively quiet at the saloon as Josh entered. He ordered a beer from the bartender and then took a seat at an out-of-the-way table near the rear of the establishment. As he settled in, he hoped that he wouldn't have to wait long for his contact, and he was pleased when he saw Blackie Jones enter the place.

Josh eyed the informant anxiously. If what the man had indicated in his letter was true, this was the break he'd been waiting for.

"Afternoon, Taylor." Blackie grinned as he approached the table. "I think you should buy me a drink. What do you think?"

"Get whatever you want and put it on my bill," Josh said hurriedly, wanting to get on with their business.

"I'll do just that." He returned to the bar to get a beer and then joined Josh at the table.

"What have you got for me?" Josh asked as Blackie sat down.

"That depends on what you got for me," the informant countered.

"If the information you give me plays out, it's worth three hundred dollars to me."

"And when do I get paid?"

"When I meet the Benton brothers."

"Wait a minute!" Blackie balked. "I can tell you where they are right now, but I ain't setting up any meeting with them. I don't mess with their kind."

"You afraid?" Josh sneered.

Blackie eyed him defensively. "If you are smart, you'd be afraid to mess with them. They're bad blood all the way."

At an impasse, the two men drank deeply of their beers as they assessed each other.

"Taylor, you pay me three hundred dollars and I'll take you to them, but I don't want to be involved in any way. They're the type who'd just as soon kill you as look at you and I don't want nothing to do with them."

Josh felt no fear as he thought of dealing with the Bentons, and he met Blackie's nervous gaze with an icy one. "One hundred dollars."

"Nope. It ain't worth it for that amount. Besides, I can get that much from the sheriff for this information."

"Two hundred then."

"When do you want to go?" Jones asked.

"Right now." Josh stood up and waited impatiently for the other man to finish his drink. "Where are they?"

"Let me see the color of your money," Blackie demanded, refusing to budge from his chair until he'd been paid.

Josh took a wad of bills from his pocket and peeled off ten twenty-dollar bills. "Now, where are they?"

Blackie drained his drink and slowly pocketed the payment, then followed the other man from the saloon. "When I left them about an hour ago, they had just taken a room at the Sidewinder Saloon. Second floor, third door from the stairs."

"You're positive?"

"I swear on my darling mother's grave," Jones told Josh solemnly.

"If your information is inaccurate, Blackie, I'll be coming after you to get my money back. Do you understand?"

Jones had no doubt as to what Taylor would do to him if he was wrong, but he was dead certain it had been the Bentons. "I ain't wrong, Taylor."

"Good." With that, the banker started across town toward the Sidewinder Saloon, one hand idly straying to the derringer he kept hidden on his person for situations like this. He found it interesting that outlaws as notorious as the Bentons were in town, and he wondered if the sheriff was unaware of their presence because of ineptitude or the closed-mouths of the lawless in the community. The latter reason seemed most likely, for Josh knew John McCrea had been following up every possible lead on the escaped convicts. Obviously the sheriff had no idea they were anywhere in the vicinity.

Though the Sidewinder was not busy, none of the few

patrons there paid the slightest bit of attention to Josh as he entered and went directly up the stairway to the second floor.

Josh felt supremely confident as he approached the room Blackie had told him the Bentons occupied, and though he kept one hand hovering near his gun, he knocked at the door with seeming casualness.

"Yeah? Who is it?" A hard, suspicious voice came through the thickness of the closed door.

"My name's Josh Taylor and I want to speak with you for a moment."

Within the confines of the cheaply furnished room, Pat and Cody glanced nervously at each other. They didn't know anyone named Josh Taylor and they definitely didn't want to open the door until they learned what was up. Reaching for their weapons, they prepared for the worst.

"This here way of speakin' suits us jus' fine," Pat responded as he drew his pistol and leveled it at the door at chest height. "What is it you're wantin', Taylor?"

Josh understood their caution, but he didn't like to discuss his business out in the open where anyone could eavesdrop. "I'm not accustomed to conducting my private affairs this way, but if you don't mind me talking about McAllister out here where everybody can hear . . ." He let the words trail off.

"Did you say McAllister?" Cody asked sharply. "What about him?"

"You botched the job." Josh said arrogantly, and the stunned silence that followed his statement convinced him that Blackie had been right. These were the Benton brothers. "Look, I'm not the law. I'm just a businessman who has a vested interest in McAllister's demise, that's all. I thought you might want to know he's still walking around in perfect health." He paused for effect. "I'd like to hire you boys to do the job right this time, if you're interested in picking up a little extra money."

In the privacy of their room, the brothers exchanged leery looks. "Who'd you say you were?"

"My name's Josh Taylor," he answered smoothly.

"Jes' a minute."

Josh smiled in triumph as he heard the key turn in the lock. Then the door was thrown open and a disreputable-looking man gestured him into the room. Another man slammed the door behind him and locked it.

"Sorry we ain't got a seat to offer ya," Pat Benton told Josh as he regarded him cautiously, taking note of his expensively tailored suit and cultured manner.

"No problem, I'd just as soon stand." Josh moved to the window and positioned himself there. Turning to face the Bentons, he kept his expression inscrutable. "I'm here to offer you a deal you won't be able to refuse."

Pat stopped him curtly by raising his hand. "First, I wanna know about McAllister. Who says it was us who tried to kill him, and how do you know he's still alive?"

Josh looked bored as he explained. "Look, I know who you are. You're the Benton brothers. It's common knowledge that you've sworn to get McAllister. Everyone knows you want him dead."

Cody and Pat nodded slowly. "And you're tellin' us he ain't? Why we saw the whole thing, there ain't no way he could have survived that explosion!"

Josh shrugged. "Rand McAllister is alive and kicking, and he knows you were the ones who set him up at the Triple Cross. Before he died, the man you planted at the mine let it slip that he was working with you."

"Damn! But how'd McAllister survive if Angelo

357

died?" Pat asked.

"I don't know the particulars. All I know is McAllister is on to you and he rode out with a posse this afternoon to track you down."

"You said somethin' about wantin' him dead. Why?" Pat wanted to know this man's motive in enlisting them to kill McAllister.

"That's strictly a business decision." Josh deflected the question quickly. "The point is we both want him dead and I'm willing to pay you handsomely to kill him. You'll get your revenge and a tidy sum from me, and I'll get what I want."

"And jes' how do we know that you won't turn us in after the job's done?"

The banker smiled thinly. "Gentlemen, it would be the height of folly for me to do such a thing. You could easily incriminate me and I, too, would be arrested. No. I think we can handle this matter with a minimum of difficulty, and in the end, we'll both be satisfied with the association."

"How much and when do you pay?"

"One thousand dollars for McAllister's death. Half now and half when the job is completed. Fair enough?"

"What's to stop us from shootin' you right now, takin' the five hundred dollars and skippin' town?"

"The promise of another five hundred dollars and the vital piece of information that I haven't given you as yet."

"What information?" Pat avidly awaited Josh's explanation.

"I know a perfect way for you to entrap McAllister, but I must have your complete agreement to my terms before we go any further."

The brothers paused, and when Cody started to take a threatening step forward, Josh drew his derringer and held him at bay.

"Just so we understand one another . . ." He smiled tensely. "I'm not stupid. I have two shots in this gun and though I may not be able to plug you both, I definitely can kill one of you. Which one will it be?" Josh waited, enjoying the expressions that flitted across their faces. "Do we have a deal?"

"Yeah," Pat agreed reluctantly, Josh's deadly ploy having won his grudging respect.

"Good. I'll leave you two hundred and fifty dollars now and you'll get the rest of the five hundred tomorrow when we meet," Josh stated.

"What's wrong with now?" Cody Benton started to argue. "You said—"

"I want the job done right this time," Josh said derisively. "And I want you both sober when we sit down to go over the plan I've devised. Do I make myself clear?"

"Yeah. What time tomorrow?"

"I'll meet with you some time after sundown. I should have all the details worked out by then. Until that time, maintain a low profile and keep your mouths shut. You're damned lucky the man who noticed your drunken escapades down in the saloon came to me rather than the law. Sheriff McCrea would be mighty pleased to have you back in custody."

The Bentons listened with little interest to his words so Josh prepared to leave.

"I'll meet you tomorrow," he declared as he handed them a wad of bills, but he did not put his derringer away until he was certain the door was closed and locked behind him.

Pat looked at Cody and smiled. "The Lord do provide! Wasn't I jes' tellin' you that not too long ago, brother?"

"Yes, sir, brother!" Cody chuckled. "I like that man Josh Taylor. He must be damned rich judging by the way he was dressed."

"Yep, and I think, once we're done with McAllister, he might jes' be next on our list. I wonder how that man makes a livin'?"

"I don't know, but I do plan to find out."

# Chapter Twenty-One

It was late in the afternoon when Lydia arrived at the ranch. She had done a lot of thinking during the ride from town, and she was filled with seething hatred for Rand and his fiancée. She fought to disguise her feelings as she entered the ranch house to face Lorelei. Lydia knew she must not make Lorelei suspicious. On the surface, she would appear happy that Lorelei and Sally had come to the ranch and delighted at the idea of Lori's upcoming marriage to Rand.

Still, Lydia meant to take full advantage of the situation at every opportunity, and she certainly planned to let Lorelei know, in a subtle way of course, that she and Rand had been involved before her marriage to Will. Smiling slightly to herself at that thought, she strode majestically into her home and accepted Juana's effusive greeting with her usual indifference.

"*Señora!* So much has happened since you left!" Juana started to tell her of Lorelei's and Sally's presence but Lydia cut her off as she spied Lorelei in the parlor.

Pretending not to have noticed the other woman's presence, she framed her words carefully, hoping to plant a little doubt in Lorelei's mind. "I know, Juana. Rand came to the hotel and we had a long discussion."

"Then you know he was almost killed last night." Juana shook her head in dismay. "If anything happens to Rand—"

"Nothing is going to happen to him, Juana." Lydia casually dismissed the old woman's worries. "You and I both know that he's more than capable of taking care of himself. He put the Bentons away once before and I'm certain he'll do it again."

*"Sí, señora."* Juana agreed somewhat hesitantly with her mistress' assessment.

"Where are my houseguests?"

"Lorelei is in the parlor and Sally is resting."

"I think I'll visit with Lorelei for a few minutes before I bathe. Bring something cool to drink to the parlor and then have someone draw my bath," Lydia ordered imperiously.

*"Sí, señora."* Juana made haste to do as she was told while Lydia moved gracefully into the parlor to confront her adversary.

"Lorelei." Lydia tried to sound happy to see her. "How nice that you're here."

"Thank you, Lydia. It was kind of you and Rand to offer us the protection of your home while all this is going on. I couldn't help but overhear your conversation with Juana, so I presume Rand told you everything that's happened." Lori had been standing by the window, but she came forward now.

"Yes, he told me everything when he came to see me," Lydia replied easily as she took the cool beverage offered by the servant. "I was quite surprised to see him in town. Why, the last time we talked, the two of you were going to be staying at the mine."

"Those were our original plans, but now the Bentons are in the area so Rand believes it's too dangerous up

362

there for Sally and me, especially since he's going to be away. When he suggested we move in here for safety's sake, Sally and I agreed."

"And he's right, of course," Lydia said quickly. "You'll be much safer here." Inwardly, she chuckled as she thought of the plan she had made with Josh. At the ranch Lorelei certainly wasn't safe.

Lori knew she had to bring her newly established relationship with Rand out into the open so she asked, "Did Rand tell you were plan to wed?"

"Yes, he most certainly did and I extend my best wishes," Lydia answered giving Lori a warm smile.

"Thank you." Lori didn't know why, but she was totally surprised by Lydia's reaction. She had expected anything but this easy acceptance from the woman she'd once thought to be her rival.

"I'm just thrilled for the both of you. Rand's such a wonderful man," Lydia declared. "I should know. We've been close for a long time, and he's been such a comfort to me since Will died."

"I'm sure he has."

Lori couldn't prevent sarcasm from creeping into her voice, and Lydia knew she'd hit a nerve.

"Now, there's no reason for you to be jealous of me and Rand," she chided. "He told me how you reacted after seeing us in the study that night when he was comforting me, but you must believe me when I tell you that absolutely nothing happened between us."

Though she managed to keep her features schooled into a mask of unconcern, Lorelei blanched as she imagined Rand telling Lydia about that encounter in the stable.

"I don't know what I would have done without him." Lydia sighed melodramatically.

"Rand is a wonderful man," Lori managed to say, but her thoughts were in turmoil.

363

"That he is. Isn't it odd that just a short time ago, he was balking at being your guardian and now you're going to be married." Lydia gave Lori a look that seemed to reflect genuine warmth and caring. "I only hope after the two of you marry he'll settle down and lead a normal life."

Lori hadn't thought of the possibility that Rand might return to his job as a U.S. Marshal after they were married. "I hadn't considered that, but I'm sure he will."

"For your sake, I hope so. Being alone is not for a woman, even one as independent as you. Why, years ago that's what caused so many problems for us—" She broke off the lie nervously, as if she'd revealed something she shouldn't have.

"Problems?" Instantly, Lori was curious. Rand had never mentioned having problems with Lydia.

"I suppose he never mentioned that to you. It was so long ago." Lydia led her on, impatient to deliver the blow that would make her doubt Rand's love.

"What was so long ago?"

"I shouldn't have said a word." Lydia sounded remorseful. "But you see, I wanted marriage and Rand did not. He wanted to be a marshal more than he wanted to settle down. When I knew there was no future for me with Rand, I married Will."

Lori had always known there had been something between Rand and Lydia, even though Rand had denied it. He and Lydia had been close. The memory of the kiss she'd seen in the stable came to her mind, and Lori hoped that had been the end of their relationship and not the beginning of an adulterous affair.

"With you, however, I'm sure it's different. Rand's much older now, and I'm sure he knows his own mind," Lydia went on, noting with pleasure Lorelei's troubled expression. "I'm sure he'll make you a fine husband.

You'll both be very happy here at the ranch, and I promise not to get in your way."

"You won't have to worry about that. I intend to live at the Triple Cross once the Bentons are captured."

Lydia gave Lori a bewildered look. "Oh, really? That's not what Rand told me in town, but I suppose you really haven't talked about it yet."

"What did Rand say?" Lori asked.

"He just mentioned that once you'd married, he wanted to live at the ranch," Lydia said with restraint. "First, of course, Rand has to catch the Bentons."

"I hope it won't take him too long." Lori suddenly wished Rand was here so she could go into his supportive embrace. She wondered if Lydia's disturbing remarks had been innocently made, and she experienced a clutching fear that this woman posed a threat to her happiness with Rand.

"So do I, but the Bentons are on the run. It might take a lot longer than we think to corner them."

"I know, but we'll just pray that it doesn't." Lori found the prospect of spending a great deal of time with Lydia wearing, and the very idea that Rand had discussed their future living arrangements with this woman disturbed her. Then again, she had only Lydia's word that Rand had said these things to her, and though Lydia appeared warm and caring, Lori felt there was more to Rand's stepmother than met the eye.

"Perhaps we could use this time to plan your wedding and get things ready so we'll be all set when Rand comes back?" Lydia pretended to be excited about the upcoming nuptials.

"Rand and I haven't made definite plans yet."

"Then you can make all the arrangements. I'll be glad to help," Lydia persisted.

"There's no rush. I think I'd like to consult Rand before I do anything regarding our wedding." Lydia was the last person Lori wanted involved, no matter how nice she was pretending to be. "But thank you for your offer."

"Of course, and if you change your mind, you know I'm more than willing to help." Lydia took a sip of lemonade to hide the scowl that threatened. Her ploy had seemed to be working in the beginning, but all of a sudden the chit had gone cold on her. Deciding that her remarks must have had some effect, however, she gave up the effort for the moment.

"*Señora,* your bath is ready," Juana announced quietly as she came into the room.

"Thank you." Lydia set her glass aside and started from the room. "Lorelei, I'll see you at dinner. It's so nice to have you here, and I can't wait to see Sally again. I really do appreciate your company"

Lori watched pensively as the other woman disappeared down the hall toward the wing of the house that contained her suite of rooms.

Rand searched the hidden campsite, his temper flaring at his own stupidity. He wondered how he could have been so careless. The Bentons had been within striking distance of the mine for several days judging by the state of things in the deserted campsite, yet he had been totally oblivious of their proximity. An icy chill went through Rand as he realized these killers could have struck at any time during that period and he would have been unprepared for their attack. Saying a silent prayer of thanks for getting a second chance at life, he determined not to rest or return to Lorelei until the Bentons were behind bars or dead.

"Find anything?" Brady asked as he joined Rand.

"No. Nothing out of the ordinary. They've been gone from here for about twenty-four hours at least, so they could be just about anywhere. First thing in the morning, we're going to have to spread out and see if we can pick up their trail."

"The horses were tied up back there," John remarked as he strode toward them. "And it looks like they rode southeast."

"That's rough country," Brady supplied, thinking of the rugged mountains and the miles of desert in that direction.

"If they didn't want to be followed, that's the way they'd head before possibly doubling back . . ." Rand's eyes narrowed as he tried to figure out just where the bandits had gone.

"You think they might have headed for town?" John was worried for he'd left only an inexperienced deputy behind.

"It's hard to say." Rand shrugged, his expression grim. "If they think I'm dead, they might take off for anywhere—Tucson, Prescott, maybe even Mexico— but if they've found out I'm still alive, they're still here somewhere, hiding and waiting for the chance to do the job right the next time."

"Don't worry. There's not going to be a next time." Brady tried to sound positive. "Do you want to camp here for the night?"

"Might as well. We know it's secluded," Rand said dryly. "But we'd better not make a fire, just in case."

Later, as they sat on their bedrolls sharing a sparse meal of dried meat and water, Rand told them he planned to marry Lorelei, and he smiled wryly at John's look of surprise.

"You and Lorelei? That's wonderful! But how did this come about? The last time we talked, you'd just taken on your duties as her guardian."

"She's a special woman," Rand mused as he thought of his love.

"And beautiful too, if you don't mind my saying so," Brady put in.

"That she is," Rand agreed. "We started off all wrong, though. She resented my interference in her life and I resented being forced into the role of her protector, but we've worked that out."

"I'm happy for you, Rand. No one deserves happiness more than you." John's declaration was sincere.

"How's Lorelei's friend Sally doing?" Brady tried to sound nonchalant.

"She's just fine. She's staying at the ranch with Lydia, as Lori is, until this thing with the Bentons is finished."

"Good." Brady's relief was evident, and John glanced at him questioningly.

"You spent some time with Sally at our party, didn't you Brady?"

Brady looked slightly uncomfortable. "Yes, I did. She's quite a lady."

"She's one of the nicest women I've ever known. Maybe you should pay her a visit." Rand's affection for Sally was heartfelt.

"I've been meaning to for some time now. In fact, her cousin Roger suggested it when I saw him before he left town, but I've been so busy following up leads on the robbery for the Wells Fargo Office that I haven't been able to get away."

"Have you turned up anything new?" John asked.

"No, but I'm beginning to suspect that we were closer to the Bentons than we thought."

Rand looked up quickly. "It does fit. The gang came out of nowhere and then disappeared. There were four, then three, and now that Angelo's dead—"

"It bears keeping in mind." John saw the connection. "We're going to have a lot to ask these boys when we finally catch up with them."

"That we are," Brady answered, rubbing idly at his still-sore shoulder.


Harley left the mining camp under the cover of darkness and went straight to Josh Taylor's home for it was late and there was little time to arrange a meeting at the saloon. Josh had just retired for the night when he heard a furtive tapping at a side window, and when he went to investigate, he was dismayed to find Harley.

"What are you doing here? I thought you understood you were never to come to my home?" he snarled as he let Oates in the back door.

"I got to tell ya what's been goin' on."

"I heard," Josh answered arrogantly as he locked the door and ushered the man into the privacy of his study. Drawing the drapes, he lit a single lamp and turned to face him.

"You did? How?"

"McAllister was in town today. Everyone knows that the Bentons blew up the mill at the Triple Cross in an effort to kill him."

Harley smiled slyly. "I know, but it wasn't the Bentons who set the explosives at the stamp mill."

"You?" Josh was surprised and pleased.

"Yep. I wondered what McAllister was doin' out at the mill with that Angelo fella, but I thought you wouldn't mind if he got killed. Accidentally, you know what I mean? Thought it might be worth a little more to ya if he was dead. Too bad that stupid Angelo hit McAllister before the explosives blew. That was what saved his life."

"I wondered how he managed to survive when the man standing beside him was killed," Josh said. He nodded thoughtfully. "So you were responsible for the destruction of the mill, but the Bentons got the blame."

"That's right." Harley grinned, quite pleased with himself.

"Good . . . good. There's no way suspicion will be directed toward us. You've done very well, Harley."

"Thanks. You know, without their own stamp mill they're gonna hafta keep shippin' ore overland. Might jes' run them outta money real quick like."

Josh smiled for the first time that night. One way or the other he was going to have that mine. "You may consider your debt to me canceled, Harley."

The miner nodded, "Anything else you'll be needin' from me?"

"Just one thing."

"What's that?"

"I want to know the shipment schedule to the mill. Can you get that information?"

"I already know it. Mondays and Thursdays when things is goin' right. Lately"—Harley grinned again—"things ain't been goin' right."

"Mondays and Thursdays, eh?"

"Yep, that's it."

"Good." Josh went to his desk, withdrew a small bag containing gold dust, and tossed it to his hireling. "That's for a job well done. Just keep your mouth shut and no one will ever know of our involvement. We'll just let them keep thinking it was the Bentons."

Lorelei knew that she should be sleeping, but the thought of Rand chasing the bloodthirsty bandits across the territory filled her with dread. Every time she'd closed her eyes in an effort to rest, visions of the demolished mill haunted her. She knew that the Bentons would stop at nothing to kill him. Getting up from the wide comfort of her bed, she pulled on a silken wrap, and opening the French doors that led

370

onto the patio area, she stepped out into the quiet of the night.

"You can't sleep either?" Sally's voice surprised her.

"What are you doing out here?" Lori asked as she moved to join her friend on a small bench near the center of the courtyard.

"I was thinking and one thing led to another. I thought the night air might help me fall asleep," she replied distantly.

"Thinking about Brady Barclay, were you," Lori teased.

"Am I that obvious?" Sally was mortified.

"Heavens, no!" Lori's denial was immediate. "I'm probably the only person who knows how you feel about him."

"Thank goodness."

"I don't know if that's good or not."

"What do you mean?" Sally blinked in confusion.

"Well, if Brady had known how you felt about him, I'm sure he would have come calling by now."

"Maybe not, Lori. He's so different from all the men I've ever known . . . I might have done something to offend him."

"I wouldn't worry on that account. You wouldn't know how to offend anybody, even if you tried!" Lori chuckled good-naturedly.

"Then why haven't I heard anything from him? I mean he escorted me back to the hotel yet I haven't heard another word."

"You have to remember that life is different here. We're not in St. Louis where men work normal hours and come calling in the evening and on weekends. Brady's a guard for Wells Fargo. Maybe he's back on duty. I'm sure you'll be hearing something from him soon."

"I hope you're right, but, Lori, if he's back at work as

371

a guard on the stageline, he could be shot, even killed!" Sally found that thought totally appalling.

"I know." Lori grasped her friend's hand. "I'm having the same worries about Rand. I *know* where he is and it terrifies me. The minute the Bentons hear he's alive, they'll be going after him, guns blazing. They aren't apt to fail twice."

"Rand's too smart for them, Lori. He'll come back to you. I just know he will."

"I wish I could be as positive of that as you are, Sally. If anything happens to him after all we've been through—"

"He'll be fine."

The young women sat together in comfortable silence then, thinking of the men they loved and imagining that Rand and Brady were somewhere safe staring up at the same night-blackened, moonless sky.

"You seemed to be getting along with Lydia at dinner tonight," Sally remarked after some time passed. "Are you finding it easier than you thought to be around her?"

"I'm not quite sure how I feel about her. We had a long talk this afternoon when she first arrived from town, and I couldn't quite decide whether she's really being friendly or it's all an act."

"What do you mean?" Sally was puzzled for she'd found Lydia to be a charming hostess at the evening meal. "Why would she be acting?"

"I don't know, but several things she mentioned 'idly' during the course of our conversation seemed calculated to me. I felt she wanted to make me doubt Rand's love."

"How?"

"Well, when she first came in, she told Juana that Rand had sought her out at her hotel room in town, she phrased it so I might think they'd had a rendezvous."

"And?"

"Then she managed to insinuate that many years ago she and Rand had been . . . close."

"Close?"

"That's as specific as she got. She just said that she hoped for my sake that he would give up his job as a marshal because his work had been the reason things hadn't worked out between her and Rand and that was why she'd married Will. It irritated me that she was brazen enough to bring up their past relationship, but in a way I was glad she did."

"Why?"

"Because that explains the kiss I saw in the stable that morning, and I hope I'm right in thinking that it wasn't the beginning of an affair I witnessed that day, but the end of one."

Sally paused to consider her friend's observation. "You're making sense."

"Rand told me he would never lie to me, and I believe him now," Lori concluded firmly.

Sally smiled brightly. "Do you know how long I tried to convince you of his finer points?"

Lori managed to look slightly ashamed. "I know you were right, but I had to find out in my own way just how wonderful Rand is."

"Well, as long as you're sure of him now, everything is going to work out just fine."

"I know. I love him Sally and I can hardly wait until he gets back."

A few minutes later, feeling better because they'd talked, the young women started back to their rooms, totally unaware of the horrors that faced them in the near future.

# Chapter Twenty-Two

Clad in dark, nondescript clothing, his derringer hidden on his person, Josh entered the Sidewinder Saloon and made his way directly to the Bentons' room. As he saw it, the plan he'd devised was infallible. If the outlaws followed his directions, everything would work out perfectly. Knocking sharply, he waited impatiently for them to respond.

"It's me, Taylor."

Pat turned to Cody with a smile, and nodded, indicating that his brother admit the banker. They had asked some questions of their own during the course of the day and they were now well aware of Josh's position at the bank. Their knowledge pleased them. Robbing banks had been one of their specialties before McAllister had put them away seven years ago.

"Come on in," Cody said as he opened the door and Josh calmly entered the room. "We've been waiting for you."

"I've been looking forward to our meeting this evening," Josh replied as he walked over to the window and then turned to face the two desperadoes. "I take it you passed an uneventful day?"

"We did what you said," Pat snarled, angered by

Josh's condescending attitude. "Now, let's see you come up with the rest of the money."

"First, I want your undivided attention while I explain the plan I've mapped out. I think you'll find that it will be easy to execute and will entail a minimum of bloodshed."

"We ain't wastin' any more time on you until we see the color of your money," Pat said pointedly, his eyes icy.

Josh looked disgusted, but he took out a roll of bills and tossed it onto the bed next to him. "It's all there—the additional two hundred and fifty dollars."

"That's what I like"—Cody leered—"a man who pays his debts on time."

"This is hardly a debt," Josh countered. "You've been hired to do a job and you're being paid an advance. I owe you nothing. *You* owe me."

Pat counted the bills and then waved aside Josh's remark. "It's all here. Now tell us this plan of yours and the extra piece of information that'll get us McAllister."

"His fiancée."

"Fiancée? What fiancée?"

"McAllister has just gotten engaged to Miss Lorelei Spencer. They are in love and are planning to be married just as soon as he's captured you."

"Oh, yeah?" Pat glanced at his brother. "I think this is one wedding that might not take place. What do you think, Cody?"

"I think you're right, brother. What's your plan, Taylor?"

"My plan is this. I will lure Lorelei Spencer into town from the Lazy Ace Ranch. I'll send her a note telling her it's imperative I get her signature on some papers involved in our mutual business dealings. I will send one of you as a guard to accompany her on the trip. Once you've got her away from the ranch, she's all

375

yours, but you must first use her as bait to draw McAllister to you. Set him up. Kill him. The girl is yours and so is another five hundred dollars."

Pat nodded thoughtfully. "That sounds easy enough. When do we move? Those false trails we left on our way back from the mine ain't gonna fool him for too long."

"Day after tomorrow. There are a few things I have to take care of. Until then, sit tight and stay out of trouble. I'll be in touch."

"I think we may enjoy this job." Cody was excited by the thought of holding a woman hostage.

"Just make sure he's dead, and the girl too. I don't want either one of them around to stir up trouble when this is over. Understand?"

"Yes, sir," Pat drawled mockingly. "Whatever you say, sir! You are payin' our bills."

"That's right and don't forget it."

When Josh had gone, Pat and Cody exchanged smug looks. "He's gonna be in for a big surprise."

"He sure is," Cody replied.


Lydia was pleased that she was alone when Josh's note arrived the next day, and she promptly retired to her bedroom to read the missive. She was thrilled to learn that he had at last made contact with the Bentons, that arrangements had been made and his plan was to be carried out the following day.

Lydia was delighted that Lori would fall into the Bentons' hands. The more time she'd spent with Lorelei Spencer, the more she had come to despise her, and she could hardly wait until tomorrow when the little witch would get her due. Fearful that Josh's note might be found, she quickly destroyed it, not wanting her involvement to be discovered.

\*     \*     \*

376

It was late afternoon when Rand tipped his hat back farther on his head and wiped the sweat from his brow as he contemplated the arid land to the east. The Bentons' trail had played out some miles back and for the last few hours, they could find no trace of them.

"I think they must have been expecting someone to follow them," Brady said as he reined in beside Rand.

"Their kind usually do," McAllister agreed tightly. The discovery of another false trail left him puzzled. He'd assumed that the Bentons had thought him dead in the explosion, so he was surprised to find that they had taken such precautions. "We'll double back to our last sighting and take it from there. If that doesn't develop into anything, we'd better head back to town. Maybe they've been spotted or there's been a robbery."

John rode up, frustrated by their futile search. "Nothing," he spat out. "It's almost as if they disappeared into thin air."

"Well, we know they're out there somewhere." Rand smiled grimly as he let his gaze sweep across the horizon.

"That's what's bothering me," John put in. "I just hope they haven't led us on a wild goose chase while they're in town causing trouble."

"I was just telling Brady, we'll head back after checking out that last lead."

The three men, sun-bronzed, and bone-weary, wheeled their horses around and started back the way they'd come.

Lorelei was finding her days at the ranch tedious. She was used to being busy at the mine so the long hours of idleness were driving her to distraction. She was most excited when she spotted an unidentified rider coming toward the ranch.

One of the ranchhands standing guard stopped the

horseman at the gate and, after a short discussion, sent him on up to the house.

"Sally!" Lori rushed to her friend's room. "There's someone coming!"

"Do you think it's someone from town with word from Rand or a messenger from Hal with news about the mine?" Sally quickly followed her back to the entryway.

"I don't know. I didn't recognize him, but that doesn't mean anything. Where's Lydia?"

"I haven't seen her since breakfast," Sally answered as they went out to greet the stranger who'd just reined in before the house.

"Good morning," Lori said brightly.

"Mornin', ma'am," Pat replied with a servility that irked him, but Taylor had insisted upon it. "My name's Mason, ma'am, and Mr. Taylor at the bank sent me out with a message for a Miss Lorelei Spencer." He took out Josh's letter.

Lori's hope of news from Rand were dashed, but she quickly covered her disappointment.

"It's nice to meet you, Mr. Mason. I'm Lorelei Spencer and this is my friend Sally Westlake," she said politely as she took the envelope he offered her. "Why don't you come in and have a cool drink while I read this letter. It may require a response."

"Yes, ma'am. Thank you, ma'am." Pat followed her inside, his gaze hungrily devouring her lush curves. He found the woman McAllister was planning to marry most attractive, and he struggled to keep from leering lustily at her.

As they went inside, Juana appeared.

"A messenger has just arrived from Mr. Taylor. He's going to stay while I read the note he sent. Could you bring him a cool drink, please?" Lori requested politely as she headed toward the parlor.

378

"Of course." The servant made haste to do as she was bid.

Having noted the man's arrival, Lydia came forth to join them, knowing it would seem strange if she did not. "We have company?"

"Yes, a messenger from Josh Taylor," Sally explained as Lori read the banker's missive.

"Is there any word in there of Rand?" Lydia asked.

"No. According to Josh's note there's been no news, but he says I must come into town to sign some business agreements. Since he knows how dangerous it is for us right now, he's sent Mr. Mason along to act as a guard on the trip."

"Well, a trip to town will certainly be a nice diversion," Lydia observed blandly.

"Do you want to come along?" Lori's invitation was directed to Sally and Lydia.

"I don't have any business there right now. As you know, I just returned." Lydia knew "Mason" was a Benton and she wanted as little to do with him as possible.

"I'll come," Sally replied, for she hoped to run into Brady Barclay in town.

Pat had been told to act like a disinterested hireling, but when the other girl invited herself along, it was all he could do not to take matters into his own hands. Only his knowledge that armed guards were posted outside kept him in restraint. Shooting his way through them with a woman in tow and getting himself killed would not bring him any closer to getting McAllister.

Controlling his urge to defy Taylor, he eyed the other young woman speculatively. She was not as strikingly beautiful as McAllister's fiancée, but she certainly was not hard to look at. With two women, he was sure he and Cody would enjoy themselves to the fullest. Pat was almost sorry that the blonde hadn't decided to go along for he found her pale, sensual beauty appealing, but there was little he could do about that. Maybe later, when McAllister was out of the way, he'd come back and sample her charms. At the moment, he had to concentrate on Taylor's plan.

Lorelei was pleased that she'd be getting away from Lydia for a while, and she and Sally hurried to their rooms to pack a few things for the trip while Lydia ordered a buckboard brought around from the stables. It did not occur to Lori that making a trip to town would be going against Rand's instructions. She had promised him not to go to the Triple Cross, but he'd said nothing about making short excursions into Phoenix for business purposes.

Pat excused himself on the pretense of seeing to his horse and he waited outside, checking out the exact location of the guards and trying to estimate the difficulty he would have should any trouble start. Pleased when he could only spot the two armed gunmen he'd noticed before, he figured he had a fifty-fifty chance of making it out alive if someone caught onto him.

Leaning casually against the waiting buckboard, he drew his sidearm and nonchalantly spun the chamber to make sure that it was fully loaded. At the sound of the women's approach, he slid the pistol back into his holster and turned toward them, his expression respectful.

"We're ready to go," Lorelei said cheerfully as she approached with Sally and Lydia following her.

Pat took the small bags Sally and Lori had packed and loaded them in the back before tying his horse to the rear of the buckboard. Handing the two women up onto the seat, he climbed up after them and took up the reins. As he did so, he noticed one of the guards coming toward them and a knot of tension grew in his stomach.

Slowly, he let his right hand drift down to hover near his sidearm.

"Miss Spencer!" The ranchhand called out as he approached.

"Yes, Tex?"

"Fred down at the stables told Jack that you were makin' a trip to town, so Jack ordered me to ride along, just in case."

Lori marveled at Jack's conscientiousness. "Mr. Mason is armed."

"I know, but Jack insisted, ma'am. He thinks one guard wouldn't be enough if the Bentons decided to try something."

"All right then," she agreed.

"I'll get my horse and be right with you." Tex headed for the stables.

Pat had been ready to draw and fire at the slightest provocation, but now he was frustrated. It had been bad enough that the other girl had decided to come along, but this was a more serious complication—a ranchhand was accompanying them. Swearing silently to himself, he knew he was going to have to act and act fast when the showdown came.

Tex joined them within moments, and the group started off.

"Have a safe trip," Lydia called out as they drove away. She knew the additional guard might present a problem, but she was certain the Bentons would dispose of him easily. They were, after all, killers who'd been hired to do a job.

Pat found something in the blonde's manner annoying, and when he directed a cold-eyed glare at her, a shiver of fright raced down Lydia's spine. As her eyes met his, she knew how his victims felt just before they met their maker. Hurrying back inside, she shut the door quickly and tried to subdue the fear that left her trembling and weak.

"Is something wrong, *señora?*" Juana's question shocked Lydia and she gasped.

"Oh, no. Nothing's wrong. Everything's just fine."

"But you seem so pale."

"I do feel a bit weak, but I think it's only the sun. I'll rest for a few minutes."

*Sí, señora,"* Juana was puzzled for she'd never known her mistress to be affected by the heat. Nonetheless, she withdrew.

When the servant had gone, Lydia drew a deep steadying breath and then managed a self-satisfied smile. She wondered why she'd felt so threatened when it was Lorelei and Rand the Bentons wanted, not her. She was safe. The thought of a long nap in the cool quiet of her bedroom was appealing, and Lydia disappeared down the hall, eager to enjoy the comforting safety of a locked door.

Lori and Sally were totally unaware of the danger they faced as they rode along with their two guards. Tex was not a talkative man and he concentrated solely on the surrounding terrain as he rode along beside the buckboard, keeping a careful watch out for anything out of the ordinary.

Pat, too, remained quiet, speaking only when spoken to. He was nervous and angry over the unexpected changes in the plan, and he hoped Cody didn't make any mistakes when they reached the designated rendezvous some distance down the road. They had picked that spot because it was so isolated and they needed seclusion to do what they intended, even more so now since there was the guard and another woman to consider.

Lori and Sally were oblivious of their driver's murderous thoughts, and they chatted on idly, enjoying the feeling of freedom the trip offered. Lori's musings inevitably turned to Rand and she speculated openly on the possibility of his success.

"I hope I hear something from Rand soon—something good."

"I'm sure you will," Sally said encouragingly. "If anyone can catch those awful Bentons it'll be Rand."

"But what if they catch up with him first?" Lori worried.

"Now don't even think such a thing!" her friend scolded. Rand will be back before you know it and then you'll be married."

"That sounds nice. Married—and to Rand. A few weeks ago I would never have dreamed it would work out this way, but now . . ." Lori gave her friend a wide, delighted smile.

Pat almost sniggered at her words. There would be no wedding, and if everything went smoothly, this little lady would never see McAllister alive again.

"You know, Lori, I hope to see Brady while we're in town," Sally admitted.

"I had a feeling that was the reason you agreed to come along."

Sally flushed becomingly at her friend's perceptiveness. "Well, if he's not going to come to me, I'm just going to have to go to him."

"I'm sure he'll be happy to see you. He certainly paid enough attention to you at the party."

"I know." Sally sighed as she remembered that night and Brady's confusion because he'd believed she was Roger's wife. It seemed humorous now, and she smiled to herself. If she was going to be a wife to anybody, it would be to Brady.

Sally and Lori lapsed into silence then, and the miles passed slowly and monotonously as the Arizona sun beat down fiercely upon them.

A calmness overtook Pat as they neared the meeting

383

place. Up ahead there was a bend in the road, just as it passed through a massive rock formation, and the ranchhand, though he might be a good gunman, was not going to know what hit him. Tex had insisted on riding slightly ahead and to the left of the wagon so Pat had a clear unobstructed aim at his unprotected back.

As they neared the rocks, Pat drew his gun and when Lori looked at him questioningly, he told her, "Just in case, ma'am. It wouldn't do to get caught unprepared, even with Tex up ahead. If anybody's plotting anything, this'll be the place they'll try it."

Lori nodded tensely, aware for the first time of some unidentifiable danger, and she glanced at Sally, giving her friend a reassuring smile.

Pat's carefully aimed shot exploded unnervingly, and Sally screamed as she saw Tex crumple and fall from his horse, dead before he hit the ground.

Lori reacted instantly, reaching for her reticule which she'd kept with her.

"No, ma'am." Pat spoke slowly as he turned toward them, six-gun in hand. "You two jes' sit there and I promise you you'll live a *little* longer. Yo! Cody! Where are you?"

Lori froze for a moment as she recognized the name he'd called out, and then, realizing this was her last chance for a one-on-one situation, she drew the gun she always carried and fired. Only Pat's lightning-fast reflexes saved his life, for Lori managed to get off two shots in quick succession, one grazing his right side and the other missing him completely as he threw himself upon her to wrestle the gun from her hand.

"You stupid little bitch!" he snarled as burning pain seared his side, and he slapped her viciously.

Sally was stunned by his unexpected viciousness, but she soon recovered and came to Lori's aid. Launching herself at the man attacking her friend, she managed to

384

land several blows about his head before he knocked her away. Caught completely off balance by his thrust, Sally tumbled to the ground and landed on the rugged terrain with a jolt that left her dazed and bruised.

Pat again struck out at Lorelei, enjoying the feeling of power he got from having McAllister's woman at his mercy, and he laughed as she lay beneath him, her lip bloodied, her cheek swelling and already beginning to discolor.

"Don't ever try to pull a gun on me again, woman. The next time I won't be satisfied with givin' you jes' a little beating!" He touched his flesh wound gingerly and then untied his bandana and pressed it to the injury to staunch the flow of blood. "Cody! Where the hell are you?"

"I'm here, Pat," his brother replied, revealing himself for the first time. He'd been confused by the outrider and the extra female and had wanted to make sure Pat was with them before beginning his attack. Reining in, he swung down out of the saddle and yanked an unresisting Sally up into his arms, crushing her against him. "You all right?" he asked Pat.

"I'll live, but no thanks to this little hellcat. When I get the chance I'm gonna—" He almost struck Lori again, but held back. Taylor had said he didn't care what they did with the women after McAllister was killed, so he would wait until the job was done.

"Which one's McAllister's?" Cody asked as he approached the buckboard.

"Mine," Pat replied thickly as he stared down at Lori who lay sideways beneath him on the driver's bench. Her fiery hair was in disarray, and her eyes were wide yet, curiously, not frightened. She looked angry and defiant in spite of the treatment he'd just given her, and he suddenly laughed out loud. "I know why McAllister picked this one. She's a wild one, and I'm gonna enjoy

385

being the man who tames her."

"You'll never tame me, Benton!" Lori suddenly fought to free herself from his painful grip, but he only smiled wider.

"I know now that pain won't stop ya, but how 'bout a little pleasurin'?" Pat trapped both her hands in one of his and then placed his free hand on her heaving breasts, making Lori moan as she tried to get away from him. "If I can't defeat ya by beatin' ya, maybe I'll jes' try somethin' else." Slowly, his eyes staring directly into hers, he began to unbutton her blouse.

"Lori!" Sally cried, as she looked on in helpless horror.

Pat's expression didn't change as he bared Lori's breasts and then, with deliberate, sensual caresses, began to explore their sweet fullness.

"No." Despite her revulsion and her desire to resist, Lori's body began to respond and terror appeared in her eyes as she realized what he was doing to her.

Pat read her reaction and laughed loudly. "C'mere, Cody. Ya wanna touch her?"

"Sure." Cody dragged Sally along as he came to the buckboard and reached out to savagely squeeze Lori's tender flesh. Then he grinned at his brother. "Let's get these two outta here. The sooner we trap McAllister, the sooner we can have us some fun."

"Tie up the one you got and get her up on one of the extra horses you brought. I'll take care of this one."

"Right."

As Cody moved off to do what he was told, Pat looked down at Lori and smiled. "Are you gonna do whatever I tell you to do?"

Lori's throat was tight as she realized how helpless she was. Her gun was gone, and there was no hope of rescue. Since hitting her had not brought about the desired result, this man would go to insidious lengths to

386

subdue her.

Pat expected instant submission from her and when he didn't get it, he again began to fondle her leisurely, arousingly. "I see that you've already forgotten the lesson I taught you."

"I hate you!" she whispered through battered, bruised lips.

"I said, are you gonna do whatever I tell you?"

"Yes," she answered in a strangled voice as she vowed silently to do whatever was necessary to stay alive. Alive so she could find a way to help Rand.

"Good," Pat released her only long enough to grab a piece of rope. Then, snaring her wrists, he pulled her upright and quickly tied her hands behind her back. "Jump down," he directed, and she scrambled to do his bidding.

"My blouse . . ." she said, feeling far too vulnerable with her breasts laid bare to his gaze.

"Shut up. I want you to stay that way, so you'll remember what I'm gonna do to you if you try anything else," Pat answered his eyes glittering.

"What are you going to do to us?" Lori asked as he climbed down and stood beside her.

Her query was rewarded with a lecherous look. "Do you mean now or later, after we kill your boyfriend?"

"You bastards!" Her fear for Rand's life made her forget her reluctant resolve to do as she was told.

Pat grabbed her by her hair and jerked her to him. "I wouldn't do no name callin' if I was you, pretty one. 'Specially when a little later you might find yourself beggin' me to be nice to you. Know what I mean?"

But Lori was mindless in her fury, and she spit in his face.

Pat's eyes turned to gleaming chips of ice as he slowly wiped the spittle from his cheek. "Girlie, you're gonna pay for that one."

"Pat! Not now! Come on, we gotta get a move on!"

His icy fury faded at his brother's words, and he savagely pushed Lori away, watching with indifference as she stumbled and fell to her knees. "You got that note, Cody?"

"Yeah, right here." Cody strode toward his brother, leading his horse and the horse upon which Sally was seated, and he opened a saddlebag and took out an envelope.

"Good. Give it here." Pat took the missive and after putting it in the box beneath the driver's seat, he climbed onto the buckboard and took up the reins. Turning the buckboard around, he let the reins drop and climbed down. He untied his own mount from the rear of the wagon and then swatted the buckboard's team with his hat, sending them back to the Lazy Ace. He and Cody knew that it would probably take a while for the horses to find their way back to their stable and that was fine with them. The longer the horses took, the more time they had to make it to their chosen hideaway and stash the women.

Pat watched until the wagon was out of sight, then he turned back to his brother. "Get his guns and let's take his horse along. We can always use an extra mount."

"Right." Cody hastily complied.

Picking up Lori's gun, Pat stuffed it into the waistband of his pants before he walked over to where she stood, silently watching him.

"Let's go," he snarled, almost hoping that she would give him another excuse to force her to comply to his wishes, but Lori was quick to obey and she walked hurriedly to the other horse Cody had brought along.

Unable to mount with her hands bound behind her, she cast a quick look in Pat's direction and saw that he was coming toward her.

"Need some help, do ya?" he asked with some

amusement as he clasped her familiarly around the waist and lifted her into the saddle. His gaze lingered lecherously on her exposed flesh and he reached up to touch her with brazen presumption.

Lori tried to jerk away from his hand, hunching her shoulders and shifting away in the saddle, but her desperate movements disturbed her mount and the horse shied skittishly almost throwing her from its back.

"Ya better jes' be still." Pat grinned at her nervousness, and he would have continued to torment her had Cody not come striding back, leading the dead ranchhand's horse.

"Let's go, Pat," he urged, and his brother regretfully swung up onto the back of his own horse. Taking up the reins to Lori's mount and Tex's, he led the way from the site of the murder, not caring that Tex's body lay only a short distance away.

Sally had been silently praying for some kind of miraculous rescue, but when she and Lori were led away she knew there would be no quick resolution for them. They would have to endure.

Casting a covert glance at Lori, she wondered how her friend was holding up. Lori's cheek and lips were swollen and bruised, and her blouse was hanging open, exposing her delicate bosom to the hot, desert sun. The Bentons had been particularly cruel to Lori because they knew she was Rand's fiancée, but Sally knew her own situation was not much better. The outlaws had seized them for a purpose, and she'd heard that these two desperadoes did not leave anyone who could identify them alive.

She and Lori were going to have to help themselves if they wanted to get away from them in one piece. Lori looked up and met her friend's sympathetic gaze. When Sally gave her a reassuring smile, Lori tried to return it, but her lips were so misshapen that her expression was more of a grimace. Sally understood and she nodded in acknowledgment as she fought to keep her balance on the back of her now-trotting mount while the Bentons led them across the rocky, barren land toward their secret hideaway.

## Chapter Twenty-Three

The exhausted, lathered horses, still pulling the empty buckboard behind them, raced into the stable-yard of the Lazy Ace late that afternoon. Hearing the commotion, Fred went out to investigate for nobody was due back yet.

"Dear God," he muttered to no one in particular as he stared in stunned horror at the foam-flecked team and the empty wagon. The realization of what had happened forced him to action, and he shouted, "Jack! Someone go for Jack! We got trouble!!"

A young wrangler hustled to obey. Swinging onto a saddled horse, he raced off, returning within minutes with the foreman.

"What's happened, Fred?" Jack asked worriedly as he dismounted.

"Looks like bad trouble, boss. This here is the buckboard the ladies rode out in. The horses are run out. Looks like somethin' terrible's happened!"

Jack methodically went over the buckboard and it's contents looking for some clue. As he was doing so, he found the letter addressed to Rand. Without thought, knowing that he was in charge, Jack tore open the missive and began to read. The cowboys noticed that the boss paled as he read the note, and they waited tensely for his orders

"I have to go speak with Mrs. McAllister. While I'm gone, get ten men ready to ride and have them take extra ammunition. We've got ourselves a kidnapping and things could get pretty ugly."

"Yes, sir!" Fred replied. "What about Tex?"

"I don't know, Fred. I just don't know." Jack was already back in the saddle, heading for the house to report to Lydia.

Lydia had been expecting "terrible" news for several hours, and she was ready when Jack rushed into the house with the letter.

"Mrs. McAllister!!" he bellowed from the entryway.

Lydia left the parlor and went to meet him, taking special care to seem startled by his unexpected appearance.

"Why, Jack, what is it? Is something wrong? Has something happened to Rand?"

"Something's wrong all right," he began. "Perhaps you'd better sit down while I explain."

"Explain what? This sounds serious, Jack. What happened?!" Lydia reached out to grip his arm for support, using an age-old female ploy.

"It's Rand's fiancée, Mrs. McAllister," he told her.

"Lorelei?" she managed to look puzzled.

"Yes, ma'am. She's been kidnapped by the Bentons!"

"Oh, my god . . ." Lydia managed to fake a half-swoon, and Jack took her in his arms and carried her to the sofa in the parlor. "Tell me it's not true. How do you know?"

"The wagon they were riding in just came back without them, and there was this note in it." He showed her the letter.

"Let me read that!" Lydia scanned Josh's missive and then turned terrified eyes to Jack. "It only mentions Lorelei. What about Sally and Tex?"

"I don't know, ma'am. I've got men saddling up now and we're going out to try to track them, but it's so late I don't think there's much hope of finding them. They've had quite a headstart."

"I have to get word to Rand. He has to know. After all, it's him they want."

"I'll have a man ride to town," Jack offered.

"No! This is something I must do myself! Have my horse brought around and tell two men to ride with me. I'll go into Phoenix. Hopefully someone in the sheriff's office will know how to get word to him."

"But it's too dangerous!" Jack protested.

"It's too late to worry about that. Besides if they've taken Lorelei hostage, they certainly aren't going to concern themselves with me."

"Yes, ma'am." Realizing she was one of the owners, Jack conceded. "I'll have your horse brought up to the house."

As Jack hurried away, Lydia summoned Juana. "There's been a terrible tragedy! The Bentons attacked Lorelei's buckboard and took her hostage! I'm riding into town right now to see if I can get word to Rand. If he should show up here, tell him to come to me as soon as possible. I'll have their letter with me."

"*Sí, señora.*" Juana was incredulous. "But how did this happen, *señora?* Tex was with them and also that Mr. Mason."

"I don't know, Juana. But they're holding her until Rand comes to them—unarmed. It's all here in the letter, that's why I've got to find him."

"And Sally? What of her?"

"They made no mention of her in the note. I don't know if they killed her or took her captive."

"We must find Rand!" Juana knew he was their only hope. Only he was brave enough and strong enough to conquer such evil. "But if they are holding Lorelei hostage that way—"

"I know. It's too terrible to think about. I must hurry. If you need to contact me, I'll be at the hotel in town.

*"Sí, señora!"*


Hour after hour dragged on as the outlaws and their hostages rode across the dry, rocky land. Several times, they stopped to erase their tracks and they often ventured away from their primary direction, weaving false trails that would confuse anyone who tried to follow. They skirted all the main roads as they headed due south, and it was almost dusk when they finally reached their hideout.

They'd chosen to hide the women on a boulder-strewn mountainside at the end of a box canyon. They had used this place as a refuge years ago before they'd gone to prison, and when they'd checked it out before the kidnapping to make sure it was still safe, the single room shanty was still standing.

Now, as they urged their horses up the narrow, winding trail that led to the shack, Pat and Cody felt certain that they had chosen the best possible place to keep the women. No one would be able to take them by surprise here, and that was the most important thing. It was only a matter of time before McAllister was theirs.

"It won't be long now," Pat gloated as he looked over at Cody.

"I know and it feels good! Wonder if that wagon made it back to the ranch by now?"

"Prob'ly," his brother replied as they stopped near the rundown building. "I wish I could be there when McAllister finally gets the news. 'Course that could take days, ya know?"

"Yep." Cody grinned malevolently as he glanced at the two exhausted women. "Days . . ."

"You take care of the horses," Pat directed as he dismounted. "And I'll get these two settled in. Then we have to talk. I've got an idea I think you're gonna like."

"You do?" The seriousness of his brother's tone struck Cody, and he wondered what Pat had in mind. He was sure it was something exciting.

"I do, so hurry with your chores and take real good care of them horses."

"I will." Cody jumped down and then pulled Sally off her mount.

Lori was not to be as lucky for Pat just stared at her, waiting. "Ain't ya gonna get down?"

Lori glared down at him, her hatred clearly reflected in her eyes. She knew, with her hands bound, it would be impossible for her to dismount without falling, yet she also knew that Benton wanted to see her lying in the dirt at his feet. Her pride warred within her as she fought being submissive to this animal who called himself a man, but common sense won out. She would do whatever she must to stay alive. Bone-weary though she was, Lori kept her back straight as she started to swing her leg over the horse's back.

But, amused by her show of determination, Pat reached up and dragged her off, holding her tightly against him as he chuckled in her ear. "You're learnin', bitch. I think we might get along jes' fine if you keep this up."

Though she wanted to be brave, Lori couldn't stop the tremor of apprehension that surged through her, and again Pat laughed.

"Yep, you're learnin' real good. Now"—he shoved her roughly away from him—"get inside and I don't wanna hear a word from either of you!"

Lori stumbled, then regained her footing and

hurried toward the shed, hoping to have a moment alone with Sally. Her friend followed her lead, and together they stepped into the shadowy interior of the dirty ramshackle hut.

"What are we going to do?" Sally whispered as she huddled close to Lori.

"I don't know." Lori's mouth was still swollen, but she managed to answer softly so they wouldn't be overheard. "All we can do is bide our time and hope for a chance to escape. Maybe if they leave us alone for a while, we can get these ropes untied."

"What do you think they want to do with us?"

"Right now, I'm the bait they're using to bring Rand to them. Later . . ." Lori's eyes met Sally's in painful acknowledgment of their fate at the hands of these desperadoes.

"No . . ." Sally was shaken to her depths.

"That's why we must try to escape. It's the only way."

"But how?"

"I—"

"I thought I told you bitches that I didn't want no talkin'!" Pat bellowed as he entered the shack and found them whispering together. He stepped menacingly toward Lori. "Is it time for another lesson?"

Lori's expression turned mutinous for just an instant, but she quickly subdued her rage. "No."

"That's a shame. I think I would have enjoyed another lesson." He let his gaze drop to her breasts. "Maybe next time, though, we'll teach your friend a few things." Pat eyed Sally with interest.

"I'd rather die than let you touch me!" Sally stiffened under his lascivious regard.

"We might jes' help you do that, sweetie." Pat grinned as he grabbed her by her upper arm and jerked her forcefully to him. "Since you weren't part of the

396

deal, everybody prob'ly thinks you're dead anyhow."

With deliberate slowness, he lowered his head to hers and kissed her, his mouth raping hers as one hand intimately explored her hips and the other pressed her against him. At his vile touch, Sally's knees buckled and the blessed forgetfulness of a faint claimed her.

Pat released her abruptly as he felt the fight go out of her, and she fell in a crumpled heap at his feet. He stood threateningly over her, a look of disgust on his features, and he was of a mind to kill her right then and there.

"What happened?" Cody entered the building to find "his" woman lying unconscious on the floor. "You didn't hurt her none yet, did ya?"

"Naw, she jes' fainted. Weak little thing, she is." He dismissed Sally without another thought. "Bring me some more rope. I want to tie their feet, so I kin be sure they ain't gonna go no place."

"Right."

Cody returned shortly with the additional rope, and Pat made short order of shoving Lori down in a dirty corner of the hut and binding her ankles.

"If I find out you've moved from this corner, I'll make sure you don't move again for a long time," he told her coldly.

Sally was just starting to come around, and she gasped in terror as she became conscious and found Cody looming above her.

"No!" she cried.

"Shut up!" Cody snarled. He wanted to slap her as Pat had done with the other girl, but he didn't want to mar her looks. Later, when he'd had his fill of her . . .

Sally's limbs were quaking when Pat roughly tied her legs together. As he worked at the ropes, Cody slipped a hand up her split skirt to torment her, and both men smiled leeringly as they noted how horrified she was.

"C'mon." Pat gave Cody a little slap on the shoulder to draw his attention away from the bound, helpless beauty. "We got some plannin' to do."

Reluctantly, Cody relinquished his intimate contact with Sally and followed his brother outside. "Damn, but I can't wait to get a piece of that."

"I know, but there's one thing we gotta do first and you know what that is."

"You think now?"

Pat nodded. "I figure tomorrow will be jes' the right time to rob Taylor's bank. What d'ya think?"

Cody gave a hoot of laughter as he pounded his sibling on the back. "We done it again, Pat! We outsmarted that banker! The last thing he's gonna be expectin' is for us to show up in town tomorrow!"

"I know. I figure they'll all be out lookin' fer us around where the kidnappin' took place. Shouldn't be too many people in town who could cause us any real trouble."

"When do we ride and what do we do with them?" he gestured toward the house.

"We'll ride out at dawn. That should put us in town before high noon. Things should be pretty quiet there then."

"And the women?"

"We'll jes' make sure they're trussed up so good they cain't move. That way we'll be sure they won't go anywhere on us while we're gone. With any luck, we should make it back before sundown."

"Then we'll have it all . . . money . . . McAllister's woman . . . and, in another day or so, McAllister, himself."

"That's right."

\*　　　\*　　　\*

Lydia rode into town at a gallop, reining in before the sheriff's office. Jumping down from her winded steed, she raced inside, "Help! John? Anybody!"

As she burst into the office, Angus Lowe, John's deputy, jumped up nervously, dropping the paper he'd been reading. "Yes, ma'am! Sheriff McCrea ain't here, but I'm his deputy and I'll be glad to help you. What's wrong?"

"I need to find Marshal McAllister right away!" she told him excitedly.

"Well, ma'am, that ain't rightly possible. You see, the marshal rode out with the sheriff days ago and I don't know where they are."

"You don't know how I can reach him?"

"No, ma'am, I don't. The sheriff just told me the posse was gonna start trackin' the Bentons up by the Triple Cross Mine and then—"

"I know all that! The information I have concerns the Bentons. That's why I have to get a message to Marshal McAllister right away," she snapped.

"You know something about the Bentons?" Angus was startled by this news, and he feared the killers were heading his way.

Lydia knew she must seem desperate, and this clod of a deputy was making it easy for her. "Yes! They've kidnapped the marshal's fiancée, and they're holding her for ransom. I've got to send word to him!"

"Those dirty, low-down . . ." Angus thought of a poor helpless female in the hands of the notorious outlaws and he stalked across the room to get a rifle from the gun cabinet. "I'll go find the marshal myself. Things have been pretty quiet here in town."

"Thank you, deputy," Lydia gave him a weak smile. "I hope you can find him quickly. I'm so worried about Lorelei."

"Yes, ma'am. I'll go looking for them as soon as I can

get Jacobs over here to take over the office."

"Please let me know the minute you get back. I'll be waiting at the hotel for word."

"Yes, ma'am. Just as soon as I find them, I'll be back."

Lydia exited the office feeling quite pleased with her performance, and she found the ranch hands who'd served as her guards on the ride in waiting for her.

"Where to now, Mrs. McAllister?"

"You two head on back to the ranch. I'm going to be staying in town until there's some word from Rand. If Jack returns to the ranch with news about Lorelei and Sally, please send word to me."

"Yes, ma'am," one cowboy said. Then the two men began the long trek back to the Lazy Ace.

Lydia stopped at the bank on her way to the hotel in the hope that Josh was there so she could fill him in on the progress of their carefully devised plan.

"Mrs. McAllister! Is something wrong?" Horace asked as she entered the outer office. He had never before seen her looking less than perfect.

"Yes. I must see Mr. Taylor at once."

"Of course, ma'am. Just a minute, I'll get him for you." The clerk hurried to knock on his boss's door. "Sir, Mrs. McAllister is here to see you and she says it's urgent!"

"Send her in," Josh replied.

Horaced opened the door for Lydia and stood back as she swept into the privacy of Josh's inner office. Only after the door had been closed, did she speak.

"Everything's going perfectly, Josh," she said as she went into his arms.

"Good. Now, if the Bentons follow their orders, we'll be running this town by the end of the week."

"There was only one small complication."

"Oh? What was that?"

"The Westlake girl insisted on riding into town with Lorelei, and Jack sent a guard along. They probably killed the guard, but they may have taken her hostage along with Lorelei."

Josh shrugged indifferently. "What does it matter as long as Rand turns himself over to the Bentons? When he and the Spencer girl are dead, it'll be all ours, love."

"I can hardly wait," she replied breathlessly. After he kissed her passionately, she asked, "Will you come to me tonight? I'll be waiting."

"Of course. I could never stay away from you. You're a fire in my blood, Lydia."

Deep-throated laughter gurgled from her as she remembered the look one of the Bentons had given her and fleetingly considered Lorelei's fate at that man's hands. "I wonder how sweet little Lorelei is doing?"

"Do you really care?" Josh asked, his tone reflecting his disinterest.

"Yes," Lydia replied venomously. "I want her to suffer. My only regret is that I can't be there to watch."

"I can think of much more pleasurable things to do," he drawled, and as he claimed her lips in another lazy, seductive exchange, Lydia let all the tension drain out of her.

"Perhaps you're right," she murmured as she gave herself over to his expertise.


When Juana heard the thundering of horses' hooves, she hurried outside, lantern in hand, to greet the returning riders. She noted with horror that Tex's body was thrown over a horse. "Jack . . . did you find them?"

"Only Tex, Juana." Jack's voice was heavy with

anger and disappointment. "And he was back-shot. We found him down the trail, dead. There was no sign of either woman."

Juana breathed a sigh of relief. At least, Lorelei and Sally had not been killed immediately, there was still hope. "Did you try to track them?"

"We followed their trail for about a mile, but then we lost them in the rocks." Jack swung down from his weary mount. "Men, take care of Tex and then go to bed. We'll be riding out again in the morning." He turned to Juana. "Did Mrs. McAllister return from town?"

"No," she replied. "The *señora* will probably stay there until she hears from Rand or the sheriff."

He nodded slowly. "That's best. I wouldn't want her here if we happen upon anything."

"*Sí.* I understand," Juana's voice was sad.

"Have extra food ready in the morning. We're going to try to pick up their trail again, but I don't know that it'll do us much good. These guys are slick. They don't want to be followed so I'm sure they've used every trick in the book to disguise the direction they took."

"You'll be careful?"

"We will," Jack replied as he led his horse slowly toward the stable. "I just hope we locate them before it's too late. If anything happens to Miss Lorelei . . ."


Rand sat before the small campfire, lost in thought. It comforted him to know Lorelei was safe at the ranch, so he let his thoughts drift sweetly over their time together, relishing the memory of her warm willing body in his arms. He smiled slightly to himself as he remembered their first union in the mine and the searing excitement of their mating in the stable, and desire for her grew in him. He wanted to see her, to hold her once again. His need to be with her, even for a few minutes, was overpowering, and Rand decided that in the morning, when they started back for town, he was going to make a detour to the Lazy Ace, with or without Brady and John.

# Chapter Twenty-Four

The night had been a long one for Lori and Sally. They had spent it on the filthy, rough-hewn floor, and they were so tense over their situation that despite their exhaustion they could find no rest. Hour after hour, they remained unmoving, fearful that the slightest sound might attract the Bentons' attention.

At first light, the outlaws were up, and Lori and Sally anxiously watched as Pat approached them and untied their feet.

"Get up!" he ordered tersely as he towered over them.

"Why? What are you going to do to us?" Sally asked, but she immediately regretted doing so when he turned his malevolent gaze on her.

"I'm gonna take you outside so you can take care of yourselves." He sneered, annoyed. "That is unless you don't want to?"

"Come on, Sally," Lori urged as she awkwardly got to her feet. "You'll need to untie our hands."

Silently, the desperado stripped away the restraints and both women rubbed their chafed, sore wrists in relief as they started outside into the brilliance of the early morning sunlight.

"Hurry it up. We ain't got all day," Pat ordered, and though the women were embarrassed by his presence, they knew they had little choice but to obey his orders.

Within minutes, he herded them back inside and again tied their hands behind them. "Now, sit down in opposite corners."

They did as they were told and then watched in alarm as he got two longer lengths of rope.

With a wide smile, he noted Lori's trepidation, "My, my, you done learned your lesson real well. Kinda afraid of me, are ya?"

Lori glared up at him, defiantly. "I'll do whatever you tell me because I have no other choice."

"You're right." His voice was cold as he hunkered down beside her and expertly tied her feet together. Then, without warning, he unceremoniously flipped her over onto her stomach and planted a knee firmly in the small of her back as he tied her hands and feet together.

Though Lori wanted to struggle and try to escape, she knew it was useless so she remained passive as he finished binding her. Pat restrained Sally in the same manner, then he left them without a word. Minutes later they heard the pounding of horses' hooves and in a short time only silence.

Lori glanced over to where Sally lay unmoving on the far side of the room. "Sally . . ." She called her friend's name through still-swollen lips.

"What?" Sally looked up at her friend nervously.

"We've got to try to get out of here!"

"I know, but how? I can barely move!"

"There has to be a way. We've got to get these ropes off." Lori glanced around the interior of the hut, seeking a sharp or pointed object, but the only useful thing she spied was the glass-chimneyed lantern on the rickety table. "The only thing in here that might work is

405

that lantern."

"But how do we get to it?" Sally was filled with despair.

"We'll have to knock it off the table somehow," Lori responded, rolling onto her side and inching her way slowly across the floor. "Try to make your way over to the table. If we can knock the lantern down and break the chimney, we can try to cut the ropes with the pieces of glass."

"I'm willing to try anything if it'll get us out of here before they come back," Sally declared. "I just don't want them to touch me, Lori."

"I know." Memories of Pat's abuse were fresh in Lori's mind. "But you have to remember the alternative."

Sally shivered and didn't bother to respond.

It took them less time than they'd expected to reach the table, and Lori bumped into it with as much force as she could, tumbling the lantern to the floor. When the chimney shattered as they'd hoped, Lori maneuvered herself so she could pick up the largest piece of glass. It's sharp edges cut painfully into her hand and she gasped.

"Lori?"

"I just cut myself, but it doesn't matter as long as we get out of here." She scooted closer to Sally. "Roll over so we can be back to back, and we might have a chance."

Slowly and painstakingly Lori sawed at Sally's bonds.

"Sally!"

"What? Did you hear something? Are they back?"

"No. I think I've almost cut the rope all the way through. Tug on it as hard as you can."

Sally strained and fought against her bonds, but could not break free. Frustrated, but not giving up,

Lori began again and this time her frantic efforts succeeded and Sally was able to pull one wrist loose. Their tearful celebration of the promise of freedom was short-lived, however, for they knew they had to get out of there and fast. Struggling with Pat Benton's difficult knots, Sally finally managed to free her other wrist and to untie her ankles.

"Lori!" She stared at her friend's bloodied hands, aghast.

"What?"

"You're bleeding." She hurried to loosen Lori's bonds.

"It's not as bad as it looks, Sally. There's only one cut. Let's just get out of here!"

As soon as Sally had freed her, Lori tore a strip of cloth from her blouse and then wrapped the painful slash on her palm. Then, buttoning her blouse, she was on her feet and ready to flee. Cautiously, they peered from the shack and were immensely relieved to find that they were alone. Sally started to smile at Lori, but Lori's troubled expression surprised her.

"Lori? What's wrong?"

"I was afraid of this, Sally." She was staring in the direction of the empty rope corral.

"What?"

"They turned the extra horses loose when they left."

"To make sure we didn't go anywhere." Sally finished the thought for Lori. "Is there any way we can walk out? Do you know where we are?"

"I've got an idea, but I can't be certain until we're out of this canyon. Let's see if we can find something to carry water in. That'll be our biggest problem."

"That and food." They hadn't eaten since they'd left the ranch the day before for the Bentons had not bothered to feed them.

"I'll look around outside, you see if they left anything

in here. We have no idea where they went or how long they'll be gone so we'd better hurry."

And they began their search, hoping to find what they needed to see them safely through their flight to freedom.


Since they'd started out at first light, it was still early in the morning when Rand and Brady rode expectantly up the main road toward the ranch house, and they were totally unaware of the chaos that reigned there. John, worried about the state of affairs in Phoenix, had ridden on into town, but Brady had agreed to accompany Rand to the Lazy Ace for a short visit. He knew Sally was staying there, and he was anxious to have the opportunity to speak with her again.

Everything seemed in order as they came in sight of the main house and Rand waved in acknowledgment to the guard who was posted at a vantage point near the entry gate. Only when the ranch hand raced down from his position did Rand realize that something might be wrong. Reining in, he waited for the man to come to them.

"Something wrong, Rand?" Brady wondered.

"I don't know," he answered as he watched the cowboy hurry toward them.

"Mr. McAllister!" Walt hollered as he raced in their direction. "It's good you're back!"

"Why, Walt? What's the matter?" Rand tensed and quickly looked around. "Where's Jack?"

"They've all gone, sir."

"Gone? Gone where?"

"After the Bentons. Jack and some of the men have gone after them."

His statements only confused Rand and Brady.

"The Bentons were here?" Rand's eyes narrowed dangerously.

"No, sir, but they attacked the buckboard that was carrying the women and—"

"They what!" Rand leaped off his horse's back and grabbed the cowboy by his shirt front. "Where are the women?"

"Juana can tell you everything. She knows." Walt was cowed by the savage side of his boss, and he stammered as he tried to explain.

In disgust, Rand released the hired hand and swung back into the saddle, spurring his horse across the short distance to the ranch house. Leaping from the horse, he was unmindful of Brady who was right beside him as he ran inside to seek out the servant.

"Juana! Where are you? What the hell is going on around here? Where's Lorelei?" he shouted at the top of his voice as he stalked purposefully through the foyer and the parlor.

Juana had been on the patio praying for Rand's return, but at the sound of his voice she came rushing back inside.

"Oh, Rand. Thank the heavens, my prayers have been answered! You have returned!" she cried, nearly collapsing in his arms.

"Juana. What's happened? Walt tried to explain, but he said you were the one who knew."

"It is so terrible." Juana sobbed as he led her into the parlor to sit down. "The Bentons have kidnapped the women."

"What!" Rand and Brady exclaimed in unison.

"What were they doing out in a buckboard?" Rand asked.

"It was yesterday . . . a messenger came and said he was from Mr. Taylor at the bank. He had a letter that said Taylor needed Miss Lorelei's signature on some papers. Late in the afternoon the buckboard came back without them, but there was another note."

"A note? Where is it? I want to see it!" Rand asked fiercely.

"The *señora* has it."

"Lydia wasn't with them?"

"No, she had just returned from town and didn't wish to go back," Juana hastened to explain.

"Then get her! Now!"

"I can't, she went to town to try to locate you or the sheriff. She said she would be staying at the hotel until she heard from you."

"Damn! Those bastards! Do you have any idea what was in that note? What about Jack? Walt said Jack had gone out to hunt them down."

"The *señora* told me they were going to hold Miss Lorelei hostage until you came to them." Juana shrugged helplessly. "That's all I know."

"And Sally?" Brady could no longer refrain from asking. "What about Sally?"

"We don't know," Juana answered honestly, reading in his expression the depth of his feelings for the young woman. "She had gone on the trip with Miss Lorelei, but they found no sign of her last night. Tex had ridden along as their guard, and Jack found Tex. He was dead—shot in the back."

"They're tracking them now?"

"Jack took a group of armed men out with him this morning, but he knew that the Bentons had too great a headstart so he was doubtful he would find anything."

"We know the feeling." Brady and Rand exchanged glances as they headed for the door and their mounts.

"Where are you going?"

"To town. I've got to find out what the Bentons are up to," Rand answered curtly as he paused at the gun case to get extra ammunition.

*"Vaya con Dios,"* Juana said softly, but the men were already out the door.

Lydia reflected on how smoothly everything was going as she preened happily before the mirror in her room in preparation for her luncheon engagement with Josh. She had met with John a little earlier and had told him the details of the kidnapping. When she'd mentioned her desperate search for Rand, John had told her that Rand had planned to stop by the ranch on his way back to town and he assured her that, once Rand learned what had happened, he would undoubtedly come to town. Lydia had expressed her relief at the thought of Rand's supportive presence, but in reality she was overjoyed that Josh's plan was working so well. Once Rand got the note, it would be almost over.

Staring at her reflection, Lydia smiled, confident that she looked beautiful. Her hair was curled and artfully arranged, and the dress she'd just purchased that morning highlighted her near-perfect figure while its becoming shade of blue set off her eyes and emphasized the fairness of her complexion. Knowing it would probably be awhile before Rand made it into town, she would have plenty of time to enjoy her meal with Josh, so she gathered her purse and left her room, expecting to meet him in the small lobby of the hotel.

The streets were almost deserted this noon as she glanced out of the hotel, and accustomed to Josh's habits, she thought it a bit unusual that he was late. He always made it a point to close the bank for the midday meal, so, assuming he'd been delayed by business concerns, Lydia left the hotel and started down the street to meet him.

\*     \*     \*

Cody and Pat were thrilled that they had timed their arrival in town so perfectly. They'd tied up their horses in the alleyway near the private side entrance of the bank and had then entered the building through the front door just a few minutes before the regular noon closing to find only a clerk and Taylor present. The rest of the robbery had been accomplished with remarkable ease. They'd held both men at gunpoint, locked the door behind them, pulled the shades, and then forced Taylor and the clerk to fill their saddlebags with money.

"You'll never get away with this," Josh swore vehemently, silently cursing himself for thinking he could trust the Bentons.

"And jes' who d'ya think's gonna stop us, Taylor? You?" Cody sniggered malevolently.

"I'll get you for this, if it's the last thing I ever do!" Josh vowed.

"It might jes' be the last thing you'll ever do! If I was you, I'd jes' shut up and be glad that we're taking care of your other business for you," Pat replied coldly as he watched Horace putting money in his saddlebags.

"Mr. Taylor, what are they talking about?" Horace asked his boss nervously.

"Shut up, Horace!" Josh snapped as he shot Pat and Cody a baleful glare.

"He's talkin' 'bout the business deal he made with us, Horace." Pat enjoyed humiliating the arrogant banker. "He hired us to get rid of Marshal Rand McAllister, but we thought his price of a thousand dollars was jes' a little too cheap for all the work we'll hafta do. That's why we're here now, to take what's our due."

"Mr. Taylor, what they're saying can't be true." The clerk was horrified.

"You mean you ain't tol' nobody all about your plans, Taylor?" Cody taunted, snatching his saddlebags away from Josh who'd finished filing them. To the clerk he said, "You should ask him again later. Maybe he'll feel like tellin' ya all about it. Now, let's go."

As the Bentons were herding Josh and the clerk into the office and out of sight, Lydia arrived at the front door. Slightly surprised to find everything looking so normal, she went on around to the side entrance expecting at any moment to run into Josh coming to meet her. When she reached the side door, she found it unlocked and walked in to find out what was causing his delay. What she saw when she stepped inside and shut the door shocked her.

"Josh!" she cried. He and Horace were being held at gunpoint by two men she assumed were the Bentons.

"Mrs. McAllister!" Horace called out. "Run!"

Pat and Cody swung around, annoyed and fearful at being discovered, but when Pat saw the beautiful blonde from the ranch he grinned in evil delight.

"Well, well. Lookie, what we got here. Mrs. McAllister, is it?"

Lydia was completely unnerved as she met his obsidian gaze. What was going on here? The Bentons were supposed to be working for Josh, yet they were holding their guns on him.

"Taylor, you didn't tell us that there was a Mrs. McAllister." Pat leveled his sidearm at Lydia.

"I am Will McAllister's widow," she responded in a whisper. "What are you doing? I thought you were working for Josh."

"Taylor's high-handed ways kinda wore on us and we decided that we wanted it all, not jes' the little piece he offered us. Now that you're here, I jes' may add you to my list." He leered at her hungrily.

"No! Josh!" Lydia's fright was real as she wheeled and tried to bolt from the room, but Cody was too quick. He reached out and snared her arm in a viselike grip.

413

Josh had been waiting for this chance, and he used the momentary distraction to slip his derringer from his sleeve and fire his only two shots. Cody was felled by his accurate aim, but his other bullet went wide, and Pat turned and fired rapidly, his bullets tearing through Josh and Horace. It was over so quickly that Lydia could do nothing but watch in horror as Josh and Horace collapsed to the floor.

"One word out of you and you'll join them!" Pat told her savagely as he knelt beside his brother's lifeless body. Though he wanted to take Cody with him, he knew he had to get out of town, so he threw the two pairs of saddlebags over his shoulder and, grabbing Lydia, started cautiously out the door. "I don't know if anyone heard the shots or not, but I do know I gotta get out of here. If you want to stay alive, jes' walk out to the horses real casual-like. Understand?" His hold on her was bruising and she nodded in mute horror. "Good. Now, let's go."

With his gun pressed hard against the small of Lydia's back, Pat used her as a shield as they started out the side entrance. He could hear footsteps heading in their direction so he tied the saddlebags on and mounted quickly, dragging Lydia up before him, his arm tight about her waist.

"There goes somebody, sheriff!" a man's voice called out at the end of the alleyway.

Pat wheeled about and shot down the man who was pointing him out. Then he spurred his horse and charged from the alley at a gallop.


When John returned from his hunt for the Bentons, Angus met him on his way into town, and the deputy told him of the kidnapping and of Lydia's presence at the hotel. Without resting, John had gone straight to Lydia to find out exactly what had taken place. The news she'd imparted to him had left him stunned and furious. Lorelei had been lured away by a phony message, kidnapped by the man who'd delivered it, and she was now being held hostage until Rand turned himself over to the Bentons.

John went back to his office to await Rand's arrival from the ranch. He was mulling over what to do next when Jacobs came running, yelling that he'd heard shots fired down at the bank. Grabbing up his rifle, John had headed in the direction of Taylor's bank, Jacobs well ahead of him. When the part-time deputy was shot as he stopped before the bank's adjacent alleyway, John was caught off guard, and he barely got any shots off as a single rider burst forth at full speed from the passageway, holding Lydia McAllister before him.

Racing to Jacobs' side, McCrea was devastated to find that his long-time friend was dead, and as a crowd began to gather, he directed them to see to him while he went to check out what had happened in the bank. Slowly and with the utmost caution, he entered the building. Inside, to his horror, he discovered the bodies of Cody Benton and Josh Taylor. Only Horace was still alive.

"Sheriff," Horace groaned hoarsely as he clasped the lawman's hand with the last of his strength.

"Horace, we'll get the doctor for you, just hold on." John tried to reassure the wounded man, then he ordered one of the men who'd followed him inside to get the town physician.

"It was Taylor," Horace gasped, wanting desperately to reveal the betrayal of the man so many had trusted.

"What was Taylor?" John asked, leaning close to try

415

to hear him.

"He was in it with them . . . so was she." Horace choked.

"Josh was involved with the Bentons?" John was startled by the clerk's accusation, and when the dying man gave a tight nod of acknowledgment, he could only stare down at him in confusion. Respectable Josh Taylor in cahoots with the Bentons?

"Her, too," Horace managed to say, and determined to tell McCrea what he'd learned in those few, apocalyptical moments, he said, "Mrs. McAllister."

"You've got to be mistaken," John replied automatically.

"No."

Horace breathed his last as the town doctor finally arrived on the scene, too late to be of any help.

John backed out of the room, bewildered by what the dead clerk had just told him. He tried to piece the information together, to make some sense of it. Josh and Lydia were involved with the Bentons—but why and for what? They were both well off and respected. Knowing that there was no time to lose if he was going to pursue the remaining Benton, he rushed back toward his office, intending to get another posse together.

"Rand! Brady!" John saw them coming and he hurried to meet them. "The Bentons just robbed the bank!"

Rand and Brady had ridden at top speed from the ranch, and they'd gone directly to the hotel, intending to speak to Lydia, but the woman behind the registration desk had informed them that Mrs. McAllister had left the hotel a short while before. Not sure where she'd gone, they were going in search of John when he called to them.

416

"How long ago? Let's go after them!" Rand responded.

"Cody was killed, I guess by Josh Taylor, but Pat rode out of town and, Rand, I'm sorry about this, but he had Lydia with him."

"What!? Where's Taylor? I want to know what's going on."

"Taylor's dead and so is my deputy Jacobs. Benton headed due east from town and he's riding double so I don't think we're going to have any trouble catching him. I've already put out the word that I need riders. We should have a full posse in ten minutes."

"Good. I won't be able to find Lorelei unless I catch up with Pat Benton, but why did he take Lydia with him? Seems to me, she would only slow him down."

"He used her as a shield as he rode out and Rand . . ." John hesitated to tell him Horace's condemning words.

"What?" Rand tensed as he studied John's expression, and he knew a moment of terrible dread for he expected John to tell him she was dead.

"Before Horace died, he said that Josh and Lydia were involved with the Bentons."

Rand could only stare at his old friend as the accusation penetrated his mind. Lydia and Josh . . . together with the Bentons . . .

"My God, why didn't I see it before?" He spoke more to himself than to Brady and John as it all suddenly made sense. Josh and Lydia had both wanted him out of the way, and they had teamed up together to plan his demise. Lydia hated him because she now controlled the Lazy Ace and because he'd refused her advances. Though Rand could only speculate about Josh's motives, he felt sure that the banker had wanted to take over the Triple Cross because of the newly discovered

417

lode. If he and Lorelei had been killed by the Bentons who'd sworn vengeance on him, Lydia and Josh would have gained everything—the ranch and the mine—and without attracting any suspicion.

"What do you mean?" Brady and John looked at him questioningly.

"I've got to search through Lydia's things and find that note." Rand stormed over to the hotel and went straight to her room. Without hesitating, he broke the lock on the door and searched through all her belongings until he found the note that had been left on the buckboard.

*McAllister—*

*We got your woman. If you want her to stay alive, meet us Friday at Apache Rock near Willow Creek. Come alone and unarmed. If we see anyone with you or if you're armed, you'll never see her alive again.*

*the Bentons*

Rage surged through Rand at the thought of Lorelei being held captive because of Josh Taylor and the scheming Lydia. Praying that Lorelei was still alive, he strode from the room. He was going after Pat Benton and Lydia right now, and he wouldn't rest until he had Lorelei back and Benton was dead. As for Lydia, Rand didn't even want to think about facing her again.

## Chapter Twenty-Five

The heat was oppressive as Lori and Sally slowly made their way down the sun-drenched canyon. Desperate to get away before the Bentons returned, they pushed onward, resting only occasionally in whatever shade they could find. They had decided to stay away from the trail for fear of running into their captors, so they were traveling across a rugged, rock-strewn landscape.

It was not an easy trek under the best of circumstances, and the lack of food and water began to tell on them as the hours passed. They had eaten what little dried meat had been left at the hut, but had been unable to find anything that would serve as a canteen. Hot and thirsty, they struggled onward down the barren canyon, needing to escape its confines as quickly as possible.

Rand had vowed that he was not going to let Pat Benton get away. The last surviving Benton was his only connection to Lorelei, and he had to capture him alive in order to learn her whereabouts. His nerves stretched taut, he led the posse in pursuit of the outlaw, having given them strict instructions not to shoot to kill. This time he had no difficulty following the desperado's trail for Benton had had no time to cover his tracks or disguise his direction, and the posse steadily gained on the fleeing murderer.

Lydia held onto the pommel of the saddle for support as Benton guided the exhausted horse up another steep incline. She was frightened. Neither she nor Benton had spoken since they'd left the bank and she wondered what his plans were now that the posse was closing in on them.

"Why don't you just give up?" she finally felt brave enough to ask as she spied Rand and the others in the distance.

"Shut up!" he seethed. "I ain't done with McAllister yet, not by a long shot."

Although Pat could see the posse coming after him, he was in no mood to give up without a fight. He had headed for high ground when he'd left town, and he was now picking his way through the rocky terrain, searching for the best place to make a stand. He hoped somehow to surprise his pursuers, but he knew with only one rifle and a sidearm there was little hope that he could hold off an entire posse. His luck was about to run out, but before it did, he wanted one last chance to kill McAllister.

As they rode behind a big boulder, Pat sensed his horse's fatigue, and he knew that pushing his mount any farther would mean death for the overworked animal. Reining in, he dismounted and pulled Lydia down after him. Quickly, he tied her wrists so she could pose no threat to him; then he gagged her with his bandana to insure her silence. This would be his only chance to get McAllister, and he did not intend to let her give away his position. Hobbling the horse, he took his rifle and canteen and, pulling a reluctant Lydia along with him, scrambled up to the top of the boulder to set up an ambush.

Rand sensed rather than saw Benton's presence, and just as he turned to direct the rest of the posse to be on alert, shots rang out. Rand dove for cover as Pat's carefully aimed bullets struck the rocks near his head. Pulling his rifle from its scabbard, he crouched low and began to work his way among the rocks and boulders in the hope of getting behind the outlaw and forcing him to surrender.

John and Brady knew how desperately important it was that they take Benton alive, and they ordered their men to fire only to offer protection for Rand.

"Give it up, Benton!" John shouted, thinking he might talk him down.

"No way!" Pat yelled back, and when Lydia tried to break away, he grabbed her by the hair and threw her to the ground. "And if you want to see any of the women alive again, you'd better let me go—now! I got one with me and it ain't gonna matter one way or the other, if I shoot her now or later."

"We can't let you go, Benton, and you know it. You're never going to win, so why don't you just admit defeat? Let Lydia go and tell us where the other two women are and, I promise you, I'll put in a good word for you with the judge," John shouted.

"Hah!" Pat sneered. "I know all about judges and courtrooms—and prisons. I ain't never goin' back to one. I'd rather be dead!"

Pat fired another volley of shots to emphasize his seriousness about not returning to jail, and the posse was forced to return his fire.

Rand had almost worked his way above Benton when it happened. Lydia, terrified and knowing that she was facing death, bolted just as Pat began to fire again. Furious that she was getting away, Pat stood up to get a clear aim at her, and he shot her in the back as she fled.

Unable to stomach watching a man shoot down a helpless woman, one of the younger members of the posse took advantage of Pat's momentary exposure to fire at him. His aim was excellent, the bullet striking the outlaw in the shoulder, but Benton lost his balance and fell from the top of the boulder. His screams echoed across the land as he pitched forward to land with an agonizing thud on the uneven ground. He lay broken and still among the rocks.

Praying that Benton wasn't dead, Rand was beside him in an instant. He had to find out where Lorelei was. Turning Pat over, he shook him in violent frustration. "Where are the women, Benton! Where did you hide them?"

Pat stared up at Rand with pain-glazed eyes, and seeing his very real agony over his missing fiancée, he managed a small, victorious smile. "Dead," he whispered, and his head lolled lifelessly to the side.

"What did he say?" Brady demanded as he rushed to Rand's side.

Rand was unable to answer for Benton's words had seared his soul.

"Rand?" Brady repeated.

"He . . . he said they were dead, Brady." Rand's voice was choked, but he fought to control his riotous emotions. "Lydia . . . where's Lydia? She might know something. Benton could have been lying."

Rand let Benton drop to the dust as he stood up and ran around the side of the rock to where Lydia had fallen. John was bending over her, removing her gag and untying her hands.

"She's still alive, Rand," he said hopefully. "How's Benton?"

"Dead." Rand knelt beside John. "Lydia . . ."

"Rand?" she whispered.

"I'm here," he replied.

She opened her eyes and stared up at him, and the hatred he saw in her gaze shook him.

"Lydia . . . where are Lorelei and Sally?" he pressed.

"I don't know." She smiled faintly. "Bentons had them."

"And you and Taylor were involved!" Rand bellowed, giving vent to his frustration. "Didn't they tell you where their hideout was?"

"No," Lydia managed to say. "And I'm glad."

Rand started as if she'd struck him. "Lydia, if you know, tell me. There's no reason for them to die."

"I don't know." Her voice was fading. "They're probably dead already, knowing the Bentons."

"Lydia . . ." Rand was about to shake her, but John restrained him.

"Rand, no. It's too late."

He looked down. Lydia was dead and so was his only hope of finding Lorelei and Sally.

"Rand?"

"We've got to keep looking, Brady." Rand's expression was wooden as he stood up. He would not accept Lydia's or Benton's word. "No matter what Benton said, I can't stop searching for them. I won't believe they're dead until I find their bodies, John," Rand declared. "I won't give up. I can't."

"I'm with you Rand," Brady swore solemnly.

"I'll take care of things here for you," John offered.

"Thanks," Rand responded grimly.

"Where do we start looking?" Brady asked.

"We start right here. We're going to comb every inch of the territory within a half-day's ride of town until we

423

find them," Rand vowed. He refused to acknowledge Lorelei's death. She had to be alive—she had to!

The blackness of the desert night enshrouded the land, and chilled by the sudden drop in temperature, Lori and Sally huddled together beneath the protective overhang of a low-rising cliff. They had not seen any sign of the Bentons and for that they were extremely grateful, but they desperately needed water and food. Lori had brought along a sliver of glass to use as a knife, and she'd managed to cut open several cacti during the course of the day, but the liquid from the pulp had not been sufficient and weakness was claiming them.

"Lori," Sally said through chattering teeth.

"What?"

"Do you know where we are?"

Summoning a bravado she did not feel, Lori replied, "I think so. It was too dark when we reached the end of the canyon to be sure, but I think we're east of town."

"And we'll be able to make it back in?" Sally had been brave and uncomplaining during their trek, but the heat had drained her and she felt depressed.

"Of course, after we rest a little." Lori was reassuring though she doubted they could save themselves now that they were free of the outlaws. She knew how to survive in the desert—her father had taught her how—but she had never had to attempt it without the most of rudimentary tools. Though she didn't want to admit it to herself, she was frightened. "First thing in the morning, we'll start heading due west. We can't be more than a half day's ride from town and hopefully we'll run into someone heading our way."

"You make it sound so easy." Sally sighed, allowing herself the luxury of believing Lori.

"It won't be easy, but we can do it." Lori smiled in the darkness. "Just remember who'll be waiting for you when you get to town."

"Brady."

"And Rand." Lori expressed her own wish. "That's why we've got to hurry. I don't know what the Bentons had planned, but I do know they were going to use us to try to entrap him. We have to let him know that we're safe."

"We'll make it."

"I know. We have to."

They were silent then, each woman lost in speculation on what the next day would bring. Sally eventually fell asleep, but Lori found slumber more elusive. Only after she put her fears from her did she feel more peaceful. Thoughts of Rand and of the security of his embrace finally comforted her, and she closed her eyes in blissful remembrance, then drifted off to sleep. Her last conscious thought was of the sweetness of his kiss.

They started out again at dawn, and though they made steady progress in what they hoped was the right direction, by noon they were once again seeking shelter. The sun was relentless, its heat draining all energy from them as they staggered wearily onward, ever looking for a shady spot in which to rest until the heat began to wane.

"Lori!" Sally gasped as she sank to her knees in exhaustion.

Lori, who'd been several steps ahead of her, quickly turned back, "Sally, you have to get up! If you stay here you'll die."

"I don't think I can go any further."

"Come on," Lori urged, slipping an arm about her friend's waist and drawing her to her feet. "I'll help you."

425

Lori braced herself so she could support Sally, and then they started off again, their pace ever slower and more agonized.

"Where do you want to search next?" Brady asked as he reined in alongside Rand. They had just spent the entire day tracking the area of the shootout in the hope that Benton had been on the way to his hideout when the showdown had occurred, but to their disappointment they'd turned up nothing.

Rand wiped the sweat from his brow as he stared off at the red-gold western sky. The sun was setting, yet he was no nearer to finding Lorelei than when they'd started out that morning.

"According to the note, I was supposed to meet them Friday at Apache Rock near Willow Creek. They might have holed up near there."

"Let's ride," Brady said. He refused to believe, as the sheriff did, that the Bentons had killed Sally and Lori, and the possibility that they were tied up and helpless somewhere filled him with a determination that matched Rand's. "We've got at least another hour of light."

Rand didn't bother to respond, he just put his heels to his horse and started off in the direction of Apache Rock.

Lori knew that they could not last more than another day or two at the most. She had managed to find a shady place and they'd rested several hours after Sally's collapse. Even so, in the sweltering heat, that had done little to revive them. They were hungry and exhausted, and desperate for water. When the sun lost some of its devastating force, they emerged from their shelter and started out in a westerly direction. They kept moving until darkness forced them to seek a protected place in which to spend the night.

At dawn they struck out once again across the wilderness, but Lori knew if they didn't find help soon, they would never make it back to civilization. She had done her best and had managed to keep them alive for two days, but their strength would not hold out much longer.

By noon, they topped the last rise of the rocky, mountainous country they were leaving, but the vastness of the cactus- and Joshua tree-studded land before them was unnerving. As far as the eye could see, there was no sign of life, and for the first time Lori really doubted that they would survive.

"Lori," Sally croaked hoarsely, her throat parched. "I don't think I can take another step . . . I've got to rest for a while."

"I know." Lori's body ached. "Let's go over by those rocks and see if we can find some place to stay until the sun starts to go down."

Weakly, Sally nodded, and they slowly hobbled in the direction of the boulders. As they climbed through the maze of rocks, their usually cautious manner forgotten in their desire to get out of the sun, they didn't notice the rattler coiled tightly on a ledge.

Sally's scream rent the air, and Lori rushed to her aid as the reptile slithered away through a narrow crevice.

"Where did it get you?" she asked quickly.

"My leg." Sally gasped as she clutched her left thigh. "Oh, God. Lori, am I going to die?"

"No," Lori answered emphatically as she lifted Sally's skirt to reveal two puncture wounds. "You're strong and healthy. You'll feel better just as soon as I get some of the poison out of there."

"What are you doing?" Sally's eyes widened as Lori

427

pressed the sharp edge of the blade of glass against the bite.

"It's the only way to get the poison out, Sally," Lori explained. "Are you ready?"

Panting and feeling a certain tightness in her chest, Sally nodded and then leaned back, turning away from the sight of the wound. She felt the initial cut and nothing more for she fainted. Lori was relieved, for it took her some time to tend the wound and she knew her friend would have suffered had she been awake. After cutting across both bite marks, she sucked at the wound trying to draw out the snake's deadly poison; then she tore off a strip of material from Sally's skirt and wound it about her thigh in a makeshift tourniquet. When she'd finished, she sat back on her heels and wiped the dripping sweat from her brow. Her own blouse was clinging wetly to her, and she knew a moment of intense longing for easy life back in St. Louis—servants and baths, hot meals and comfortable, safe surroundings.

Shaking her head at her ridiculous daydreams, Lori studied her friend closely. Sally did not look well. Her color was ashen in spite of the heat, and her breathing was rapid and shallow. Lori was torn between the need to go for help and the desire to stay with her friend. Knowing she could make no decision right away, she sat quietly beside Sally and waited for her to regain consciousness.

Nearly two hours passed before Sally began to stir.

"Lori . . ." Sally gazed up at her friend with feverish eyes.

"Sally! I'm so glad you're awake." Lori smiled down at her. "I've been so worried about you."

"I'll be all right," she whispered as her eyes drifted closed.

"Sally?" Lori knew a moment of very real panic for

she thought her friend had died.

"Lori, you can't stay here." Sally opened her eyes as she spoke, but her voice was barely audible. "You must go on." Speaking was difficult for her, but Sally knew, even through her haze of agony, that they had no hope of rescue unless Lori went on.

"I can't just go off and leave you here!" Lori protested.

But Sally shook her head weakly. "We have no choice. I know I can't make it now, but you can. Please . . . go for help and then come back for me."

Lori knew her friend was right. If she stayed, they were doomed, and if she went . . . It was the only way.

"I'll go as soon as it cools down a bit," she promised, her heart breaking at the thought of abandoning Sally in the wilderness.

"Good." Sally sighed, and then she rested almost peacefully.

It was late afternoon when Lori shared the moisture from a cactus with Sally before starting out again, alone. She had always enjoyed the serenity of the desert, but she had never dealt with it as a killer. Now that she'd discovered the dark, dangerous side of this arid land, she hated it. Ignoring her own discomfort, she forced herself on as she trudged across the desolate countryside, searching anxiously for help.

Lori did not stop at dusk, but continued on well into the night, using the moon and stars as guides in her quest for civilization. She did not know how long she'd been walking, when she thought she saw the flickering flare of a campfire ahead. Eager to reach the elusive glow, she tried to run before it occurred to her that she didn't know whose campfire this was. Forcing herself to go more slowly, she decided to sneak in closer to get a better look before making her presence known.

Ol' Roscoe Davison sat before his small cook fire,

pouring himself a cup of steaming, strong coffee. He had covered a goodly amount of territory on his monthly trek to town for supplies, and he was looking forward to arriving in Phoenix the following day and reaping some reward from his long days of hard work. His claim was not a rich one, but it yielded enough gold dust to keep him in whiskey whenever he made the trip, and he smiled now as he thought of the smooth, mellow bourbon they served at the Gold Nugget Saloon.

His burro Moses was tied up a short ways away from camp, and when the beast shifted nervously Roscoe quickly grabbed his shotgun and doused the fire. He knew you could never tell what kind of creatures were lurking out in the dark on the desert, and he didn't want to be a sitting duck for any two-legged varmints. Silently, he moved in the direction of his tethered companion, cautiously searching the darkness for some sign of furtive movement.

When he doused the fire, Lori wondered if she'd been hallucinating, and she stumbled in the sudden blackness. Unable to prevent her fall, she cried out in muffled pain as her ankle twisted, and in that instant, a tall man towered over her prostrate form, his lethal-looking shotgun aimed directly at her.

"Hold it!" His voice was sharp, and Lori froze, afraid to move lest he fire.

"Please . . . I need help."

Roscoe was totally stunned to hear a feminine voice. "What the—"

"Don't shoot!" she pleaded.

"'Course not," Roscoe said gruffly as he lowered his gun and moved closer. "Are you alone?"

"Yes . . . no. My friend was hurt and I've got to get back." Lori was relieved to find that this man was not hostile, and she started to get up. He quickly came to her aid.

"You say you have a friend with you?" He glanced over his shoulder to see if he could spot anyone else in the paleness of the moonlight.

"Sally was injured and I had to leave her behind. I came on alone."

"So that's what you're doin' way out here on foot. Well, come on back with me now, and I'll start the fire up again while you tell me about it." A sociable fellow, Roscoe was amazed at this unexpected encounter. He rarely came across anyone on the desert, let alone a woman. "My name's Roscoe Davison."

"I'm Lori Spencer," she told him shakily as she allowed him to guide her back to his campsite.

"Spencer, eh? Knew a man name of Spencer in these parts once. Good fella. Prospector, he was." Roscoe's tone was kindly as he helped her sit down and then started to rekindle the blaze he'd so recently extinguished.

"My father's name was George and he prospected around here," Lori told him.

"George, you say?" Roscoe paused in his endeavor. "Yep, I reckon that was him. He's dead?"

"He died just a few months ago, in a landslide."

"Happens to a lot of us up in these mountains. It's a wild, mean land." He waited for the fire to spring to life. "You got to be careful all the time."

In the brightness of the glowing flames, Lori saw her rescuer clearly for the first time. Roscoe was not overpowering in size, but his grizzled white beard and his long hair made him seem larger than life. Had they not spoken before, in the dark, she might have been disturbed by his wild appearance, but she relaxed as his pale eyes gazed compassionately upon her.

"Thank you," Lori told him gratefully as he passed her his canteen.

"You're lookin' right peaked," he said. "Drink up.

After that, I've got a few bites of dinner left you can have."

Lori flashed him an appreciative look as she drank deeply of his water. It was acrid and warm, but to her it tasted like the sweetest nectar. She took the food he offered and quickly devoured it before speaking again.

"I don't know how I can ever thank you, Mr. Davison."

"Well, you can start by callin' me Roscoe, little gal, and by tellin' me what you're doin' out here in the middle of the desert on foot."

Lori knew she should tell him the truth and she didn't hesitate. "My friend Sally and I were kidnapped by the Benton brothers. Have you heard of them?"

"Yep, I heard of 'em. I think everybody in the territory's heard of the Bentons. Weren't they in ja.l?"

"They broke out just a short time ago. Anyway, they were keeping Sally and me tied up in a little, deserted cabin in the box canyon some distance back, but when they left us alone for a while, we managed to get away. We've been trying to find our way back to town ever since."

"And what happened to your friend?"

"Sally was bitten by a rattler. It happened after we'd been walking for days. I didn't want to leave her, but I had to. If I'd stayed, we'd both have died. Can we go back now? Tonight? I only left her this afternoon. I can show you where she is." Lori felt guilty because she was safe while Sally was braving the desert night all by herself, injured.

"Now, now." Roscoe tried to calm her. "There ain't no point in chasin' outta here in the dark. You get some rest, and we'll head back for your friend first thing in the morning."

"But—"

"There ain't no reason to be hurryin'," he insisted.

432

It's too blamed dark tonight anyways. Morning will be soon enough."

Roscoe got up and brought her his blanket, draping it about her shoulders.

"You just rest for now. You'll feel better if you sleep for a while, and as soon as it's light we'll pack up old Moses and go back for her."

"Moses?"

"My furry friend over there," the old-timer nodded toward his droopy steed.

Lori nodded and smiled slightly. She understood the closeness that developed between a lone prospector and his pack animal. Years ago, when she and her father had been roaming the territory, they had had a burro they'd been fond of.

"Rest now, you hear?" ·

"I will," she sighed, and as a great mental and physical weariness stole over her, she snuggled more deeply into Roscoe's blanket. She was soon fast asleep.

The old man watched her for a long time as she slept, his thoughts troubled for he feared they might meet up with the Bentons. He'd heard of them many times when he'd paid his visits to town, and it surprised him that two women had gotten away from them alive. He worried about the condition of the girl who'd been left behind, and he hoped it wouldn't be too late to save her in the morning. Snake bites usually weren't fatal, but there was always danger with them. Shifting his position, he finally closed his eyes and sought sleep, knowing that his trip into Phoenix was going to have to be postponed for a few days.

Rand faced Brady across their campfire. They were both bone-tired from their endless hours in the saddle, and their supplies were running low.

433

"We're going to have to go into town for supplies soon," Brady remarked. He had firmly believed when they'd started out that they would be able to locate Sally and Lori, but their long days of searching had yielded nothing and his hopes were beginning to flag.

"I know." Rand knew despair as the reality of their situation bore down on him. "In the beginning, Brady, I had hoped Benton had been lying. In fact, at the time I would have bet my life on it, but after all this time . . ." His eyes met Brady's across the fire. "Now I'm hoping he was telling the truth."

Brady nodded in understanding for he, too, was devastated by the thought of the two women bound and helpless in some hellhole in the middle of the desert.

Their morale low, they said no more as they prepared to turn in for the night, yet both men knew that at first light they would be up and ready to ride again for they could not yet admit the hopelessness of their cause.

## Chapter Twenty-Six

Lori knew both excitement and concern as she caught her first glimpse of Phoenix in the distance, and she cast a nervous glance at Sally who was making the trip to town on burro-back courtesy of Moses. Since she and Roscoe had returned to find Sally feverish but still alive, Sally had made steady improvement under the old miner's care. They had camped for two days until Sally had been strong enough to travel, and now they were finally on the last leg of their trip into town.

The thought of making it to safety, filled Lori with elation, but she couldn't help but wonder about the Bentons. Perhaps they were somewhere nearby, watching for her or Rand. The idea frightened her, and she knew that somehow she had to get word to him, warn him.

"I can't believe we're almost there," Sally exclaimed in delight. The past week had been a nightmare for her, and she was thrilled to think that they were now so near to civilization. "I have to tell you, Lori, there were times when I really didn't think we were going to make it."

Lori smiled in acknowledgment. "If it hadn't been for Roscoe, Sally, we wouldn't have made it."

"Shucks, ladies"—the old man grinned proudly—
"I'm glad I was there for you, and I hope when we get
into town we find out that the law's caught up with
the Bentons and they're already six feet under."

"Me, too," Lori agreed. "And I hope Rand's safe."

Lori had told Roscoe the whole story of their ordeal
so he knew how worried she was about her fiancé.

"We'll find out shortly, but I wouldn't be too
concerned. The way you described him, he sounds like
a mighty capable man, being a U.S. Marshal and all."
Roscoe wanted to ease her mind. "Why, if he's already
taken care of the Bentons, he's probably out leading a
posse, looking for you right now."

That possibility pleased Lori, and she smiled.


Sitting across from Brady at a secluded corner table
in the Gold Nugget, Rand stared down at his empty
glass and wondered where the liquor had gone.
Moments before the glass had been full. Reaching for
the bourbon they'd brought with them to the table, he
poured a hefty drink and setting the bottle aside, he
downed half the contents of his glass.

"Say, big guy, you're drinking that kinda fast, aren't
you?" Pearlie Gates sashayed over to the table and put
her arm around his shoulders as she smiled down at
him. She'd been watching the two men drink since
they'd come into the saloon around noon and she
wondered why two such good-looking men were alone
and so intent on getting drunk. "That's potent stuff."

Rand pinned her with a glacial glare as he swallowed
the rest of the bourbon and then refilled the glass with
the last of the contents of the bottle.

"I know," he replied coldly. Then, ignoring her
presence, he shouted to the barkeep. "Bring us another
bottle."

"I'll get it for you, sweetie." Pearlie pressed against him suggestively before strutting to the bar to get the bottle the bartender had put out. When she brought it back and placed it before Rand on the table, he tossed several silver dollars in her direction.

"Pay the bill and keep the rest for yourself," he directed indifferently as Brady looked on, mystified.

"Oooh," Pearlie cooed, excited at the thought of bedding this big spender. "I'll be right back to keep you company."

"No." Rand's answer was quick and cutting. "I don't want your company. I want you to leave us alone. Just take the money and make sure we're not bothered.

Pearlie was dismayed by his brusque dismissal. She thought him the handsomer of the two and had been looking forward to bedding him, still, she did not want to argue when easy money was available. She smiled at him pointedly as she scooped up the coins.

"Whatever you say, sweetheart." As she hurried away to the bar to pay his bill, she hoped he would change his mind and come to her later. There weren't many customers at the Gold Nugget who passed up a chance to sample Pearlie Gates's favors.

Rand watched her walk away, his expression blank. He was drunk, he knew it and he didn't care. His express purpose in coming to the saloon had been to drink himself into forgetfulness, and he was doing his best to achieve that goal. He did not want to think, he did not want to feel. He only wanted to lose himself in the welcoming comfort of inebriation and put from his mind, if only for a while, the pain of his sorrow.

Lorelei was dead. He would never see her again or hold her again or touch her again. Inwardly, he berated himself for not having been there when she'd needed him most, and he thought of the horrors she must have suffered at the hands of the Bentons before she'd found

437

solace in death. Unnerved, he fumbled for the bottle, tilted it to his lips and drank greedily of its contents.

"Give me some of that." Brady pushed his empty glass across the table top toward Rand.

"Sure." Rand splashed a healthy dose of bourbon into his tumbler.

"I'm glad you bought her off," Brady remarked nodding toward the dancehall girl. "She's been over there near the bar for the last few hours, eying both of us."

"The last thing I want or need tonight is a woman." Rand glanced quickly in Pearlie's direction, noting her painted face and voluptuous figure. "There's only one woman I want and . . ."

Silence suddenly stretched between them then as they relived the last few days and their final, terrible decision to give up the fruitless search for Lorelei and Sally.

"Damn it, Brady! Lorelei and Sally are dead and it's all my fault!" Rand stated with barely controlled fury.

"Rand, you can't blame yourself. The Bentons are the ones who did this, not you."

Rand snorted sarcastically at Brady's attempt at consolation. "I might as well have killed Lorelei and Sally myself!" he raged. "If it hadn't been for the grudge they had against me, the Bentons wouldn't have returned to Phoenix, and they certainly wouldn't have kidnapped two women I cared about so they could use them to get me."

"You don't know that. The Bentons were killers. They don't need any excuse to murder innocent people. That's why they were sent up in the first place."

"Brady"—Rand shook his head slowly in defeat—"I don't want to talk about this any more. I don't even want to think about it."

"Rand, we did our best."

"And it wasn't enough," he declared bitterly, taking another deep drink of bourbon.

Brady knew there was no point in arguing for he felt the same way. The Bentons had won, and though they'd lost their lives in the process, they could not have devised a more hellish torture for Rand than the one he was now enduring.

Dust-covered and aching from exhaustion, Lori, Sally, and Roscoe arrived in Phoenix at sundown. Prospectors were a common sight in town, so they made their way through the streets practically unnoticed. Roscoe finally stopped Moses before the Gardiner's Hotel.

"Is this the place you were talkin' about stayin' in tonight?" he asked as he helped Sally dismount from the burro.

"Yes. We've stayed here before, so I don't think we'll have any trouble getting rooms," Lori answered.

"I'll help you get settled and then I'll be on about my own business," he offered, keeping a supportive arm about Sally's waist as they entered the lobby.

The lady behind the desk eyed them coldly, and Lori could easily understand why. They were filthy. Their clothes were dust- and sweat-streaked, their hair was unkempt and disheveled. They looked exactly like what they were—refugees from the desert—and they bore no resemblance to the sophisticated young women who'd arrived in town just a few weeks before.

"Can I help you?" The clerk's question was less than enthusiastic.

"I'm Lorelei Spencer and we'll be needing two rooms, please." Lori approached the woman in a most dignified manner, despite her shabby appearance.

As recognition dawned, the desk clerk gasped in

surprise, "Miss Spencer . . . you're alive?!"

"Quite." Lori smiled.

"Thank heavens! Why, when we heard the story . . . Everyone thought you were dead."

"Luckily, we're not," she replied as she took the two sets of keys the woman offered. Lori had no idea whether Rand was in town or not, so she decided to talk to John first to find out exactly what was going on. "Would you send word to the sheriff that we're here and would like to meet with him as soon as possible?"

"Well, yes . . . of course." The woman had heard the gossip about the murders at the bank and about Lydia McAllister's possible involvement, but she wisely held her tongue. That news should be imparted by the sheriff. "I'll send for him right away." She glanced at Sally who was leaning heavily on Roscoe and added, "Do you need the doctor?"

"Yes, and have two baths brought up for us, please," Lori requested as she turned to help Roscoe maneuver Sally up the stairs.

"Lori, do you think it's really necessary to have the doctor come?" Sally protested for she was feeling better except for a slight weakness.

"It can't hurt, Sally," Lori said firmly. "Roscoe did a wonderful job and I'm sure you're going to be fine, but we might as well take advantage of the doctor's help while we're in town."

"All right, but I've already caused you so much trouble."

"Don't be ridiculous!" Lori looked at her friend in amazement. "I'm just glad that we got out of this alive." She turned a warm gaze on Roscoe as they reached the top of the stairs and started down the hall to their rooms. "And we both know who we have to thank for that."

For the first time in more years than he could

440

remember, Roscoe blushed. "I told you before I was happy to help you and I was."

"Well, I want you to know that if you ever need a job, there's one ready and waiting for you at the Triple Cross," Lori offered.

"The Triple Cross?" Roscoe's eyes widened. "You're that Spencer?"

"I'm that Spencer and I'd be honored to have you at the mine, Roscoe," she told him as she unlocked the door to the first bedroom and opened it.

"I'll remember that if my claim ever gives out," he told her seriously as he guided Sally to the bed. "Do you want me to stay until the sheriff and the doctor get here?"

"It's not really necessary," Lori assured him. "I know you've got pressing business of your own."

"That I do, but I'll tell you what. I'll come by later and see how you're doing. How's that?"

"We'll be looking forward to your visit, Roscoe," Sally pressed his hand, her eyes warm with gratitude. "And thank you, again."

"You're welcome." He beamed and then left them on their own.

The liquor he'd been consuming had taken its toll, and Brady's eyes were glazed at he stared across the table at Rand. "You got a place to stay tonight?"

"Here's good enough," Rand mumbled. He knew he did not want to go back to Gardiner's for his memories of Lorelei were far too strong there. The remembrance of their first kiss by the fountain assailed him and he fought against it, not wanting to recall the sweetness of her touch and the glory of possessing her.

"I'll go pay the barkeep."

"I'll go with you. Let's bring the bottle along, might

want some more during the night." He got up unsteadily and was surprised to find Pearlie beside him slipping a helping arm about his waist. "What do you want?" he demanded harshly, finding her cloying artificial beauty a mockery of Lorelei's pure loveliness.

"I just heard you talking and I came to help you upstairs. I got a real nice room and you're welcome to spend the night there with me," she said as she leaned against him insinuatingly.

"Thanks, I'll get my own room," he answered as he disentangled himself from her. He'd intended to discourage her, but Pearlie only smiled.

"Whatever you want, big guy, is fine with me." She walked with him to where Brady was waiting.

"We got the two rooms at the end of the hall," Brady said as he moved off toward the steps.

"Good." Rand followed him, ignoring Pearlie.

However, she watched with interest as he disappeared upstairs, and she wondered if he'd change his mind as the night went on.

John could not believe the message he'd just received and he almost ran all the way to the hotel.

"Which room is the Spencer girl in?" he demanded as he strode to the desk.

"I gave the ladies twenty and twenty-two," the clerk hurriedly informed him. She was fascinated by all the happenings of the day. Rumors that the Bentons had killed Lorelei Spencer and her companion had been rife, and now the young women had showed up out of the clear blue. Eagerly, the clerk waited to see what the sheriff would have to say when he came back downstairs.

John raced up the steps two at a time. He was trying to keep a tight rein on his emotions, but the thought of

Lorelei and Sally turning up alive after he'd given up all hope of finding them was the best news he'd had in ages. He stopped before room twenty and knocked softly.

"Lorelei?" he called out, and he broke into a wide grin when the door swung open and a disheveled but very much alive Lorelei stood before him. "Dear God, it's true!"

Lori read the amazement on his face and smiled. "John, come in. Sally's here, too. We're waiting for the doctor to arrive."

"Doctor?" Instantly concerned, he looked from one woman to the other. "You were injured?"

"Sally was bitten by a snake, but she's doing much better now," she explained. "I just wanted the doctor to take a look at her to be sure she's completely recovered." Her expression suddenly turned serious as she thought of the Bentons and Rand. "John, there's so much I have to tell you, but first you must get a message to Rand, right away! Do you know where he is?"

"He's still here in town somewhere, I think." John had not spoken with Rand since earlier that day when he and Brady had returned to town after calling off their futile search. At the time, Rand had been frustrated and filled with anger over their lack of success.

"He's in town? Thank God!" Lori's face was alight with joy for her love was so near. Anxious to be reunited with him, she said quickly, "I've got to see him, to let him know we're safe. Do you know where he is so we can get word to him? And I want him to know that the Bentons are plotting something."

"Lorelei, honey"—John could see how upset she was about the outlaws' devious plan and he put a comforting arm about her shoulders—"the Bentons

443

are dead. You won't have to worry about them ever again."

Lori and Sally both looked up at him in stunned surprise.

"They're dead?"

"One was killed trying to rob the bank here in town and the other got it in a shootout with the posse."

Lori and Sally exchanged relieved looks as they absorbed the news.

"They're really dead. When?" Lori asked.

"Almost a week ago," John explained. "They attempted to rob the bank, and evidently Josh Taylor managed to shoot one of them before he was killed."

"Taylor's dead?"

"It was terrible, just terrible," the sheriff related sadly. "The clerk was killed during the robbery, and so was one of my deputies. Pat Benton escaped unharmed, but he took Lydia with him."

"Lydia?"

"Seems she and Taylor were involved in a conspiracy with the Bentons to murder Rand," he explained, and Lori blanched with the news.

"Lydia was involved." Lori glanced at Sally. "Then she must have known all about that 'messenger'. No wonder she decided not to go to town with us!"

"What are you saying?" John asked.

"The messenger who came to the ranch with Taylor's note was Pat Benton," Sally told him. "We invited Lydia to come to town with us, but she refused. Now we know why! She set us up for the Bentons as part of the plan to kill Rand."

"Where is she now?" Lori demanded, ready to face the treacherous bitch who had nearly cost them their lives.

"She's dead, Lorelei," John replied solemnly, and Lori smiled in grim satisfaction as he continued. "After

444

we lost the Bentons' trail when we were searching for them after the explosion at the mine, Rand stopped off at the Lazy Ace with Brady to pay a visit to you two ladies. That was how he found out about the kidnapping."

Sally brightened at the news that Brady had joined in the search for her and had actually gone out to the Lazy Ace to see her.

"Lydia had come into town, she wanted to locate Rand, she claimed, so he headed back here right away," John continued. "Brady came with him. They had just ridden in when the outlaws struck at the bank. We got a posse together and headed out after Benton, and since he and Lydia were riding double, we had no trouble tracking him."

"Did Lydia go with him willingly?" Lori had to know the depth of that vicious woman's connection with the desperadoes.

"No. Any involvement with them had been handled by Taylor. I think she accidentally happened upon the robbery and Benton just grabbed her and took her with him as a hostage. When we finally trapped him, Lydia tried to escape, but Benton shot her down in cold blood."

"I've never rejoiced at anyone's death, but I feel no remorse over hers," Lori stated coldly.

"I don't either," Sally declared. She wondered how Lydia could have so cruelly and calculatingly plotted their kidnapping and Rand's demise.

"There's one other thing," John remarked, and in response to their questioning looks, he went on. "Rand and Brady both think you're dead."

"What?" Lori and Sally chorused.

"After the shootout, but before he died, Pat Benton swore to Rand that you were both dead. He refused to believe him at first, so did Brady, and they kept

445

searching for you on their own until just this morning. It was a terrible blow for them to admit that their quest was futile."

"Brady was looking for us?" Sally was delighted.

John gave her a warm, understanding smile. "Indeed he was. He and Rand were very upset when they rode in earlier."

"Where do you think they are? We'll go to them right now." Lori knew how desperately concerned she'd been over Rand's dangerous situation, and she could imagine what he'd gone through when Benton had told him she'd been killed.

Before the sheriff could reply, however, there was a knock at the door. When Lori responded, several maids entered, bearing the necessities for the bath she'd ordered.

"Why don't I go see if I can locate Rand and Brady for you while you two bathe?" John offered quickly as the servants bustled about the room.

"Do you have any idea where they could be?" Lori asked. She had been so afraid that something terrible had happened to Rand, and now, knowing he was alive and well, she could hardly wait to be with him again.

"I'm not sure," John hedged. "He might even have gone back to the Lazy Ace. Let me ask around for you, and I'll let you know as soon as I find something out."

"We'll wait right here until we hear from you," Lori agreed happily.

"Good." John was relieved that she'd consented so readily for judging from the state Rand and Brady had been in earlier that day, he had a good idea just where they'd gone when they'd left his office, and it wasn't back to the ranch. "I'll be back just as soon as I can."

Rand wanted to sleep. He did not want to be awake, but no matter how much bourbon he drank, he could not pass over the edge into complete oblivion.

Lying on the lumpy, stained mattress in the cheap, rented room above the Gold Nugget Saloon, he silently swore at his inability to put Lorelei from his mind. Always, she was there—her sweetness and beauty searing his very soul. Nowhere could he find a moment's peace. Rand closed his eyes, but a vision of her danced before him, her arms outstretched in a welcoming gesture that beckoned him nearer, her eyes were aglow with the fire of love. Groaning, he flung himself from the bed and snatched up the bottle of liquor from the night table, drinking deeply of its potent contents.

He was swaying as he stood there in the middle of the room, and when he looked up he was disgusted by his reflection in the cracked mirror over the wash stand. Blankly, he stared at his reflection, dispassionately studying the man before him, taking in his unshaven features and filthy, wrinkled clothing, and the star that shone brightly on his chest even in the dimness of the room.

The star . . . Suddenly, the badge he'd worn so proudly for so many years became the symbol of his loss. If it hadn't been for his job, he would never have become entangled with the Bentons in the first place and Lorelei and Sally would still be alive. In a moment of frustrated rage, he threw the bottle at the mirror full-force, and he watched in drunken pleasure as the glass shattered into a thousand sharp shards that crashed to the floor.

Suddenly Rand knew he had to get out of the room, and staggering toward the door, he flung it open and then started down the hall. Rand didn't know where he was going; he only knew he needed to be outside. The confines of the stifling room were aggravating his misery.

Pearlie was busy plying her trade with the cowboys

in the Gold Nugget, but when she saw the tall, handsome marshal come down the stairs, she walked away from her other potential clients without a backward look.

"Where you goin', big guy?" She blocked his path and looked up at him, coyly batting her thick lashes.

"Out." Rand's answer was brusque and he gave her only a cursory glance before stepping around her.

"Want some company?" She trailed eagerly after him. Since he'd gone upstairs she'd tried to distract herself with the other men in the saloon, but none of them had measured up to him and she still hoped to get him to bed her.

Rand didn't even bother to answer as he strode across the crowded room and Pearlie, remembering how blunt he'd been earlier, took his silence to mean yes.

Hurrying over to the barkeep, she told him excitedly. "I'm going with him. I'll be back later."

"What about the rest of the customers, Pearlie?" the man argued.

Giving him a pained look, she said, "Have Myra and Susie come downstairs for a while. I ain't gonna be that long."

When Pearlie glanced up Rand had already disappeared through the swinging doors so she rushed after him.

Lori sat in the tub of warm water, feeling blissfully happy as she thought of how well everything had turned out. She and Sally had made it back alive and in good health, and Rand was safe. Her heart beat wildly as she thought of her love, and a quiver of excitement shook her when she imagined herself once again enfolded in his strong embrace. Delightedly, as she

448

rinsed the soap from her hair, she began to hum the same melody she'd been singing the night Rand had first kissed her by the pool in the courtyard. Soon—very soon—he would come to her and then life would be wonderful again.


Although Rand had been trying to flee his memories of Lorelei, he was now driven to return to the hotel courtyard where they'd shared their first kiss. Quietly, he stood at the edge of the patio, staring at the splashing waters of the pool and remembering their fiery first embrace. It seemed a lifetime ago, yet he knew it hadn't been all that long since they'd kissed so fervently here in the moonlight. There was a constricting tightness in his chest as he thought of the moments they'd shared in the courtyard, his bittersweetness driving him to desperation.

*God!* he argued almost violently to himself. *It can't be over. . . . It can't be.*

His hands clenched into fists as he acknowledged, in agonizing pain, that it was. Lorelei was dead—murdered by Pat and Cody Benton—and he would never have the chance to love her again.

He heard it distantly then, the lilting, exotic melody that Lorelei had sung that first night by the pool. He knew the voice couldn't be Lorelei's, he knew she was lost to him, but he couldn't stop himself from desperately searching for her. Suddenly it seemed to Rand that he saw her, standing slightly away from him in the deep, concealing shadows of the night.

"Lorelei?" His voice was hoarse with emotion as he took several steps in the phantom woman's direction, and a thrill surged through him as he heard her huskily speak his name.

She was in his arms then, warm and willing, and

Rand closed his eyes to enjoy the rapture of holding her close. He kissed her passionately, never questioning the reality of the situation but molding the woman's soft curves to him and relishing the feel of her in his arms once again.


Lorelei continued to sing as she completed her toilette. Then, wrapped in a clean, soft towel, she turned down the oil lamp and went to the window overlooking the courtyard. There she and Rand had first discovered their passion and there they would be reunited. She smiled as she remembered the explosive excitement of their kiss by the pool and her aggravation with Rand afterward. How silly she'd been! Rand had been no ruthless womanizer. All her terrible suspicions had been ill founded. He loved her and they were going to be married just as quickly as it could be arranged.

It was then that she heard a man in the courtyard say, "Lorelei . . ." She thought the man sounded like Rand and she leaned farther out the window to catch a glimpse of him, thinking that John had found her love and Rand was on his way to her. But she did not see Rand looking up at her. Instead, she got the most devastating shock of her life. The man she'd heard speak her name had been Rand, but he had not been talking to her. Lori stared in horror as Rand heatedly embraced another woman in the privacy of the patio.

She felt nauseated as she watched the pair. Unable to speak, unable to think, she finally drew back and stood just beside the window, shivering uncontrollably. So this was the man who had been so distraught at thinking her dead. Tears stung Lori's eyes, and though she fought to hold them back, they fell unheeded as she laughed aloud at the thought of what a fool she'd been.

Rand might have been unhappy for a moment or two, but obviously he'd already managed to replace her with another. Deciding that her first assessment of him had been true after all, Lori shook her head despondently, thinking herself foolish for having believed in him.

Almost blinded by her tears, she walked to the bed and collapsed across it, clasping the pillow to her breast as she tried to decide what to do. The first lightning strike of pain had diminished, leaving a dull emptiness within her, and her only sustaining thought was of the Triple Cross. She wanted to go home, would have left immediately, but she knew it was impossible for her to make the ride before daylight.

Nervously, she eyed the door to her room, fearing that at any moment, John would return with Rand and she would be forced to face him. Lori knew that seeing Rand right now would destroy her. She had fought so hard to stay alive, suffered so much humiliation at the hands of the Bentons, just so she could come back to Rand, only to discover that it really hadn't mattered to him if she'd lived or died.

Sighing, she buried her face in the softness of the pillow as she tried to force herself to think rationally. There would be no future for her with Rand. She was silently thankful that she now knew she was not pregnant with his child, for the break between them would have to be complete and final.

Rand tried to lose himself in the woman's kiss, but there was something wrong, something subtly different about the feel of her in his arms. Finally despite his liquor-fogged senses, he drew back and looked down at her. He was jolted at finding the dancehall girl in his embrace.

"What the hell!" he ground out, releasing her as if

451

he'd been stung.

"What's wrong? Don't you like me?" Pearlie leaned closer and brushed her ample bosom against his chest.

Rand backed farther away from her and rubbed his eyes in an effort to make sense out of what had just happened. He had thought she was Lorelei. A shudder of disgust shook him at the realization that he had mistaken Pearlie for the woman he loved.

"It doesn't matter," he muttered, feeling completely lost in his drunken haze.

"What's wrong, sugar?" she coaxed, trying to understand what his problem was. "Why don't you come up to my room? I know how to make you feel good. I can show you tricks you'll never forget." Pearlie tried to take his arm, but he pulled free.

"No. You're not the one I want."

She thought he meant he wanted another girl from the saloon. "C'mon. I'm much better than the other girls. Let me show you. I can make you forget every other woman you've ever had."

Rand looked down at her, his expression suddenly intense for he longed for Lorelei. "I almost wish you could," he said, then he turned his back on her and stalked off across the courtyard, disappearing into the darkness.

Pearlie watched him go, angry with herself for having wasted so much time on him. Finally, straightening the bodice of her low-cut gown, she stomped off toward the Gold Nugget, hoping that the other girls hadn't taken all the business for the night.


John was frustrated. He'd checked out every saloon and bar in town and had turned up no sign of Rand or Brady. He stopped by the other hotels to see if either man had taken a room, then gave up his quest and returned to Gardiner's to tell Lori and Sally that the men must have returned to the ranch.

John knew the young women were eagerly awaiting him, and he felt badly because he hadn't located Rand and Brady. Thinking that Sally might be resting, he went first to Lorelei's room.

"Yes?" Lori called out in response to his knock.

John thought her voice sounded slightly muffled. "Lorelei, it's John."

"Just a minute." Thinking he had Rand with him, Lori panicked and hurriedly began to pull on her clothes. When she was finally dressed, she took a moment to compose herself before letting him in. Then she unlocked and opened the door, expecting to be confronted by John and Rand. To her surprise, John stood alone in the hallway.

"You didn't find him?" Her relief was real, but John mistook it for disappointment.

"I'm sorry. I looked everywhere, but I couldn't find Rand or Brady. They must have gone back to the Lazy Ace this afternoon."

Lori knew better, but she was not going to mention the scene on the patio. "I guess they did. I really appreciate your trying, John."

"I just wish I could have found them for you. I know how eager you are to see him again. It's just a shame that he's already left town."

"Well, just knowing he's safe is enough for me. I'll see him soon." She gave John a slight smile that did not reveal her true thoughts.

He nodded. "You'll tell Sally? I didn't want to disturb her since she's recovering."

"She does need rest, but the doctor said she's going to be just fine. I'll tell her your news. Thanks again, John."

"You're welcome, Lorelei." He smiled. "I'm glad

453

everything's worked out for you."

"So am I." Lori closed the door as he headed down the hall, and she waited until she was sure he was gone before leaving her room to go speak with Sally.

Sally eagerly bid her enter, but her excited expression faded when she saw that Lori was alone.

"John just came to my room."

"And?"

"And he couldn't locate Rand or Brady."

"I'm sorry, Lori. I know how much you wanted to see Rand." Sally tried to cheer her friend. "But we'll find them tomorrow. I promise."

"Oh, no, we won't." Lori finally gave vent to the feelings she'd been holding in, and Sally who was sitting on the bed, looked up questioningly at her.

"What?"

"I don't ever want to see Rand McAllister again," Lori declared furiously.

"Lori." Sally was completely bewildered by her declaration. "What are you saying?"

"I'm saying that John may not have been able to find Rand, but I did."

"I don't understand. If you found him, then where is he?"

"Right now? I imagine Rand is in some woman's bed." Lori's voice was filled with bitterness.

"Lori!" Sally was shocked. "I don't believe you said that!"

Lori rounded on her, her eyes dark with pain. "Sally, earlier, right after we had our baths, I heard a man talking out in the courtyard. I thought he sounded like Rand, so I looked out the window. It was Rand, Sally, and he was kissing a woman. I couldn't see her clearly, but she was in his arms, kissing him passionately."

"Surely you must have been mistaken," her friend argued. "You know how much he loves you."

"I thought I did, but, Sally, I did see him. It wasn't a dream, although I wish it had been."

"You've got to talk with him about this. You know what happened the last time you saw him kissing another woman."

"Don't talk about that." Lori turned away, her heart broken. "In the morning, I'm returning to the Triple Cross. I know you're probably too weak to travel yet, but I can't stay here. I must get away before I run into Rand."

"You're going to have to see him sometime."

"Maybe, but when I do see him again, it's going to be when I choose to do so," Lori said flatly.

Sally's gaze was compassionate. "I understand, but if you go, I'm going with you."

"No you're not! The doctor said you needed bedrest. Besides, I'm sure Brady will be looking for you in the morning."

But Sally would not agree. "I am not going to let you go back to the mine by yourself. We'll hire a buckboard, and we can leave as soon as you're ready. If I survived our trek across the desert, I'm certain a half-day's ride to the mine won't kill me!"

Lori gave her friend a warm look. "Thank you, Sally."

# *Chapter Twenty-Seven*

Though Lori tried to rest when she returned to her room, the surcease of sleep was denied her. Still lying awake in her bed at the first sign of dawn, she summoned one of the hotel maids and sent word to the stable that she wanted to hire a driver and a buckboard for the journey to the mine. To Lori's surprise Sally was awake when she went to her room, and after a quick breakfast in the hotel dining room, the young women left a short explanatory note for Roscoe at the desk and then started on their way to the Triple Cross.

Lori had been tense and edgy as they headed out of town for she feared a confrontation with Rand, but now that she was safely away she was both relieved and disappointed. The innocent romantic in her had been secretly hoping that Rand would come dashing up to her at the last minute to apologize and to declare that what she'd seen the night before had all been a terrible mistake, but in reality, right this minute Rand was probably in that woman's bed, sleeping off a night of wild, abandoned lovemaking.

The thought devastated Lori, and it infuriated her. How could Rand dismiss what they'd shared so easily? He and Brady had continued the search for them after the others had given up, but only yesterday he'd decided she was dead and last night he was already seeking another woman's favors.

Lori reviewed in her mind the embrace she'd witnessed in the courtyard, and she was firmly convinced that Rand had been a willing participant. It infuriated her to find herself reliving the misery she'd experienced as a child when she'd seen him kissing Lydia in the stable, and she tried to push all thoughts of Rand from her mind. She had allowed him to hurt her twice and that was foolish. Turning her anger toward her own naïveté, she hardened her heart against any softer emotions she harbored for Rand.

What had existed between them had been merely a physical attraction, Lori decided. Rand had shown her last night that any woman could assuage his needs so no doubt any man could satisfy hers, though at the moment that thought sickened her. She'd been taught the beauty of love and sex and marriage, but Rand had made a mockery of them.

With firm resolve, Lori straightened on the buckboard's seat, determined never to let Rand near her again. She would face him when the time came, for she knew there was no way to avoid it, but she would never allow him to touch her heart. What had existed between them had been potent and powerful, but it was over, as dead as he thought her to be.

Sally had been watching the grim play of emotions on Lori's face, and her heart ached for her friend.

"Lori, do you want to talk about it?" she asked.

"There's nothing more to say, Sally." Lori denied her inner turmoil.

"Well, you know I'm here."

"I know, but nothing can be accomplished by rehashing everything that's happened. I'm going home, and with Hal's help I'm going to make the Triple

457

Cross the most successful mine this territory has ever seen."

"I'm sure you will," Sally agreed, and though she would have liked to press Lori to open up and release some of her pain, she said nothing more. Perhaps later Lori would feel the need to discuss her feelings for Rand. Now they were just too raw and painful.

Brady opened one eye, experimentally at first, and he immediately regretted his action and raised his arm to protect his eyes from further torture. Light, bright and shining, filled the room and its glare sent frissons of pain pounding through his head. Yes, he decided miserably, it certainly was daylight.

With a groan, Brady swung his long legs over the side of the creaking bed and he sat unmoving, silently suffering, his head bowed in tormented tribute to his excesses of the night before. As the throbbing subsided somewhat, he took a quick glance around the sparsely furnished room, and a disgusted expression appeared on his face as he tried to figure out exactly where he was. Vague memories of last night came back to him, in snatches, but he could not place his current surroundings. The last definite thing he could remember was Rand ordering another bottle of bourbon in the saloon and then telling the dancehall girl to leave them alone.

Though it required a major effort, he got to his feet and slowly crossed to the window. Below him, life went on at its usual pace. Nothing seemed to have changed. But the woman he had come to care for was dead. A vision of Sally swept warmly into his mind. She had been the most wonderful woman he'd ever encountered and now she was gone, forever.

Brady, too, had known the failure and despair Rand had experienced last night, but he was not a man who could easily express what he was feeling so he'd kept his agony to himself. He had been on his own since he'd been orphaned in his early teens, and Sally's brief presence in his life had given him a glimpse of what love could be like. Brady knew it was going to be very difficult to go back to his solitary existence now that he'd experienced a little of life's brightness.

Girding himself for a future alone, he turned away from the window and moved back to the bed. After pulling on his boots, he stood up and strapped on his gunbelt before heading from the room to find Rand. He wanted to say good-bye to the man who'd become a good friend before he returned to the Wells Fargo office and his old way of living.

As he emerged from his room, Brady hazily remembered Rand had taken the next room down the hall and he knocked on the door, hoping to find Rand up and about. Brady was surprised when the door swung slightly open at his touch, and he pushed it wider to take a quick look inside. Finding the room deserted, he set out to find Rand.

Rand was riding slowly toward town, his expression as grim as his thoughts. His mistaken encounter with Pearlie in the courtyard had sobered him considerably, and desperately needing to get away, he'd sought solace in the vast stillness of the desert. He'd camped out alone under the star-studded sky, and as the sun had risen in the East, his anguish had turned to bitterness. In an instant of pain-filled anger, he had torn his marshal's badge from his shirt and had sworn never to wear it again.

Rand's life was a shambles. He had already decided that he would send a wire to Marshal Duke tendering his resignation, for he knew there was no way he could continue to be a lawman, not when he harbored such bitterness. He wasn't sure what he'd do next. Lydia's death had left him the sole owner of the Lazy Ace, and though he hated the very thought, he was now in complete charge of the Triple Cross. Both responsibilities weighed heavily upon him. Today, he planned to return to the ranch, but first he was going to find Brady and John, and thank them for their help and support.

John stood in the doorway of his office, casually surveying his domain. The knowledge that Lorelei and Sally had survived their seizure by the Bentons had left him feeling good about life, and he was in a mellow mood as he watched his fellow citizens go about their business. The sound of his name interrupted his musings, and he glanced up to see Brady heading his way.

"Brady! I thought you'd left town." John's voice reflected his sudden excitement at seeing the Wells Fargo man again.

Brady was puzzled by John's attitude. "No, not yet. I was hoping to catch up with Rand before I left. Have you seen him this morning?"

"You mean he's still in town? Then where the hell were you two last night? I was looking everywhere for you?"

"You were?" Brady frowned, assuming instantly that there had been trouble. "Why? What happened?"

John suddenly beamed as he clapped Brady on the shoulder. "We had some late arrivals in town yesterday."

"Late arrivals?" The younger man was befuddled.

"Seems an old prospector stumbled upon two young ladies making an escape from some outlaws who'd

460

been holding them hostage and he brought them safely into town."

"What!" Brady felt a surge of joy. "Sally? Lori?"

"Yep." John smiled widely. "They're at Gardiner's right now. C'mon, I'll take you to them."

"How did this happen? They escaped from the Bentons?" He was amazed.

"Lorelei told me the whole story. Now"—John paused as he prepared to tell Brady about Sally's encounter wtih the snake—"Sally was snakebit, Brady, but Lorelei assured me last night that she was going to be fine."

"Snakebit?" Barclay tensed at the news. What kind of hell had Sally been through?

"The doctor saw her last night and she was doing fine."

"Thank God."

"Where were you, anyway? I looked damned near everywhere for you."

"Rand and I were at the Gold Nugget. We took rooms there."

"I should have known you wouldn't have gone back to the ranch, but when I checked all the saloons and hotels I just figured that you had."

They entered Gardiner's Hotel, and as John led the way upstairs to the rooms Lori and Sally had occupied the night before, Brady grew nervous at the prospect of seeing Sally again. Just minutes before he'd thought her dead and now . . .

John knocked sharply on the door of Lorelei's room and his surprise was evident when a maid opened the door.

"Yes, Sheriff?"

"Where's the young woman who occupied this room last night?"

"She checked out," the woman replied.

"She what?"

"Both of them," the maid went on. "They left at sunup, rented a buckboard from the stable. They seemed in pretty much of a hurry."

"Did they leave any messages? Did they say where they were going?"

"They left a note at the desk for somebody named Roscoe Davison, but other than that they didn't say much."

Brady turned to John. "Who's Davison?"

"He's the prospector who brought them into town," the sheriff replied. "And as to where they went, I'm almost positive they've gone to the Lazy Ace."

"The ranch?"

John nodded. "Last night when I couldn't locate you, I figured you'd both gone back to the ranch and that's what I told them. They were pretty keyed up about seeing you again, so I'm sure that's where they're headed."

"And Rand doesn't know any of this?" Brady confirmed.

"No. I haven't seen him. In fact, I was surprised to see you this morning."

"I'm sure glad you did." He was feeling a lightness in his heart, a sensation he hadn't known since early childhood. "Let's go see if we can find Rand. This is one bit of news he definitely needs to hear."


Rand tied up his horse in front of the telegraph office and strode inside, anxious to have this bit of business over with. After giving his message to the clerk and paying for it, he headed off to find Brady. His stop at the Gold Nugget proving futile, he nodded to the sullen Pearlie who was lingering by the bar as he left. Deciding to try John's office next, he was disappointed to find it deserted, but knowing that the sheriff was probably just out making his rounds, Rand settled in behind the desk to await his friend's arrival.

"Damn!" Though Brady was not usually given to swearing, the aggravation of having good news and not being able to find Rand to tell it to him was driving him to distraction. "Where could he have gone? The last I saw of him, he was going into his room at the Gold Nugget late last night."

"I don't have any idea." John was sympathetic.

"What worries me is that Sally and Lorelei are going to show up at the Lazy Ace and we're not going to be there."

"Do you think Rand would have gone out to the ranch without saying good-bye to you?"

"I don't know." Brady considered John's thought. "I'd hope not, but he was pretty strung out last night. Why don't we check out the stables and see if his horse is still boarded?"

"Good idea."

Their walk to the stables took them past the office and they caught sight of Rand at the same time.

"There he is, thank God!"

"Rand!"

"Hello, John, Brady." Rand's demeanor was calm as he stood up to greet his friends, paying no attention to their unusual exuberance. "I was hoping to see both of you. I've decided to leave and—"

"You're damned right you're leaving. Get your things. We're leaving right now! We should have left hours ago," Brady blurted out.

Rand eyed him in confusion. "Just where is it we're going?"

"To the ranch! Rand, Lori and Sally are alive!"

463

Rand paled at the news.

"What is this, some kind of cruel joke?" he demanded harshly, his eyes narrowing in disbelief.

"It's no joke, Rand," John hastened to assure him. "They arrived in town late last night. I tried to find you then, but I couldn't so I mistakenly told Lorelei that I thought you had gone home."

"How was she?" he asked, his throat tight and his voice choked with emotion.

"She was fine, just fine, and real anxious to see you," John answered truthfully. "Now I suggest you two hit the trail. If Lorelei and Sally rode out of here at dawn hoping to find you at the ranch, they're going to be two mighty disappointed women when they find out you aren't there."

John's words goaded Rand from his momentary stupor. "I'll see you later," he said. Flashing the sheriff a wide grin, he raced from the office with Brady following close behind.

Hours later Rand and Brady faced Juana in the parlor of the ranchhouse at the Lazy Ace.

"They're not here?" There was disbelief in Brady's voice.

"No. I haven't seen or heard from them. In fact, the last news I had was that they were dead," Juana explained. "Where else could they have gone?"

"The mine?" Brady wondered.

"Knowing how Lorelei feels about the Triple Cross, it's conceivable that she would go there." Rand tried to understand what she'd done, but he sensed that all was not as it seemed. "Let's ride. If we push the horses, we can make it before nightfall."

"You will let me know how they are?" Juana asked as she accompanied them from the house.

"I'll send word," Rand promised as he swung up on his mount.

Juana nodded and waved as they raced off toward the mine.

Lori stiffened at Hal's casual question. "I haven't spoken with Rand yet," she said quickly.

"You mean he doesn't know about any of this yet?" Hal was surprised.

"No. The sheriff couldn't locate him in town so he figured he must have gone out to the ranch, and once I found out that the Bentons were no longer a threat, all I could think about was coming back here."

"Then Rand should be showing up real soon." Noticing her discomfort, he asked, "You did send word to him, didn't you?"

Lori's eyes were flashing fire as she turned on him. "No and why should I?"

Hal was caught off guard by her vehemence. When Rand had left with Lorelei and Sally to escort them to the Lazy Ace, it had seemed that this pair had finally worked things out. His expression reflected his confusion as he gently reminded her, "Because, among other things, he is your legal guardian, Lorelei."

His reproach annoyed her. "Technically, he may be my guardian, but that's as far as it goes."

"I don't understand. When you left here, you two seemed happy, but now, after everything you've gone through, you don't even want to see him?" Hal was mystified. Isolated as he was at the mine, he had not known what had been going on, and the story Lori and Sally had just told him seemed incredible. It was hard for him to believe that Lydia McAllister and Josh Taylor had been in cahoots and working with the Bentons to set up Lori's and Sally's kidnapping in an effort to lure Rand to his death. And he was even more bewildered by Lori's new attitude toward Rand. Hal knew McAllister had been worried about Lori's safety. That had been Rand's primary reason for wanting the young women to live at the ranch while he went after the Bentons. "I'm sure he cares about you."

Lori snorted. "Well, I'm not. Look, Hal, I really don't want to discuss this any further."

"But don't you think Rand deserves to hear from you?" He would not be put off. "If you don't send him word that you're still alive, how do you expect him to find out? He's probably worried to death."

She shot him a derisive look. "That I seriously doubt."

Hal glanced in exasperation at Sally.

"I'm sure Rand will be here soon, Hal, so I wouldn't worry," Sally put in, feeling confident that John would give Rand and Brady the news as soon as he saw them again.

He was perplexed. "Well, I'd better get back to work, then. I'll speak with you later this evening."

"Fine," Lori dismissed him wearily, not wanting to discuss the events of the last few weeks anymore. She had thought she would be happy upon returning to the mine, but since she'd arrived the joy she and Rand had shared on their last night here had haunted her. How very much she'd wanted to marry him . . . then.

When Hal was gone, Sally spoke up. "You aren't going to be able to hide from him forever, you know."

"I don't care," Lori stated flatly.

"If that were true, you wouldn't be so upset."

"Sally," Lori ground out, "John said that Rand and Brady had only given up on rescuing us yesterday morning! How could he have gone straight into another woman's arms if he was upset about me being 'dead'?"

466

"I don't know," her friend admitted slowly. "But one way or the other, you're going to have to face him. You know that, don't you?"

"Yes." Lori's reply was barely audible.

"And do you know how angry he's going to be when he finds out that you're alive but you didn't let him know?"

"What was I supposed to do, Sally? Find out what room he was sharing with that woman and knock on the door and announce that I'd returned from the grave!"

"I know you're hurt, but think about how Rand is going to feel when he learns you're alive and haven't even bothered to contact him. The last time he saw you, he thought you were going to become his wife!" The longer she'd thought about it, the more firmly Sally believed that Lori had acted childishly in fleeing town that morning without seeing Rand.

"Yes and the last time I saw him I firmly believed he was going to become my husband. But after all we'd been through, seeing him in another woman's arms . . . What would you have done, Sally?" she countered.

Sally had expected this question and she met Lori's challenging gaze levelly. "I think I would have faced him then and there. I don't know what might have happened, but I do know if I loved a man, I would be willing to fight for him. This situation is entirely different from the time you saw Rand kissing Lydia. You were a child then; you're not now. You two had declared your love for one another and had promised to marry. Think about it."

"I'm going to lie down for a while," Lori said, and she disappeared into the privacy of her room.

Stretching out across the bed, she considered everything Sally had said. She knew that her friend's

467

arguments made sense, but they didn't heal the hurt or eliminate the devastation she felt over Rand's betrayal. Closing her eyes, she let exhaustion overcome her and she slipped into a deep sleep that was filled with tormented visions of Rand, of the glory that had been theirs when they had been together and of the desolation she'd felt at the sight of him making love to another woman.

When the guard at the mine saw the two riders approaching, he stepped out, gun in hand, to stop them. "Hold up there! Oh, Mr. McAllister. Good to have you back!"

"It's good to be back," Rand returned absently as he scoured the mining camp for some sign of Lorelei.

"Miss Lorelei and Miss Sally are both up at the main house," the guard offered helpfully.

Rand's and Brady's relief was complete, and they put their heels to their horses, eager to reach the women they loved. "Thanks."

Totally unaware of the reason Lori and Sally had returned to the mine and not particularly caring about it at this time, they thundered toward the house, anxious for their long-awaited reunion.

Sally heard the commotion and stepped outside to see what was happening just as Brady reined in at the rail.

"Brady . . ." Her breath caught in her throat at the sight of him, and when he dismounted and turned toward her, she launched herself into his embrace.

"Sally! I can't believe you're really alive!" His voice was husky as he stared down at her in joyous fascination, and then, mesmerized by the fact that she was actually in his arms, he lowered his head and kissed her.

It was ecstasy to, at last, be in Brady's arms, and Sally felt she was transported to the heavens at the touch of his lips, so warm and inviting.

He broke off the kiss but did not release her from the encirclement of his arms. "I . . . we"—he cast a quick glance at Rand who was starting to stride past him—"we thought you were dead."

"I know," she replied. Then, noting that Rand was about to enter the house in search of Lori, she called out to him. "Rand, wait! I've got to talk with you!"

Rand stopped just as he was about to open the door, and he looked back at her curiously. "Isn't Lori inside?"

"Yes, but there's something you must know before you talk to her." Sally was very fond of Rand, and she wanted to let him know exactly what he was about to face.

"Is Lori all right?" He did not miss the seriousness of Sally's tone. "Brady and I wonderd why you came here instead of going to the ranch."

"It's a long story and one you should hear before you see Lori again," she confided as she moved slightly away from Brady.

"Did the Bentons hurt her? If they did—"

"No. It has nothing to do with the Bentons, although that wasn't an easy time for us." Brady's arm tightened protectively about Sally's shoulders and she looked up at him, giving him an adoring smile.

"Then what?" Rand was at a loss as to what she was talking about and he was rapidly losing patience. He'd been through hell searching for Lorelei, but now Sally was telling him he had to wait even longer before he was reunited with her.

"Lori and I got back to town late yesterday and we were lucky enough to get rooms at Gardiner's Hotel."

"We knew that. John told us this morning."

"Well, John went to look for both of you. He was going to bring you to us, so we were to wait in our rooms at the hotel." She paused, flushing slightly as she realized what she now had to say to Rand.

"And?"

"And, Lori saw you last night, Rand." Sally glanced at him nervously. "In the courtyard area of the hotel . . . with another woman."

"That's impossible. I wasn't with a woman last night." Rand frowned. "Far from it. I ended up camping out, alone, on the desert, and I didn't return to town until this morning."

"That's right, Sally," Brady put in. "We were drinking at the Gold Nugget, and then we took rooms over the saloon for the night. But we didn't bother with any women. Rand bought off the only one who tried to approach us."

"Pearlie." Rand groaned her name as the scene on the patio came into hazy focus in his mind.

"Pearlie?" Brady asked. "She's the one you paid to leave us alone, isn't she?"

"Yes. But she followed me when I left my room later last night." He cursed under his breath as he imagined what Lori had witnessed. "Where is Lori, Sally? I have to explain."

"She's in her room resting, but, Rand, just like she did with Lydia, she's believed the worst."

"Thank you for the warning, Sally." He kissed her affectionately on the cheek before turning and disappearing indoors.

When Brady would have followed him, Sally took his arm. "Brady, as upset as Lori is, I think we'd better let them have some time alone."

He nodded as he faced her, his eyes meeting hers in soft, sweet promise. "There's a lot I have to say to you, Sally, things I should have said the night of the party."

"And I think they're things I want to hear."

As she gave him an open, loving smile, Brady's fear that she might reject him vanished. "Walk with me, Sally?"

The sun was dipping low on the western horizon as, hand in hand, they headed slowly away from the bustle of the camp.

## Chapter Twenty-Eight

In his barely controlled eagerness to see Lorelei again, Rand strode quickly across the main room toward her bedroom. His heart was near to bursting with the joy and excitement he was feeling, yet he paused briefly before the door to decide the best way to approach her. He wanted to do more than to sweep her into his arms and proclaim his love, but he could well imagine the shock she had suffered last night when she'd witnessed him embracing Pearlie on the patio, the hurt that had been hers when she'd thought he was seeking another woman.

Rand smiled to himself at the thought of any other woman taking Lorelei's place in his affections. Lorelei was the only woman he'd ever truly loved. Confident that once he'd explained the circumstances she would understand, he quietly turned the doorknob and entered her bedroom.

As he'd hoped, she was sleeping peacefully so he silently closed the door behind him and remained where he was, letting his eyes feast on her loveliness. The simple daygown she was wearing clung softly to her ample curves, and he ached to strip away that garment and press heated, cherishing kisses to every inch of her satiny flesh. Her hair was unbound, spread around her in a pool of fiery splendor, and Rand longed to run his hands through its silken length. He felt himself harden in anticipation of tasting of her sweetness as, like a man possessed, he moved closer.

The agony her 'death' had caused him was swept away as Rand sat carefully on the edge of the bed. Lori was here, she was alive; and he knew only his need to reaffirm their closeness. They had both been through hell, and Rand had no intention of letting last night's mistaken embrace ruin their future. He would awaken her slowly, gently, and then explain everything. Softly, he brushed an errant curl from her cheek as he leaned nearer to kiss her.

Though still deep in sleep, Lori stirred at the touch of his lips, and already caught in the grip of a sensuous dream of Rand, she moved restlessly on the bed and sighed his name.

Her seductive murmuring of his name entranced Rand, and he kissed her again, his lips brushing hers in a soft, exploratory caress. Though logic told him he should awaken her so they could discuss what had happened and settle everything between them, his need to possess the sweetness of her body urged him to make love to her now and talk later. Her willing response to his kiss was all the provocation Rand needed to give himself over to the wonder of his love.

Lori's dream of Rand was so vivid it seemed real, and she wasn't sure whether she should fight the erotic sensations flowing through her or just enjoy them, since they were, after all, just her own imaginings. For hours she had tossed and turned, plagued by tormenting visions of the Bentons, of her harrowing escape across the desert, and of Rand embracing another woman. But suddenly her nightmares had ceased, and she was being swept into an erotic fantasy so powerful

473

it was arousing her even as she slept.

In her dream, Rand was with her—kissing her, touching her—and she was on fire with need for him. All the hatred she felt for him had been swept away by his caresses and she didn't care about anything except the desire to be one with Rand again. Enraptured, Lori moaned in excited expectancy and she reached out for her dream lover, drawing him to her and glorying in his heated kisses. In her dream, her clothing was being stripped away and her lover's mouth was gently suckling her breasts. Her passions spiraled, and when he parted her legs to stroke her intimately, she surrendered eagerly to his expert touch. His agonizingly teasing caresses took her to the throbbing heights of pleasure, and in her passion, she cried out Rand's name, sobbing in exhausted delight.

It had been a dream unlike any other she'd ever experienced, and when Lori slowly came to realize that its overpowering sensuality had awakened her, she did not open her eyes. The power of the desire her fantasy had aroused embarrassed her, and she lay unmoving upon the softness of her bed, wondering how the memory of Rand's lovemaking could affect her so completely. She was lost in this silent contemplation of her body's response when a deep, satisfied chuckle shattered her peace. Horrified, she opened her eyes to find Rand beside her, his eyes dark with passion and sensual expectation.

Humiliation washed coldly over Lori as she stared up at him, reading in his expression an arrogant confidence that reflected his sense of total control over the situation. Her humiliation quickly changed to fury at the thought, and she struggled to sit up so she could get away from him.

"You! How dare you come into my room and . . ." She was conscious of her naked state, yet so angry she didn't really care about it.

"And what?" Rand smiled seductively. In his mind, her explosive response to his caresses had reaffirmed her love and her need for him, and now, filled with desire, he was ready to make love to her. He reached out to caress her breast. "Love you?"

"Love!" Lori shrieked as she slapped his hand away. "You don't know the meaning of the word! Get out of my room!"

He had expected her to be angry so he listened to her diatribe calmly. "Ah, but I do know the meaning of the word, darling, and I'm not going to leave this room until I've shown you just how much I do love you."

Rand's confidence that he'd mastered her and that she was going to meekly surrender to him pushed Lori to the limit. He'd betrayed her love when he'd thought her dead, and now, upon finding she was alive, he had the gall to return to her as if nothing had happened! Well, he'd better think again; she wanted nothing more to do with him. He had shown his true colors; he was the rogue she had always thought him to be. It was over between them, and Lori knew she'd been foolish to let their involvement go as far as it had.

Rand was completely unaware of the depth of Lori's anger. Having just heard her murmur his name in her sleep, he felt sure that she loved him and he stood up to undress, wanting only to hold her close and make her his own once more.

Lori couldn't believe what she was seeing as he gave her a heated look and, unbuckling his gunbelt, placed it carefully on the table beside the bed. He thought she wanted him to make love to her! The realization astounded her. Was there no end to this man's conceit? She didn't want him! Just because she'd responded to his touch while she was asleep, didn't mean that she felt the same way when she was awake! Feeling desperate and knowing that she had to act, Lori reached out quickly and snatched his gun from its holster.

"I said get out of my room and I meant it!" Lori declared vehemently. "Now, move."

Rand heard a telltale click and he pivoted quickly to find himself looking down the barrel of his own sidearm. "What the—" His words died in his throat as he noted the deadly expression in her eyes.

"You heard me, Rand."

The desire he'd been feeling slowly drained from his body as his gaze met hers over the cold, glinting steel. "Lorelei, we need to talk. Let me explain."

"I don't want to listen to a thing you've got to say."

"I love you. This is all a mistake."

"You're right about that much. Allowing myself to care about you was the biggest mistake I ever made," she seethed, hardening her heart against anything he had to say.

"I want to . . ." Rand's gaze was riveted upon her as she braced herself on her knees upon the bed, her hair falling about her shoulders in a red-gold cape of curls, her bare breasts heaving in her indignation.

"I know what you want, Rand McAllister." Lori sneered contemptuously. "And you're not going to get it from me! Go find the woman you were with last night! Maybe she'll want you in her bed. I certainly don't!"

Angered by her obstinate refusal to listen to his explanation, he said, "Can you deny the joy and satisfaction you just experienced in my arms?"

"I was dreaming, and that is all it was. *A dream!* The man I thought I loved, the man I was dreaming about and responding to, doesn't exist."

"You were responding to *my* touch."

Lori gave a brittle laugh. "You may like to think so."

"I know so. You called my name, Lorelei."

476

She shrugged. "Your whore last night probably did, and no doubt Lydia did too . . . before she married your father!" At his surprised expression, Lori smiled grimly. "Oh, yes. Your dear departed stepmother couldn't wait to insinuate to me that you two had been lovers. How cleverly you phrased it when we talked about it. 'I was not involved with my stepmother.' Wasn't that what you said?"

"Lori," Rand regained control of his temper for he really wanted to relieve her of her baseless fears. "I can explain everything you saw last night, and I know you didn't see much. You couldn't have because nothing really happened."

"Just shut up! I don't want to hear any more. Whatever existed between us is over. I made a bad error in judgment where you're concerned, but I'll never make it again. Get out, now!"

His eyes narrowed as he considered disarming her and forcing her to admit the love they felt for one another, but common sense ruled. He would bide his time.

"I'll go, if that's what you really want." He tried to sound casual.

"It is." Her reply was unwavering.

"I'm leaving your room, Lorelei, but not your life," he added determinedly. "You're a fool if you think it's over between us. We've barely begun, love."

"I'm not your love!"

"Oh, but you are." Rand's gaze met and challenged hers.

"That's your misfortune, then, because I hate you!"

"You may feel that way right now, but I'm not about to give you up. If you choose not to accept me as your lover or your husband, you still have to deal with me as your guardian. I planned to live here at the Triple Cross until the loan has been repaid and I see no reason not to do so."

"I can make the mine pay by myself. I don't need you or your help!"

"I see things differently."

"But I don't want you here!" Lori felt trapped.

"That's too bad, because I'm going to remain here from now on. I've resigned my job and I intend to dedicate myself to making the Lazy Ace and the Triple Cross successful."

Lorelei had hoped he would be returning to his job, and she paled at the news that he'd quit.

"I'll be overseeing everything, just like before."

"It won't be 'just like before'," she declared hotly as the memory of their lovemaking intruded on her thoughts.

"No. It won't," he agreed smoothly. "It's going to be better." She didn't want to hear what he had to say, but Rand went on unconcerned. "I love you, Lorelei, and you're never going to be rid of me. Never. The days I spent searching for you and knowing you were in the Bentons' hands were the worst of my life. And when I finally had to admit defeat and give you up for dead . . ."—his voice turned husky at the thought of the pain that had been his when he'd thought her lost to him forever—"well, I didn't care about anything. I got drunk with Brady that night—real drunk. But all I could think about was you."

"You expect me to believe that?" Lori scoffed. "You missed me so much and loved me so much that you went right out and found another woman! You've got until the count of three to get the hell out of my room. After that I start shooting."

Rand eyed the gun pointed squarely at his chest, and he knew this was not the time to push her any further. Without another word, he turned and left the room.

Lori watched as the door closed behind him, then she

began to shiver uncontrollably as the emotions she'd held in check overwhelmed her. Seeing him again had been worse than she'd imagined. Her emotions were fragmented. She hated him yet, despite her denials, she had responded wildly to his touch. How was it possible to hate him and to crave him? And how could she have responded to him knowing what she did?

Lori was confused and upset, and she was frightened by the power Rand exerted over her. Even in the beginning it had been difficult to deny her attraction for Rand, but now that she'd known the pleasure that could be hers in his arms, it would be even harder to stay away from him. But she must. It was over, and she had to get on with her life.

Setting Rand's gun aside, Lori rose from the bed and slowly began to pull on her clothing. She didn't want to leave the haven of her room; she wanted to stay there, safe from the potency of Rand's presence, but she knew she could not allow him to think that he had that much power over her. She had professed to hate him and she was going to make sure that he believed her. This was her home, not his. Straightening her shoulders in an unconscious gesture of strength, she struggled to prepare herself for future run-ins with Rand.


Brady and Sally paused near the top of the rise behind the main house to stare out across the desert. Their view was panoramic, and as the sun continued its glorious descent, bathing the land in vibrant shades of red and gold, they stood in silence, admiring the timeless wonder of the moment.

"It's beautiful, isn't it?" Sally remarked as she gazed at the desert's ever changing façade.

"Yes, but I think you're much more beautiful than any sunset could ever be," he proclaimed boldly as he gazed down at her.

His ardent words sent a thrill of excitement through Sally and she turned to him, her eyes warm with unspoken love. "Thank you."

"Sally, I know this is probably going to sound strange to you, but I feel as if I've known you all my life," Brady began awkwardly. He had never declared himself to another woman and he wasn't quite sure how to go about it. Should he blurt out everything he was feeling or hint at the depth of his emotion and see if she responded?

"It doesn't sound strange to me, Brady," Sally said encouragingly. "I feel it, too."

"You do?" He was amazed.

Sally nodded, smiling slightly. "From the first, in fact."

"The first?"

"When you spoke to me for the first time in Maricopa, when I got on the stage . . ."

He grinned. "I thought you were the most beautiful woman I'd ever seen, and when I woke up after being shot—"

"I was so worried about you," she put in fiercely. "And I didn't want to leave."

"I'm just glad I was able to find you again. I was afraid that you were only passing through this territory. I got the surprise of my life when I found you at the McCreas' party." Brady chuckled and then shook his head ruefully as he remembered believing she was married to Roger. "I hit both the heights and the depths that night. I was furious when I thought you were married."

Sally laughed lightly but the expression in her eyes was serious. "I am very glad that I'm not, Brady."

He swallowed a trifle nervously. "Sally . . . I, uh . . . I love you and I want you to marry me." Before she could answer one way or the other, he rushed on. "I know you don't know me every well, but I'm willing to wait for as long as you want. I mean—"

"I know what you mean, Brady, and you're a dear, sweet man to even consider it." She knew he was nervous and she wanted to reassure him. "But . . ."

His heart sank at the words *a dear, sweet man*. It hardly sounded like she was in love with him, and he suddenly felt very embarrassed by his bold proposal. Only by forcing himself to listen to the rest of what she was saying, did he come to realize that she wasn't rejecting him. Not at all!

"I don't need any more time to make up my mind. I don't need to know more about you than I already do. You are honest, strong, and handsome, and I love you with all my heart. We don't need to wait, Brady. I'll marry you."

He stared at her, thunderstruck. "You will?"

"I will." Sally nodded firmly.

"Oh, Sally . . ." He groaned as he pulled her into his arms. "You don't know how happy you've made me! Yesterday, I thought you were dead, gone from my life forever, and now . . ."

Choked by his emotions, Brady could say no more so he kissed her, his mouth taking hers possessively and staking his claim on her heart.

Sally surrendered to his embrace eagerly. Her previous experience with men was limited, but the first time Brady had kissed her she'd known that his lovemaking would be special. He was the man for her, and she didn't want to put off their marriage any longer.

Oblivious to everything save Sally's nearness, Brady held her in his arms, enjoying her softness. Finally, his lips left hers to explore the sensitive cords of her throat, and his hands slid up from her waist to trace patterns of teasing arousal on her breasts. Sally had never allowed a man to touch her so intimately before, and she couldn't prevent the soft moan that escaped her at the onset of Brady's sensuous play. When he cupped the sweet fullness of her bosom through the material of her blouse and brushed his thumbs across a taut, aching peak, her knees buckled and she was forced to clutch his shoulders for support.

Overwhelmed by Sally's response, Brady slipped his hands lower to mold her hips to his hardness.

"That's how much I want you, love," he said huskily.

"Oh, Brady . . ." Sally had never been sensually aroused before and she clung to him weakly. "You feel so good to me."

"We're good together," he whispered before kissing her deeply. "And we will be forever."

Brady knew instinctively that she was as excited as he was, but he held himself back, refusing to give free rein to his desire. This was hardly the place. There would be plenty of time for lovemaking later, once they were married. He wanted their wedding night to be a night of joy and discovery. Until then he would take care to control his need for her. As he ended the kiss, he drew slightly away, and Sally, sensing his withdrawal from her, opened her eyes to look up at him questioningly.

"Brady? Is something wrong?" His touch and his kisses had thrilled her, and she didn't want him to stop.

"How can you ask that?" he reached up to gently caress her cheek. "Everything's perfect, sweetheart."

"Then why did you stop kissing me?" she asked, the erotic ache within her refusing to subside.

Brady found her innocence endearing, and his smile was wry as he tried to answer plainly. "I stopped because my need for you is great, but if I'd kept on kissing you, we wouldn't be only kissing."

Understanding dawned on Sally, and she blushed

prettily as she glanced around and realized they were standing out in the open where almost anyone could see them. "Oh."

"Now, don't go getting embarrassed on me." He chuckled and pulled her close. "I want our lovemaking to be something special, Sally."

"It will be if this is a sample," she said candidly, and Brady's laugh was appreciative.

"It'll be better than this, love. Much better."

His lips sought hers once more, but this time he controlled his passion, telling her instead by a soft cherishing exchange that he adored her and would never hurt her in any way. When they finally moved apart, they were both smiling.

"We'd better go back." Brady was aware that the shadows were deepening around them.

"I know," Sally agreed reluctantly, for she'd enjoyed this time alone with the man she loved. "I hope Rand was able to explain everything to Lori."

"I do, too," he said. "I want them to be as happy as we are."

"I don't know if anyone else can be this happy." Sally's eyes were sparkling as they started back down the hill. "But it would be nice if they were."

"Look. There's Rand now." Brady pointed as Rand emerged from the house.

"I wonder where Lori is?"

They said no more but went forward to speak with Rand.

When he saw Brady and Sally coming toward him looking blissfully content, Rand felt a stab of envy. Damn Lorelei and her stubborn ways! If she'd only given him a chance to explain, they could be as happy as Brady and Sally were.

"Rand." Sally hurried up to him, but seeing his glowering expression she knew the answer to her question before she asked it. "It didn't go well?"

"She didn't want to listen to anything I had to say, Sally," he replied curtly.

"I'm sorry, Rand," she murmured. "I had hoped that seeing you would change the way she was feeling."

"It didn't." When Sally looked tearful, Rand hastened to add. "Don't worry, though. I have no intention of giving up so easily."

"You don't?" she brightened.

"I love her, Sally, and I really believe that in spite of everything she says she loves me." Then, not wanting to discuss Lori any more, he changed the subject. "Enough about our problems, what about you two?"

"We have wonderful news," Sally beamed.

"Sally has agreed to marry me, Rand," Brady said, gazing adoringly upon his love.

"That's wonderful. I'm happy for the both of you." Rand meant it, he couldn't help but think that he and Lori should also be sharing bliss.

"Thank you," they replied.

"When's the wedding?"

"We haven't decided yet," Brady answered. "But the sooner, the better as far as I'm concerned."

"I think I'll go tell Lori our news, I won't be long," Sally promised, starting inside, but Brady drew her back to him for a parting kiss before letting her go.

Sally knew Lori had been dreading her reunion with Rand, and she hurried to her room and knocked on the door. "Lori?"

"Come on in, Sally." Lori was relieved to find that it was her friend and not Rand.

"How did it go?" she asked as she entered the room and shut the door behind her.

"The way I'd thought it would." Aware that Sally trusted and liked Rand and that she would always give him the benefit of the doubt, Lori answered obliquely.

"Meaning?"

"Meaning, I told him that I didn't want any more to do with him."

"And what did he say?"

"What could he say?" Lori challenged. "I told him to get out and he did."

Sally saw Lori's expression harden, and her hopes were dashed. Obviously seeing Rand had not softened her toward him.

"I'm sorry. I'd really hoped that he would have a good explanation. What did he say happened last night?" she queried gently.

"He didn't explain." Lori sounded bitter.

"Rand didn't tell you?" Sally was surprised.

"I didn't give him a chance!" her friend declared hotly.

"But why? You said you loved him, yet you didn't care enough to listen to his explanation?"

"I don't love him!" Lori argued. "I thought I did, but I was wrong. And I didn't let him explain because I didn't want to hear any more lies or half-truths! Now, if you came in here to badger me about Rand, you can just stop."

"I came in here to see how you were and to see if your reunion with Rand was as happy as mine was with Brady. Obviously, it was not."

"Brady's here?"

"Yes, he rode in with Rand and we've just talked."

"And?"

"He's asked me to marry him and I've accepted," Sally stated excitedly.

"Oh, Sally, that's wonderful." Lori embraced her friend. "But are you sure? You haven't known him that long."

"I know everything I need to know about him," Sally declared staunchly, and at Lori's skeptical look, she

485

went on. "Brady's different from all the other men who've courted me. I can't really put into words what the feeling is, but I know I can trust him with my life—and I know I want to."

"If you're sure—"

"I am." There was no doubt in Sally's mind. "And Brady feels the same way."

"I'm glad for you, Sally. I really am." Lori fought to hide her own unhappiness. "How soon are you going to be married?"

"I don't know. We haven't discussed it yet, but I really would like Brady to meet my family before the wedding."

"And I'm sure they'll want to meet him."

"I hope they'll like him." Sally suddenly wondered what her family would think when they met Brady.

"Why wouldn't they?"

"You're right. He's wonderful and they're going to love him as much as I do!" Sally sighed. "I just hope Brady won't mind going to St. Louis."

"You'd better talk about making the trip soon."

"Come on, I'll ask him now." Sally started from the bedroom, but stopped at the door. "Lori?"

"What?"

"Will you be my maid of honor? There's nobody else I'd rather have."

"I'd be thrilled, Sally!" Lori hugged her friend.

"Good. Now, let's go find my husband-to-be, and I'll see if we can make some plans."


Several hours later they sat around the table in the main house, relaxing after dinner. Hal had joined them, and he'd been fascinated with their tales of the Bentons.

"So the posse managed to track down the last

486

remaining Benton and that was when Mrs. McAllister was killed?"

"That's right," Brady replied. "And before he died, Pat Benton told us that Lorelei and Sally were dead. Rand and I refused to believe it at first, but we finally gave up the search."

"You kept looking for them even though he told you they were dead?" Hal was impressed.

Rand nodded. "The Bentons would have done anything to get even with me, and simply murdering the women would have been too 'clean' for him. He would have wanted to make them suffer first, then use that against me."

Lori and Sally both shuddered at the accurate portrait Rand had just painted for Hal. The Bentons had been cold-blooded and vicious, and the women knew that a horrible fate had been in store for them had they not escaped.

"I'm just glad Lori figured out a way for us to get out of there," Sally put in. "Why, she's the one who thought of smashing the lamp and using the glass to cut our ropes. If it hadn't been for her, I'd be dead by now. We could not have survived very long in that cabin, not the way they left us."

Brady took Sally's hand in a comforting grip. "It must have been terrible for both of you."

"It was," Lori agreed in a flat voice as she remembered the desperadoes' vile hands upon her, the sensations they'd deliberately aroused. "I'm sure they intended to have their fun with us. We were just very lucky that they were killed."

"I'm glad you had presence of mind to escape. I'm only sorry that Brady and I weren't able to rescue you." Rand's deep voice cut across the conversation.

"I didn't need you then, Rand, and I don't need you now." Lori's hostile reply briefly silenced everyone.

Rand didn't bother to answer her, but his expression was slightly mocking as his fathomless gaze settled upon her.

"Well, I'm glad you're safe," Hal said, hoping to break the tension. "And it's good to have you back. There's a lot to catch up on around here, Rand."

Lori seethed as Hal discussed mining business with Rand, but she couldn't prevent him from doing so. Nothing had changed except that she knew the truth about Rand now and she would never again be fooled by him.

"We'll get on with it first thing tomorrow. We still have that loan to pay back and I don't want to risk foreclosure by the bank," Rand was saying.

"And you're going to be leaving us, Miss Sally?" Hal inquired, knowing that she and Brady were to be married.

"As a matter of fact, Hal, Brady and I have decided to return to St. Louis. We'll be going into town tomorrow to send a wire to my folks, letting them know of our wedding plans, and then we'll be catching the stage to Maricopa the following day."

"How are you going to like going back East?" The foreman turned to Brady.

"I'm sure it'll be different, but I think it's important that I meet her family before the wedding. Besides, wherever Sally is, I want to be."

"When is the big event?"

"Hopefully we'll be able to hold the wedding within a month of our arrival back home," Sally explained. She was pleased that Brady had been quite willing to return to St. Louis with her, and she was anxiously looking forward to introducing him to her family.

"I wish you the best of luck."

"Thank you. Lorelei will be going to St. Louis, too, but we don't know just when yet."

Rand looked quickly at Lori, wondering why she would return to St. Louis. She'd said often enough that she had no desire to go back, that she loved the territory and didn't want to leave it, yet now she was planning to . . .

"You see, she's agreed to be my maid of honor." Sally gave Lori a warm, loving look before continuing. "As soon as we set the date, I'm going to wire her so she can arrive in time for the wedding."

Rand's question was answered by Sally's explanation, but he was disturbed by the prospect of Lorelei's trip. Roger Westlake and God knows how many other men were all back there, just waiting for a chance to win her love. If she returned, feeling about him as she did right now . . . He scowled blackly at the thought and immediately remarked on the effect her absence would have on the mine.

"Lorelei, you know that you have a responsibility to the Triple Cross. The next few months will determine whether the loan is paid off on time." Rand's cool, controlled tone gave the lie to his true feelings.

Lori glanced at him sharply, infuriated by his attitude and by his attempt to manipulate her. She had not planned to go to St. Louis until the week before the wedding, but since Rand had issued a challenge, she was determined to show him that he had no control over her.

Turning calmly to Sally, she told her, "Sally, I think I've changed my mind."

Rand felt some of the tension go out of his body. He was certain that she was about to agree with his assessment of the situation, that she had decided not to be Sally's maid of honor. His shock was complete when Lori openly defied him.

"I think I'll return with you and Brady now." Her gaze was icy as she glanced at Rand. "There are many acquaintances I'd like to renew, and this will be a good time for socializing, don't you think?"

"Lori, that would be wonderful, but what about the mine?" Sally asked.

Though she felt that she was betraying her father, Lori knew that Rand had to be taught a lesson so she shrugged casually. "Rand's made it perfectly clear that he's in charge here, so he can just take over. I'm sure the work I do could easily be accomplished by hiring another miner. Don't you think so, Hal?"

Hal glanced nervously from Rand to Lorelei, sensing the undercurrent of anger between the two and not knowing quite how to deal with it. "Well, that is true to some extent, Miss Lorelei."

"There, you see?" She cut him off before he could say any more. "Everything will work out fine. I'll be leaving with you tomorrow, Sally, and I'll plan to stay in St. Louis until after the wedding."

"That will be wonderful," Sally exclaimed delightedly. "But do you think you should be away that long? I mean, I know how much you love the Triple Cross—"

"Don't be silly," Lori brushed aside her friend's concern. "Rand is perfectly capable of running the mine without me and with Hal and Cam here, I'm sure everything will go smoothly. Don't you agree, Rand?"

Rand was infuriated by her defiance, and his eyes glittered dangerously as they met hers across the table. "We'll do what we must," he answered enigmatically, and Lori was chilled by the hidden meaning in his reply.

"Fine, it's settled then. I'll be going with you," she said with more bravado than she was feeling. "And, right now, I think I'd better start packing."

"I'm going to be calling it a night, too, Miss Lorelei." Hal rose to leave. "Brady, you can bunk in the room Roger was using while he was here. Rand can show you where it is."

"Thanks, Hal."

"Good night. I'll see you in the morning."

"Good night, Hal."

Brady and Sally stood up to follow him outside, wanting to enjoy a few moments together before going their separate ways, and suddenly, Lori found herself alone with Rand.

She gave him a tight smile as she started to turn away. "Well, good night, Rand."

"Lorelei." His voice was so soft it caressed her taut nerves.

She stiffened. "What?"

"You won't be able to get rid of me that easily, love." His dark eyes were upon her.

"You are the most arrogant, conceited man I've ever had the misfortune to meet. I can't believe you think I'm going back to St. Louis just to be away from you!" she told him haughtily. "I'm going back because I want to." With that, she stalked away and slammed her bedroom door behind her.

# Chapter Twenty-Nine

It was late, hours after midnight, and Rand sat alone in the darkened main room of Hal's house, a half-empty bottle of bourbon before him on the table. He had retired at the same time as the other men, but sleep had refused to grant him surcease from his turbulent thoughts. Frustrated, he'd gotten up and sought the liquor Hal kept on hand. But drinking only seemed to heighten his turmoil as he sat in night-shrouded solitude trying to come to grips with his situation.

Lorelei was leaving the Triple Cross. She would be gone in the morning and would probably not return for some months—maybe never considering her current frame of mind. Roger, Rand had no doubt, would welcome her with open arms, and he wondered just how many other men in St. Louis were in love with her. Those thoughts drove him to tilt the bottle to his lips and take a deep draught of the powerful brew.

He didn't want to let her go, but he didn't want to force her to stay. Technically as her guardian, he could do that, but he realized that Lorelei would only fight him harder if he tried.

Remembering the ecstasy he'd given her that afternoon, Rand stifled a groan, and desire for her welled up inside of him. God, how he wanted her! His desperate search had ended in frustration, and after he'd given her up for dead, she'd turned up alive, and now . . . Now she hated him for that one kiss—a kiss that had been meant for her actually.

Rand shook his head at his own stupidity. If he hadn't been drunk, it never would have happened. Suddenly he was conscious of the bottle in his hand and with a vicious curse he pushed it away. Liquor had been the cause of the whole mess, and he certainly wasn't going to help matters if he drank himself into another stupor.

He stood up and strode from the house. There was only one way he could stop this foolishness. He had to show Lori just how much he loved her.

Rand's tread was catlike as he entered Lori's house, unerringly crossing the main room and steathily entering her bedroom. After closing the door behind him, he approached the bed, determined to pick up where they'd left off that afternoon. He knew she might fight him at first, but at this point he didn't care. She planned on leaving tomorrow and this would be his last chance to prove his love to her.

Emboldened by the bourbon he'd consumed, Rand hurriedly stripped off his clothing and slipped into bed beside Lori. Drawing the lightweight cover back, he was thrilled to find that she was clad in only a sheer nightdress.

Lori stirred restively as she suddenly felt slightly chilled, and without opening her eyes, she reached out sleepily to pull the cover back over her. But what she touched was not a blanket, and she shrieked in fright as her hand made contact with the hot, hardness of a male body. She jerked away and started to bolt from the bed, only to be pulled unceremoniously back onto its softness.

"Oh, no. You're not leaving me, not yet," Rand murmured, and silencing her protest with a passionate kiss, he pinned her down with his body.

Rand! Lori's initial fear was immediately replaced by anger. Did he think he had free access to her bed any time he pleased? She fought him, hating his arousing touch, as his hands explored her intimately through the sheerness of her gown. Lori could feel her body beginning to betray her to his expert touch, and she knew she must get away from him before the havoc he wreaked on her senses overwhelmed her. Unwilling to give in to the exquisite torture that was his lovemaking, Lori tried to squirm from beneath him, but his weight held her immobile. Only when he ended the kiss did she have a chance.

"Let me up this instant, Rand, or I swear I'll scream for help!" Lori's voice was firm.

To her dismay, he merely clamped a hand over her mouth, effectively silencing her.

"I have no intention of letting anyone interrupt us tonight."

Rand could see that her eyes were widened by a mixture of fear and anger, and he smiled down at her crookedly.

"You look as if you hate me, love, but we both know that's not true and I intend to prove that to you, right now."

Rand grasped the front of her gown and with a single pull, rent the delicate material, baring her bosom to his heated gaze.

"I know how you like me to caress you here . . . and here . . . and here," he said hoarsely as he cupped and molded her satiny, exposed flesh.

Lori held herself stiff in his embrace. She did not want him! He was a womanizer! He had betrayed her once and she would never let him do so again! Yet, even as her mind struggled to hang onto that thought, her breasts began to ache with the need to feel his lips upon them.

"I love you, Lorelei." Rand's eyes met hers for a single moment before he lowered his head to press heated kisses to her bosom.

He suckled gently at each crest until she moved restlessly beneath him, instinctively seeking more, and he moved over her then, slipping easily between her thighs and trapping the hardness of his desire between them.

Lori felt the heat of him so close to her own need, and it was all she could do, not to wrap her limbs around him and lose herself in his embrace. She wasn't sure whether to curse him or love him as every nerve in her body screamed for the release only he could give. His touch sent shudders of ecstasy through her, and Lori could only gasp when Rand thrust his hips suggestively against her, letting her know of his own readiness.

Lori's eyes reflected her inner torment, and Rand knew that she was close to the edge. He took his hand away from her mouth as he whispered.

"Tell me now just how much you hate me."

Lori was torn. A part of her still did hate him, but her body was on fire. "I . . . I hate you," she sobbed, hating him for forcing her to love him.

Her words infuriated Rand. Hate him, did she? He lost what little control he still had then, and he brushed aside her gown and sought the center of her with a questing, practiced hand while his mouth claimed hers once again in a passionate exchange. Deliberately, he teased her to the heights, bringing her to the edge of ecstasy several times until she was moaning and all but crying out to him to give her that ultimate satisfaction. Only when she was quivering with need, did Rand seek the hot, wet core of her womanhood and bury himself deeply within her.

Lori did cry out softly as Rand moved powerfully against her, his every thrust spiraling her desire higher until, a moment of sublime rapture, her passions exploded in a white-hot frenzy. Sated, Lori collapsed beneath his driving weight as he continued on to seek his own peak, and she smiled slightly when she felt him convulse in the throes of his own pleasure.

"I love you, Lorelei." His breathing was hoarse and rasping in her ear as he rested above her.

Lori, too exhausted to speak, closed her eyes, and as a contented peace filled her, she thought maybe, just maybe, she really didn't hate Rand.

Rand waited for her to reply, but her silence only served to reaffirm what he had come to believe during their tempestuous mating . . . maybe it was too late for them.

The realization left him feeling sordid, and he withdrew from her and left the bed to pull on his clothing. When he turned back, she appeared to be sleeping, but thinking that an act prompted by a desire to avoid speaking to him, he quickly quit the room, this time taking his gun and holster with him.

The sky to the east was just beginning to brighten as Rand returned to his quarters, and only a short time later when Hal emerged from his room, ready to begin the new day, he found Rand, bedroll in hand, heading out of the house.

"You're leaving?" Hal was surprised to see Rand up, let alone carrying his bedroll.

"I just need to make a short trip back to the ranch. I won't be gone long—a day, maybe two," he assured him. "Give the others my best when they leave this morning."

"I will, but wouldn't you rather stay and do it yourself?"

"No. It's better this way. I'll see you in a couple of days. If you need me for anything, just send word to the Lazy Ace."

"I will." Hal watched perplexedly as Rand headed for the stables to get his mount.

Lori came awake slowly, her sleep-drugged senses still pleasantly dulled and insulated from reality. As she yawned in lazy contentment and started to stretch, the sweet soreness between her legs sent shock waves of realization through her and she suddenly became conscious of what had taken place during the night. The memory of Rand's forceful yet passionate love-making assaulted Lori then, and she flushed as she recalled her own unbridled responses. She had gloried in his domination, and though she knew she should be outraged by his boldness, she found herself secretly delighted.

For a moment she pictured him embracing the other woman and her spirits were dampened. Then she recalled Rand's profession of love and the bliss she'd found in his arms, and she realized that a part of her would never stop loving him.

Climbing out of bed, she stripped off the ruined nightdress and hastily pulled on her clothes, eager to go in search of Rand. Perhaps Sally had been right; perhaps she had been wrong to condemn him so completely. Knowing that she'd never really given him a chance to explain the scene in the courtyard, she felt a certain amount of guilt. If what had happened that night had truly been as innocent as he'd claimed, maybe there was hope for them.

Lori felt almost carefree as she left her room, and she smiled brightly at Sally who was already enjoying a cup of coffee at the breakfast table.

"Good morning, Sally."

Sally regarded her questioningly. "Good morning, yourself." She smiled. "You seem awfully happy this morning."

"I am," Lori answered lightly. "Have you seen Rand anywhere?"

"No, not yet. Why?" Sally sensed a change in Lori's attitude and she wanted to know more.

"I just needed to talk with him for a few minutes."

"That's about all the time you're going to have if you're planning on leaving with us. Brady's already gone to bring the buckboard around and he plans on heading into town some time in the next hour."

"Oh." Her eyes widened as she remembered that she was to return to St. Louis with Brady and Sally. "Then I'd better hurry."

Lori stopped by Hal's house and finding it deserted, she went to the mine in the hope of locating Rand. On the level where the cave-in had occurred she finally managed to catch up with Hal.

"Morning, Miss Lorelei. I'm surprised to find you down here today. Do you want to take a last look around before you leave?" he asked cordially.

"No, I was trying to find Rand. Have you seen him around this morning?"

"Yes, as a matter of fact, I did. Right at sunup."

"Then he's down here somewhere?" She glanced eagerly around.

"Oh, no, Miss Lorelei. He's gone."

"Gone?" she was shocked.

Hal nodded. "He headed out at dawn. Said he had some business to take care of at the Lazy Ace and that he'd be gone a few days. He also said to tell you and the others good-bye for him."

Lori blanched at the news. "He did?"

"Yes." Hal noticed her troubled expression. "Is there

498

something wrong, something I can help you with?"

"No. No, Hal, everything's fine. Thanks anyway." With an effort Lori brought her emotions under control. "Brady's already bringing the buckboard around and we're planning on heading into town within the next hour."

"I'll be up to see you off, then."

"Thanks." She gave him her best smile as she started up the tunnel to the lift that would take her out of the mine.

Rand was gone and Lori was devastated. How could he have left without saying good-bye? Had his lovemaking just been a lustful demonstration of the control he had over her senses? Had he wanted to prove that he could master her at anytime he chose? As she left the lift and walked blindly toward the house, her heart sank. Although Rand had professed his love in the dark of night, he had not cared enough for her to try to stop her from leaving. Brokenhearted, she knew what she had to do.

"Did you find Rand?" Sally called cheerfully from her bedroom when she heard Lori reenter the house.

"No," came her monotonic reply.

At the dull sound of Lori's voice, Sally hurried out to speak with her, "No?"

"He left early this morning for the ranch. He told Hal to tell us all good-bye for him," Lori explained tightly.

"Lori, I—"

"Don't worry about it Sally," she said curtly as she strode to her own room. "It's probably better this way."

Feeling helpless in the face of Lori's unhappiness, Sally returned to her packing, silently hoping that the trip to St. Louis would help her friend sort out her confused emotions.

*     *     *

499

It was dusk and Rand stood on the porch of the ranchhouse, staring off into the sunset with unseeing eyes.

"Rand? Will you be eating anything? The food is on the table." Juana stood at the front door.

"No, Juana. Not tonight," he answered distractedly.

Puzzled by his strange mood, the servant retreated to instruct the maid to clear away the carefully prepared meal.

When she had gone, Rand left the porch and strode to the stables, driven by a need to return to the scene where he and Lorelei had once made love so passionately. He knew she was still in town, for she would not catch the stagecoach to Maricopa until the following day, yet he could not bring himself to go after her. It was over between them. She did hate him. She'd said so even as he'd taken her to the heights of ecstasy. There was nothing more he could do. She was lost to him again, and this manner of losing was no less painful for him than it had been when he'd believed her dead.

Resignedly, Rand drew a deep steadying breath and forced his thoughts away from Lorelei. He knew the ranch would continue to prosper under Jack's management, so he decided to concentrate on making the mine the most successful venture the territory had ever seen. If Lorelei wouldn't accept the gift of his love, then he would present her with a paying gold mine that would make her wealthy. His heart heavy, he started back to the house, hoping that the hard work ahead would keep his mind free of her haunting presence.

## Chapter Thirty

Lori accepted the glass of champagne from Neil Michaels. "Thank you, Neil."

"You're welcome, Lori," he replied, his eyes feasting on the sight of her. He had been one of many swains Lori had left behind when she'd returned to her home out West and he'd been delighted to find that she'd come back to St. Louis. "Have I told you yet how marvelous you look this evening?" As he spoke, his gaze lingered appreciatively on the cleavage her low-cut gown revealed.

"Why no, but thank you," Lori answered, growing increasingly uncomfortable under Neil's hungry regard. She had originally accepted his invitation to this party so she could renew some old acquaintances and just enjoy herself, but the evening had turned out to be as dull as the other outings she'd attended since she'd returned four weeks ago. Lori knew that wasn't anyone's fault. She just couldn't seem to find any enjoyment in the endless rounds of dances and parties.

Sipping her champagne, she assumed an attentive expression as Neil discussed his investments and his plans for the future. She supposed he was trying to impress her, but she had little interest in his money or his future and she had to restrain herself from pointedly telling him so.

Money would not make her happy. She knew that. Only one thing would make her happy, and she knew that would never be. Without Rand, her life seemed to have little purpose. She'd become a social butterfly, flitting from man to man, seeking someone who could replace him in her heart, but no one had even come close to challenging his memory.

At the thought of Rand, Lori sighed softly, and Neil, hovering attentively at her elbow, quickly asked, "Would you like to go out into the garden for a breath of fresh air?"

"Yes, please. That sounds heavenly." Lori thought a few moments away from the crowd might improve her spirits.

Neil smiled to himself as he took her arm and guided her easily through the maze of dancers to the double French doors that opened onto a garden now in full bloom.

The moon was a sliver of silver in the late evening sky as Lori walked the path at Neil's side. Outwardly, she seemed contented enough, but her mind was not on the beautiful array of scented blossoms. Instead, she was thinking of the vast magnificence of the cactus-studded Arizona desert and of the man whose hold on her had not lessened.

When Neil led her up the steps and into the secluded gazebo at the center of the garden, Lori didn't protest, and when he took her in his arms, she glanced up at him in the half-darkness of that romantic summer house and imagined for a moment that he looked just like Rand. He was tall and his shoulders were wide, and his hair was dark. Lori closed her eyes as Neil drew her to him, pretending it was Rand who was holding her, kissing her.

For an instant, she almost believed she was within Rand's embrace, but when Neil broke off the kiss to whisper her name, panic surged through her. He wasn't Rand! He never would be!

A sob tore from her as she pulled away and stared up at him as if he were a stranger, shocked to realize just how desperately she'd wanted him to be the man she could never have.

"I'm sorry, Neil. I think we'd better go back inside now." Seeing the heated desire in his gaze, she backed slightly away from him.

"Lori, you're so beautiful and I want you so badly. Marry me and let me love you as you were meant to be loved." Neil thought Lori the most gorgeous woman in the world, and he was undaunted by her sudden withdrawal. Snaring her wrist, he pulled her back against him.

"Neil!" Surprised by his move, she struggled against him. "Let me go."

"No. Not until you give me your answer. I want you, Lori, and I mean to have you." His voice was thick with passion.

"Neil Michaels, if you think for one moment that I would marry you, you are sadly mistaken!"

When he still refused to free her and instead tried to press hot kisses across the top of her breasts, she kicked him in the shin with all her might. Neil grunted in surprised pain and quickly released her.

"I don't love you Neil, and I definitely don't want to marry you," Lori told him plainly. "Especially after being so manhandled!"

"Lori, I . . ." Neil tried to apologize, but she turned her back on him and stalked away.

"I'll find my own way home. You needn't consider yourself with me any longer," she said as she headed for the house.

Neil watched her in silent amazement until she had gone indoors.

Lori caught sight of Sally and Brady as soon as she entered the ballroom and she hurried to join them.

"You look a little pale. Are you feeling all right?" Sally inquired.

"No. As a matter of fact, I'm feeling a little faint and I was thinking of returning home early tonight."

"Brady"—Sally turned to her fiancé—"would you have one of the servants bring our carriage around."

"Right away," he replied.

"Thanks, Sally." Lori breathed a bit easier knowing that she would soon be back in her room at Sally's parents' house.

"Do you need us to go with you? Brady and I can leave, too," Sally offered.

"No. I'll be fine once I have a chance to lie down for a while," Lori assured her.

"If you're sure . . ."

"I am. You two just relax and have a good time."

"What about Neil? Does he know you're leaving?"

"I've already taken care of him," Lori said curtly.

"I see. Well, Brady's motioning to us from the foyer." Sally led the way to the front hall. "Has the carriage been brought around?"

"Yes. It's out in front. Do you want us to go with you, Lori?" he asked solicitously.

"No. You stay and enjoy yourselves, and I'll see you first thing in the morning."

Brady slipped a possessive arm about Sally's slim waist as they watched Lori, assisted by the driver, climb into the carriage. When it had rolled off into the darkness, he asked.

"What do you suppose happened?"

"I don't know, but she certainly didn't sound too pleased with Neil."

Brady nodded. "I don't know about you, but I've got the feeling she misses Rand more than she's willing to admit."

Sally gave him a warm smile. "I think you're right. Maybe she's beginning to realize just how much he really means to her."

"Lord, I hope so. I know how much he loves her, and I'm sure it was hard on him to let her go like this."

"It may have been hard, but it was probably the best thing he could have done."

"Why do you say that?"

"Because if he had forced her to stay with him, her resentment would only have grown. This way, she's proving her own independence, but at the same time she's coming to understand that being on your own isn't always the best way, especially if there's someone you truly love."

"And you believe she still loves Rand?"

"I know it. She just hasn't been willing to accept her own feelings for him. Until she does, I think she's going to be pretty miserable. It doesn't matter whether she's here or in Phoenix."

"I sincerely hope you're right."

"We'll be finding out pretty soon." Sally was suddenly very smug.

"Why?"

"Because I sent Rand an invitation to our wedding, and I have a feeling he'll come."

"Have you heard from him?"

"No."

"Then how can you be so sure?"

Sally slanted him a knowing, feminine look. "Call it intuition if you want, but if you'd been away from me for over a month, wouldn't you want to see me if you could?"

"I'd want to do more than see you," he growled

505

huskily in her ear.

"Well, I'm counting on Rand to feel the same way. Come on." She tugged almost playfully on his arm. "We have to get back to the party."

"Do we have to?" he protested good-naturedly. "Can't we go for another walk in the garden?"

"We have to." She paused before adding meaningfully. "But maybe we could fit in one more moonlight stroll."

The look she gave him was inviting, and Brady's reluctance melted away at the prospect of sharing stolen kisses under the starry sky.


"You coming in yet?" Hal asked Rand.

The younger man stood outdoors smoking a cheroot. "Not yet," he replied, his gaze fastened on the pale, luminescent slice of moon that hung low on the horizon.

"Well, I'm going to bed. See you in the morning."

"Right."

"And, Rand . . ."

"Yes?"

Hal hesitated. It really wasn't his place to speak up, but somebody had to give Rand the push he needed, "If I were you, I'd go to the wedding. Cam and I will make out just fine while you're gone. We've already accomplished a minor miracle in these last few weeks. If things keep on this way, we should have the loan paid back early, so why don't you go on and enjoy yourself."

Rand's expression didn't change as he replied distantly, "I'll think about it."

"Don't think about it, do it. And while you're there, convince Lorelei to come back with you."

"I'm afraid I don't have much influence over Lorelei anymore," Rand stated.

"I don't know, Rand. I don't think she would ever have left the Triple Cross if something hadn't upset her real bad, and I figure it was something that happened between you two. Damned if I know what it was and I don't want to know. That's your business," Hal said sagely. "But you two seemed to be happy before the Bentons seized her, and I don't know why you can't be happy again. You were made for each other."

"I think Lorelei would argue that point, Hal," Rand drawled derisively.

Hal shrugged. "I'm just telling you the way I see it. Think about what I said, and at least go to St. Louis for the wedding. You do care about Brady and Sally, don't you?"

Rand nodded but didn't speak.

"Then go." Hal clapped him on the back. "But you'd better make your decision soon. It'll take you the better part of a week to make the trip and the wedding is only ten days away." He paused, waiting for Rand to say something, but when he got no response, he added, "I'm calling it a night."

"Good night. And Hal?"

"Yes?"

"Thanks."

When Hal had gone inside, Rand flicked the remains of his cheroot into the desert darkness and then ran a hand wearily through his hair. Was Hal right? Should he go back East for Sally and Brady's wedding or should he stay here and work the mine?

He thought of Sally's wire urging him to come, telling him they would be delighted if he did, and he wondered just who the "they" were. Lorelei certainly wasn't included, he mused bitterly. He hadn't heard from her since she'd gone and, in truth, he hadn't expected to. He'd known how she'd felt when he'd left

507

her bed that night, and he'd regretted taking her that way ever since. At the time, he'd hoped to convince her of the sincerity of his feelings, but his plan had backfired and he'd only proven that he could overpower her by a combination of brute strength and sensuality.

Though he'd been working constantly since she'd gone, the weeks without her had been miserable and he wanted, no needed, to see her again. His decision made, Rand was alternately elated and tense as he strode back inside to begin making his plans.

Brady pulled Sally into his arms and kissed her fervently, letting her taste his desire for her.

"Mmmm," Sally purred when the kiss ended, and she nestled safely against the broad comfort of his chest as they shared a few moments alone in the parlor of the Westlake home. "I love you, Brady."

"And I love you." His voice was a deep, sensuous growl. "Tomorrow night, I'm going to show you just how much."

Lifting her head so she could gaze up at him, she whispered, "I can't believe that the time has gone by so fast."

"I know, but I'm glad it did," he admitted, hugging her close.

"You aren't sorry you came, are you?" Sally wanted to make sure he was as happy as she was.

Brady chuckled as he looked down at her in surprise. "Sorry? Certainly not. You mean everything to me, love."

Her smile brightened at this reassurance, and she drew slightly away so she could face him squarely. "And you are really happy about taking a job in the family business?"

"It's the best opportunity anyone's ever given me, Sally. I feel honored that your father offered it to me, and I fully intend to live up to his expectations."

"You won't miss the territory?" His love for the West had been a major concern for her, and she knew if he professed a need to return to his duties with Wells Fargo, she would go with him without hesitation.

"Darling, you mean more to me than anything in the world. I do love the Western way of life, but that's because I've never known any other. I've come to like the city, and your family is here. This is where we belong."

Sally sighed and went back into his arms. "I'm glad you feel that way. I know they like you a lot."

"Well, I like them, and I think we're going to be very happy here."

Sally kissed him then, showing him by that gesture just how pleased she was that everything had turned out so well. As Brady felt the fires of his need flame to life, much as he wanted her, he broke off the embrace.

"Love, I think we'd better call it a night." He gave her a crooked half-smile.

"But why? We've finally managed some time alone and—"

"And if you don't go to bed right now, you may be getting a taste of your wedding night early."

"But Brady . . ." She pouted as she moved restlessly against his chest.

He found himself unable to resist one more kiss, and Sally took full advantage of it, enjoying the womanly power she had over him. Looping her arms invitingly around his neck, she pulled him down upon her on the sofa, relishing the feel of his big body pressed so intimately to hers. The evidence of his arousal was hard against her thigh, and Sally gloried in the knowledge that he wanted her.

How she loved this man! He had given up a great deal to return home with her, and she had every intention of making certain that their years together would be filled with joy and love.

Brady wanted Sally as he had never wanted another woman. He was alive with the need to make her his own. Her breasts were crushed enticingly against his chest, and despite their clothing he could feel their pointed peaks inviting him to taste their succulence. The thought of kissing those full, tempting orbs sent a shaft of pure desire through him, but he fought to control his passion. He would wait until they were married.

Sally could feel how tense Brady was as he held himself in check, and though she longed to break his strong-willed control, she knew that he wanted their wedding night to be their first time together. When he ended the kiss and shifted his weight from her, she reluctantly let him go.

"Tomorrow, Brady, we won't have to stop." Her voice was husky with promise.

"I know, sweetheart, and that's the only thing that's keeping me going right now." His eyes were dark with passion as he stood up and gazed down at her. "Come on, let's go to bed. The faster we get to sleep, the faster tomorrow is going to get here."

"I hope I can get to sleep," she told him ruefully.

He grinned at their discomfort. "I know, believe me, I know."

Sally took his hand and allowed him to draw her up and into his arms, and they stood in silent rapture, imagining the bliss that would be theirs in a scant twenty-four hours. They walked out into the hall then and mounted the stairs together, parting at her bedroom door with a sweet gentle kiss that belied the burning desires raging within them both.

510

Sally sighed deeply as she entered her room. One more day and she would be Mrs. Brady Barclay. The thought sent a thrill of expectation through her and she knew she would get little sleep this night. Excitedly, she slipped out of her clothes. Then, drawing on a gown and wrapper, she tiptoed from her room to knock quietly on Lori's door.

"Lori? Are you still awake?" she asked in a soft voice. She had almost decided to return to her own room when she heard Lori's muffled reply.

"Yes, come on in."

"Lori," Sally began as she stepped inside, "I am so excited I just can't sleep. Do you feel like talking?"

"Of course, I haven't been able to sleep either," Lori confided as she turned up her bedside lamp. "The thrill of it all is getting to you, is it?" she teased once Sally had settled herself on the bed, the intimacy of the moment reminding both of them of the many times they'd shared their thoughts and plans during the years at school.

"I am beyond excitement," Sally laughed. "Oh, Lori, I love Brady so much, I can hardly wait for tomorrow night! Do you know how wonderful it's going to be to make love to Brady?"

Lori gave her a wry smile. "No, thank heavens, I don't. I don't think you'd consider me your friend if I did. Not that he's not attractive . . ."

Sally blushed as she protested. "I didn't mean it that way. I just meant that I'm so tired of this damned self-control."

"You should feel honored that he cares enough to wait, Sally. But I can assure you, after tomorrow he's never going to think about 'controlling' himself again. I'm sure he wants you just as badly as you want him."

Sally's expression was rapt. "I know."

Lori felt a twinge of jealousy. How nice it must be to

know that the one you love with all your heart loves you just as deeply. Sally was fortunate to have found the man of her dreams. As hard as she'd tried not to think of Rand that night, he slipped into her thoughts—sensuous overpowering Rand—and Lori could not shake the feeling of desolation that overcame her.

Sally noticed the sudden change in Lori's mood and quickly asked, "What's wrong? Is it Rand?"

"You know me so well, Sally." Lori gave a sad little laugh. "Sometimes, I think you know me better than I know myself."

"I know you're a very proud person, Lori, and that's generally good, but lately I think that your pride has caused you a lot of pain."

"What do you mean?"

"I mean that you love Rand. You always have and you probably always will." As Lori began to protest, Sally went on. "But your pride won't let you admit it. You feel you've been wronged and you won't allow yourself to try to understand what really happened, to forgive and forget, even at the cost of your own future happiness."

Her words were softly spoken, but their impact was fully felt.

Lori sighed shakenly as she confessed, "I don't want to think about Rand, Sally, but he's always there in the back of my mind, haunting me. All the men I've been seeing since we got back . . ." At Sally's nod, she continued. "Well, I've been trying to find someone who could replace Rand, but no one measures up." Lori covered her face with her hands and tried in vain to suppress the shudder that shook her. "What can I do, Sally? I've tried everything!" Her desperation was real.

"There's only one thing to do, Lori," her friend soothed. "Admit to yourself that you still love him and then go back and get him."

"But he doesn't love me!"

"Why do you think that? Because he wasn't there to see you off the morning we left?"

"Yes."

"He might have cared so much he couldn't bear to watch you leave."

A flicker of hope glimmered to life within Lori's heart. "Do you think that could have been his reason for leaving so abruptly?"

"I don't know, but it would certainly make sense if it was. If he didn't care, why would he have bothered to leave so suddenly?"

Lori smiled tremulously. "But what about that woman?"

"I don't know. That's something you'll have to ask him. But, Lori, even if he did spend the night with her, is that any reason to make yourself suffer so much? You weren't married yet, you'd exchanged no vows, and he did think you were dead."

"Could you forgive Brady if he did that?" Lori countered, refusing to put aside her doubts.

"I love Brady. I wouldn't like it and I'm sure I'd be angry, but if it had been under the same circumstances, I'd certainly try to put it from my mind. Love does conquer all, Lori, if you let it."

Lori was thoughtful for a moment before giving Sally a quick hug. "I'm going to try, Sally. As soon as your wedding and reception are over, I'm going home. It may not work, but I've got to do it. I care too much not to."

"Lori, I'm so glad!" They hugged excitedly. "Somehow I think you're going to end up as happy as I am."

"I hope so. You two look as if your love was made in heaven."

"It was." Sally smiled.

## Chapter Thirty-One

"Do you, Brady Barclay, take this woman, Sally Marie Westlake, to be your lawfully wedded wife, to have and to hold, for richer or for poorer, in sickness and in health?" the priest asked solemnly.

"I do." Brady's voice was deep and sure.

"And do you, Sally Marie Westlake, take this man, Brady Barclay, to be your lawfully wedded husband, to have and to hold, for richer and for poorer, in sickness and in health?"

"I do," Sally replied, no trace of doubt or nervousness in her tone.

"Then, by the power invested in me, I now pronounce you man and wife. You may kiss your bride." The priest smiled at the joy on the faces of the newly wedded couple.

Lori watched, enthralled, as Brady lifted Sally's gauzy veil and then took her into his arms for an adoring kiss. She was observing their embrace with quiet joy when she suddenly sensed that someone in the church was staring at her. Surreptitiously, she glanced at the guests gathered in the pews but noticed no one looking in her direction. All eyes were riveted on Sally and Brady. Shaking off the feeling, she turned her attention back to the ceremony as the priest completed the blessing.

When the organ music began again and Sally and Brady led the procession from the altar, Lori took Roger's arm and allowed him to guide her from the church.

Having arrived after the ceremony had begun, Rand had remained standing in the shadows at the back of the church while the ritual was performed. Sally looked lovely in her bridal gown of white satin and lace, but he had given her little more than a passing glance for his gaze had immediately sought out Lorelei.

Rand's heart stirred at the sight of her for she was breathtakingly beautiful as she stood in attendance on Sally, and he knew he'd been a fool to think he could let her go. She meant everything to him. Mesmerized by her nearness, he could not look away, and he felt his blood quicken at the remembrance of her in his arms.

As the ceremony ended and Brady kissed Sally, Rand couldn't help but wish that he and Lori had been exchanging their vows that would bind them together. When Lori turned and glanced quickly about the church, Rand stepped back into the deeper shadows. He did not want her to be aware of his presence until they were able to speak privately, and he tensed as he wondered what her reaction to him would be.

As the music began signaling the procession from the altar, Rand saw Roger take Lori's arm and he felt a surge of fierce jealousy. He wondered just how much time they'd spent together during her visit here. Roger's love for Lori was no secret, and Rand feared they might have become close.

Knowing that they were going to walk close by his present position, Rand made a quick exit from the church. He did not want to risk a confrontation now. He would see Lori that evening at the reception.

\*     \*     \*

The reception had been going on for several hours in the ballroom of the Westlake home. All the while Lori had pretended that she was having a wonderful time, but she was not. Sally's and Brady's happiness only seemed to emphasize her loneliness, and she longed to flee the merrymaking and head for home. She had been away long enough. It was time to correct the mess she'd made of her life.

"Dance?" Roger asked as he joined her.

"Of course," She went into her arms readily, feeling quite comfortable with him.

"Is something troubling you, Lori?" he asked perceptively. He noticed a haunted, almost pained expression in her eyes when she wasn't aware she was being watched.

"Why do you ask?" she countered quickly.

"Oh, I don't know. Maybe the way you've been watching Sally and Brady. You seem sad somehow."

"I was just homesick, that's all." She tried to dismiss his observations.

"I thought you swore you were never going back?" he teased, remembering her determination to stay in St. Louis when she'd returned.

"That was then."

"And now?"

"I left more than just my home behind, Roger," she said truthfully.

"Rand?"

Again his perception caught her off guard. "You know?"

"Sally told me that you were in love with him. I hope you don't mind my knowing."

"No, but—"

"But you're surprised that I'm taking it so well?" He grinned disarmingly.

"Well, considering everything that's happened between us—"

"Don't worry, Lori. If I can't have your love, I can't think of anyone else I'd rather see win you. Rand's a good man," Roger said, his tone serious.

"I do love him, Roger, but I'm afraid it's not as simple as you think." She sighed.

"This dance is about over. Why don't we get away from the crowd and go somewhere where we can talk?"

"Thanks, I'd like that." Lori really wanted to be away from all the celebrating.


Deliberately arriving late at the reception, Rand was greeted warmly at the door by Sally's parents.

"Good evening." Sally's father shook his hand as he entered. "I'm Jim Westlake and this is my wife, Delight."

"It's nice to meet you. I'm Rand McAllister," he replied courteously.

"So you're Rand?" Delight Westlake smiled widely. Sally had told her all about Rand. "Sally's often spoken of you."

"Good things, I hope." He smiled.

"Definitely," Jim put in. "I'd personally like to thank you for saving their lives during the stage robbery. Sally and Roger both told us how bravely you defended them. Being a U.S. Marshal must be dangerous work."

Rand was surprised by their interest. "It is, but I've resigned my post to devote more time to the ranch and to Lorelei's mine."

"That's right. They did mention that you were her guardian. She's here in fact, I just saw her dancing with Roger. I'm sure they'll be delighted to see you. Why don't you go on in?" Jim suggested as more guests began to arrive.

"I will. Thanks." Rand started into the ballroom, but his thoughts were dark.

So Lorelei was dancing with Roger, was she? He had been her partner at the wedding and now he was her escort for the evening. Rand silently cursed himself for letting her return here; then he headed to the bar to get a drink. Tumbler of bourbon in hand, he moved nonchalantly through the guests. As his gaze swept over the dancers, he spotted Lorelei waltzing smoothly about the floor, in Roger's arms.

"Now she's monopolizing Roger!" The woman's remark reached Rand's ears and he paused to listen.

"It's almost scandalous the way she's been throwing herself at men since she got back. First Ron, then Paul, and then Neil. I wish she'd stayed in Arizona or wherever it was she went!" The second woman's tone was condemning.

Rand stiffened at their condemnation of Lorelei and his knuckles whitened as his grasp tightened on his glass. So, Lori had been throwing herself at every man here, had she? He gritted his teeth at the thought. He had introduced her to the delights of loveplay and now she was eager to try out that knowledge with any man who would come to her.

Scowling blackly, Rand moved away from the gossiping females. He wanted nothing more than to stalk out onto the dance floor and drag her bodily from the room, but he knew better than to cause such a scene for it would only add fuel to the already heated talk about her. It infuriated him that she was so willing to share her body's joys with any man in town, and he felt an almost primitive rage when he saw Roger lead her from the ballroom and disappear down a side hall.

His white-hot temper barely under control, Rand set his glass aside. He was just starting after Lorelei when Brady and Sally caught sight of him.

"Rand!" Sally greeted him excitedly. "You came!"

"Of course," he replied tightly. "I wouldn't have

missed it. You make a lovely bride."

"Thank you, Rand." She kissed his cheek affectionately.

"It's good to see you, Rand." Brady shook his hand.

"Thanks, and congratulations."

"Thank you. I feel I'm the luckiest man alive tonight," he gazed down at his wife adoringly. "Have you had a chance to meet anyone yet?"

"I've just arrived." Rand's answer was terse, but they seemed not to notice.

"What about Lori? Does she know you're here? Have you seen her?" Sally asked anxiously as she glanced about the room, searching for her friend.

"No," Rand lied. "But I'll find her."

"I'm sure she'll be thrilled to see you," she went on.

Rand was about to deny that when Sally and Brady were summoned from his side.

"Go find her, Rand," Sally urged as Brady drew her away. "We'll speak with you both a little later."

Rand watched their progress through the crowd for a moment before turning to head in Lori's direction.

Bright moonlight was streaming through the floor-to-ceiling casement windows in the Westlake study as Roger led Lori into the room. He paused long enough to turn up the lamps and then partially closed the door to afford them a little privacy. Relieved to have escaped the throng of guests, Lori felt much lighter of spirit.

"So you're really going back to Arizona," he was amazed.

"First chance I get," she answered buoyantly. "But you know, I'm really nervous about seeing Rand again."

"Because you think he hates you?"

Lori nodded. "He didn't even bother to see me off when I left, and now I'm going to return to the mine and tell him I love him? I think he's going to find that a

519

bit hard to believe, especially after the last fight we had. I didn't even bother to let him explain a situation that had distanced me from him. I even told him that I hated him, Roger."

"Well, you'll just have to convince him that you still love him. Telling him you're sorry you didn't give him a chance to explain might help. He'd be a fool not to want you back," Roger said encouragingly.

Rand had become even more infuriated at finding that Roger had taken Lorelei into the study, and as he approached the room he was feeling quite violent. He was reaching to push the door open when he heard part of their conversation, and he froze. Lori had just confessed that she loved him. His anger drained from him and he paused only an instant before entering the room unannounced.

"And I'm no fool." Rand's deep voice caught Lori and Roger unaware, and Lori gasped in surprise as she came to her feet.

"Rand?" Her eyes were round with wonder as she gazed at the man she loved. "You're really here?"

"Yes, Lorelei." He crossed the room toward her. "And I want you back."

"Oh, Rand . . ." Without hesitation she went straight into the warm, safe haven of his arms. "It's been so terrible without you. I thought I could forget you, but I couldn't. I'd never be able to . . . I love you, Rand. You're the only man I'll ever need."

Noting the joyous expression on Lori's face, Roger started to retreat to give them some privacy.

"Roger." Rand's call halted his progress.

"Yes?"

"Thanks." Rand felt he needed to thank somebody. When he'd started down the hall, he'd been filled with bloodlust. He'd wanted to kill every man he suspected of touching Lorelei, but he knew now that what he'd overheard had just been malicious gossip.

"You're welcome," Roger answered. "She's all yours. Make sure you take care of her."

"I will. You can be sure of that," Rand vowed, and Roger nodded in response as he exited the room and shut the door behind him.

When Roger had gone, Rand stepped slightly away from Lorelei to stare down at her, his expression serious.

"I love you, Lorelei," he told her solemnly, still having trouble believing all that had just happened.

"I love you, Rand, and I'm sorry." Her eyes grew luminous with tears as she thought of the needless heartache they'd been through.

"Shhh . . ." He tried to quiet her, so they could just savor the specialness of the moment, but Lori refused to be silenced.

"No. I must tell you everything. I was so cruel to you . . ."

"There's no need to talk about it."

"But there is! I think I went a little crazy when I saw you kissing that other woman. I was so jealous and hurt."

"I'm sorry for that. If I'd known you were alive, it never would have happened."

"I know. You tried to be honest with me. You tried to tell me the truth about that night, but I was too proud to listen."

"I was drunk, Lorelei. Very drunk," he explained slowly, reliving the misery of that terrible time. "But drunk as I was, I couldn't forget you. You were in my thoughts, haunting me, and I was driven to return to the courtyard. I thought maybe, just maybe . . ." Rand paused as he drew a shuddering breath. "Anyway, Pearlie had been after Brady and me all day at the saloon, and when I left for the courtyard, she followed

521

me. I was out of my mind with grief, remembering you and thinking you dead, and when I saw her in the shadows, I thought she was you. God, I was desperate for you! I had admitted your death, but I couldn't accept it." Lori went to him as she witnessed his very real anguish. "I kissed her, but only once. It took me a minute, drunk as I was, to realize that she wasn't you. That must have been when you saw me."

Lori nodded, but didn't speak.

"I broke off the kiss and left her. Then I spent the night on the desert somewhere."

"I'm sorry for all the pain I've caused us."

"I'm sorry, too. You mean the world to me and if I had only known—"

"It's over, darling. I love you with all my heart." She reached up to him, needing his kiss to heal all the misunderstandings and distrust that had existed between them.

It was a soft kiss at first, a tentative brush of lips that both promised and pledged. Totally enthralled, Rand drew her near, savoring the sweetness of having her once again in his arms. Lorelei was his, and he would see to it that they would never be parted again.

Lori melted against Rand as she reveled in the joy of their reunion. Sally had been right all along! He did love her! Tingles of excitement traced down her spine as she realized that her happiness was now complete.

"I need you, Rand," she whispered, and he could restrain himself no longer.

His mouth slanted possessively across her lips, his tongue dueling sensuously with hers, tasting of her and showing her by imitation what he wanted to do. Then his hands strayed lower, and he pulled her tight in the cradle of his hips letting her feel the power of his own need for her.

Lori groaned at his erotic touch and she moved

sinuously against him, silently cursing the barrier to intimacy their clothes created. She wanted him! Craved him with a hunger that would never be fully assuaged and she longed for some time alone with him so she could show him just how much he really meant to her.

As she leaned invitingly closer, Rand slipped a hand within the confines of her bodice to caress the silken flesh of her breast, and Lori moaned at the exquisite sensations that flowed through her as he teased a pink crest to hardness.

"Rand . . . please . . ." she sobbed, her long-denied need for him flaming to life.

At her words, Rand stopped his play and Lori looked up at him questioningly.

"What is it?"

"I want you, Lori, more than anything. But not here, where we could be interrupted at any moment."

"I know." She leaned more heavily against him, her legs suddenly too weak to support her.

Rand took her hand and pressed an ardent kiss to her palm. "Do you trust me?"

"Completely," Lori answered.

"Then wait here for me. I'll be right back."

"Where are you going?"

Rand's smile was quixotic as he kissed her softly. "I'll be right back." With that, he left her standing in the middle of the study, ablaze with desire for him.


Lorelei smiled up at Rand as she looped her arms about his neck and pulled him down for another flaming kiss. "You surprised me, Mr. McAllister."

"I did, Mrs. McAllister?" he asked as he pressed kiss after passionate kiss on her waiting lips.

"Um . . ." She sighed as she rubbed her bare breasts

523

against his hair-roughened chest, glorying in the feel of his manly form. "You completely swept me off my feet tonight."

"Once I knew how you felt, love, I could see no reason to delay our marriage, and since Roger was all too willing to give me directions to the nearest justice of the peace"—he grinned down at her lazily—"I thought it was time that I claimed you for my own."

Lori returned his smile as she insisted throatily, "Past time."

"We'll never be parted again," he vowed, shifting his weight lower.

"I'm glad," she said softly. "Rand?"

"What?"

"Do you suppose Sally and Brady are enjoying their wedding night as much as we are?"

"I certainly hope so, love," he growled sensuously. "They deserve this joy, too."

Then, as Rand expertly stroked and fondled her breasts, Lori forgot all about Sally and Brady. Soon, afire with the need to feel his lips upon her, she cried out as his mouth descended to claim one throbbing peak. Clutching at his shoulders, she moved restlessly beneath him as he continued to caress her, his hands slipping lower to explore the warm center of her femininity. His touch, so practiced, sent her senses reeling, and Lori found herself moving against his hand, arching and straining upward in a search for release from the heightened desire he'd evoked. Lori sobbed wildly as he took her to the crest of excitement, then she shuddered as love's peak swept over her in wave after wave of breathtaking ecstasy. Sated, she then lay in Rand's arms as she slowly became aware of her surroundings again, and she smiled faintly as she heard Rand's triumphant chuckle.

"I love how you respond to me, wife," Rand told her

as he pressed his very evident arousal against her.

"And I love how you respond to me, husband," she grinned as she reached down to touch him.

Rand tensed and caught his breath at her bold caress, and she now chuckled victoriously as she brazenly urged him onto his back. Delightedly dominating him, she took her pleasure, teasing him with her lips and tongue until he, too, was mindless with need. Lori moved over him then and with Rand guiding her, she positioned herself above him and slowly lowered her hips to take him deep within her. Rand groaned at her possession, and he held her hips tightly to him as he began to move.

"Kiss me, Lorelei," he demanded, and Lori did so, her breasts brushing teasingly against his chest as they continued to move in love's embrace.

They reached the peak together, this time, exulting in the joy of their oneness. Then, knowing that they had never before experienced such perfection, they lay wrapped in each other's arms, momentarily fulfilled and both very aware of their enduring love.

"Rand," Lori murmured contentedly.

"What, love?"

"Can we go home soon?"

"As soon as you want," he told her, and as they lay in each other's arms, they watched the sky brighten with dawn, knowing that their future would be filled with love.

## BESTSELLING HISTORICAL ROMANCE
### from Zebra Books

PASSION'S GAMBLE                                    (1477, $3.50)
by Linda Benjamin
Jessica was shocked when she was offered as the stakes in a poker game, but soon she found herself wishing that Luke Garrett, her handsome, muscular opponent, would hold the winning hand. For only his touch could release the rapturous torment trapped within her innocence.

YANKEE'S LADY                                       (1784, $3.95)
by Kay McMahon
Rachel lashed at the Union officer and fought to flee the dangerous fire he ignited in her. But soon Rachel touched him with a bold fiery caress that told him — despite the war — that she yearned to be the YANKEE'S LADY

SEPTEMBER MOON                                      (1838, $3.95)
by Constance O'Banyon
Ever since she was a little girl Cameron had dreamed of getting even with the Kingstons. But the extremely handsome Hunter Kingston caught her off guard and all she could think of was his lips crushing hers in feverish rapture beneath the SEPTEMBER MOON.

MIDNIGHT THUNDER                                    (1873, $3.95)
by Casey Stuart
The last thing Gabrielle remembered before slipping into unconsciousness was a pair of the deepest blue eyes she'd ever seen. Instead of stopping her crime, Alexander wanted to imprison her in his arms and embrace her with the fury of MIDNIGHT THUNDER.

*Available wherever paperbacks are sold, or order direct from the Publisher. Send cover price plus 50¢ per copy for mailing and handling to Zebra Books, Dept. 2010, 475 Park Avenue South, New York, N.Y. 10016. Residents of New York, New Jersey and Pennsylvania must include sales tax. DO NOT SEND CASH.*

## THE ECSTASY SERIES
### by Janelle Taylor

SAVAGE ECSTASY (Pub. date 8/1/81)          (0824, $3.50)

DEFIANT ECSTASY (Pub. date 2/1/82)          (0931, $3.50)

FORBIDDEN ECSTASY (Pub. date 7/1/82)   (1014, $3.50)

BRAZEN ECSTASY (Pub. date 3/1/83)          (1133, $3.50)

TENDER ECSTASY (Pub. date 6/1/83)          (1212, $3.75)

STOLEN ECSTASY (Pub. date 9/1/85)          (1621, $3.95)


Plus other bestsellers by Janelle:

GOLDEN TORMENT (Pub. date 2/1/84)      (1323, $3.75)

LOVE ME WITH FURY (Pub. date 9/1/83)   (1248, $3.75)

FIRST LOVE, WILD LOVE
(Pub. date 10/1/84)                                      (1431, $3.75)

SAVAGE CONQUEST (Pub. date 2/1/85)      (1533, $3.75)

DESTINY'S TEMPTRESS
(Pub. date 2/1/86)                                        (1761, $3.95)

SWEET SAVAGE HEART
(Pub. date 10/1/86)                                      (1900, $3.95)


*Available wherever paperbacks are sold, or order direct from the Publisher. Send cover price plus 50¢ per copy for mailing and handling to Zebra Books, Dept. 2010, 475 Park Avenue South, New York, N.Y. 10016. Residents of New York, New Jersey and Pennsylvania must include sales tax. DO NOT SEND CASH.*

## SIZZLING ROMANCE
### from Zebra Books

**REBEL PLEASURE**             (1672, $3.95)
by Mary Martin
Union agent Jason Woods knew Christina was a brazen flirt, but his dangerous mission had no room for a clinging vixen. Then he caressed every luscious contour of her body and realized he could never go too far with this confederate tigress.

**PASSION'S PARADISE**             (1618, $3.75)
by Sonya T. Pelton
Angel was certain that Captain Ty would treat her only as a slave. She plotted to use her body to trick the handsome devil into freeing her, but before she knew what happened to her resolve, she was planning to keep him by her side forever.

**TEXAS TIGRESS**             (1714, $3.95)
by Sonya T. Pelton
As the bold ranger swaggered back into town, Tanya couldn't stop the flush of desire that scorched her from head to toe. But all she could think of was how to break his heart like he had shattered hers—and show him only love could tame a wild TEXAS TIGRESS.

**WILD EMBRACE**             (1713, $3.95)
by Myra Rowe
Marisa was a young innocent, but she had to follow Nicholas into the Louisiana wilderness to spend all of her days by his side and her nights in his bed. . . . He didn't want her as his bride until she surrendered to his WILD EMBRACE.

**TENDER TORMENT**             (1550, $3.95)
by Joyce Myrus
From their first meeting, Caitlin knew Quinn would be a fearsome enemy, a powerful ally and a magnificent lover. Together they'd risk danger and defy convention by stealing away to his isolated Canadian castle to share the magic of the Northern lights.

*Available wherever paperbacks are sold, or order direct from the Publisher. Send cover price plus 50¢ per copy for mailing and handling to Zebra Books, Dept. 2010, 475 Park Avenue South, New York, N.Y. 10016. Residents of New York, New Jersey and Pennsylvania must include sales tax. DO NOT SEND CASH.*